Feather Dali

Adventures from the Rainbow Bridge

Tremor

Eric Fish and Amanda Fish

Dedication Page

Dedicated to:

Neuro Dan – Feather Dan (2014 – 2018)

As well as to those who've had to say 'goodbye' to a loved pet. They will forever live in our hearts and we are better humans for having them in our lives no matter how briefly.

Special Thanks:

We would like to extend a special thank you to Carrie Huntington. Your skill as an editor, your passion, and the countless hours you spent seeking out any detail that was overlooked are priceless. Thank you for helping to make this story into a book we're proud to release to the public. It wouldn't have been the same and certainly not as good without you.

Eric and Amanda Fish.

Prologue

Motionless, Tremor crouched on the lower branches of a mighty mahogany tree as he took in the world around him. The jungle heat was stifling. It was the type of heat that made most animals find whatever cool spot they could and just collapse until the humidity lessened. A hurricane had savaged the area for two days before finally passing just a few hours ago near daybreak.

Tremor knew the storm had been a monster. He was in awe at what it had done. It changed the entire landscape as it moved through. It was almost unrecognizable. Entire hillsides had been transformed. Mudslides had torn entire swaths of forest away. No tree had been spared. Branches were scattered across the forest. Ancient hardwoods had been no match for the battering wind and their massive root balls now cut off game trails. Rivers and streams were dangerously swollen. It would be perilous to try to use them as a water source until they calmed but he knew where else to look when he got thirsty.

The only sounds he could hear were the constant dripping of water through the leaves, the occasional rustle of rocks falling as water continued to erode the Earth and the various chattering of birds. The birds were beginning to stir. Most of them were now without nests that would be capable of providing suitable or safe shelter and they were carefully scouting for anyplace to build a new home.

Tremor listened closely, his ears swiveling to catch every sound. This was the jungle after all and while those were the dominant sounds that could be heard there was a lot more going on. Predators and prey alike hadn't eaten in days. Hurricanes were a great equalizer in the jungle. They were just as deadly to all of them regardless of their station in the food chain.

Tremor was the top of the food chain. He was a black panther and not just any panther. He was massive with muscles that flexed beneath his short rough fur with every step. At over three hundred and fifty pounds he was considered a giant even among his own species. His head was enormous. His jaws could encircle and snap the neck of another panther with ease. His height and size were a tremendous advantage and he had faster than normal reflexes as well.

Whenever he encountered his own kind the result was the same. They would take one look at him, bow their head, lower their tail between their legs and scamper away. Those who he let escape counted themselves lucky. He would kill other predators for no other reason than sport and just because he could. Even worse, he would kill prey just to keep other predators from having food. He had a reputation for being ruthless, cruel, and most believed his heart was filled with pure evil.

Despite his size and tremendous weight Tremor moved through the forest silent as a ghost, sticking to the larger branches that could support his weight. He was unconcerned with what his future in this newly transformed landscape would be. He'd survived the storm, which was all that mattered. He was well aware of his place in his world and as far as he was concerned everything that lived in the jungle lived in his world.

Tremor had already hunted at daybreak. He'd killed and eaten three rabbits and part of a wild boar to fill his belly. He was now scouting to learn the new landscape in the hurricane's aftermath. Knowing there would be other animals displaced from the flooded river, he made his way there. The river was more swollen than he'd ever seen in all of his dozen years of life. He stopped on the limb of a tree and watched the rapids smash fallen branches to pieces. Nothing would survive falling in the river this day.

The river's roar drowned out nearly all sound but Tremor could still hear a high pitched, panicked, squeal. He'd already smelled the fear emitted from the wild boar in its panic. A glimpse of movement a dozen yards away helped him know where to focus his senses and he moved in. Each step slow and deliberate, he moved across tree branches towards the disturbance. A wild boar had fallen into a gaping hole which had been left after one of the hardwoods toppled. The fallen trees' massive root ball stood like a wall blocking the boar's exit to higher ground.

Tremor watched the boar. The large male tossed its head about slashing at the ground with its old curled tusks while dragging an injured rear leg as it struggled in vain to escape. Tremors whiskers twitched as he caught another more familiar scent wafting through the humid air. He lifted his head and sniffed again. He knew the animal the scent belonged to. Her name was Kaldra. She was another panther. She was smaller than most of their species making her his opposite in size but not in spirit. She was exceptional at hiding and despite her smaller size she was an impressive hunter. He could feel her eyes on him now. She must have been watching the wild boar's predicament as well and spotted him as he approached.

Tremor positioned himself above the boar on a tree branch, his enormous weight causing the branch to sway. He knew that the sound of the boar's frantic squeals combined with the thundering roar of the river would make it impossible for him to hear anything else approach or flee. His reputation would prevent anything from attempting to take him on and he knew Kaldra well enough to know she didn't flee. She would want to see what he was going to do with the boar.

Kaldra would know how he felt about the situation; all of the predators in the jungle would. This was an easy kill and a quick breakfast for someone. That wasn't something Tremor would allow in his jungle. He was proud of Kaldra for not taking the easy kill. He liked her and would have been displeased if he had to kill her for doing so.

Tremor believed in the hunt. The hunt was life. Every meal should be earned. Easy meals made predators lazy and weak. He took pride in every predator he allowed to live in his jungle. He made sure that each one of them earned their place as a predator every day by forcing them to hunt to survive. If they couldn't hunt then they'd starve to death. It was well known that if he caught any of them taking an easy kill for a meal that he would hunt and kill them. That was the way of the hunt. That was life in Tremor's world because that is what he allowed.

Tremor focused on the boar. It would never escape the hole it was in. If the river didn't rise a few more feet and claim him then he would starve. The storm made everything more difficult and it would be weeks before a sense of normalcy returned. The trapped boar would be a terrible temptation for another predator. They were all hungry. Hunger was supposed to be nature's motivator and help refine a hunter's skills but it could also be a weakness.

Weakness was unacceptable. There was no sound as Tremor dropped out of the tree. His massive body struck the boar eliciting one loud squeal before he slammed it to the Earth knocking the wind from its lungs. Tremors massive jaws closed over the boar's throat and squeezed. The boar kicked and thrashed but couldn't bring its razor sharp tusks to bear or kick free. Within moments it was still.

Tremor never let go of its throat as he dragged it up the side of the hole and towards the river. He carried the corpse to the top of the bank and in one fluid motion slung it into the thundering river. The river was so loud he couldn't hear the boar's body splash but he watched as the rapids picked it up and carried it away. In just a few yards the raging current pulled it under and it disappeared from view.

9

Tremor turned and stalked back into the storm devastated jungle. He surveyed everything around him looking for the eyes he knew were watching him. He knew Kaldra was watching but he could sense others as well. Predator and prey alike were out there and he was glad. They needed to witness him in these moments. They always needed to be reminded that it was he who allowed them to live. It was he who made them stronger by not allowing them to take easy kills.

Chapter 1 – Rainbow Bridge

Feather Dan, a small orange tabby cat with bright yellow eyes and a sweet face, sat comfortably on a cloud at the top of the Rainbow Bridge. The Rainbow Bridge was the biggest most beautiful multicolored rainbow that ever existed. The rainbow stripes were made of many colors that all blended together so beautifully that it could be hypnotic to look at them gradually blending together. Dan had tried to count all of the colors a few times but there were so many he never could manage it. Since he'd first arrived at the Rainbow Bridge the colors reminded him of one of those giant boxes of crayons. Not just the big box either but the biggest box there ever was that held more colors than he ever thought there could be.

He looked a few dozen yards ahead of him where the bridge arched down towards Earth. The vibrant colors of the Rainbow Bridge gradually descended into a swirling grey and white mist before completely disappearing into a giant fluffy white cloud. That giant fluffy white cloud was affectionately known as Fluffy. Fluffy served as a visible veil between the world of life and the world of spirit. The top of the Rainbow Bridge existed in the spirit world and magnificently arched high above Fluffy. It stretched from Earth, across the heavens and into the clouds of paradise. When all pets passed away on Earth, their spirits traveled across the Rainbow Bridge to reach pet heaven.

Feather Dan briefly thought back on his own journey across the Rainbow Bridge. There was a touch of sadness but mostly curiosity, wonder and an eventual understanding and pride once he realized his true purpose for being at Rainbow Bridge. Pets can always see the Rainbow Bridge, even when they're alive and on Earth. Feather Dan, like most pets, would often stare intently at it while he was on Earth. Sometimes he could even see a pet making the passage. Humans, however, only catch a small glimpse of it on occasion. There usually had to be rain and sunshine at the same time for a human to see it. Even then they could only see a fraction of what it consisted of. Many times what humans actually saw was the Rainbow Bridge reaching out to gather pets who had passed away.

As beautiful as the Rainbow Bridge was, it wasn't often that pets would sit and stare at it like Dan was. Today Dan had a very important job to do; a job that he was greatly humbled and honored to have. He was very excited and vigorously licked at his fur to make sure his orange and white stripes were spotless while he waited. The minutes continued to tick by but he didn't get impatient. What was happening was something that all pets at the Rainbow Bridge considered sacred. Today there was a pet that had died on Earth and was in the process of finding his way up the Rainbow Bridge. Every pet had their own unique crossing over experience. Some of them came over quickly. It was like they blinked and poof, here they were. Sometimes the journey up the Bridge was more difficult. When a pet was tightly bonded with a human, it was difficult to let go of that bond and the sadness of their loss. Once a pet reached the end of the Bridge and learned of their greater purpose, the sadness would fall away and be replaced by understanding that brought happiness, love, and peace.

Feather Dan watched as the clouds finally began to glow. A moment later he could see the silhouette of a cat walking across the bridge towards him. The clouds shimmered and a slim medium sized white and orange cat stepped out of Fluffy, into the grey and white mist then out into the light. Feather Dan was excited. He knew who this was. His name was Remy.

Remy was walking slowly, not with a sense of caution but with uncertainty. After a few steps he looked farther up the Bridge and saw Dan. His light golden eyes widened a bit in surprise, his head was upright and alert and he had a slight bend in his lifted tail. Dan could tell that Remy was still confused. Once in a while it took a little extra time for a pet to completely come to the realization of where they were. That was one of the reasons why there was always another pet there to greet them as they crossed the Bridge. It was Dan's job, at the moment, to help Remy with his transition to the heavens.

Dan smiled his friendliest smile, held his head and tail high and calmly walked down the Bridge a little way to greet him. "Hi Remy. My name is Feather Dan." Dan sat back on his haunches, signaling his intent to wait on Remy to acclimate to his surroundings. "I'm sorry your time on Earth has come to an end. Your human mom, Patti, asked me to be here for you and to help you figure things out."

Dan took a moment to take in Remy's appearance now that he was closer to him. Remy's face was mostly white with orange patches and orange ears. His ears perked up and his golden eyes shone bright when he heard Patti's name. "But how do you know my human and how do you know me?" Remy appeared sad and his ears drooped after a moment. Dan figured Remy was likely missing Patti something terrible.

Dan smiled at him again, "Your mom prayed extra hard and asked me if I could help you cross the Rainbow Bridge and show you around. She prayed so hard that everyone up here could hear her. She sure must love you a lot." Dan's tone was calming and compassionate to help put Remy at ease.

Remy managed to softly tell Dan, "She was crying when I closed my eyes for the last time." His voice was shaky and it cracked a bit, the pain of her loss easily conveyed in his words.

Dan lowered his head out of respect and understanding. Remy's emotions were still very raw and his bond with his human was obviously a strong one. This was not at all uncommon. In fact, most of the cats at Rainbow Bridge had that same experience and it was

13

hard on all of them. It became easier as they began to understand their new reality. They all became excited when they learned about their purpose.

Dan walked up to Remy and rubbed shoulders with him. Dan knew additional words wouldn't help. It was just going to take time for Remy to grieve in his own way. Dan turned and took a few steps away from where Remy stood. He looked over his shoulder back at Remy in an invitation to follow. Remy understood he was being asked to follow, and was soon walking a few steps behind at Dan's left shoulder.

As Dan began to lead Remy across Rainbow Bridge to where it ended, he continued talking. "Well Remy, she was crying because she loves you so much and is going to miss you. Don't worry though. You'll see her again. It takes time to recall everything when you first cross over so I'll try to explain and help you remember."

Remy nodded for Dan to continue.

"All animals cross the Rainbow Bridge when their time on Earth is done. There is always another animal that has crossed over waiting to greet them and explain things. Usually it's another animal that they grew up with and love but sometimes it's different. Sometimes they don't know anyone else who crossed over and then someone who experienced the same thing comes to greet them. Sometimes it's like now, where your human prayed hard and asked me to come. If a human asks hard enough and with enough love their message makes it to the heavens beyond the Rainbow Bridge where all of the pets waiting for their humans are."

"Why did Patti ask you to come help me?" Remy asked.

"It's a bit of a long story." Dan responded. "The short version is that while I was still on Earth she got to know me on social media. I was just a kitten at a shelter looking for my forever home. She almost adopted me but someone else did first. I had some pretty serious physical disabilities when I was on Earth. I couldn't run and it hurt to walk. I had a neurological disease that made life challenging for me."

Remy looked Feather Dan over from nose to tail. Dan knew he didn't look anything but healthy and he had no visible physical disability. Figuring Remy would be confused by his lack of disability now, he explained further. "My neurological disability was so severe that I was named Neuro Dan while I was at the shelter. Later my mum gave me the second part of my name which is Feather Dan. We don't have any disabilities at Rainbow Bridge. We are all whole, healthy and full of energy to play. Now I just go by Feather Dan. Anyway, my mum at my forever home started up a social media page and she and dad shared my stories with my social media friends every night. Patti kept up with me and she even became great friends with my mum. She knew I had already passed and she prayed that I would take care of you here when you passed. I heard her prayers so I came to find you."

Remy nodded at Dan and asked, "So we get to play with each other forever? Are there toys? What else do we do?"

Dan chuckled. Remy was coming around quicker than many who first crossed over. "Well sort of and yes, but we do have a greater purpose. When we were on Earth and just kittens we could remember that but as we grow up we forget. Once we cross the Rainbow Bridge we have to wait for our humans.

"You see, we actually choose them. They think they pick us out but that's not really correct. When we spot the human that speaks to our heart we capture them with love and the humans are unable to resist. That's why it doesn't always make sense why some people choose the pets they have."

15

What is it that we are waiting for our humans to do?" Remy asked Dan.

Dan stopped walking and turned his head toward Remy, "We're waiting on them to die, of course."

A look of surprise crossed Remy's face. Dan continued. "It's the job of all pets to wait for their humans. We are the first to greet them when they cross the veil between life and death."

Remy looked hard at Feather Dan. His fur had a shiny luster to it. Remy looked down at his own fur and his ears went back in surprise. Dan knew he would see that it also shimmered sort of like they were both lightly dusted with glitter. Dan had been waiting for him to notice that as well. It always took a minute for things to register after crossing the Rainbow Bridge. The transition could be confusing and each cat got their bearings in their own time.

Dan explained it to Remy before he could even ask, "When our humans time on Earth is done we feel their spirit approaching and glow extra brightly. That's when we know it's time to run to the top of the Rainbow Bridge to greet them. When humans experience the crossing, they always see a light that helps guide them where they are supposed to go. They see the light at the end of a dark tunnel and feel compelled to go into the light."

"That light that they see is actually us. All of us at the Rainbow Bridge have fur that shines and shimmers. The more we groom the brighter and more sparkly we shine. We try to stay as clean as possible to create a bright enough light to make it easier for our humans to find the entrance to the Rainbow Bridge where we can be reunited." Dan paused for a moment to give Remy a chance to process the importance of what he was being told.

Because he had been waiting on his mum and dad for a while now, Dan now remembered why cats groom so much and could share that with Remy. While on Earth the grooming instinct for cats is very strong, even if most adult cats no longer consciously know why they do it. Grooming always seems to be such a high priority because their subconscious understands why it's necessary and prompts them to groom frequently.

Dan noticed a tiny spot on his orange fur that was a little less shiny than the rest. He sat down on his haunches and licked it until it was as bright as the rest of his fur. While Dan was cleaning his shoulder Remy looked around. Dan was already aware of a human spirit sitting at the foot of the Rainbow Bridge gazing into the clouds. Dan noticed when Remy saw the spirit and said between licks, "It's incredibly rare but every now and then a human who already passed away ends up at the entrance to the Rainbow Bridge to greet a loved pet that they left behind. Those are very special humans and most of them cared for special needs animals, ran pet rescues, or just loved their pet so much they refuse to go without them. The tremendous sacrifices those humans made on Earth allow them to be here but they cannot leave the Rainbow Bridge. They must stay ever vigilant and while their hearts and minds may wander, their spirits stay right here. Hopefully her pet arrives soon and her vigil is a short one."

Satisfied with the shine on his shoulder, Dan continued their walk over the Rainbow Bridge. As they neared the top of the arch Dan said "Pets have to wait on their humans and while we wait we enjoy a wonderful life. If you can imagine it you can enjoy it. If you had a favorite toy, a plump cushion, or even a cozy cat bed you particularly enjoyed, you can wish for it and it will be here for you to enjoy again. This is a wonderful land filled with happiness and joy."

Dan saw the sadness slowly melting from Remy's shoulders and his eyes lost some of their pain. Remy must be attuning himself to the incredible sense of peace and happiness that was the very fabric of pet heaven. Dan thought that was a very good thing for any new soul to pet heaven. Soon Remy would be at perfect peace here.

"What happens when our person gets here?" Remy inquired with an intent and focused look at Dan.

Dan's eyes lit up with his excitement at Remy's question. Once again, Remy was proving to be quite the clever cat. "That's a fantastic question. Humans who love their pets demonstrate a pure and selfless love for their pets. Because of that, it's our job to make sure they have a peaceful transition to what comes next in the afterlife. When a person crosses they aren't supposed to stay at the Rainbow Bridge. When a person crosses there is a huge parade. Everyone in the land of the Rainbow Bridge gets together and the pet goes to their human. Together they get to walk into the Beyond."

Ears set forward to show his alertness and curiosity, Remy asked, "What do you mean by the Beyond."

Dan explained, "The parade ends in a giant sparkling cloud. The only time an animal spirit can walk into it is when they are with their person. The human we chose to be ours on Earth is the only one who can take us to the land beyond the bridge. That's part of why the bond between a pet and human is so special and hard to explain."

Dan paused then said, "Now and then a pet doesn't go with their human to the beyond. That's rare and only happens when the pet still has to wait on another human. Sometimes we choose more than one human and when that happens we have to stay and wait for all of the humans we've chosen."

As they crested the top of Rainbow Bridge, the rest of cat heaven opened up in front of them. Dan stopped walking to sit and give Remy time to take it all in. Rainbow Bridge ended into a large clearing at the top of a cloud. The ground swirled with fine white mist that felt cool and refreshing to cat paws. To the right of the clearing was a massive city made up of cat trees and empty boxes of every shape and size. Some of the cat trees were so tall that they towered over one hundred feet into the air. Dan told Remy it was named Cat Tree City. Beyond Cat Tree City was an enormous mountain made of clouds that looked like a mile high stack of rainbow colored blankets. Beyond the rainbow colored mountain was the horizon. The horizon was filled with pure white clouds that stretched on for as far as Remy could see. The clouds looked like a majestic mountain range.

The city's main street came right up to the edge of the clearing. Towering cat trees lined either side of the street and led to the center of the city. The city center overflowed with every cat that was waiting for their humans. There were many kinds of cats. They were all scrambling down cat trees, leaping out of boxes and rushing to the main street, named surprisingly enough Main Street. Happy cheers erupted when they got there and they twirled and danced as they ran towards Rainbow Bridge.

To the left of the clearing where Rainbow Bridge ended was a large path that wound to the top of a cloud. At the end of the cloud was yet another cloud. That cloud was the purest of white and sparkled brightly.

Dan saw Remy looking and said, "That's the cloud I told you about where we go with our humans to the beyond."

From that cloud all the way to Rainbow Bridge and the Main Street entrance to Cat Tree City a huge crowd of cats had gathered. There were cheers and celebrations and Remy realized that a parade had formed.

The parade consisted of a few humans and around them all of the animals they had ever had were beginning to materialize. There were cats, dogs, hamsters, guinea pigs, lizards, birds, snakes and creatures Remy hadn't even seen or heard about before. The animals were all gathered around their people and the people were smiling and hugging all of them.

Dan got excited at seeing the parade and said, "Everyone celebrates the reunion at the bridge. All of the pets the humans had that are waiting on them come and the reunion is beautiful. It's very rare that other animals cross into the kingdoms of other species except for parades. Dogs have their own kingdom and birds have theirs. All of the animals have their own kingdom where they can wait in the way best suited to themselves. Time moves very differently between the Rainbow Bridge and Earth. We don't have parades every day so we all celebrate when we do."

As they walked down the end of Rainbow Bridge and neared the back of the parade, Dan started pointing out different cats in the crowd on the side of the streets. He called several of them by name and they waved a paw back to him in greeting. He pointed out, a black and white cat, who Dan said was one of many of his spirit siblings he never met on Earth that were waiting with him for his mum and dad.

He pointed out Bandit and Sassy, a pair of Siamese cats with black masks. They were identical and the only way to tell them apart was by their collars. Bandit had a blue collar and Sassy had a pink collar when they arrived at Rainbow Bridge. Dan told Remy that they were good at heart but were so curious that they were always causing trouble. They were so involved with themselves that they didn't even hear Dan. Dan knew they had showed up at the Bridge together. They had died together after getting into mischief on Earth.

With the parade about to start Dan stopped to celebrate with everyone. Dan cheered with the rest of the crowd and Remy found himself caught up in the excitement and cheered as well. It was an emotional experience shared by all. Some had a glimmer of a tear in their eyes but they were happy tears. The sense of love through the fulfillment of the family reunions was overwhelmingly a joyful experience for all participants. Dan knew it would make Remy feel better and ease the loss of Patti.

There were a dozen humans in the parade and each one had several animals with them. One by one they walked up the trail toward the giant sparkling cloud. As they passed through the cloud it shimmered and glowed brightly. The glow was so bright Dan almost had to look away. As each of them entered, waves of pure love pulsed out over the Rainbow Bridge that left everyone feeling peaceful and refreshed.

When the last person in the parade got to the cloud they stopped. The man knelt down to talk to his cat and asked what was wrong. The crowd was so quiet everyone could hear. Dan whispered to Remy that this very rarely happened and was considered a sacred occasion to them all. The cat mushed up against his human's legs and told him he had to stay behind. There were a few other cats, three dogs and even a pair of hamster's sitting at his feet waiting patiently to cross.

They listened intently as the cat told his human how much he loved him but he had to wait for another human. He told him that his wife still needed him to be her light and it wasn't time for her to cross over yet. He couldn't leave until she crossed. It was his sacred duty and he loved her too much to go just yet. His human nodded in understanding, thanked his beloved cat and hugged him once more. Then he stood up and together with the rest of his pets walked into the shimmering sparkling cloud.

The other animals in the crowd came over and hugged the cat. They told him he had been very brave and were so happy for him that he had another person on Earth that had loved him enough that he was duty bound by love to stay. Dan told Remy that he would be a celebrity now until his other human came along. Dan said very few cats got to be in the parade more than once.

As the parade dispersed Dan and Remy walked and talked. Remy asked Dan what they could do and Dan told him that he was taking him someplace special. As they continued walking many other cats greeted Dan. Almost all of them said, "Hi," as they walked by, all of them at least nodded in greeting and they all smiled when he was near.

Curious, Remy asked, "Why do you get so much attention? I see that most of the cats just pass by each other unless they are obvious friends."

Dan turned his head and mumbled something under his breath. Remy nudged him and asked him again. Dan rolled his eyes and said with a sigh "I may be a bit of a celebrity, or… ugh, some of them consider me to be royalty here."

Remy stopped in his tracks and asked him, "Royalty? What does that mean?"

Dan stopped with him and pointed with his paw to the giant cloud mountain that looked like it was made of rainbow colored blankets. "That's Blankets Mountain. Blankets Mountain didn't exist in the land of the Rainbow Bridge until I arrived. Remember I mentioned that while I was on Earth I was actually a disabled cat who could barely walk? My humans had to be creative in finding ways to care for me and they created a Blankets Mountain for me to perch on. While I was on Earth I was the king of my mountain. That's where I spent most of my life. I would sit on it and play with feathers that friends from all over the world sent me."

"How did you get people from all over the world to send you feathers?" Remy asked next.

Dan replied quickly hoping to change the topic from his notoriety. "Remember my mum made me that social media page? Somehow I wound up with tens of thousands of friends from all over the world who really loved me. They loved me so much that they sent me presents. They still love me. Even now, when their pets die, some of them pray hard and ask me to meet them at the Rainbow Bridge and show them around. Just like Patti did for you."

Remy was staring at Dan in what Dan recognized as wonder. Remy was learning a lot, most of it probably felt more like he was simply being reminded of something he already knew but the story of Blankets Mountain wasn't something he could have remembered. No matter how many times Dan explained it, he was still embarrassed when he was stared at like Remy was doing.

Dan continued his story, "I started getting requests right away, even on the first day I was here. I was fortunate and remembered everything that I was supposed to really quickly. I knew right away how to go greet the ones I'd been asked to and show them around. The more I helped with their crossing the more friends I made. I became good friends with many of my social media friend's cats who were crossing. We all wanted to stay together but didn't have a place to stay like that." Dan told Remy, remembering it just like it was yesterday.

"One day I got a notion and I grabbed a part of a cloud from the horizon. I pulled it to a spot no one was using and thought about my Blankets Mountain on Earth with all my heart. The next thing I knew there was a poof sound. That piece of cloud I pulled over sprung up right underneath me. I found myself standing on top of a rapidly growing cloud mountain. It was rainbow colored because my Blankets Mountain on Earth had been a random patchwork of blankets of all colors and sizes." Dan thought it looked a lot like his blankets back home and was just as comfy.

"When the mountain finally stopped growing, I was on the very top of the biggest mountain in all of the land. All of the cats of the Rainbow Bridge were staring at me in amazement and wonder. Even the elders were awed and fascinated. They had heard of such things happening in legends. They called that type of permanent creation a 'Miracle Manifestation' but not one of them had ever actually witnessed such a thing happen. We can imagine anything we want to play with and it will be created, but only temporarily. Our toys aren't actually real and will go away as soon as we're done playing with them. Blankets Mountain isn't like our imagined toys. It is very real and is now believed to be a permanent part of Rainbow Bridge."

Feeling embarrassed, Dan mumbled, "That's when they started calling me King of Blankets Mountain. Somehow I managed to stumble into being a celebrity of sorts just like I had been on Earth."

Dan perked back up and smiled, "I decided that since my Blankets Mountain had the same colors as the Rainbow Bridge that everyone would be welcome to come and rest and play on it with me. Everyone who I help cross the Rainbow Bridge I bring to Blankets Mountain and invite them to stay if they want to."

Remy was staring at him wide eyed and said, "I can't believe that a king came to greet me."

Dan bumped into him and said, "Please don't actually call me a king. My head isn't that big. I've had to work hard to get people to stop using that nickname and just call me Feather Dan or Dan. Patti knew that we would become great friends just like her and my mum on Earth. That's why she asked me to meet you."

Remy's curiosity was evident in his next question. "What are we going to do next?"

Dan smiled back at Remy. "Well, we're going to go to Blankets Mountain of course."

24

Chapter 2 – Blankets Mountain

Their walk to Blankets Mountain took them clear through Cat Tree City. They started at the Rainbow Bridge end of Main Street and had to follow it all the way to the other end of the city. The outside end of the city where Main Street let out had, of course, been named the Blankets Mountain entrance of Main Street. There was even a street sign put up with that written on it.

Remy enjoyed his walk through Cat Tree City. The place was enormous. The Main Street was filled with cats of all types. Hundreds of alleyways sprung off either side of the road and led to different types of neighborhoods. There was friendly chatter everywhere. Cats from all over the world came here when they crossed and Remy was in awe of all of the different languages he was hearing. He was shocked as well to realize he could understand everything being spoken.

Everyone continued to wave at Feather Dan. Many came up, said hello and introduced themselves to Remy. They were asked if they wanted to play with different toys several times. Each time Dan would thank them but tell them they were on their way to Blankets Mountain. Each visitor nodded and went about their business; that business being playing with toys. The toys were unbelievable. Remy thought it was like they had access to the world's biggest and most eclectic pet toy store ever! Dan promised Remy he would show him how to think a toy into existence after they got to Blankets Mountain. He also reminded him that the toys would disappear when he was finished playing with them but that was okay because all he had to do was think of them again and they'd show back up.

After some time walking through Cat Tree City, they finally came to the end of Main Street. Towering before him was Blankets

Mountain. It was a short walk from the city to actually start climbing the mountain. There were a few cloud trails easily visible and Remy could tell that the one Dan was heading towards was the most heavily traveled by how wide it was.

As they began walking up the path Dan began to explain in more detail the different aspects of Blankets Mountain. They only made it up a little ways when they came across a couple of other cats playing chase.

"Hi Meghan! Hi Peanut!" Dan yelled to them. Meghan was a torti and Peanut was an orange stripe cat like Dan only bigger. They stopped their game of chase long enough to say hi and get introduced to Remy. They each pointed to spots along the side of the mountain not too far from where they were playing that were "their" spots to sleep in peace. Remy took a closer look and he could see that each of them had a small cloud shaped like a folded blanket that was attached to Blankets Mountain. The sleeping spots looked really comfortable.

Meghan explained to Remy, "Our beds are considered *our* spots. That means that nobody else bothers that spot and if you're sleeping there's no sneaky ambushes or anything." She gave Peanut a funny look and said "Right, Peanut?"

Peanut looked around like he had misplaced something and muttered, "Yup, that's right."

"That's the way it's *supposed* to be." She gave Peanut a little shove and turned her attention back to Remy. "The cloud beds are even moveable!" Meghan's voice betrayed her excitement. "You can drag them anywhere you want." She gave Peanut another funny look, "That means if we want to go spend time on a different part of Blankets Mountain all we have to do is drag our cloud with us." She stared at Peanut and said, "Isn't that right, Peanut?"

26

Peanut continued to glance about in a distracted manner but responded, "Yes, yes, that's right."

Feather Dan chuckled and told the two of them to behave. They resumed their walk up the path. Remy continued to look around and could tell that there had to be hundreds of cats living on Blankets Mountain. A look of pure amazement was evident on Remy's face. The more he saw and learned the more amazed he became.

"Blankets Mountain always has enough space. When another cat says they want to live here until their human comes I just grab a bit of a cloud and bring it over. I imagine it being a comfortable blanket and poof, it appears under the new cat. Then it floats up Blankets Mountain. When their bed gets to a spot they're happy with, it transforms into a rainbow blanket cloud."

Remy was fascinated by the concept of thinking a cloud into existence the way Dan was describing it. He had to know more about it. "How do you pull away a piece of a cloud?"

Dan paused to answer. "Did you ever see Patti eat cotton candy?"

"Yes." Remy nodded remembering a few occasions when she had some in the house with friends.

"Well," Dan said, "It's kind of like pulling off a piece of cotton candy. The cloud is soft and a little sticky just like cotton candy. It even starts to dissolve so I have to move kind of fast. I don't know how it exactly works but I'm pretty sure there aren't too many rules here for us to worry about."

Remy shook his head in quiet contemplation. He sure was learning a lot and knew Dan wasn't even close to being done telling him things. He could tell that Dan definitely liked to talk and tell stories. He thought that was fine and even smiled. He enjoyed hearing Dan explain everything and he was grateful Patti had managed to get Dan to greet him.

Dan glanced around and continued, "Blankets Mountain has really become a giant community. We've got a great reputation and it's known as one of the most peaceful places at the Rainbow Bridge.

"Many of the pets that come to the mountain, like me, were disabled during their time on Earth. Once they left their bodies behind the disabilities were left behind as well. Most of us spend the day doing things we were unable to while on Earth. There's always a cat with the zoomies and there are races all of the time. We even have long jump and high jump competitions."

As they began to near the mountain's top Remy asked, "Where do you sleep?"

Dan looked all the way up to the top, "Up there. When Blankets Mountain appeared I was standing on top and that's where I decided to sleep. I get the best view of the land from up there."

Dan got a gleam in his eye and Remy could tell he was about to tell him something that he was excited about. "I've also got a very special spot up there. I call it the Hall of Feathers."

"While I was on Earth, I was obsessed with feathers. They were absolutely my most favorite thing to play with ever. My disability prevented me from having fun with the zoomies like other cats, but feathers were a blast to play with. I'd pounce, swat them and the most fun part of all was when I chomped on them. The bigger feathers made a fantastic crunching noise that drove me wild and made my humans laugh."

"When Blankets Mountain appeared there was something about it I didn't know about right away." He glanced at Remy. Remy was still focused and listening closely to Dan's words. "Blankets Mountain is hollow."

"Wow." Remy exclaimed with surprise.

"Well," Dan continued, "not completely hollow. Not like a balloon kind of hollow but there are caves and lots of passageways."

They finally made it to the very top and Dan pointed to a part of the side of one of the blankets. "Can you see it?"

"See what?" Remy was staring right at where Dan was pointing but all he saw was the side of a green and white spotted cloud that was shaped like a blanket. He looked really hard but didn't see anything any more unusual than anything else. Of course pretty much everything he'd seen that day was pretty unusual so he knew he must not be seeing something.

"That's the entrance I first found." Dan walked up to it and scratched at the seam in the blanket. It silently slid open to reveal the entrance to a cave. Remy walked up and looked in. There were ledges resembling steps going down and he could see it opened up after a bit into a large cavern.

Dan pointed to his blanket bed just a few feet away from the cave entrance. "I slept just a few steps away from it for weeks before I figured out it was there." Dan looked at his bed and got a big smile. His blanket was covered with the names of different cities from all over the world.

Remy looked and noticed it too, "Your bed has names on it?"

"Sometimes," Dan said. "My blanket bed changes every night. When I was on Earth my humans changed out the blanket on top of Blankets Mountain any time it got dirty or too covered in fur so that top blanket got changed out a lot. I'm not sure why but it still does it here too. I rather enjoy it though. Each day I get a different one that looks like one of the ones from my Blankets Mountain on Earth and it brings back good memories."

Dan shook his head, "Sorry, I got distracted. Anyway, after I explored the caves I knew right away what I wanted to do with it." Dan puffed up his chest and lifted his head. Remy could tell he was very proud of what he'd done and seemed pleased to show off his accomplishment.

"It's much more fun to show you than to try to explain, so come on," Dan said and he led the way into the tunnels. "This is the Hall of Feathers, my pride and joy of Blankets Mountain."

They went down quite a distance, hopping from ledge to ledge until they got down to the first cavern. "I don't keep the Hall of Feathers locked up or anything but I do ask the other cats for privacy on this part of the mountain. They're always welcome to visit but I do love to show off the feathers and tell the stories of how I got each one so I ask that I get to be here anytime someone comes for a tour."

Remy nodded, he could appreciate that. Dan had wide happy eyes and a big smile when he continued talking.

"When birds cross over they fly from the Rainbow Bridge over the cat realm and out past the cloud mountains where they disappear. We all love it because we get to see them again and they look just as happy as we are. I started following a bird once because I'd never seen one with its coloring before. It noticed me and sang me a pretty song while it flew. Before it went out of sight it dropped a feather for me.

"I hurried over to where it landed and it was beautiful. I decided that it was way too pretty to chomp on and that I needed a special place for it. That's when I got the idea for the Hall of Feathers. I brought it back here and found a special place for it. I thanked the bird for the feather and set it down. As soon as I did, a beam of sunlight came out and illuminated the feather.

"I was amazed and I stared at it for a long time. Then I realized I could hear the song of the bird that had dropped the feather! I immediately decided that I had to get more bird feathers to add to the collection. It didn't take long and I got hundreds. I think the birds enjoyed sharing their song and a feather as much as I enjoyed watching and listening to them. I made it my goal to get one of every feather of every bird that ever existed and put it in the Hall of Feathers."

As Remy looked away from Dan and out into the cavern his yellow eyes went wide with wonder. The cavern was huge. It stretched ahead a long way forward but it wasn't too wide or very tall. It wound out of sight to the right many yards away. The walls were lined with exactly what Dan had described; feathers. Every feather Dan collected rested on its very own special blanket, each a color that best helped the feather stand out. Remy couldn't tell where it came from but each feather was illuminated by a ray of sunshine. He walked up to the closest feather and as he got near he listened closely and he could even hear the song of the bird that feather came from.

Remy turned and gazed at Dan in wonder, "How did you do all of this? How did you get the birds songs to come through like that? It's one of the most beautiful things I've ever heard."

Dan shook his head at the question, "I don't know. I just loved the feathers so much and as soon as I set them down the blanket's color changes to compliment the feather, it's covered in sunshine and then I can hear the bird song. As far as I can tell it just happens on its own."

Dan looked around fondly, "I spend hours here admiring each feather and listening to the sounds that the birds sing."

31

He moved Remy between two feathers and told him to listen. Remy could hear the sound of both birds and they were singing together in unison.

Remy shook his head in disbelief, "Dan this is incredible. You deserve the name Feather Dan, that's for sure."

Dan shook his head. "We could spend all day right here but there's something really special that I want to show you! Follow me!"

Dan turned and trotted down the cavern towards where it branched off to the right. Remy ran along beside him and Dan began to explain what he wanted him to see.

"It was the only thing I found in the caverns when I searched the first time. It must have appeared when Blankets Mountain sprang into existence. I don't know, maybe I just happened to be standing on something that was buried. I haven't been able to figure it out but it's really neat."

"What is it?" Remy asked.

"It's an ancient Native American headdress. It's obviously hundreds of years old, maybe even older. It's adorned with what must be at least a thousand feathers of various sizes and types. They circle the entire thing. Whoever would have worn it would have had feathers not only surrounding their head but draped all the way down their back and trailing on the ground. It's got silver and gold decorations and beads that are just hypnotic."

"Oh wow! I really want to see that!" Remy said.

Dan picked up the pace as Remy followed. They hurried past several hundred more feathers that Dan had proudly displayed. Remy promised himself to come back and visit each and every one of them. Dan slowed to a walk as they approached the pedestal that displayed the headdress right where Dan originally found it.

"Oh no…" Dan sounded truly concerned.

The pedestal sat empty; a beam of sunlight shown down where the headdress should have been.

As they approached they began to hear an odd sound. At first it was faint, as if coming from a distant horizon but grew steadily louder as they got right up to it. The sound was that of drums and chanting. It was a beautiful mix and sounded like an old Native American drum circle. The sounds were faint and unlike the bird songs which obviously came from the feathers, the music seemed to be coming from all around them. The air turned cold and shadows started to flicker along the blankets nearest the pedestal. Dan stared hard at the shadows and glanced around. There was no light source that could produce the shadows they were seeing. Slowly, with what looked to be a great effort, a cat stepped through the shadows into the cavern and began walking directly toward them.

Neuro Dan and Remy stared at it in confusion. As if it were choreographed they blinked, shook their heads and blinked again. The cat was transparent! They could see right through it. It looked to be an absolutely ancient cat. Its fur was patchy and they could see where it had partly turned from black to white and grey as it had aged, particularly around its mouth. Its eyes glowed light yellow and it looked very wise. Remy thought for a second that he should run but then remembered that he was already at the Rainbow Bridge, so he didn't think he really had anything he needed to run from anymore. Plus, Dan was standing firm and didn't look threatened or frightened in the least.

The ancient cat stopped in front of them and spoke. Its voice sounded like an echo. "Feather Dan, I am Doba. I am here from the

Beyond; the place beyond the Rainbow Bridge. I am here because there is trouble and the Rainbow Bridge needs you."

Feather Dan cocked his head sideways, his golden eyes squinting as he stared at Doba. "Nice to meet you Doba. How did you come back from the Beyond? What kind of trouble is there?"

"My person was a Navajo Indian Chieftain and that headdress belonged to him. Returning to the Rainbow Bridge from the Beyond in any form is nearly impossible. The emergency here is so grave that my entire tribe came back together in the Beyond to perform an ancient ritual to allow me to be here. I have only a little time before I will fade, only moments really, so I must explain quickly.

"The stolen chieftain's headdress must be returned. The headdress has mystical properties that have been forgotten for centuries. Used recklessly, it could cause terrible damage to Rainbow Bridge and Earth.

Remy looked and saw Dan with a very concerned expression and serious demeanor. Remy had just met Feather Dan but knew he was a very light hearted and happy cat. If Dan was genuinely concerned, Remy decided that he would be too. Doba continued speaking directly to Dan.

"The turquoise beads on the headdress, when clicked together, are capable of opening brief portals between the Rainbow Bridge and Earth. The feathers on the headdress are capable of jumping through the portal and to Earth itself. If another animal were to find one of those feathers and chomp on the stem it would transport them through the open portal and into Rainbow Bridge. They would appear wherever the portal was opened."

Dan shook his head in disbelief and said, "Holy Cat. This is serious."

Doba nodded and continued, "Once the portals are opened they only stay that way for a few minutes at the most unless they are reopened by clicking the beads again. All it takes, however, is for the portal to be opened once and it creates a bind point. The feather or feathers that go through the portal are bound to that location. They can allow for travel back and forth forever or until the stem of the feather no longer has any crunch left to it. All that is required to go back and forth is for the feather to be bitten.

"When the beads are clicked, if no feather has already been chosen and pulled from the headdress, a small feather will automatically release from the tail. That small feather will shoot through the portal to a location on Earth. The small feathers have only enough material to chomp for one round trip. The larger feathers on the headdress can have dozens and potentially hundreds of trips in them."

Remy suddenly gasped with excitement, "Does that mean I can bite a feather and go back to Earth to visit with my human?"

Doba turned his attention from Dan, gave Remy a stern look and said, in a commanding tone, "No, you cannot." He sighed and in a kind, understanding voice he explained further. "Once animals pass away and come to the Rainbow Bridge we no longer have living bodies on Earth to return to. We can never return in that form again, at least not with the magic of the headdress. Only animals on Earth have the ability to pass back and forth. They keep their body in both realms."

Doba turned his attention back to Dan and his voice became serious once again. "Note that it is unknown what effects, if any, result to the physical body of an animal that uses the magic to cross back and forth."

A pained look crossed Doba's face and he spoke more quickly. "Listen carefully, my time to be here is running out. Remember that while the bigger feathers can transport an animal back and forth more than once there is no way of knowing how many times they will work. When the stem of the feather no longer crunches it will no longer work. Whatever side the animal is on will be the side they stay on."

Doba's image began to flicker and fade. His voice was becoming more distant and harder to hear. "Get the headdress back and be sure to keep it safe. Two Siamese were here earlier. They were admiring the feathers you've assembled. When they spotted the headdress they were overcome with cat curiosity and ran off with it."

"Bandit and Sassy!" Dan exclaimed.

"When the parade began to form they hid it away so they could attend. Now they are traipsing around the clouds beyond your Blankets Mountain playing with it. They have no idea what they have or the damage they are doing. They are obsessed with the beads. They've been swatting at them while they run about and have already opened up three portals."

Dan groaned and said, "Oh no…"

"Already three Earth cats that have been pulled through. The feather they chomped will have returned with them in some fashion. You must find them and get them to bite the feather again to send them home."

All Remy could see of Doba now were his yellow eyes. He concentrated hard to hear his words. "Look behind the pedestal for what you need. Choose wisely which cats you summon to help you. The fates of many now rely solely on you and the choices you make." Doba was almost gone, his words were a whisper. "Find the headdress. Stop this tragedy." Then all traces of him completely faded away.

36

Dan looked over at him, his bright golden eyes coming into focus. "This is bad. I need a second to think but we don't really have time to waste"

Remy understood and he suddenly found himself sharing Dan's uneasiness. He didn't respond to Dan's statement, he didn't need to. He thought for a moment and decided that he was new to the Rainbow Bridge and he wasn't going to just think up a solution. Uncomfortable with just sitting quietly, Remy decided to take a better look around. Behind the pedestal where the headdress once sat he found two turquoise beads and three large feathers. "Look Dan, we'll need these. What now?"

Dan turned to Remy. His look of concern was replaced by one that Remy was coming to know meant he was being playful. Dan hurriedly gathered up the feathers and beads that had been left for them. Then he looked around and spotted a particular feather. Remy watched him run over and grab a huge peacock feather out of its display. Dan ran back over to him and grinned, for just a moment, at some thought Remy could only guess at. With an excited gleam in his eyes Dan said, "Get up, follow me and try to keep up. I know who can help us and how we can get them here!"

Chapter 3– Rainbow Colored Sun Puddles

Binx was bored and feeling restless. Summer had come early and with not a cloud in the sky to provide shade, it was looking to be a very hot day. It wasn't quite noon yet. Normally on a sunny day like this, it would be time for napping in sun puddles. But for some reason, he just couldn't get settled down. He'd spent the last hour grooming. He was a young Flame Point Siamese. His fur was mostly bright white with a bit of orange on his ears and tail. It generally took him twice as much time to keep cleaned up as it did most other cats. Dirt stood out in obvious contrast on his white fur. He looked himself over with his bright blue eyes and was satisfied. After his hour-long bath he was spotless. There wasn't a speck of dirt from his oversized, orange tipped ears all the way to his slender orange tipped tail. Usually a full on grooming session that took that long was enough to get him perfectly relaxed for a good two or three hour afternoon cat nap. Today that just wasn't the case.

He was sitting in the living room, in front of a large sliding glass door. The sun was shining through and he was enjoying the warmth. He glanced up at the big leather couch and saw his brother and sister, Leroy and Amelia. They were both sprawled out and sound asleep. That's normally what Binx would have been doing as well. He stood up, arched his back in a big stretch and took a look outside. Sometimes there were birds passing through but there were none to watch at the moment. He listened quietly for a bit but didn't hear the owl that passed through the neighborhood and that he suspected had a nest nearby. With the owl silent, he thought maybe he'd get a peek at the squirrel family.

There was a squirrel family that lived in the trees in the wood line just a few yards beyond the porch. All of them enjoyed watching the squirrels jump between the trees. One of the squirrels had been there for years before Binx had joined the family. His siblings referred to him as Mr. Squirrel out of respect. There was an outside cat named D.J. who had hunted Mr. Squirrel for years. Leroy and Amelia said they'd watched the drama play out many times. When D.J. would pounce, Mr. Squirrel would take to the trees and lead D.J. on a wild tree climbing chase. Once Mr. Squirrel got to the very top he'd leap to a different tree leaving D.J. stuck high up in a tree top. Recently, Mr. Squirrel found himself a Mrs. Squirrel and now there were also baby squirrels to watch.

Binx sighed; nothing was stirring outside either. Apparently he was the only one unable to nap. He couldn't figure out why he was feeling so restless. He decided he would just go walk around and pace for a while and see if maybe he could just shake it off.

He turned back towards the couch, glanced at Leroy and Amelia again and stretched out his long white legs. He dug his claws deep into the tan carpet and gave them a quick sharpening. He sat down for a second and did just a little bit more grooming. Even if he was just going to go and aimlessly wander around he wanted to look his best. He didn't believe there was any excuse to look less than amazing.

When he finished he decided to walk a circle through the living room. He jumped up onto dad's desk to see if there was anything new or fun to knock over. He didn't find anything there except for the usual stuff. He looked around and decided he'd go checked out his mum's desk next. There was nothing new or exciting to play with there either so he wandered over to the couch. He stopped briefly to give Leroy and Amelia a sniff but they were sound asleep.

Bored with the living room, he strolled into the kitchen. No one had left anything good to eat lying around on the floor or the counters. It was a small kitchen so he got bored in there pretty quickly. He stood on the kitchen counter trying to decide where to go to be bored next. He decided that he'd go take a walk down the hall to the guest bedroom. He didn't usually spend too much time there. Unless dad's mom was visiting, they rarely had guests. That meant nothing in that room ever changed.

He trotted down the hall, turned right and strolled into the bedroom. He hopped up on the bed and decided that since he didn't have anything else to do that he'd do a little more grooming. Leroy often accused him of being obsessive over his grooming but it took quite a bit of work to keep his white fur perfect. His big orange tipped ears perked up. He stopped and looked around but didn't see anything. As soon as he went back to cleaning his shoulder he heard something again. He was hearing something odd, which wasn't really unusual. They lived in an apartment so you never knew what strange sounds would come from the neighborhood's other apartment units.

He shook his head and resumed grooming. He decided he would simply ignore it but after another minute it began to sound like it was coming from inside the bedroom. He stopped grooming and decided he was going to figure out what it was. He perked up his ears as tall as he could, which was significant as his ears were huge compared to other cats, and listened intently. He closed his eyes and focused, trying hard to identify the sound, or at least what direction it was coming from. The harder he listened the more he thought that it sounded like the beating of drums. Not the drums that someone's child might bang on to learn to be in a band but like something he'd heard on T.V. It was one of the oddest sounds but he was pretty sure it was Native American drums. It sounded like it was in the room but at the same time it sounded like it was somewhere a long way off.

Binx stood up and looked around. He decided he was going to check out every corner of the room to figure out where it was coming from. He hopped off the bed and wandered over to the closet. He saw Feather Dan's old Blankets Mountain stacked neatly where it had been placed for over a year. It was made up of thirty or so blankets, each one completely different, all folded up neatly and stacked one on top of the other; it stood several feet tall.

Binx inspected the area on the ground around it but nothing was out of the ordinary. He started examining it further. He looked up towards the top and saw nothing on one side but as he walked around it he discovered something he'd never seen before. It was something remarkable. There was a part of a peacock feather poking out from between two blankets about halfway up. It was the most unusual peacock feather he had ever seen.

Binx had seen many feathers since he'd been adopted and fallen in love with his forever home. Feather Dan loved feathers while he was alive. Even though Dan had been gone for over a couple months before Binx had been adopted, there were still hundreds of feathers around to play with. There were even a few peacock feathers left so it wasn't as if he'd never seen one before. Despite being the youngest of his siblings he felt he was quite qualified in stating that the particular peacock feather that was sticking out of Blankets Mountain was the most unusual feather he'd ever seen. It might well have been the most unusual *anything* he'd ever seen. It was rainbow colored and shimmery like someone had poured glitter on it. It swayed gently as if moved by a soft breeze but there was no fan in the room. The air conditioner wasn't even on.

Binx climbed up the side of Blankets Mountain to give it a proper inspection. He put his pink nose up to it and gave it a sniff. It smelled strange but not bad, just something that he had never smelled before. If he had to guess, he'd say it smelled like a cloud. He swatted at it with his paw to make it bounce and it shimmered when it moved. He grabbed it with his mouth and tried to give it a good pull to get it out but it tasted funny and wouldn't budge. He pawed at the blankets around it to see if he could dig it out. When he did he was surprised. Light flickered out from between the blankets!

Binx quickly pulled his paw back and stared at the spot the light had come from in wonder. He reached back out and pulled on the blanket and again light flickered out from inside of Blankets Mountain. He stopped and studied it hard. This was just incredible and he had to show Leroy and Amelia! He turned and raced off as fast as he could back to the living room. He jumped up on the couch right between them and immediately started excitedly babbling about a rainbow feather and lights in Blankets Mountain.

Amelia hissed in annoyance. She put one of her giant six toed polydactyl paws over her head. "Stay out of the catnip Binx," she fussed at him, "and quit interrupting nap time!" She had a short solid grey coat and was a bit overweight. She gave a groan and rolled over so her back was to him.

Leroy was the largest of them by far. He was easily fifteen pounds but tall, long and muscular. He was orange and white striped with white mittens for feet. He was the oldest but wore his age well. Depending on his mood, his facial expressions could look very wise or just plain dopey. He stretched all four of his legs out as far as he could covering nearly two thirds of the couch. He opened one dark yellow eye and glared at Binx.

"Put my toy nip banana back where you found it right now!"

Binx was exasperated. "I promise I haven't been in the nip. I don't even know where your nip banana is!" He couldn't let those two distract him or blow him off like they usually did, "There is light coming out of Blankets Mountain! There is a rainbow colored sparkly feather! I was hearing drums and it smelled odd in there. Really! You have to see the rainbow feather!"

42

Leroy groaned, closed his dark yellow eye and started to go back to sleep. Binx refused to be ignored this time. This was too exciting. He pawed at the bottom of Leroy's big white feet. "I'm not telling stories! I haven't been in any catnip! You have to come see what's going on. It's incredible!"

Leroy's feet were very ticklish and they twitched. He opened both of his eyes and glared at Binx. "Quit tickling my feet before I bop you on top of your head! It's nap time now. Shut up!"

"Leroy, Amelia, come on you have to see this!" Binx was highly excited and had no intention of leaving them alone until they came and saw it for themselves. "I've never even heard of a rainbow peacock feather before! Why is there light in Blankets Mountain? I promise I'm not telling stories. You have to come see for yourself!"

Leroy groaned, rolled over and stood up. He stretched his back and gave Binx a very ugly look. "Fine, but after I look I'm going to go back to sleep and better get left alone for the rest of the day."

Leroy hopped off the couch and Binx excitedly hopped off behind him. Binx was tiny next to Leroy, less than half his size. He watched Leroy's shoulder muscles roll while he walked. Leroy was known mostly for being a gentle giant but Binx could tell he wasn't happy about nap time being interrupted and he really didn't want to get bopped on his head.

Amelia, having been too disrupted to fall back asleep, got up and with a huff of irritation and jumped down to join them. She was larger than Binx but much smaller than Leroy. She was a big fan of extra treats and had a bit of a chubby frame to show for it. Not yet fully alert, she slowly followed them down the hall into the guest bedroom.

Binx ran ahead of Leroy as fast as he could and kept telling Leroy to hurry. Leroy took his time despite Binx's excitement for

43

him to come see what he'd found. Leroy took one look at Blankets Mountain and stopped dead in his tracks. Amelia walked into Leroy's back side and hissed.

Now they could see the rainbow colored peacock feather sticking out of Blankets Mountain. Binx ran over and jumped up to it. He pawed at it and pulled on it but it wouldn't budge.

"I told you so! Look how it shimmers! Have you ever seen anything like it? And look at this." He let the feather go and pawed at the blankets and when he did light flickered from between them. Binx looked back at Leroy and exclaimed with satisfaction. "I told you so!"

Leroy took a moment to stare at Blanket Mountain. "What is this?" He cautiously walked over to Blankets Mountain and sniffed around.

Amelia, the most cautious of the bunch, kept her distance while Leroy examined things. She leaped up on the bed and watched from there. Binx kept pawing at the blankets and tugging at the feather but it wouldn't budge. Leroy hopped up to take a closer look.

"Leroy, you're the strongest. See if you can get the feather out." Binx gave him an expectant and excited look.

Leroy pushed it with his nose and watched it shimmer just like Binx had. He opened his mouth and bit it hard. Holding onto it as hard as he could he pulled and tugged on it. The feather didn't budge. He set his feet and used his entire body to try to drag it out. It didn't move; not even a centimeter.

Leroy stopped and studied it, "That's really stuck in there."

Binx climbed over to stand next to Leroy. "I tried to pull the blankets aside so I could see where the light was coming from but

I'm not strong enough. See if you can pull up the blankets and I'll try to see what that light is."

Leroy nodded his head in agreement. He climbed up to get in a position above the feather where he'd have the best leverage. He dug his claws deep into the blankets and braced himself. Once he was set he gave it a mighty pull.

The blankets weren't stuck like the feather was and they moved. Bright light spilled out into the room. Amelia emitted a surprised gasp. She hopped down off the bed to get a better look. Binx didn't waste any time. He poked his head right in and looked around.

Leroy grunted as he lifted the blankets a little higher. "Well Binx? What do you see?"

"Pull it up some more Leroy, just a little higher." Binx was small and almost able to squeeze in.

Leroy gave another good tug and the blankets pulled back several inches. It opened up more than wide enough for Binx to be able to crawl inside. Binx poked his head in and looked around. He was looking at a big cave made of blankets like the ones on the outside of Blankets Mountain. There was a lot of light that was coming from higher up. The stem of the Peacock Feather was sitting in a rainbow colored sun puddle on the floor of the cave a few feet in. It registered with Binx that the cave was bigger on the inside than Blankets Mountain was on the outside but he'd seen unbelievable things already that afternoon that he didn't even question it. He took a couple of steps inside the cave to get a better look around.

"Leroy it's incredible! It's a big blanket cave and there's lots of light coming from somewhere up at the top. The feather... It's stuck to a rainbow colored sun puddle!"

"Quit making up stories Binx, what's really making that light?" Leroy replied to Binx.

Amelia cautiously entered behind Binx and she gasped. "Leroy, he's not making up any stories at all!"

Leroy grunted as his muscles flexed. "Hold on. I'm going to drag this blanket aside so I can look for myself. Don't go anywhere until I'm there with you!" Leroy continued to drag blankets aside. "Binx, I know you never met Neuro Dan but this was his Blankets Mountain and it's something that we consider to be sacred." Leroy lectured. He was soon able to hop through to join them.

Leroy made it down into the cave and walked around Amelia to stand next to Binx. They all looked stunned by Binx's discovery. There was no way that this cave could fit inside of Blankets Mountain. It would take at least a dozen Blankets Mountains to house just the part they could see from where they were standing.

Amelia asked in awe, "Leroy, do you think that this has been here all along? I wouldn't be surprised if Neuro Dan still has secrets we don't know about. Maybe this was a fort he kept hidden."

Leroy was looking around. Binx knew he could be very patient about things that he didn't understand. Binx's curiosity wouldn't stand for being patient waiting on Leroy to make up his mind to investigate further. Leroy looked over at Amelia and said, "I'm not sure but we have to investigate this."

Together and side by side they went further in. Leroy walked over to examine the rainbow colored sun puddle. It took them several steps to get to it and it was hypnotic and beautiful. Binx reached out to touch it with his paw and before Leroy could stop him they heard a shuffling from somewhere not far above them.

When they looked up they saw Feather Dan with his wide and happy bright golden eyes and big goofy smile looking down at them. He looked exactly the same as before he passed away; except he had a fascinating bright sparkle to him. It was the same sparkle that was on the peacock feather. Dan looked so excited that he looked like he was about to spring into a happy dance.

Leroy and Amelia seemed to be paralyzed with shock. They stood there stunned, mouths hanging open, and just stared.

Binx looked up, and cocked his head in curiosity and asked, "Who are you?"

Dan's whiskers pushed forward in excitement and his ears perked up eagerly. He was smiling from ear to ear, "Hi, Binx. I'm Feather Dan. The Rainbow Bridge is in trouble and I need your help."

That was Neuro Dan – Feather Dan! But it couldn't be. Dan died well over a year ago! What were they looking at? Was it a ghost? Binx could hardly believe this was happening.

Chapter 4 – Sink Bath Cats

Dan looked back over his shoulder and said, "Okay, Remy, pass me those feathers now."

A moment later Leroy saw the tips of three feathers poke out over the ledge right next to Dan. Dan gave them a quick look then one by one pushed each off the ledge. Tumbling sideways and end over end, they floated down to the ground in front of the group. Seeing three large eagle feathers float down broke Leroy out of his daze. He was struggling to process what was going on. Dan was right in front of him. He hadn't been in the nip in three days so it couldn't be a hallucination. Leroy blinked a few times and looked back up at Dan. "Dan, how is this possible?"

Dan stared at Leroy, his wide eyes full of excitement and joy, he gave him a wink. With tremendous amounts of affection in his voice he said, "Hi, Leroy and Amelia. I sure have missed you two." He looked behind him and nodded to someone. When he spoke again his voice was all business. "I don't have time to explain at the moment but I will as we travel. Right now, I need each of you to pick a feather. Don't *ever* lose that feather. I'll explain in a bit but for now I need you to give the stem one great big giant chomp. Just one chomp though, that's very important."

Leroy was puzzled, "What do you mean as we travel?"

Binx had closed in on the feathers. He gave the feather a gentle swat and watched it shimmer with that glittery look that everything had inside the cave. The eagle feather was huge. Even with his orange tipped tail sticking straight out behind him it was almost as long as he was. He gave it a sniff. It smelled just like the peacock feather had. He shrugged his shoulders, reached down and picked it up by the stem with his teeth. Just like Dan had instructed, Binx gave the feather one fierce chomp.

Amelia was still too slow to stop him. Leroy watched as Binx chomped the feather and disappeared into thin air. Amelia's eyes went wide and she took a step back. Leroy was staring, open mouthed, at the spot where Binx had been standing. He looked around frantically but didn't see him anywhere. Binx had disappeared!

"Binx!" Leroy shouted and quickly looked back to Dan. A bit of panic had set in. As the eldest among them, Leroy considered himself responsible for the wellbeing of them all. "Neuro Dan – Feather Dan!" He shouted a bit of panic in his voice, "What happened to Binx?!"

Dan turned around and looked behind him. Leroy heard someone else say "Got him." and Dan turned back towards them again.

"Binx is fine. He's up here with us."

A giggle escaped from Binx. Leroy thought he said something had tickled his tummy. Then they could hear Binx start yelling in excitement. "Leroy! Amelia! I'm up on the ledge with Dan and his friend. You have to see this place. Hurry up already!"

Leroy couldn't make out what he was saying but he could hear Binx talking to someone. He sounded like he was asking a hundred questions all at once.

Dan looked at Leroy and smiled. "I don't have any more neurological problems now, Leroy. I'm just called Feather Dan now. You'll confuse people if you keep calling me Neuro Dan."

If it were possible Leroy looked even more amazed. To think of Dan without any of his physical disabilities that had limited him his entire life was a wonderful thing to imagine. Leroy got lost in thought for a moment. Amelia came up to him and bumped his shoulder. That brought him back to the present and he remembered their predicament.

Amelia looked at Leroy and said, "I suppose we better chomp the feathers and go. If something happens to Binx we sure will be in trouble. You know he's likely to wander off on his own. We can't let anything happen to him."

"Yes, you're right." Leroy nodded in agreement and stepped up to a feather. Amelia followed suit and stepped up to the last one. They both sniffed at them. Leroy couldn't detect any particular smell from the feathers.

Amelia looked over to Leroy and said, "Shall we? On the count of three we chomp at the same time."

Leroy took a deep breath and sighed. He wondered what in the world they were about to get into. He nodded at Amelia and said, "One."

Amelia took a deep breath and said, "Two."

"Three," they said in unison.

They each chomped down on their feather at the same time. For a brief second they felt the sensation of falling in their stomachs. In the time it would take to blink, they were standing at the top of the ledge with Dan and another cat. The feathers they had chomped had become decorative collars around their necks with a miniature version of the eagle feather hanging from it. Leroy looked to reassure him that Binx remained nearby. Binx was trotting his way, looking at his and Amelia's feather collars.

He sniffed theirs and said, "Your feathers smell like clouds too! Did it tickle your belly? This is the best adventure day EVER!" Binx was rambling nonstop. "Hey, this is Remy. He's new here too but he came through the Rainbow Bridge not by chomping a feather."

Dan looked at them and got a confused look on his face. He said, "Oh dear, you don't shine."

Leroy, Binx and Amelia looked at each other then looked at Dan and Remy. Sure enough, they just looked like normal cats while Dan and his friend had that Rainbow Bridge brightness to them.

Dan said, "It must be because you still have your bodies. This is all very new to us too. I haven't figured out how bringing you here works yet. I just found out how to do it a few minutes ago. No matter, we'll figure it out as we go."

Binx was getting too curious to be still. He was starting to wander off and snoop around but hadn't gone far yet because his head was filled with questions. "Look at all of the ledges! How far up does it go Dan? What's around that corner? What about that corner? Jeez Dan, how big is this place? How'd you fit it all inside your Blankets Mountain in the closet? Is everything made of blankets? It would kind of be weird if all of Rainbow Bridge was made of blankets. I mean, I like blankets and all but this is a lot of blanket stuff going on. Maybe we should talk about different decorations later."

Leroy scowled at him, "You stay close Binx. Do NOT wander off without us. We need to figure out what's going on and why Neuro Da… Sorry, Feather Dan brought us here."

Dan shook his head at all of the questions Binx was asking. "This is the Rainbow Bridge. No the Rainbow Bridge is not made up of blankets. Only my Blankets Mountain of clouds is made up of blankets. I'll get to other questions later but right now we need to get moving. I'll explain but there's trouble and we need to go."

Dan hurriedly led them through the series of connecting caves and tunnels within Blankets Mountain. They went up several ledges and by the time they got to the Hall of Feathers it felt as if they'd climbed from the bottom of a mountain clear to the top.

As they traveled together, Dan explained, "This all really just unfolded about an hour ago. I had just welcomed Remy to the Bridge, showed him around Cat Tree City and welcomed him to Blankets Mountain. I was showing off my feather collection in the Hall of Feathers when I noticed the Native American headdress was missing."

"The what?" Amelia asked.

"It's the showpiece in my collection. It's beautiful and covered with feathers and shiny pieces and turquoise beads. It was there when I created Blankets Mountain and it's been on a cloud pedestal ever since."

Leroy sounded astonished. "You created a Blankets Mountain at Rainbow Bridge?"

Binx giggled, "Why would you put a dress on your head?"

Leroy gave Binx a stern look and said, "You hush and let us work this out."

Dan continued, "When we got to the empty pedestal we could hear drums and chanting."

Binx perked up, "I could hear drums in the room when the peacock feather was sticking out of your Blankets Mountain."

"A spirit named Doba from the Beyond appeared to us and told us that the headdress had mystical properties. One of the things it can do is send animals back and forth from Earth to the Rainbow Bridge. Click a couple of beads, toss in a feather and poof!"

Leroy shook his head, "Simply incredible. That's how you got us here."

Dan nodded his head, "Yup. Unfortunately, Siamese twins have stolen the headdress. They have no idea about its abilities either. The spirit told us that they are running around in the clouds playing with it. When we talked to him he said they'd already opened three portals and that there are three cats lost in the clouds beyond Cat Tree City. Doba said I needed a team because they would be too scared and untrusting of spirit cats like us. That's why I need you guys. I need help in rounding up those cats, plus however many more Sassy and Bandit, the Siamese twins, have managed to bring through. We have to get them to chomp their feathers so they can go home. It would not be a good thing if they became stuck here."

They hopped up to another ledge, rounded one more corner and stepped into the Hall of Feathers. The newcomers stopped to take it all in for a moment. Amelia walked over to look at a white and blue speckled feather and became enamored with the sounds of the bird song. Leroy took in the scene from the center of the room. He was so impressed he didn't know what to say. It was a beautiful collection.

Leroy noticed when Binx bounded off towards the opposite wall to get a look at some larger feathers. Binx wasn't staying with the group and was about to scold him when Remy spoke up.

"I'll help Leroy keep an eye on the kid, Dan. I think we need to be moving though." Remy volunteered.

Dan led Leroy and Amelia further into the Hall of Feathers, leaving Remy and Binx to keep up on their own. Leroy could hear Remy remind Binx he would miss out on their adventure if he didn't keep up. Leroy knew how much of a handful Binx could be. Remy would likely soon regret offering to babysit.

Dan looked over at Leroy. "There's a lot to learn once you get to the Rainbow Bridge. You know, it's pretty easy to check in on you. I peek in all of the time to see how you guys and mum and dad and gramma are doing."

Amelia brushed up against Dan and said, "It was really hard when you left us. We were all heart broken and I don't think I've ever seen mum and dad stay so sad for so long."

Dan nodded, "I saw that. I wished so hard I could tell them not to cry so much. I think if they could have known how much fun I was having and how good I felt they would have been happy instead."

Dan sniffled. "There are some things that are harder for me to check on and I'm curious. How is Mr. Squirrel? Has outside cat D.J. stopped trying to catch him yet? And Mr. Owl, is he still around?"

Amelia snorted and rolled her eyes when he mentioned Mr. Owl. "How many times did you try to convince me to hand deliver a note to Mr. Owl to see if he would give you one of his feathers?" She snorted again, "Hand deliver, Dan, really you could be something else. I had no intention of being Mr. Owl's, breakfast, lunch or dinner!"

Dan smiled as many wonderful memories flashed before him. "Well, I really, REALLY wanted one of Mr. Owl's feathers."

Amelia shook her head, "He's still around alright. I think he's got a new nest not too far away from where Mr. Squirrel has his home now."

Leroy smiled and said, "Mr. Squirrel met Mrs. Squirrel last year and now they have a little family right across from our porch. Although I do worry with Mr. Owl so close, I love to watch those little rascals run about. I've actually been wondering if they haven't worked out some type of truce because not one of the younglings has been snatched."

Leroy knew Mr. Squirrel was unique for a squirrel. He'd sit outside the glass door on their porch and chat with Dan for hours; or until D.J. wandered around and chased him off. He was a really nice squirrel and was always willing to keep his eye out for feathers in exchange for any nuts that mum or dad happened to bring into the house.

When they stepped out of the entrance to the Hall of Feathers and onto the top of Blankets Mountain, the view was breathtaking. They were on the highest point in Rainbow Bridge and they could see forever. The clouds were beautiful. They were white, fluffy and in various shapes. The clouds resembled rolling hills and mountain ranges. They stretched on endlessly. There were many cats playing all over the clouds that were closest to Blankets Mountain and Cat Tree City.

Amelia took one look at Cat Tree City and she started to tear up. Leroy knew she absolutely loved cat trees. She liked to scamper on them, jump off them and sleep on them. They were her favorite spot to be. She looked over the thousands of towering cat trees and looked happy taking them all in.

Binx was running in circles around everyone. He raced over next to Amelia and looked at Cat Tree City. Then he raced over to Leroy and looked at all the other cats playing on the clouds. He was out of breath from all the running and couldn't speak.

Remy kept a close eye on Binx and asked Dan, "Where do you think we should start looking?"

Dan shook his head, "I'm not sure. I suppose we're going to have to start asking around to see if anyone has seen the twins. They should be pretty easy to spot dragging that big old headdress around. They won't exactly be able to stay very inconspicuous."

At that moment Binx's orange tipped, two sizes too big ears perked up. He was hearing something he wasn't expecting to hear. He stood up on his hind legs, turned his ears in all different directions and looked around like he'd heard something.

Other than having unique markings on his fur because of his breed, Binx had one other feature that stood out and was impossible to miss; his ears. Binx had giant ears that were two sizes too big for his head. People would chuckle at him and ask if he was ever going to grow into them but it was obvious he wasn't. Binx never got hurt feelings about how they made people laugh. Leroy had asked him about it and come to the conclusion that he was too much of a happy cat and far too curious to worry about what other people thought. Those ears, however, gave him a kind of superpower. Leroy knew he had exceptional hearing.

Remy noticed and asked, "What is it Binx? What are you hearing?"

"Does anyone else hear that?" Binx stopped swiveling his ears and they focused in on a specific spot.

Leroy stepped up next to Binx and looked in the direction his ears were pointing. "What do you hear kid?"

"I hear," Binx paused for a second as if to make sure he wasn't mistaken. "Yup, I hear barking. It's coming from out towards those clouds."

Dan perked up and said enthusiastically, "Oh that would be Grace! I'm sure glad she decided to visit today." He turned towards a trail that twisted down the side of Blankets Mountain towards the clouds. "Come on let's go greet her." They started heading down

Blankets Mountain and it didn't take long before the others could hear the barking too.

Remy asked, "How did a dog manage to get into the cat clouds. I thought you said that all of the animal kingdoms were in different realms."

Dan nodded, "It's true but there are some exceptions. Most of the time different animal species are separated into their respective realms. Mostly the only times different animals are seen together are when they are with their human and walking to the Beyond Cloud. Each realm can see that path from the Rainbow Bridge to the Beyond Cloud without interacting with the other realms."

Remy nodded. "So how is it we are going to meet a dog?" he asked Dan.

Amelia spoke up. "Grace isn't just any dog. She was my best friend. Grace passed away just a few months before Dan did. Losing both of them so close together was hard for all of us." Amelia's tail was quivering, betraying her excitement. "Dan, is Grace really here?"

Dan smiled, "Yes, Amelia. To answer your questions Remy, Grace was raised as a pup with cats. She lived her entire life with cats. I'm honestly not sure if she thought she was a cat or if she thought we were dogs like her. She was also a guardian to me. She seemed to understand my disability and she looked after me. Now, she just shows up whenever she wants to check up on me. She has no problem at all navigating the cloudscapes."

As they made their way down the mountain they passed several other cats who Dan had helped cross over. They were looking at Leroy, Binx and Amelia as if the circus had come to town. One of them, a beautiful Norwegian Forest Cat, asked Dan, "How did they get so filthy?" She wasn't intending to be insulting, she was just in shock. "They don't shine! Dan, are you going to give them a sink bath?"

Amelia flattened her short ears across the top of her grey head, glared at the long haired silver and black cat and hissed. The other cat looked absolutely offended and turned away.

Dan quickly stepped in. Amelia was known to be quite the sassy pants and wouldn't be hesitant at all to express her opinion. "No," he told her, "They are different but special. They are with me and we're on a very important mission."

Other cats were starting to gather around and stare at the group. The crowd got big enough that Dan decided he'd take advantage of it and see if they could get some extra help. "Has anyone seen or heard from the Siamese twins, Sassy and Bandit?"

The crowd looked amongst themselves but before any of them could speak up, everyone's attention suddenly shifted out towards the clouds where there was a commotion. Grace was chasing a cat. Chasing wasn't exactly the right word to use though. Grace was actually herding the cat. Grace was a small black and white Border collie. While she had been alive, she became an amazing herding dog. She was so good that she had gotten the reputation of being a grade 'A' professional cat herder. Now it was easy to see that she was herding a cat directly to Blankets Mountain.

Like him, Leroy noticed that the cat didn't shine. One of Dan's friends yelled out to Dan that Grace was bringing in her second sink bath cat of the day. Leroy watched Dan look around. Sure enough, crouched on one of the blankets near the bottom of Blankets Mountain was another cat that didn't shine. Its fur was bristled and its tail high in an effort to look bigger and more menacing. Any time another cat tried to get near, the cat's hackles went up, his ears went flat and he hissed and growled.

Grace rushed up with the second cat and got it corralled on the same blanket cloud as the other one. Amelia ran right up to Grace, purring as loud as she ever had. She showered Grace with kisses and rubbed up against her with mushes until she'd circled Grace four times.

"Oh Grace, how I've missed you so!" Amelia said in a big happy voice.

Grace looked happy to see Amelia. Her whole back end was wagging not just her tail and she was panting showing a big toothy grin. Grace looked toward Dan and saw Leroy and two other cats standing next to him. Leroy nodded at Grace and told her, "Hello, old friend. I've missed you a great deal."

Grace raced over towards Dan and Leroy to give them a good sniff and a few licks. Then she looked at Dan, glanced at the cats she had herded, then back to Dan. Dan nodded in understanding and told her "It's a long story. I'll explain. First, let me introduce you to Remy, who has newly crossed over. This here is Binx and he came with Leroy and Amelia."

It took a few minutes for Dan to explain to Grace what the situation was. When Dan finished Grace said, "I was coming for a visit today when I noticed a cat without any shine to it. I knew something was wrong. So, I crouched down so he wouldn't see me and watched. He just sat there and kept clawing at his neck. I couldn't figure out why until I noticed he managed to pull off a small collar and toss it on the ground." Grace nodded at Leroy, "The collar looked a lot like the one Leroy, Amelia and Binx have but with a smaller feather. I didn't know what to do but I figured if anyone could figure it out, it'd be you."

She glanced over at the two herded cats. They were sitting close together and were watching the other cats warily. "Anyway, I knew something was wrong and even if you didn't know what to do. You'd at least have room on Blankets Mountain for them."

Grace looked back out towards the clouds, "Once I got that one here and you weren't around I thought that if there was one cat like that out there that there could be more. I decided to go look and I found that one. She's got more of a temper than the first one too."

Dan looked and he could see from where he was sitting that the other cat didn't have the collar on either. He knew they were going to have to get those back if the cats were going to have a chance to make it back home.

"Leroy, would you please go talk to them. We need to know where they left their collars. Try to explain things to them, please. I don't want them to be so scared. You look like them so I expect they'll at least listen to you."

Despite Leroy's intimidatingly massive size, his calming demeanor and lack of shine was enough for the other two cats to let him approach and talk to them. He explained the situation and told them to just stay put and stick together. He told them the group would go find their collars so they could go home but to just stay safe where they were and not get lost.

It only took Leroy a few minutes to get the cats somewhat more relaxed. When he returned he told Dan, "They don't have any idea where their collars are. They became completely disoriented when Grace started chasing them. They couldn't even guess how far out they were."

Dan looked at Grace. "Lead the way friend. It may have been by chance, but you found us a starting point. You've given us a trail of clues to follow. The twins can't be far off from where you found the cats."

The group got to their feet. Amelia had to be awakened. She'd curled up against Grace and been snuggling so hard she'd dozed off. Grace started off towards the mountain range of clouds and the others followed.

Chapter 5 – Bandit and Sassy

The two Siamese, Bandit and Sassy, were taking turns dragging and playing with the headdress. It was huge, much bigger than both of them combined. The feathered tail of the headdress trailed several feet behind them. The beads and other decorations which adorned it clattered together as it was dragged along. At the moment, Sassy was doing her best to carry it. She was staying close to the side of one of the large cloud mountains in order to avoid being seen from Blankets Mountain. The headdress was heavy but not so heavy it took both of them to walk with it. The real challenge was the sheer size of it. It was so big that it kept them from being able to move quickly.

Bandit, walking beside her, was watching the decorative beads and other shiny pieces sway back and forth and clatter together. He was studying it very carefully. They had seen four tiny feathers fly off the tail of the headdress, dance in the air then disappear. They hadn't completely figured out how to duplicate it themselves but they knew it had to be some specific combination of the decorations touching or maybe even a specific noise. It could even be a combination of something they hadn't noticed yet.

When it happened the first time it was a complete surprise. A tiny white feather popped up off the tail of the headdress and danced in the air for several feet. Sassy pounced at it out of reflex but it evaded her then simply vanished. They stared at the spot where it had disappeared and waited to see if it would come back but it was gone.

After a long discussion about how fascinating it was they decided that one of them would carry it and the other would watch closely to see if another feather would pop up and fly off. Sure enough not long after the first one appeared another one flew off the tail. Bandit pounced at that one but he didn't have any more success than Sassy and in just a matter of a couple of seconds that feather vanished as well.

They swapped positions and Bandit carried it while Sassy took her turn to trying to figure it out. It took longer for the third feather to launch off. Sassy was fast but the feather moved faster and very erratically. Had it been there for more than just a couple of seconds she may have had a chance to catch it but she only got one chance to pounce on it and poof it was gone.

It was after it happened the fourth time that Bandit thought he was beginning to identify a correlation between some turquoise and silver beads and the launching of the feather. They decided that Sassy would just carry it for a while and see if Bandit could get it figured out. Bandit watched the swaying of the beads closely, paying particular attention to which combination of beads were making contact with each other. Every step Sassy took caused the beads to sway and different decorations would touch each other. One step and a silver bead and a piece of bone would touch. The next step and a turquoise bead and a red bead would touch. Each time they touched they would make different kinds of clicking and clacking sounds.

Then Sassy tripped and a bunch of turquoise beads bounced around. Bandit's eyes went wide as he saw another tiny white feather shoot off the tail and dance into the air. He tried to anticipate which way it was going to zig or zag and pounced but he missed it and the feather vanished.

Despite missing the feather Bandit looked at Sassy and smiled. "I think I figured it out!"

Sassy set down the headdress, eager to hear what Bandit had to say.

"When you tripped you made those turquoise beads..." Bandit went silent in complete surprise.

Exactly where the feather had disappeared stood a cat. It had appeared from absolutely nowhere. One second it was empty space and the next there stood a cat. They were shocked and gaped at it. The cat was a calico and had the dirtiest fur either of them had ever seen since they crossed the Rainbow Bridge many years ago. The cat was staring at them and looked just as stunned as they were.

Sassy looked it over in disgust and said, "Oh my cat. You're absolutely filthy!"

The calico looked at the two of them, flattened its ears and hissed.

Sassy continued to stare at the calico, "No need for that hissing. I'm certainly not going to touch you! Are you sick? You're not contagious are you? I didn't think we could get sick here. Bandit have you ever seen anything like this?"

Sassy's question snapped Bandit's attention back to her. "Nope, I sure haven't. I haven't even heard anyone ever talk about it either."

Before Sassy could say anything more, the calico cat interrupted with questions showing he was very curious about his surroundings. "What did you two get into? What is wrong with your fur? Where am I and how did I get here?" he demanded.

Bandit cocked his head to the side as an idea came to him. "Where did you come from? What were you doing just before you got here?"

"I was at home playing in my living room. I saw a little white feather floating down from the ceiling and when it got close enough I caught it and started to chomp on it. I didn't even blink and the next thing I know I'm standing here looking at you two. Where am I?"

"You really caught the feather?" Bandit asked excitedly. "Oh, you're at the Rainbow Bridge." He looked at Sassy excitedly, "Are you thinking the same thing I am?"

She looked a bit more apprehensive than she did excited. "Are you wondering about those other feathers that disappeared? Do you suppose other cats came through after we left?"

"No," Bandit shook his head but stopped and said "Oh I hadn't thought about it like that. He's an Earth cat. Think about that Sassy. He came from his home to here. What if those feathers work both ways?"

Her eyes went wide and together they said, "I wonder if we do catch a feather if we can go back home?"

Sassy looked at the calico. They needed to get rid of him so they could figure this out. "What's your name?"

"My name is Sam." the Earth calico replied.

"Well, Sam, welcome to the Rainbow Bridge. You need to get that fur cleaned up pretty quick. If you go back that way and walk around this cloud you'll see a giant mountain that looks like it's made of blankets. Head there, lots of cats live there."

With that said, Bandit and Sassy grabbed the headdress. They carried it together so they could move more quickly. Sam watched them run off. He was extremely confused. He also noticed that he had a strange collar around his neck that hadn't been there before. He figured it must have some purpose so he decided to leave it alone, even though it stung a little. He needed to figure out just exactly what was going on. As he watched Bandit and Sassy disappear behind another cloud he decided that he would follow

Sassy's instructions. He turned around and headed off towards Blankets Mountain.

Sassy and Bandit ran until they were two entire clouds away from where they left Sam before they stopped to rest. Sassy took advantage of the small break to ask Bandit a question. "Do you think Dan knows what the headdress does?" Sassy asked.

Bandit nodded his head, "Probably. Dan's really smart, almost as smart as we are. I can't imagine why he would keep such a treasure like this a secret though. I bet Dan can catch those feathers too. He's the best feather chaser I've ever seen. How many times do you think he's gone back to visit his family?" Sassy got a look on her face that Bandit knew well. He could tell she was thinking hard about his question so he waited to hear what she had to say. Sassy was pretty smart so it was usually in his best interest to listen to her.

"I don't know. It just doesn't make sense." Sassy said. "We both know Dan has to be the most generous cat at Rainbow Bridge. I just can't imagine he'd horde anything that would make everyone happy."

Bandit thought about what Sassy said. "Yeah, you're right. Dan is a generous cat and he likes to share. He really must not know what this thing can do. He's been missing out." No reason he had to miss out, or Sassy had to miss out though. They could just keep this to themselves until they had it all figured out.

"Probably, either way we need to keep moving." Sassy reminded him.

She was right, it would ruin their fun if they got caught with the headdress. They wandered a few clouds farther out not really paying attention to the direction they were headed. When they stopped for another rest break, they both agreed to try to get the headdress to do its magic again.

66

"Let's just set it down here." Bandit said. "I've been watching it closely as you ran. I think the turquoise beads are part of what made the magic work." Bandit had noticed that when they hit each other a feather showed up. "Get ready, Sassy, I'm pretty sure I know how to get this to work now."

Sassy crouched low prepared to pounce as Bandit started to swat at the turquoise beads. He hit them a few times before he got them to click just right. When they did, a small white feather shot off into the air. Sassy launched herself into the air to catch it. Just as she landed on it, it poofed and was gone.

Sassy sighed, "Those feathers are seriously fast!" Sassy sat back on her haunches and looked at Bandit.

Bandit knew she was a great hunter but he could tell she was getting frustrated every time she missed catching a feather. "Do you think that maybe if we just bring it back to Dan he'd catch one for us? It sure would be nice to visit home."

Bandit missed their human a lot and would love to do more than a quick check in from the Rainbow Bridge. It had been a long time, more years than he could remember, since they'd gotten ear rubs. Bandit was tempted by the idea of seeing Hope again. But he knew Dan well enough to know he wasn't a risk taker and would be more likely to take the headdress away from them and not let them near it again. "Dan would be too cautious; especially if he doesn't already know about its magic." he told Sassy.

Then another thought occurred to him. "You don't think another Earth cat is going to show up do you?" If Earth cats started showing up all over the place, they were going to be in big trouble and Dan would hunt them down sooner rather than later. There was no telling where those feathers went after they disappeared. He'd only just seen the one cat show up. It had to be just a coincidence. Surely that cat had simply been in the right place at the right time to see the feather.

Bandit wasn't quite ready to quit trying to catch a feather before Dan spoiled all their fun. "Come on let's go over to that cloud and try again." He knew Sassy was as eager as he was to keep trying until they figured it out.

Bandit hadn't made it three steps when he heard a laughing sound behind them. He stopped in his tracks at the same time Sassy did. He glanced at her and she looked at him and in unison they both turned around to see there was a goat standing there chewing something in its mouth. It looked at each of them, its ears twitched and it bleated what was probably a question at them. It was the same laughing sound as before. The goat bleated again and Bandit thought it might have been asking them a question. Since he didn't speak goat and he knew Sassy didn't speak goat, he couldn't guess what it was asking and had no idea how to answer it. He looked over at Sassy wondering what she was thinking they should do.

Sassy looked at Bandit and said, "Um, well this is interesting. I don't know what to do about this one."

Well if she had no idea, he certainly had no idea. It was probably best to just pretend it never happened and get away from the scene of the crime. Bandit looked back at Sassy and with his most level voice said, "We just walk away. We don't know anything. I didn't see any goat and neither did you."

Bandit glanced at Sassy and said, "We're going to run for it but we'll have to carry the headdress together. Let's back up slowly to get away from it, then when we get far enough we turn around and run fast when I say now."

She nodded her agreement with his plan, never taking her eyes off the goat in front of them. Then Bandit and Sassy both backed up ten paces and turned around. Bandit made sure his teeth had a strong grip on the headdress before saying, "Now! "And they started running.

The goat bleated again. Bandit was glad he didn't speak goat. It was probably saying mean things at them based on the angry way it kept bleating at them. He wasn't surprised when he heard hoof beats indicating it was chasing after them. "Run faster Sassy it's gaining on us!" Bandit yelled as the hoof beats sounded directly behind them. He knew goats would eat anything and he wasn't about to lose the headdress to a goat. With the motivation to not lose their prize to a goat, Bandit and Sassy sprinted faster still carrying the headdress between them. Bandit thought it was a good thing they had practiced carrying toys just like this many times. At full speed, even dragging the headdress, they were soon outrunning the goat.

As they disappeared around the side of the cloud, Bandit knew the goat wouldn't be able to see them. He could still hear the goat bleating but it wasn't far away yet. "Stop!" said Bandit through his teeth. Sassy stopped and looked at him, breathing hard from their run. Bandit quickly dropped the headdress to say, "we gotta find a good spot... to hide…. from the goat. I know... just where to go... Follow my lead." Picking up the headdress, he saw Sassy nod and they started running again. Bandit was out of breath from running, but this was shaping up to be a very exciting day.

Chapter 6 – Smelling Clouds

Grace led the way as Feather Dan, Remy, Leroy and Amelia started out on their journey. They traveled towards the nearest cloud to Blankets Mountain. Leroy thought it felt funny to be walking on wispy clouds. It felt like walking across cotton balls. Dan said it just felt like walking on a soft carpet to him. There were obvious differences in sensations and experience with cats that didn't make it to the Rainbow Bridge the traditional way. Leroy wanted to be a bit cautious with everything they did but Binx was eagerly inspecting everything and seemed to be having a good time experiencing the different sensations.

Leroy explained to Dan why the other Earth cats, he refused to refer to anyone as a sink bath cat, said they took the collars off. "The other Earth cats told me that their collars stung and felt like they were burning their necks."

Dan motioned to Leroy's collar, "Does yours sting?"

Leroy shook his head, "Not at all. It just feels like a normal collar to me."

"Nope, it's no bother at all." Binx chimed in as he jumped into a small swirling cloud. When he landed in it he vanished for a second and the bit of cloud broke up and scattered as if he'd jumped into a pile of leaves. Remy stayed close to Binx, which now and then meant simply running circles around the group in order to keep close to him.

They speculated back and forth on why the cats that the twins were bringing over were having the issue. Remy shared his idea. "Doba said the small feathers were only good for one round trip. He said the bigger feathers could be used for multiple trips. What if the collar stings to warn you that you only have one chomp of the feather left? You know, so you'd know if it's safe to use it again?"

"Brilliant sleuthing, Remy!" Dan exclaimed. "That must be it. A way of warning the user so they wouldn't be trapped here and not be able to help their person."

Leroy nodded in appreciation, "Very wise of who or whatever created the headdress."

The group rounded the side of a cloud. After a few more steps Grace stopped and sat down. Looking back at Dan she said, "This is where I found the first cat. He wasn't at all far from Blankets Mountain. He was just wandering around, obviously lost. I could tell he had no idea where he was or where to go."

Everyone stopped and looked around the area where Grace was sitting. "I came up to try to help but as soon as he saw me he hissed and made the ugly growls at me. He really doesn't like dogs. I even tried to talk to him in cat so he'd feel more comfortable but even that didn't work. I wasn't sure what else to do so I barked at him and got him to run. I herded him to Blankets Mountain," Grace informed the group.

Dan nodded, "That was the right thing to do. Did he have his collar on when you got to him?"

Grace shook her head no. "Nope, I never saw a collar on him."

"Well," Dan looked around, "we need to start looking somewhere and it might as well be here. Everyone spread out. We'll have to do one of those things we've heard people call a grid search."

Dan quickly explained what he wanted them to do and the six of them spread out in a line. They all walked forward together, each of them searching the swirling mist of cloud below and around them.

They sometimes had to brush some thicker patches of swirling clouds aside to see under them. They walked forward for about a hundred feet, then turned, moved the line farther away from the cloud mountain and traveled back towards where they started. After the third pass, and what felt like a very long time searching Binx stopped and started sniffing the air.

"I smell the same thing I did in the guest bedroom back home when I first found the peacock feather sticking out of Blankets Mountain." Binx eagerly sniffed all around him searching intently.

Amelia looked at him and asked, "What are you talking about? You keep telling us you smell something odd but nobody else smells anything at all. You aren't making up stories again are you?"

Leroy gave Binx a stern look, "Binx, I never smelled anything either. This search is very serious and no time to play games. Are you sure about this scent you say you smell?"

"I'm not playing or telling stories, I promise. I don't know how to describe it except to say it smells like what I would expect a cloud to smell like."

Amelia snorted, "Well if you smell clouds try looking around. You do realize we're walking on clouds right now?"

"Let me see if I can smell it too," Remy said as he walked over near Binx to see if he could smell anything. When he got close to where Binx was sniffing he spotted the collar. "Hey," Remy got everyone's attention. "Look, the collar is right here!"

Remy reached down to pick the collar up but cried out, "Ow," as soon as his paw touched it. He immediately released it, as if it bit him. "That was no little sting! That burned bad!"

Leroy was concerned for Remy's safety. He bounded over to make sure he was okay. "What's wrong Remy?"

Remy, licking his orange paw, nodded at the collar. "I can't touch it. It felt like touching fire. Also, I couldn't smell anything like clouds."

Leroy looked at the collar and gave it a quick but gentle swat. He didn't experience anything painful about touching it. He gave it another tap and carefully moved it a few inches. He still didn't feel anything except a tingle so he picked it up with his paw. As soon as he held onto it he felt a slight sting but it didn't really hurt it was more irritating than anything else; kind of like stepping in water and not being able to shake it off your paw. Leroy let the collar drop back to the cloud at his feet.

He looked at Dan and said, "It doesn't really bother me. Just a little stinging tingle like when a foot falls asleep."

Dan walked over and touched it quickly with a tap of his right paw. He gasped when he did. "Yep, it burns just like Remy said." Dan stepped back from it. "That's the first time since coming to the Rainbow Bridge that I've experienced anything like pain. I didn't think pain could exist here."

Amelia touched it briefly with her paw, then held her paw on it a little longer. "It's not painful to me. It doesn't bother me much. Give it a try Binx, and see if it bothers you."

Binx sniffed at the collar then put his paw on it. "Nope it doesn't hurt much at all. It sure does smell like clouds though I'm pretty sure that's what I smelled."

A shrewd look crossed Amelia's face. Leroy could tell she was deep in thought about something before she spoke. "I was thinking about what you said Doba told you. I'll bet it's a defense mechanism of some kind to keep the angel kitties from trying to use a feather."

Dan looked at Amelia as she spoke. Then he nodded, catching Leroy's attention. "That's some great detective work, Amelia. I'm sure you're right. Who knows what would happen if a Rainbow Bridge cat chomped on one of those feathers. But I wonder why the bigger ones we got for all of you didn't have the same effect?"

Remy nodded his head in agreement. "We really don't know much about how the headdress works." Remy added. "I agree with Amelia. I think that makes sense for it to be a defense mechanism."

Dan nodded, "You're right Remy. We don't have time right now to worry about how it works. It's important that we get the headdress recovered as quickly as possible. We need to stop Sassy and Bandit before something terrible happens."

Dan was quiet for a second, then turned towards Grace, "Grace, do you remember which cat this one came off of?"

Grace shrugged, "I know which cat was here but I have no idea where he took off his collar. It could be his or the others but let me sniff it and see if I can tell by the smell."

After sniffing it for a minute she nodded, "It definitely smells like the first cat."

"Okay," Dan said, "I wonder what would happen if we give the wrong collar to the wrong cat? If the collars are linked to the bind point created by the beads do you suppose that if the collar went to the wrong cat they would end up back in the wrong house?"

Remy groaned, "That would be awful. The humans wouldn't have any idea what had happened and be really confused."

"I spent time considering the best place to create the bind point for your feathers." Dan said while looking at Leroy and Amelia. "I wanted you to have a way back home that was safe and well hidden, but still accessible. Who knows what kind of bind points the twins were creating by just opening them randomly."

Leroy gave it some thought. Dan was right. His careful planning made sure that it wasn't an accident that they found the feather portal. He put it in a place he knew only they could find it. He might not have been counting on Binx to find it first though. That thought made Leroy chuckle inwardly. Leave it to Binx to get the adventure started.

Dan continued "Let's keep going and try to find the other collar. We've already gone this far. I'm not ready to turn back just yet. With some luck and Binx's special nose sniffing maybe we can find the other one and get them both back home at the same time."

Leroy glanced back at Binx, and sure enough he was looking rather pleased at himself with Dan's praise. Sometimes the kitten was actually useful, but no need to let him know that. Leroy wrapped the collar around his front ankle to keep it separated from his own collar. Grace took the lead again and began to lead the group towards another cloud mountain. It took a while to get there but when she got to where she had discovered the other cat she sat down.

"This is the spot," Grace said as she looked back at Dan again.

"Okay," Dan replied, "let's do the same thing we did the first time. Spread out, same positions."

Leroy got into a line as they began their grid search of the area. He looked for a while, making several more passes, but he didn't find the collar. Neither had anyone else reported finding it. Leroy looked at Dan and saw the worried expression on his face. He knew Dan well enough to know that he was probably blaming himself for the entire predicament. "It's not your fault Dan." He walked out of line to bump shoulders and mush heads with his old friend. "We'll find the collar and get the headdress back. It just might take a bit longer than we'd hoped."

Dan nodded but the concerned expression didn't fade. "The collar's obviously not in this location. I'm not sure where to search next."

Leroy had been thinking about how Binx seemed to have a nose for finding things. He remembered that their mum and dad always said that Binx was more like a dog than a cat. Binx went for walks on a leash, came when he was called, and played fetch with his toys; all very un-cat like behaviors. Maybe somehow he had a little bloodhound in him and a dog's sniffer as well. "You know we do have a secret weapon. Binx. Mum and dad always said he might be part bloodhound. Maybe he can sniff it out since he said the feather has a smell."

"It's worth a try." Dan said. "Binx, why don't you walk up front with Grace and see if you can find a collar by smell."

"I'm on it boss!" Binx replied.

When Binx joined her up front, Grace turned to him and said, "I don't smell anything different about those collars but I'll try to catch the cat's scent again. Working together I'm sure we can hunt them down. You sniff for collars, and I'll sniff for cats."

"Hey, I just thought of something," Amelia said. "Grace, you probably don't smell anything on the collars because you belong here. I know you have a great sniffer but maybe that's the reason."

Grace responded to Amelia, "That could be. But still, it helps to have an idea of where to look to find a scent trail. Any ideas?"

Binx got a mischievous look and turned to the group. "Leroy, cover your ears. You shouldn't hear this."

There was no way he was going to do that Leroy thought. He glared at Binx to let him know just what he thought of covering his ears, his disapproval displayed by the lashing of the tip of his tail and his flighty flattened ears.

"Oh well," Binx continued. "Back home, when I'm trying to sneak off with something, like one of Leroy's catnip bananas or some food leftovers from the kitchen, I always try to stay out of the line of sight. It helps me not get caught. I'll sneak behind the couch so nobody can see me until I manage to get to where I can do what I want with my prize."

Dan's ears perked forward in amusement and he looked directly at Leroy, "Nip bananas, huh? Looks like Binx found YOUR secret stash."

Leroy looked right back and Dan with his best poker face. Leroy knew what Dan was thinking about. He'd always tried to make off with Dan's catnip toys without getting caught. Dan did a nightly inventory of them to make sure he hadn't lost any. It was a great day when he could play with a toy all day and sneak it back before Dan noticed it was missing. But it was still embarrassing that Binx could fool him. Leroy gave Binx an even sterner look and began to flip his big orange striped tail in irritation. He was going to have to be more vigilant after he found a new spot for his nip bananas.

Leroy risked a glance at Amelia. Judging by the smug look she had on her face, she was pleased she was proved correct. When she caught him looking her way, she proceeded to clean her left paw. He could hear her tell him I told ya so with that look of hers. Yeah, he'd have to find a new "really good impossible for Binx to find" hiding spot to fool Binx when they got home.

Binx didn't seem to notice Leroy's irritation. "Anyway, I bet that's what the twins would be doing if they don't want you to see them. I'm sure they're using Siamese ninja techniques of stealth. Rule number one: stay out of the line of sight. Figuring that, I'm sure they're trying to keep some of the taller clouds between themselves and Blankets Mountain. They wouldn't want to be spotted."

Binx looked around at the landscape. "If I had a prize to be sneaky with, I'd be headed there next." He pointed to the closest tall cloud. It wasn't very far away at all but it was tall and blocked their line of sight of whatever was behind it.

"That's pretty clever thinking, Binx." Remy said, sounding impressed with the younger cat's logic.

Leroy could at least admit to himself that sometimes Binx was indeed very clever. He made a mental note to be more on his toes around the kitten.

"I agree," Dan said. "Since we have no idea where to go from here anyway and knowing that the twins got the cats here in the first place, that's as likely a place to search next as any."

Grace shook her coat and stretched. Her dog tags on her collar making a metallic clinking sound. She always wore it on Earth, so when she came to pet heaven a version of it came with her. "I like that strategy. We need to find the twins anyway and I might just pick up their scent while we're looking."

Grace and Binx took positions side by side and the rest of the group fell in behind them. It didn't take long to get to the tall cloud mountain. Binx had been right, once they got behind the cloud they couldn't see Blankets Mountain. Binx stopped and looked around.

Binx was quiet for a second before he spoke next. "If I had the headdress I'd be really just dying to play with it. I bet I wouldn't go too much farther before I stopped to do just that." He walked slowly a few feet forward, nose sniffing the ground. After just a few steps he stopped. "I got it! I smell cloud feathers over here."

Leroy trotted over to search the wispy cloudy ground around Binx. He could hear the others spreading out and looking for the collar. Not a minute later, Dan found the collar. Leroy walked over to Dan and took the second collar to add to the first collar he already collected.

"Well done." Grace said. "I'm going to sniff around for just a minute and see if I can get a trace of the twins scent trail." Grace put her head down to the cloud ground and started sniffing in circles from where the collar was found.

Remy walked up to Binx and rubbed his shoulder. "Great job, Binx! That was some great deduction on where the twins might go next. I'm glad you're part of the team and helping us track them down."

"We are doing well finding the two collars," Dan said. "I think we should get those two Earth cats back as soon as possible. But we also need to find those twins before more portals get opened and we have a bigger mess to clean up." Dan looked over to see that Grace was still nearby before calling her over. "Hey, Grace. We need to figure out our next steps."

As Grace came close enough to hear, Dan called everyone's attention. "So we have two important tasks to accomplish. Get the Earth cats back where they belong, and continue to track down the twins. I hate to say it, but I think we need to split up."

Leroy agreed with Dan. "Dan's right. We have to clean up the twins' mess by getting those Earth cats back where they belong. Since I'm holding the two collars, I volunteer to get them back home. Most cats get one look at me and the fight goes out of them. I think I'm the best cat for this job."

"Thanks Leroy. I think you may be on to something there. However, I'm concerned if we split up you might not be able to find us again." Dan looked over at Grace before continuing, "Grace since you are from here and know your way around, can you help Leroy get back to the Earth cats and then come find us to help us track down the twins?"

Grace made a happy bark, her ears flopping. "Yup. I know a shortcut we can take as well. Leroy and I will be as quick as we can."

Leroy nodded. He wasn't looking forward to running all the way there and back, but he knew it was important. "Ready to go when you are, Grace."

"Thank you," Dan said. "That leaves Binx to help us find the twins' trail and Remy and Amelia to help me look for collars and more lost Earth cats. Hopefully we make headway chasing the twins down and we can wrap this whole thing up quickly."

Leroy knew Dan was looking at him and Grace in the familiar way he had to show he was grateful. It hit him in that moment just how much he had missed Dan.

"Before we head our separate ways, there's something I think everyone should know about the twins. The twins are good at heart, there's no questioning that. That being said they have never been able to control their cat curiosity and it runs stronger in them than in most of us."

"It's a Siamese thing," Binx, being a Flame Point Siamese himself, piped in. "I get it." Binx was nodding his head.

"Maybe," Dan acknowledged that Binx could be right, "but either way it's caused problems here in the past. There was one time when they took off with Willie's special toy. Willie had recreated a unique catnip toy from his childhood memory and the twins swiped it and ran off with it. Because it was unique on Earth, only one can exist like it in pet heaven. The twins were later caught by a group of Willie's friends who were helping find his toy. The twins were so high on nip that they got in a fight over the toy. It wasn't play-fighting either. It got ugly and took a whole bunch of alley cats to get them under control and make the twins return Willie's toy."

"I didn't realize there was fighting at the Rainbow Bridge." Remy sounded a bit upset.

Dan shook his head, "There isn't supposed to be. We can't really hurt each other and it's against the rules to act like that. It was a matter of who could muscle who to get the toy back. Then we had to restrain the twins until they got their wits about them again. Willie got hurt feelings and the twins later apologized but I don't want anyone getting taken by surprise if they do try to fight back."

"Okay, Grace." Dan motioned towards the direction of Blankets Mountain. "You and Leroy better get going and please be quick about it. We need you back as soon as possible."

Grace nodded, looked at Leroy to make sure he was ready, and without a word she took off running back towards Blankets Mountain. Leroy turned and charged after her. Grace's tail was held high and wagging. Leroy was leaping and bounding as fast as he could to keep up. Even as fast as they were going it would be a while before they made it back to the others. Leroy wished them happy hunting.

Chapter 7 – Feathers Time

Leroy chased after Grace as fast as he could. Grace had been very fast on Earth and she hadn't lost any speed at the Rainbow Bridge. Occasionally she stopped and yelled at him to hurry up. Leroy wasn't going slowly on purpose, Grace was just faster than he was. He was getting in a hurry himself. Those feather bracelets were starting to sting him even more. The longer he kept them on the more it was hurting. He was anxious to get them off and to the other Earth cats.

Grace led the way racing from cloud to cloud. Blankets Mountain occasionally appeared in the distance in between the cloud peaks. Leroy was relieved to see it got bigger and bigger the closer they got. Once they were almost there they passed by clouds with cats playing on them. Leroy and his dull fur stood out like a sore thumb and the cats would always stop and stare. Grace kept up the pace and never stopped to respond to any of the questions. Leroy did note that all of the cats knew Grace by name, even calling out to her in a friendly manner and none of them seemed bothered by her at all.

Grace stopped and let Leroy get caught up. She was staring at another very large cloud mountain and looked as if she were debating something. She let out a quiet whine, turned to Leroy and said "We're taking a short cut." She nodded at the giant cloud, "That's one of my favorite places here and a very popular spot. It's also the only place in the cat realm where I'm not exactly welcomed."

That piqued Leroy's curiosity. "Everyone seems to like you just fine here. Why don't they want you to go to that cloud?"

Grace started moving again but more at a light jog than a full out sprint. "This is kind of like a big colosseum. They do all kinds of competitive games here. They have a giant race track set up as well as a couple of arena fields. They hold all different kinds of races and competitions here.

"They do sprint races, long distances races, high jump competition and even acrobatics. There's also another game that's pretty much everyone's favorite game here. They have an entire league dedicated to it with lots of teams that compete. It's an entirely new sport that they created shortly after Dan arrived. It's called Feathers Time."

Leroy inwardly chuckled with amusement. While Dan was on Earth, his favorite games all involved feathers. On his social media page he always ended his stories with 'Now I declare it FEATEHRS TIME!' If there was a game here that Dan helped make, of course it would be called Feathers Time. Leroy was amazed and just couldn't get over how his little buddy not only managed to inspire tens of thousands of people on Earth but seemed to be doing the same thing again at the Rainbow Bridge.

"Well of course he called it Feathers Time." Leroy composed himself and ran again to catch up with Grace. "So what's the game about?"

Grace's tail started to wag as she explained, "When a game of Feathers Time begins, Feather Dan starts it off on top of Blankets Mountain."

Leroy looked and could see that the top of Blankets Mountain had a perfect vantage point to look down onto the cloud and the arenas. Blankets Mountain was right next to the Arena Cloud and only a few yards separated them at the bottom.

Grace continued, "Something else that's different about Dan here than the others is that something strange happens when Dan shares a feather. Once he gives someone a feather another feather appears out of nowhere just a few feet above them and it floats down to replace it. To start the game Dan gives a blue feather to one cat on each team of five cats. When the feather that floats down out of the sky gets in front of Dan he blows on it and more magic happens. It zooms off towards the arena, dancing in all kinds of unpredictable zig zags. The cats he gave a blue feather to have to get their feathers down Blankets Mountain and across the field to their team's safe zone. They also have to get the feathers to the safe zone before another team member can catch the ones Dan sent zooming out onto the field.

"When a team member with one of Dan's blue feathers from the mountain gets it to their team's safe zone they tag off with another team member. That player has to get back up Blankets Mountain. Dan hands them another blue feather and they are off again. The teams have all five of their players do that. Once a team gets their last blue feather handed into their safe zone, the team with the highest score wins."

Leroy had been imagining the game as Grace explained it and he thought it sounded really fun. "How is it that Dan was able to create the game? How is he able to do what he does with the feathers?"

Grace shrugged, "Nobody's sure exactly. Some of the elders think that because Dan had been so generous while he was on Earth that it's a kind of reward for him. Any time he shares a feather he gets one back. The ones he gets back are special. He can do fun things with them like blow on them and make them zoom away. He does that with the kittens that have crossed the Bridge and they love it."

As they approached the arena cloud a few cats came running up to Grace and started fussing at her. One silver and tan cat who was in excellent physical condition ran up first, "Grace. What are you doing here? We're practicing right now. You know you're not supposed to be here."

Another heavily muscled cat ran up next, "You are absolutely NOT to go chasing anyone and doing that dratted pit maneuver during the race!"

Grace shook her head and looked at the first cat who'd spoken to her, "Arthur, I promise I won't. I'm on official Feather Dan business and I'm in a hurry. This is just a shortcut and I don't have time to go around."

They had been so preoccupied and concerned with Grace that they hadn't even noticed Leroy until just then. "Whoa," The silver and tan cat's eyes went wide, "What's wrong with your friend here, Grace?"

"Sorry," Grace kept on moving, "No time to talk right now. We're in a hurry."

"Hey!" shouted another cat from the Arena Mountain, "That must be one of those sink bath cats we've been hearing about!"

Leroy flipped his tail in irritation but didn't say anything. He just followed after Grace and ignored the other cats. When Grace and Leroy rounded the corner of Arena Mountain, Blankets Mountain came into full view right ahead of them. A large crowd had gathered at the bottom of the mountain where they had left the other two Earth cats. There were so many cats surrounding the Earth cats, that they were going to have to push their way through to get to them.

Grace sighed at the sight, "Okay Leroy, just stick right behind me until we get to them. I'm going to lower my head and make a path through them. I may have to bark to get them to move aside."

Once they got to the back of the crowd it became obvious that Grace's herding instinct was going to work in their favor. Grace started barking, startling the cats in front of her making it easier for her to push them aside. She'd bark a couple of times and push forward again. After a few times, her barks got the attention of the cats near her and they got out of her way. Several cats stepped further back at the sight of Leroy. Soon Grace and Leroy pushed through to the front of the crowd. The Earth cats looked terrified, cowering with bristled fur and ears set forward while their eyes scanned the nearest cats. Grace and Leroy trotted directly in front of them blocking the Earth cats from view.

Grace ignored the questions being hurled at her. "We've never seen anything like this! Why are they so dirty? Do they hate their humans? Why aren't they getting clean when they groom? Where did they come from? Why don't they know where they are? Are they sick? Is it contagious? Don't they care if their humans find their way to the light?"

Both cats turned towards Grace, squared off and started growling and hissing. Grace backed up a few steps and sat down a short distance away. "There's no time for questions. Quiet!" Grace addressed the cats behind her. The Earth cat's hackles were still up but they calmed down after Grace made the other cats back off. Grace reminded Leroy which feather bracelet to give which cat by smelling them again and matching the scent of each Earth cat.

Leroy gave each of the cats a serious look. "Do these look familiar? I don't want to get them mixed up." Leroy didn't waste any time in getting them off and handing them over.

Both cats nodded and Leroy said, "Okay, give the feather on your collar a chomp. Just one chomp and you should be returned home right away."

Leroy and Grace watched as each Earth cat chomped on their respective feathers. Just after the sound of the feather being bitten, the Earth cat simply vanished. No puff of smoke or popping sound, they were just gone. There was a collective gasp among the clowder of cats behind them followed by a brief moment of absolute silence. Then the questions came in a flood. The cats were yelling so loudly over each other to be heard that Grace's answers couldn't have been heard. Grace gave a couple of very loud barks to quiet them down.

"Look everyone," Grace gazed across the gathering of upset cats, "This is one heck of a story and I kind of came in at the middle part. This story will be much better told by Feather Dan. But you'll have to wait for him to come back to tell it. If you see any other sink bath cats try to get them to come right here and get them to stay put. We'll help them when we get back. Right now we have to try to catch up with Feather Dan."

Grace and Leroy were about to head off when Arthur, the silver and tan cat they had seen at Arena Mountain came running up. "Will Feather Dan be back in time to start the games tonight?"

"I don't know," Grace panted, her long tongue curling over the side of her wide open mouth. "I expect so and I'll remind Dan of his obligation."

The silver and tan cat nodded and stepped aside, "Thank you."

Grace nudged Leroy, "We have to hurry. Dan needs us back as quickly as possible. "

Leroy nodded that he was ready. Then they were off at a run with Grace leading back the way they had come. Arena Mountain soon faded quickly behind them as they disappeared into the clouds headed toward where they last saw Dan and the others.

Chapter 8 – The Nose Knows

Dan looked to the rest of the group and in a serious tone said, "We need to get going. Binx, you lead the way." Dan looked back towards Grace and Leroy just in time to see them round the side of a cloud and disappear from sight as they raced back to Blankets Mountain.

Binx looked around and found the next likely path he thought the twins would have taken. He started walking and the rest of the group followed.

Amelia groaned, "Dan, I absolutely cannot believe you have us following Binx. We're on a critical mission and of all of the cats at Rainbow Bridge, we're following Binx?"

"He's our best option, Amelia. He's helped get us this far. Come on, we need to keep up. We don't have time to waste." Dan replied.

Binx just ignored Amelia's grumbles. Trotting along happily, he led them from cloud to cloud. He stayed close to the taller ones most of the time. He was doing his best to pretend he didn't want to be seen so he could scout the most likely path Bandit and Sassy would take. It wasn't hard because back home he spent large portions of his days either ambushing Leroy or Amelia or sneaking off with some of Leroy's catnip toys. It was a short time later and on the third cloud that he caught the smell of fresh rain.

"I smell that smell again!" He said excitedly.

Everyone fanned out and started their grid search. In less than a minute, Amelia found a collar just a few feet away from where Binx was sniffing.

"Found it." She picked it up, showed it to the others and wrapped it around her front leg for safe keeping.

Dan shook his head, "It's good we found a collar so quickly but bad because there isn't another cat anywhere in sight."

Amelia looked around and said "When I want to see what's going on or try to spot Binx when I know he's being a brat, I go to higher ground, usually the top of the cat tree." She looked around and said, "I think we should go to the top of this cloud and see if maybe we spot anything."

Dan thought about it for just a second and said, "That's a great idea. Binx, remember where you left off down here so if we don't get any leads up there we can come back and resume where we left off."

Binx, who had already started running up the cloud, stopped and looked back at Dan. "Um, sure Dan, no problem."

Remy rolled his eyes and twitched his tail, "I'll remember the spot Dan."

"Thanks Remy," Dan nodded in appreciation and the group quickly chased after Binx who was already a quarter of the way up the cloud.

It took them a minute to get there but when they finally got to the top they could see all the way back to Blankets Mountain. They could even see part of Cat Tree City just past it. Dan paused to admire the view. The rest of the group was quiet as they gazed at the view before them. Even the rambunctious Binx had stopped and quieted while he took in the view.

"I bet that's our cat." Dan said breaking the silence.

He pointed to a space below them. Trotting along between the cloud they were on and the next one was a grey cat with white spots and no shine to its fur. Dan yelled out and waved to the cat trying to get its attention. Binx, Amelia and Remy took their cue from Dan and started yelling along with him. Dan led the way as they headed towards the Earth cat.

The Earth cat heard them yelling, stopped in a half crouch and turned its head in their direction. It appeared confused initially. It watched as they hurried down the cloud toward her in an unthreatening manner. She started forward to meet them and then sat on her haunches, no longer appearing to show any signs of fear towards them.

As soon as they approached the Earth cat she started asking questions. "What's going on? Where am I? What is this place?" Her face scrunched as if she'd eaten something distasteful Binx thought as she looked Dan and Remy over. "What's wrong with your fur?"

"Hold on. Slow down." Dan said. "You've got a lot of questions. I'm sure this is confusing for you, but we are here to help you. But first, let me ask you something really quick."

She nodded at him, "Okay." Binx could tell she wouldn't wait for long before demanding answers again.

"Did you drop this feather collar on the other side of this cloud?" Dan inquired of her while motioning Amelia to step forward and show her the collar.

Pawing at her neck she said, "Yes, it was starting to burn a bit. I don't know why it was on me in the first place. I didn't like it burning me, so I took it off. Now what's going on here?" Binx could tell from her tone that she was very annoyed. He hoped Dan could get her to cooperate so they could get her back where she belonged.

Binx thought she looked at Dan like he'd been in the catnip. He had to hide his smile at the thought.

"We know how to get you back home if you will just trust me." Dan said with confidence. "Take the collar back and give that feather one good hard chomp."

She gave Dan an exasperated look before taking the feather collar back from Amelia. "Okay, I'll entertain you for now because you're cute. But I expect some serious explanations if this doesn't work."

Dan's face remained neutral as he watched her bite into the feather on the collar. As soon as the feather crunched she was gone.

"Whew," Dan said as his posture relaxed. He'd done a good job hiding his tension, Binx thought. "I wonder how many more cats we're going to find. Let's get back to where you smelled that portal Binx. I want to see if you can still smell it and we need to get hurrying again."

"Follow me," Remy said. "I remember the exact spot."

Remy led them back up to the top of the mountain so they could go down to the other side where Binx had smelled the last feather collar. When they got back to the top of the cloud they stopped to look around again. Amelia quickly spotted another no shine cat. This one was an orange cat with markings similar to Dan and Leroy and was two clouds away. It was too far for it to hear if they called out to get its attention.

Binx took careful note of what direction the Earth cat was heading in and hurried down the cloud. When they got to the bottom Binx said, "I can still smell that funny cloud smell but it is a little fainter."

Dan thought about it and said, "I bet that once the feather was used again to go back, any remnants of the portal would start to dissolve."

Remy nodded in agreement, "At least we're learning a lot about these things."

"The elders and professors will be asking us questions for weeks once this is all settled." Dan warned Remy.

Remy looked at Dan inquisitively. "Professors?"

Dan smiled back. "Yes, Remy, there is a lot that I haven't had a chance to show you or tell you about yet. I promise I'll start filling you in later."

While the others were talking, Binx began looking around to determine which way they should search for the twins next. He was looking for someplace to give them some additional height to see further when he spotted a tall cloud that would work. "I'm pretty sure the twins would have gone that way. That's a good tall cloud over there. It's wide too so they could stay hidden longer."

Dan looked where Binx indicated "I'm sure you're right but the Earth cat is walking in the opposite direction." Dan paused for a second. "I really don't want to but we're going to have to split up again. I'll take Amelia and we'll go grab the Earth cat. It was a long way off but I don't think I saw a feather collar on it. Remy and Binx, you two go look for the feather collar. Stick to the same strategy we've been using. It's worked really well so far."

"I'll keep us focused on the mission." Remy assured Feather Dan before he glanced directly at Binx. Binx knew that look. Amelia gave him that same look when she wanted him to be on his best behavior. Binx had to admit it was a good plan and this was such a fantastic adventure that he didn't want to mess it up.

It took Remy and Binx several minutes to get to the tall cloud mountain. They were now out of sight of Dan and Amelia. They barely rounded the edge of the tall cloud when Binx smelled the cloud smell again. This time they didn't even have to do a grid search, Binx found the feather collar right away. Remy said they would go back around the corner and wait for Dan and Amelia to return. Binx wanted to go explore but let Remy keep him entertained by answering questions about his favorite games.

Dan and Amelia ran as fast as they could but it still took over a half hour to catch up to the Earth cat and then led him back to Remy and Binx. The cat was just as confused as the others they had found. Dan had already explained to the Earth cat what was going on.

Binx heard the Earth cat whisper to Amelia that Dan needed to lay off the catnip. But he did give one hard chomp on the feather. The next instant the cat was gone.

Amelia was panting from all the running around. After she caught her breath, she asked, "How many more of the cats do you think there still are?" Binx knew Amelia didn't much like to run, preferring to take frequent naps instead of play with him.

Dan shook his head, "There's no telling."

"I'm seeing a pattern though," Remy chimed in. "Each time we round a cloud and can't see where we just were, Binx smells the portals. I'm guessing that means the twins play with the headdress every time they get to a new cloud then move on."

"That's what I'd do!" Binx had finished scanning the terrain and picked another likely spot to check out. "And if I knew I'd done something, like drag in an Earth cat or something I knew I shouldn't have, I'd make a quick escape too."

Amelia snorted, "Yup, and leave the mess for someone else to clean up."

Binx just ignored Amelia's dig at him. She was always making snarky comments, it didn't mean he had to listen to them. He led the way towards the next series of tall clouds.

Dan looked around apprehensively. "I've never been out this far before. Only a few cats ever go very far away from the Rainbow Bridge."

"Why not?" Binx asked. "It's fun out here!" He didn't see what there was to be afraid of. Exploring new spaces was fun and adventurous.

"None of us ever want to be too far away from the Rainbow Bridge just in case something happens and our human picks that time to come. We don't know exactly when it will happen but when it does there is nothing more important for us than to get to Rainbow Bridge right away."

When the cats reached the next series of clouds Binx didn't smell anything. He even tried a nearby cloud to check it out as well but the trail had gone cold. With nothing to find here, Dan decided they should climb up to the top again. When they got up there and looked around they spotted Grace and Leroy off in the distance about two cloud mountains away. They were running as fast as they could towards their direction. Binx knew Grace was trying to figure out which scent trail to follow once she reached the point where they had split up earlier. He jumped and waved at Grace until she spotted them. She adjusted her direction to make a straight line towards them.

They waited for Grace and Leroy to catch up. Then they caught them up on their progress with the other two Earth cats they'd found. Grace told everyone about the commotion at Blankets Mountain and how everyone had seen the Earth cats disappear. The event had gotten the kitty rumor mill going into overdrive and she warned Dan they would definitely expect him to have an explanation later.

"Also," Grace informed Dan, "Arthur asked me to remind you that your presence is required to start the Feathers Time game tonight. It's the semi-finals, isn't it?"

Dan sighed. "It is the semi-finals. I'd completely forgotten about it. Thanks for reminding me. I'll be sure I'm there to start the games. I wouldn't want to disappoint the players or the fans. I know how much it means to them and that they can't play without me."

Grace looked up at the sky and a worried whine escaped her. "It won't be long and dusk will fall. We need to get back before dusk falls."

Binx looked up at the sky too. "We've all got great night vision and I'm sure my nose will work after dark. I don't mind if you want to keep going. I'm having way too much fun to stop now anyway!"

Everyone but Dan looked at Grace as she spoke to Binx. "It's a bad idea to be out of sight of the Rainbow Bridge at night. There aren't any predators in the clouds or anything. There's no real dangers at the Rainbow Bridge per say, but the nights… the nights are different. The sky is beautiful at night, almost hypnotic you might say."

Dan took over explaining, "Grace is right. Some nights the stars shine and twinkle so bright it's almost like day time. Other nights beautiful colored lights come up and soar into the sky. It's like someone pulling several giant rainbow scarfs across the sky. There are several different things that can happen at night but one thing always happens. All of the cats always lose their sense of direction and their minds become distracted."

"Dogs too," interrupted Grace. "It happens to all of the animals in every realm."

Dan continued, "If you got stuck out in the clouds after dark and couldn't see the Rainbow Bridge or Blankets Mountain you'd have no idea where you were. By the time the sun came up you could completely forget what direction you had been going or even where you had come from. Without a landmark you could walk around forever and never find your way back. If your human came while you were gone and you weren't there to be a light for them, they might get lost forever too."

"I sure hope the twins keep that in mind," Remy voiced his concern.

"Okay, that's it for the day." Dan said next. "It's time we got back to Blankets Mountain. We can't risk spending any more time getting farther away. We're going to be pushing it just a little bit as it is."

"Do we have enough time to keep taking a look from the top of the clouds?" Remy asked Dan.

Binx knew that if the twins got lost at night they wouldn't have anything else to do but play with the headdress. They could open up dozens of portals and leave who knew how many other cats lost as well. He was feeling the urgency to get that headdress back where it was safe.

"Yes," Dan said. We can go in a straight line and climb to the top of as many clouds as we come to. Maybe we'll get lucky and spot the twins heading back. It would be good to see where they go when they return to the Rainbow Bridge."

On the trip back they did stop frequently and climb up as many tall clouds as they could looking for Earth cats or the twins. They didn't spot any other Earth cats. Neither did they spot the twins. Binx wasn't sure if that was a good thing or a bad thing.

Chapter 9 – The Night

The twins had to run around more clouds than they could count before they were finally able to get the goat off their tail. It was much faster and more persistent than either of them could have ever imagined. After what they thought must have been an hour of running, the goat had finally just stopped. It looked around and decided to climb a cloud. When it got to the top it must have liked the view because it jumped and hopped about like it was doing a happy dance.

The twins, two clouds away, watched it with a sense of relief. It would have been very difficult to sneak around with a goat following their every move. No longer under pursuit they decided to click the beads and try to catch another feather. Sassy almost had it but it but once again it was gone too fast.

"Let's hurry Bandit," said Sassy. She and Bandit both grabbed onto the headdress and immediately began to make their way to the end of the cloud. They quickly ducked around the edge of the cloud where they could watch but not be seen. If another goat showed up they didn't want to try to have to run away again. They decided to wait a minute to see if anything else would show up but nothing did.

"Okay," Sassy said, "let's go to that cloud over there and then it's your turn again."

Bandit nodded in response and they moved on to another cloud and tried again. Bandit didn't have any luck catching the feather either. The headdress was fun but it was really getting frustrating never being able to catch the feathers. They hurried off to another cloud just in case something appeared, they didn't want it following them.

"I sure wish we could tell when another animal was going to come through." Sassy was debating trying again.

Bandit nodded in agreement. "Where do you think they keep coming from?"

"I don't know but I've never seen a cat filthier than these. I bet Dan would know."

When Sassy mentioned Dan, Bandit remembered the Feathers Time games. He absolutely loved watching the games. Tonight it was even a playoff game and was expected to be one of the best games of the season. "This has been a fun adventure and all but it's starting to get a little bit boring. I'm not sure those feathers are actually catchable. We better start heading back, Sassy."

Sassy looked up at the sky and agreed. "Trying to get away from that goat took more time than I expected. One thing I do know is that we've never been this far away from the Rainbow Bridge before."

Bandit knew they had been out for a long time and it was dawning on both of them that they might not be able to make it back before dark. They glanced at each other and a shadow of fear began to settle over each of them. He knew how serious their situation was. They'd lost track of time and put themselves in a situation where they might not be able to fulfill their sacred duty to their human.

"Do you think we should just drop the headdress and run for it?" Bandit asked. He wasn't accustomed to feeling fear. His curiosity could overcome anything that would make most cats hesitant.

"I don't know, Bandit." Sassy was thinking the same thing but it just didn't feel right to her. "If we leave it here we might not be able to find it again. This is Feather Dan's most prized artifact. He'd be so disappointed in us if we lost it."

Bandit sighed, "I know. Dan is so giving with everyone. He's got to be the most generous cat we've ever known. Do you think we'd be banned from the Feathers Time games if we didn't get it back?" Bandit couldn't handle the idea of being shunned from the games; they were one of the best parts of the Rainbow Bridge as far as he was concerned.

Sassy shook her head. "I doubt Dan would go that far. That wouldn't be like him at all. I don't know what the rest of the cats would say though. We really just need to get this back and make things right."

Together they carried the headdress and hustled as quickly as they could. Time kept on passing by but they figured they had to be getting closer and were becoming less worried about making it back before dark. That was until they rounded a cloud and spotted the goat on top of the cloud in front of them. Its back was turned and it didn't see them but it was hopping about and prancing. They ducked back around the corner before they were spotted.

"Oh no," Sassy exclaimed, "not that bothersome goat again!"

"We're going to have to go around. We can't have that thing following us back to Rainbow Bridge."

Sassy nodded, "We're going to have to backtrack at least two clouds if we're going to stay out of its line of sight."

Bandit was looking at the sky and feeling even more apprehensive. "I'm not sure we have enough time, Sassy."

"Me either," Sassy agreed, "but we don't have a choice. We'll just have to try to move even faster."

They ran as quickly as they could while dragging the headdress but it took time to make the detour. They managed to avoid being seen by the goat but the sky was getting darker by the minute and they still couldn't even see the glow of the Rainbow Bridge. It was becoming frightfully obvious that they were not going to make it back before dark and a sense of dread filled their hearts. Despite being tired they pushed themselves even harder in an attempt to avoid the inevitable.

Bandit thought the stories of cats being lost in the clouds and never being seen again were the saddest stories at Rainbow Bridge. They were told to newcomers like ghost stories meant to keep children from wandering into places that were dangerous. There was a difference between those ghost stories meant to scare children and the stories about what happens to cats lost at night. The ghost stories were just that, stories but what happened to cats out in the clouds after dark was very much real. Bandit wasn't sure how dark it would have to get before he and Sassy would no longer be able to tell direction or even if they would know it when it happened.

When it started happening it was very subtle. He didn't really notice it until Sassy started tugging on the headdress because she was trying to go in different directions. After the third time, he realized what was going on and stopped running. Bandit no longer knew what direction they were traveling in. He thought they were lost. He looked at Sassy and she looked at him. Even though he told himself it was just the effects of the dark, he couldn't help feeling scared.

"How close to home do you think we are?" Sassy asked after she finally dropped the headdress and took a look around them.

Bandit shook his head in uncertainty. "I thought I knew a few minutes ago but now I can't really remember. I can't even remember what direction we were just running."

"Me either." Sassy looked around. "Do you see anything that looks familiar?"

"This is confusing. It all looks familiar, and yet it doesn't look familiar at all." Bandit said as he shook his head.

"I know exactly what you mean," Sassy agreed. "Let's climb up to the top of this cloud and see if either of us can tell where we are. Let's take the headdress with us so we don't lose it." Sassy then took a hold of the headdress again.

"Good idea. Maybe we can see Blankets Mountain or the glow from Rainbow Bridge," Bandit said. He sure hoped they found something that would point them in the right direction. He grabbed a hold of the headdress and resumed walking with Sassy.

The climb to the top of the cloud took tremendous effort, especially after they had been running for so long. Bandit pulled in one direction and then Sassy would pull in another one. He wasn't sure they were even still going toward the top of the cloud anymore. With a little coordination, they finally reach the top just as it got dark. Sprawled out before them in every direction was an endless sea of towering clouds stretching on for what had to be miles in every direction. Bandit had no idea where they were.

Instead of the preferred clear night lit by exceptionally bright stars that would help them see where they were, the aurora borealis was visible. It was a weird name for the hypnotic dancing light patterns on display in the sky. One of the cats at the Rainbow Bridge had a human who studied things like that and the human had called it the aurora borealis. The dancing lights were beautiful to watch but didn't hold Bandit's attention for long. He couldn't help the fear he was feeling at the thought of being completely lost and not being able to ever make it home again.

"Bandit, I hate to say this," Sassy hesitated. "But I think we should stay here until morning. I'm afraid we'd just get more lost if we kept going." She dropped the headdress and sat back on her haunches with her tail curled around her protectively. Her ears swiveled trying to pick up sound, something Bandit knew she did out of nervousness.

"I think so too, Sassy." Bandit agreed, dropping the headdress and laying down to rest. He knew when they started out they'd been running in the right direction. There was no telling how far off course they were now. The chances of getting further lost were too high if they kept running not knowing where they were going.

After a few minutes, Sassy appeared to relax. She laid down on her belly, with her feet twisted to the side and proceeded to groom herself. Bandit found it relaxing as well and started to groom himself as well. It was easier to spot where he was dirty by the dulled shine on his coat. It was bad to get lost, it was even worse to be dirty.

They spent the first part of the night talking as they groomed themselves. They talked mostly about Hope, their human, and how much they missed her. The last time they had checked in on her they noticed that she was getting quite a bit older than she had been when they crossed the Bridge. She was getting to that age where it was common for humans to pass away and make the crossing. On Earth, unexpected tragedies happened frequently and humans, as well as pets, could cross at any time but with her significantly advanced age the odds were greatly increased.

Bandit knew it was impossible to know when Hope's time would come and she would need them to be her light in the darkness. Bandit and Sassy shared a case of the sads as the realization that they may have let her down became a very real possibility. It was their sacred duty to be there for her and if she crossed now they both wouldn't be.

They didn't know what else to do so they decided to make sure they were extra clean so their brightness could be seen from a long way off. They even took turns helping each other get any spots that weren't perfect. That helped them to take their minds off of being sad until they ran out of spots to clean. Bandit started getting bored. After lashing his tail a few times, he looked at Sassy to see she was looking at the headdress again.

Sassy swatted at the beads on the headdress, "I want to give it one more shot. Maybe those feathers move slower at night." Sassy sounded hopeful.

Bandit thought it was worth a shot to try. He got up and moved closer to the headdress before sitting on his haunches so he could swat it with his paws. Bandit struck the turquoise beads for her and a feather launched off the tail. Sassy pounced. Those feathers didn't move any slower at night and again she missed. She hissed in frustration and sat down.

Bandit was looking at the rest of the headdress. "Maybe we should just pull a couple of the big feathers off the top. We haven't tried that yet."

Bandit's idea was interesting and made Sassy curious. "We don't have anything better to do. I really doubt either of us will be able to sleep tonight."

"Right," Bandit agreed. "We can say its research. Maybe we can learn more about it so when we bring it back we can show Dan something he might not have known. Maybe he won't be as mad if we show him something new and fun."

It was at that moment that something terrifying happened. The night became a little darker. A large black shadow covered them and the hair along their backs and tails rose as a sense of dread swept through them.

From out of nowhere a giant black figure appeared before them. It was huge and covered in short course fur that was black as midnight on a starless night. It had massive black paws, long powerful legs, a broad muscular chest and a fierce looking black face. It had the eyes of a predator. They glowed yellow and as it looked down and saw them the pupils dilated. It snarled and its growl was the loudest most horrifying sound either of them had ever heard. That was, at least, until it screamed a roar that shook the cloud. Their blood ran cold and they were both momentarily paralyzed with fear.

Sassy reacted first. She pushed Bandit hard forcing him to move and screamed "Panther! Run!"

Bandit realized that Sassy got him out of the way just in time to keep from getting swatted by the biggest paw he'd ever seen. Its claws looked razor sharp and talon like. The cloud shook where the claws had landed and bits of cloud tore off, stuck to the dagger like claws.

Bandit ran faster than he ever had before, scared to death it wouldn't be fast enough. Sassy was right beside him. He couldn't believe that something as terrifying as a panther could have come to the Rainbow Bridge. Its fur was dirty like a sink bath cat. He doubted it cared. It was unlikely that a panther would be responsible for helping any human cross over.

The beast screamed and roared behind them. Bandit looked behind him just long enough to see its glowing yellow eyes locked onto them before it charged. Next thing he knew, it landed in front of them and spun around to face them, bits of cloud flying as the claws dug in. Bandit managed to stop just before running directly into it. Sassy slid to a stop next to him. This thing was incredibly fast. Bandit was sure they couldn't out run it.

Crouching, it dropped its head low to the ground level with them. Bandit knew this panther was a killer. Everything about it screamed predator. The way it moved, the way its ears were hyper alert, its whiskers spread wide and pushed forward, the way it held its shoulders, how it was crouched and ready to pounce at any moment. It glared at them, its yellow glowing eyes causing the twins to freeze in panic. The panther's eyes shone with intelligence and cunning and something else that made him want to cower with fear. Bandit could see there was intelligence but no empathy in its eyes.

"Where am I? What is this place?" he demanded, His voice was deep and gravelly but his words were clear. Bandit was frozen with fear. He couldn't move or speak. His entire body was trembling and he knew he might pass out at any moment.

"Speak!" The panther shouted as its eyes widened then narrowed again. Its giant pink tongue licked across its massive and deadly fangs. The command shook Bandit out of his paralysis, but before he could speak, Sassy spoke first.

"You're at the Rainbow Bridge." she answered in a trembling voice. Bandit knew she was just as scared as he was. He desperately wanted to look away from the panther's stare. Looking into its eyes was like looking at death. The panther's gaze flickered to Sassy as she spoke.

"This is where pets go when they die on Earth." Bandit managed to squeak out. "We wait here until our humans cross over so we can go to the Beyond with them." Bandit's voice wasn't one he recognized as his own. But before he could think about it more, he lost the ability to speak when the panther's gaze returned to him.

"I've heard of this place," The panther snarled in disdain. "I find it appalling. Why am I here and where are the rest of you pathetic *house cats*?"

Sassy spoke up, "It's hard to explain why you're here. "It's got something to do with that headdress and feathers, but we aren't sure how it works. We don't know where the others are because it's night and we're lost." She ducked as she said it, her embarrassment at being lost evident. Bandit could count on one paw the number of times he'd seen Sassy act embarrassed.

The panther glanced at the headdress sitting a few yards away then looked back at Sassy. "What does it being night have anything to do with you being lost? Even '*house cats,*'" it spit the words out like they tasted bad, "have superior night vision."

"Well…" Bandit started to explain but stopped when the panther only became more agitated. He watched its long, thick black tail whip back and forth. Then he got distracted when the panther started pulling up bits of cloud with his claws. They were lethal looking, very uhm...sharp.

"What is this?" the panther demanded. He licked and pawed at the feather pendant that dangled from his neck.

Bandit hadn't noticed it before. It was a small white feather dangling from a cord around the Panther's incredibly strong and thick muscular neck. He realized it must not have already belonged to the panther. It might be connected to the headdress somehow, but he wasn't sure just how. "Um...we don't know."

"It stings, I like that. Pain is good, it helps keep us alert." the Panther said as if it was a small matter for something to be painful and sting. He turned his focus back to the twins, his yellow eyes glowing with curiosity and danger. "Tell me about this land of the Rainbow Bridge. Describe it, I want to know everything."

The initial fear of being in the panther's presence was overwhelming. Now that he was demanding answers, Bandit felt compelled to appease the giant predator. The panther's eyes were hypnotic in a nightmarish fashion and pulled the words right out of his soul. Before he was aware he was doing it, Bandit had told the panther all about the Rainbow Bridge. Sassy told him how it worked, about Cat Tree City and even Blankets Mountain. When they ran out of information, the panther sat up and looked off into the distance.

Released from the panther's gaze, Bandit looked at Sassy. He knew he looked as scared as he felt when Sassy mirrored the same look in her eyes that he had. They were in big trouble. If they ever got out of this alive, they would have to find a way to make things right. He still didn't know how this had happened, exactly.

The panther made a chuffing noise and looked down on the twins. "What are your names?" While it was phrased as a question, Bandit knew it was a command. He knew better than to not obey.

"I'm called Sassy." Sassy managed in a shaky voice. Her body was trembling in fear.

"I'm Bandit." Bandit managed to get out, instinctively knowing that angering the panther was not a good idea. He didn't seem like the kind of cat that had a lot of patience.

The panther nodded in approval, "At least they are not weak names. My name is Tremor. You may address me either by that or as Master. You are now my servants and are going to lead me to Blankets Mountain. If I'm going to be trapped in this cursed land of clouds with no jungles then I will be its ruler." Tremor narrowed his eyes to slits and his lip curled revealing yellow stained, sharp glistening fangs. "If you disobey me I will eat you both."

Bandit and Sassy looked at each other and their fear began to be pushed aside by desperation. Bandit really wished this wasn't happening. This was Rainbow Bridge. This was the land where all of the cats fulfilled their sacred purpose and were reunited with their beloved humans so both could go to the Beyond. There was too much at stake. He had to save Rainbow Bridge and Blankets Mountain. He looked at Sassy and saw the same determination in her eyes. He knew he didn't have to say a word when Sassy just barely nodded at him. Through all the scrapes they'd be in together, she'd know exactly what he'd been thinking. They had to get out of this mess. She would help him lead the creature as far away from Rainbow Bridge as possible.

"Run!" Bandit screamed at Sassy. He didn't pause to see if she heeded his cry before he took off in the opposite direction.

Tremor let out an angry roar. Bandit knew they were in big trouble. He hadn't made it a few yards before he felt his hair stand on end. He sensed it just before something heavy landed on top of him. His nimbleness saved him from being crushed by Tremor's giant paws. He just managed to right himself when he was struck again. Bandit found himself flipped head over tail crashing hard into a cloud.

"Bandit!" Sassy screamed in terror.

"Just run!" Bandit yelled to her as he shook his head and struggled to his feet. He shook off the blow and turned to face the panther. He arched his back, his fur standing on end. Tremor snarled and Bandit hissed back. Bandit growled and stood his ground. Tremor growled, showing his massive fangs as he stomped steadily forward preparing to attack again.

"Bandit, no!" Sassy screamed, her voice cracking in desperation.

Bandit never took his eyes from Tremor but yelled to Sassy, "I said run! You know what you have to do. Do it, now!"

Tremor snarled and growled his displeasure as he stalked closer to Bandit. "I told you, you are my servant. You will do what you are told." An evil twisted look flashed across Tremors face, "There are serious consequences for disobeying."

Bandit hissed in defiance and Tremor attacked. He struck out with his right paw before Bandit could dodge it. Bandit felt the heavy paw hit him on his left shoulder, driving him violently down and into the cloud again.

"Get up!" Tremor commanded.

Bandit got up slowly and shook his head. His ears were ringing and his vision blurred. For a second he thought he might pass out but the feeling passed.

Tremor towered over him, his right paw held up, claws out, ready to strike again. "Do not displease me anymore. I won't tolerate any rebellious nonsense. You *will* obey me."

Tremor slowly lowered his paw and held it in front of Bandit's face. He unsheathed one of his claws and gently tapped him on the head with it. "Don't disobey me again. Next time you'll get the claws."

Bandit dropped his head in defeat at being caught by Tremor. He hid his smile and sense of relief that their plan had worked. From his peripheral vision he saw Sassy sprinting around the corner of the cloud and out of sight. Tremor gave Bandit a push towards the cloud they had run down.

"Now I want you to tell me all about that headdress of feathers that you two were looking at when I got dragged into this wretched place."

Bandit was panicking on the inside. He had no idea how he would do it, but he had to distract and stall as much as possible. He just prayed that Sassy would find her way back to the Rainbow Bridge and find someone there who would know what to do.

Chapter 10 – Legendary Times

Dan knew they had to reach the protection of the city before night fell. As long as they remained within the glow of the Rainbow Bridge, they would be shielded from the side effects of the night. Feather Dan and company traveled swiftly back through the clouds. Racing up clouds only to race down others, sometimes leaping from one cloud bank to another, Dan led the way using his beloved Blankets Mountain as their true North to keep them on course back to Cat Tree City.

They arrived shortly before dark to a sight he wasn't expecting. As the small tired group drew close, they heard them before they saw them. An enormous crowd of hundreds of cats had gathered around both Blankets Mountain. Dan could also see them as far out as the stadium cloud where the Feathers Time games would shortly begin.

As soon as his group was spotted, questions were voiced loudly by the upset cats concerned with his absence impacting the Feathers Time game.

"I see him!"

"There he is. There's Dan!"

"Are the games going to go on as planned?"

"Where have you been?"

"Don't you know the games are about to start?"

"Why aren't you at the stadium?"

"More sink bath cats? Are we being invaded?"

There were too many cats, all asking questions at the same time. Every time he tried to answer, Dan would be interrupted by someone asking another question. He had an idea to get their attention. He raced up a short way up Blankets Mountain, then stepped off to the side of the path. He paused and thought of a tall straight cat tree, with a single flat platform at the top for him to sit on. The cloud under his feet twinkled and glowed. The nearest cats saw this and knew something was happening. They stopped talking to watch as the top of the platform raised Dan up and up until he was above the crowd and easy to see and hear him.

As Dan's head started to appear above them, more and more cats fell silent waiting to see what would happen next. When Dan felt the platform was high enough, he willed it to stop rising. Taking advantage of the momentary lull in noise, Dan asked if anyone had seen the twins since that was the more pressing matter.

The gathered cats looked around at each other, several calling out they hadn't seen them only to be joined by others voicing the same. No one had seen the twins recently. That wasn't good and Dan began to seriously worry for their safety.

"I could use a few volunteers to check for places the twins are often seen. Please let me know as quickly as possible if anyone here spots the twins. I'll be on the top of Blankets Mountain. They may be in danger and I need to find them quickly."

A few cats stepped forward, some friends of the twins and volunteered to see if the twins were in any of their favorite spots. Dan thanked them for their help, knowing that they would probably prefer to be watching the game. Dan hoped that they were just hiding out in Cat Tree city. It would be very bad if they were stuck outside the city when night came and they lost their way back. It was a shame they had been unable to find them so far.

One of the team captains, Roberto, yelled up to Dan and asked, "We are still having the games tonight, right?"

Dan's attention was returned to the crowd staring at him waiting for an answer to the question. Tonight was a playoff game and it had been the talk of Rainbow Bridge for the last two weeks. He knew how disappointed they would be if the games were cancelled. It was a small joy he could give them and it meant a lot to him and to them. Dan nodded his head and despite his mounting concerns said, "Of course we will still have the games!"

The crowd cheered and the mood immediately went from one of concern and skepticism over the situation with the sink bath cats to one of excitement and anticipation. When the roar of the crowd died down enough he could be heard, Dan nodded to the captain again. "I'll take my place at the top of Blankets Mountain. Get the teams ready and we'll begin right away."

The captain smiled a huge grim to show his pleasure. A split second later, Roberto had turned around and zipped off towards Feather Stadium. Dan had no doubt both teams would be quickly rounded up and headed out to their field positions.

The crowd soon dispersed all headed towards Feathers Stadium to enjoy the games. Dan lowered the platform back down until it disappeared. His friends had remained behind, soon forgotten in the crowd's excitement that the games were still on. Dan turned to his friends and motioned for them to follow him as he began the trek to the top of Blankets Mountain. Dan led the way. Remy and Binx on either side of him. Amelia and Leroy were close behind, still within hearing distance. Grace trailed behind the group, tongue hanging out, her collar jingling and tail occasionally wagging.

Binx looked at him inquisitively with his bright blue eyes, "Everyone is really excited about the games. What are they like?"

Dan knew Remy, Amelia and Leroy would be interested as well. He began explaining the game to the Binx loud enough for the others to hear him. He was almost late in starting the games, so Dan set a snappy pace for the others.

"The game is called Feathers Time. There are four teams and five players on each team. Each team has their own goal zone in the arena. To win the game the team has to have the most feathers in their goal zone. The game is played both on Blankets Mountain and in the arena below it."

Dan blushed as he explained the next part. "Because I was so generous during my life on Earth I have this thing I can do with the feathers. If I give away a feather another one appears in front of me. I can blow on the new feathers that appear and make them fly erratically in a general direction. That's how we start the game."

"I'm not sure I understand." Remy said.

Dan saw the others looked a bit confused as well. The game was hard to describe with just words. Seeing it played, it would start to make more sense to them. As the small group of friends reached the top of Blankets Mountain, there were four cats already waiting for him. Dan looked at his friends and said, "It's a lot to explain and I need to get the game started. Just watch and you'll figure it out pretty quickly. I'll explain as they play."

The four players were looking at Dan in the most unusual way and backing away from him and the group as they approached. Dan stopped and looked around and it dawned on him that Grace was still with them. There was no way Grace could resist chasing the cats during a game of Feathers Time. The temptation and her herding instincts would be too much and she'd end up spoiling the game.

He walked up to Grace and gave her a kind look. "I'm sorry, my friend, but you will need to wait in the Hall of Feathers until the game is over." Grace sighed then lowered her head. She trotted down the tunnel to the Hall of Feathers without complaint. She really was a great friend. He knew he was lucky to be considered part of her pack.

Dan looked away from where Grace had been and saw that the four players looked relieved. Dan walked up to them and set a small glowing light blue feather that was shaped like a small bird's flight feather on the ground in front of each of them. He took a step back, cleared his throat and said, "I give each of you a feather." Then he shouted loud enough that all of the cats gathered at the colosseum could hear him, "Now I declare it FEATHERS TIME!"

The players sprang into action. They each grabbed a blue feather at the same time, spun around and started sprinting down the Blankets Mountain towards the arena. The moment the cats grabbed their feathers, four new feathers appeared in the air, floating in front of Dan. The new feathers were the same size and shape of the blue feathers, but glowed a lovely white instead of blue. Dan inhaled and blew out a big breath at the white feathers. The feathers shot off quickly towards the stadium. They were flying so fast that they zoomed past the players that were racing down the mountain.

Dan looked to his friends and said, "Those zooming feathers are called Free Feathers."

Dan directed his feline companions to watch the players race down the mountain toward the playing field. Having witnessed many games before, Dan knew the players each had their own strategy to be the first down the mountain. Some of them just ran as quick as they could, while others took giant leaps down. If they got close enough to each other, sometimes they'd try to trip their opponents up to get ahead. He turned his gaze away from the players racing down the mountain.

He turned his attention to the stadium just as the Free Feathers reached it. The remaining four players from each of the four teams began trying to catch them. The Free Feathers zigged and zagged back and forth and up and down. The cats crashed into each other and did all kinds of acrobatic moves to try to catch the feathers. It was similar to watching cats chase a laser dot back on Earth, if the laser could float in the air instead of being bound to walls and floors and other physical objects.

Dan looked at his friends, "The cats I gave a blue feather to will now need to get that feather into their team's goal zone. The other cats on their team can either try to help protect them or go after the Free Feathers that I sent down to zoom around."

The friends watched the game and were beginning to get caught up in the excitement of the crowd. Binx was flattened low to the cloudy ground, ears perked up, eyes as wide as saucers and he tried to take it all in. He was absolutely still with just his eyes moving as he watched players try to catch free feathers.

The players that Dan had given a blue feather to made it down Blankets Mountain and were racing through the arena. Dan pointed their progress out to Remy and explained to his friends, "Their goal is to get the blue feathers I gave them into their goal zone." Remy nodded in understanding, a grin spreading across his face. It was pretty easy to see why the game would appeal to the inherent playful hunter nature of cats.

The Arena was shaped like a giant square. In the center of each of the walls of the square was a pyramid shaped hollow cloud. At the top of the hollow pyramid was a symbol representing each team. Each of the four teams had one goal zone.

Dan pointed at the goal zone at the far end. One of the players he'd given a blue feather to was sprinting as fast as he could towards the goal zone and was almost there. His entire team had him

116

surrounded. Two players from another team tried to flank them by getting in front and running into the side of the group. They tried to knock them off their path so they'd have to circle back around and make a second attempt to get into their goal zone but with only two against five they were unable to. Two of the players on the defending team broke off and collided with the two attackers. They got tangled up with each other and tumbled across the field. The other two team members escorted the blue feather carrier the rest of the way to the goal zone. As the blue feather carrier crossed the goal line their symbol at the top of the pyramid glowed brightly and spun quickly. When it quit spinning the number two was displayed above the symbol.

"See?" Dan asked the group. "Each team has different strategies with this part of the game. Some teams surround their blue feather carrier and escort them in while others try to knock the feather out of the cats' mouth and take it for their own team. Look over there." Dan pointed to the right side of the field. "That team is taking advantage of almost everyone being gone and staying focused on catching the remaining Free Feathers. The blue feathers I give the carriers are worth two points. The Free Feathers zooming around the field are worth one point each. That team's strategy is to try to get all four of the white feathers before their blue feather carrier loses it to another team."

"Oh my cat!" Binx was now bouncing from paw to paw in excitement. "I want to play!"

Remy chuckled at the young Binx. "Maybe we can find a way for you to play later. It looks like this is a really important game to them so let's just watch and learn."

Leroy looked over to Binx, "It looks like it would take quite a bit of teamwork, Binx. Do you think you could keep yourself under control and focused long enough to work as a team with others?"

117

Binx was nodding his head vigorously, "Oh yes, I know I could!"

Amelia snorted, "I doubt it. You can't even decide what toy you want to play with for more than two minutes most days."

"I know, I know," Binx said excitedly, "but this is different!"

Dan nodded, "It may sound strange, but Binx is right. There is something about the game that gets the younger ones focused and settled. It's very popular and keeps many of the young ones out of trouble."

The player who had scored first ran back out into the field. Another team member ran up to him and they bumped paws. The player who had come from the mountain rejoined the rest of his team and ran off towards the two remaining Free Feathers. The other player turned towards Blankets Mountain and began running up towards Dan.

Dan glanced at his friends, "Once a player scores with the blue feather I gave them, they tag off with another player on their team. The new player comes back to Blankets Mountain and I give them another blue feather. Of course that means a new free feather zooms towards the arena and enters the field of play. Each player can only come up Blankets Mountain once so they have to stay organized with each other to keep the next member to tag with close by."

By the time the second player got to Dan, all of the teams had scored. The other team's players were already on their way up Blankets Mountain as well. Dan already had a blue feather set on the ground for him and when he got to it Dan told him that feather was a gift for him. The cat grabbed the blue feather and started charging down the mountain towards the stadium. Another white feather appeared, floating in front of Dan. He blew on it and it launched away to the stadium.

The cats crowded in the arena and along Blankets Mountain were cheering and celebrating. There were thousands who had come to watch. The gathering area where the cats could watch the games expanded on its own as more cats arrived. There was always room for more to come. Soon the scores were two, two, four and four.

Dan could hear Grace whine and occasionally bark when the crowd roared as a goal was scored. Dan was proud of her for behaving and staying put. He knew how much she enjoyed chasing cats and playing with them. He knew how hard it was for her to be left out of the fun.

The third round of players soon came for their blue feathers and raced off. Ten minutes later the fourth round of players all received their blue feathers. The scores were all close by the time the final fifth round of players came to collect their team's feather.

Dan explained to the group, "When the last blue feather I gave to a player from the top of Blankets Mountain gets into the team's end zone the game is over and the remaining Free Feathers are then worth no points. They will disappear. The final scoring feather is worth five points. The team with the most points wins. Sometimes a team has to play keep away with their final feather. If they were down by more than five points their team would have to catch Free Feathers or capture another team's blue feather to get their score up enough to be able to win. There are no tie games. If a score results in a tie the team who got the final blue feather in the goal zone is the winner."

The game went on for over an hour before one cat got the last feather into her end zone. As soon as she did the remaining Free Feathers vanished and those players still trying to catch them stopped and looked around to see who won. The feather above the winner's end zone shone brightly then grew in size and turned a polished gold color. Bells chimed and the sound echoed through the streets and alleys of Cat Tree City. The crowd erupted in excitement.

The scoring feather above the goal of the team with the fewest points went dark. That team was now eliminated from the next round of the championship. The players on the field congratulated each other as they made their way to their respective goals to celebrate together. Dan knew there would be lively celebrations happening across Cat Tree City until the morning, especially for the three teams advancing to the next round.

The gatherings in the arena and on Blankets Mountain were loud and wild. As the cats spilled out of the stadium and towards the streets of Cat Tree City Dan knew he was right. There wouldn't be anyone sleeping in the city that night. Cats were celebrating and singing different songs in the streets and other public places in large groups. Others played chase or with favorite feather toys in various versions of the Feathers Time game reliving favorite moments from the game. Perhaps, he dared hope, if Sassy and Bandit were close enough in the dark they could hear the celebration and find their way home.

Some cats were more worn out from the excitement and ready to relax at home although sleeping might prove difficult that night. Dan explained to Remy that all cats had their very own favorite cat ledge to sleep on in Cat Tree City whenever they wanted to. Cats that preferred company and to snuggle so would share a ledge.

Once the excitement quieted and the cats were not racing around in the excitement of the celebrations on Blankets Mountain, Dan let Grace come back up and join everyone. "Thank you, Grace. I know it's not easy for you to wait like that with so much action happening so close."

"It's okay," Grace said. A huge doggy grin was on her face, and her tongue was hanging out showing she was happy. "I know I can't help myself. That's why I try not to be here when the games are being played."

Dan nodded, "Today is an exception, my friend."

Dan took a deep breath to steady himself. With the games behind him, he needed to get back to work. "I've fulfilled my obligation with the games for today. Now we need to get back to work and focus on our mission."

Leroy reached over and bopped Binx on the head. "Hey, pay attention."

Binx flicked his tail at Leroy, "I am paying attention. I'm paying attention to everything! Look over there! Those cats are playing a type of Feathers Time! Let's go see if they'll let us join. Dan, do you have some more feathers we could use?"

Leroy bopped him again but a bit harder.

"Hey!" Binx complained, "Cut it out, Leroy. That's not nice."

"I said pay attention. I meant pay attention to Feather Dan, not the other kittens playing Feathers Time."

"Why, what…" Binx finally focused on the group and saw everyone gathered together looking very serious. "Did I miss something? What happened?"

"Nothing," Leroy muttered. "Nothing is going to be able to happen until you pay attention. We still have a mission that we're on. Remember?"

Binx's bright blue eyes went wide, his orange tipped white ears stood up alertly. "Oh yeah, I forgot. Sorry. What do you need me to sniff out next?"

"Nothing yet, Binx." Dan inwardly chuckled. Binx really was just a kitten. It was easy to understand how he could get distracted, especially about feathers. "I just need everyone to pay attention so we all know what we're doing. Okay?"

Binx nodded eagerly, "Yup, you got it, Dan. So what are we doing next?"

Dan continued like he'd never been interrupted. "Now that the Feather Times game is over we need to get back on track. It's time we paid a visit to Aristotle."

"Who's Aristotle?" Remy asked.

"Aristotle? He's the elder cat. Aristotle's been here the longest of all of us. He's over one hundred Rainbow Bridge years old. He crossed the Rainbow Bridge when his human was very young but she wasn't so young that they hadn't bonded. His human still has loving memories of him and so he will be the light to guide her to the Bridge when her time comes."

Dan hoped that Aristotle would have some answers or wisdom on how to proceed to share. He lived in the center of Cat Tree City. His perch was at the very top of the tallest cat tree. They would have to go visit him there because Aristotle didn't go wander around very much. The view from his perch let him see all around. The only place higher at the Rainbow Bridge was Blankets Mountain.

Dan looked over to Grace, "Do you need to go back to the dog realm yet?"

Grace shook her head, "Nope, no way I'm going anywhere as long as all of my friends are back together again."

Amelia purred loudly as she mushed circles around Grace's legs. Dan could tell Amelia was perfectly happy to have Grace around. Judging by the huge grin on Grace's face, she wasn't

122

complaining either to have Amelia with her again. Dan thought that despite the circumstances, it was nice to have all his friends back together.

Dan smiled, "Grace, I have a favor to ask. I know you want to come with us but you can't climb cat trees. We're going to have to climb up really high to reach Aristotle. I could really use your help keeping an eye on Blankets Mountain. I need someone I can trust to keep an eye out for the twins. I also need someone who can manage them if they try to cause any trouble. I know they wouldn't give you any problems."

Grace nodded her collar clinking softly as she did, "Sure, Dan. I'll keep watch. Maybe we'll get lucky and they were just hiding out waiting for the games to end. They must know by now they are in big trouble. They might try to sneak back and put the headdress away. I'll keep watch. If they come back, I'll hold them here until you return."

"Thank you, Grace." Dan turned back to the others. "Stick close to me everyone. The streets are going to be much busier than normal. Binx, do not wander off please."

"Don't worry about Binx," Remy piped up. "I'll keep him focused and with the group."

With that settled the group headed out. Dan was right, the streets and alleys of Cat Tree City were packed. It was much more crowded than usual that night because of the Feathers Time game that had just finished, but not so crowded Dan thought it would be an issue.

After navigating through the chaos, Dan led the group to the cat tree that Aristotle lived on. It was very tall, with a lot of back and forth levels about six feet wide and twenty feet long, climbing ever higher. Some levels held flat platforms for sitting, others held open-ended enclosures shaped like U's, C's, squares, seashells, or circles.

Between some platforms were hammocks or tunnels. Ledges were reached by crossing platforms, ladders or runs. Some ledges had scratching posts, dangling toys or wind chimes with sparkly crystals on them. Dan thought it was truly a magnificent cat tree. Many cats loved to call it home, he could understand why.

"Okay everyone;" Dan sounded anxious, "We should do some quick grooming before we go up. It's considered an honor to ask Aristotle questions. He likes to tell stories, kind of like me, but to actually seek him out and ask for his knowledge is something altogether different."

Dan wanted to make sure his shine was as perfect as it could be. He thoroughly gave his coat a cleaning starting with his front paws and working up to his ears and head. He moved on to his back and rear legs, finishing up with his tail. Satisfied that he shined and there were no dull spots on him anywhere, he looked to check on the progress the others had made. For being new to the Rainbow Bridge, Dan thought Remy did a fine job of getting his shine perfect as well. Leroy, Amelia and Binx had groomed as well. Dan knew they were very clean, even if they didn't shine at all.

It looked like everyone was done grooming. "It's time to get moving then, everyone ready? Here we go. Try to keep moving and follow me. We are going all the way to the top." He thought it might be a good idea to put Leroy, Amelia and Binx between him and Remy. "Binx, follow directly behind me. Amelia and Leroy follow Binx. Remy I know you're new here, but you shine and they don't. I want you to be behind Leroy in case anyone raises a fuss. If they see our shining coats, they will not be as alarmed."

Making a quick hop up the first level, Dan headed straight for a ladder and ran up straight to the next level. From there he leaped to the next floor, and then crossed it to reach the other side where there was a small run up to the next level. The group moved left and right across the levels, moving upward. After quite a bit of hopping, climbing and leaping they made it to the top. Binx wasn't distracted at all by the dangling toys. The jumping and running and climbing at a fast pace probably enabled him to focus on keeping up as they climbed to the top. Dan only encountered a few cats that made comments or flattened their ears back at the sight of Binx, Amelia and Leroy following him. Dan knew it had been a good idea to have them follow directly behind him so the heaven cats would know they were working with Dan.

Aristotle's ledge was very large, cup shaped and soft. There was plenty of room for all of them to stand side by side as they approached him. Aristotle himself was a very large cat. On Earth his breed was referred to as a Maine Coon. He had a large boned body, with wide paws and gorgeous thick white ear tufts and fur between his toes. His long haired coat of flowing brown and black fur marked him as a brown tabby. His underbelly was a lighter tan color. While their large size may seem intimidating, most of the bulk of a Maine Coon comes from all their thick body hair. When they reached him, Aristotle was cleaning his enormous ringed bushy tail. His shine was even brighter than the other cats at the Rainbow Bridge which was impressive because Dan knew that with that much fur, it would take a long time to get a thorough grooming to shine that brightly.

Dan sat on his haunches, wrapping his tail around his front paws, just a few feet away from Aristotle. As was the custom, Dan waited patiently for Aristotle to finish his grooming and acknowledge their presence before attempting to speak. Binx quickly mimicked Dan's posture. Amelia lowered herself to the ground, with her front paws tucked sideways under her chest and her back paws hidden. She wrapped her tail around her to her side, and left it lying limply. Dan knew that Leroy was likely tired from all the running earlier and then all the climbing they just did. He wasn't surprised when Leroy promptly fell over flopping down, front legs straight out in front of him, back legs twisted to the side. Remy stepped up quietly, and mirrored Dan's polite waiting posture.

Aristotle's aged face lit up and he looked genuinely happy when he saw Dan. Bright green eyes that shone with wisdom and pleasure looked directly at Dan. He flashed a wide happy smile and said, "Feather Dan! What a pleasure to get a visit from you on a night such as this. Welcome my friend, and welcome to the new comers as well."

"Thank you, Aristotle." Dan bowed his head out of respect as he approached and sat down in front of him. He introduced the others and briefly explained why three of them didn't shine.

"Yes," Aristotle was staring at Leroy, Amelia and Binx with intense curiosity. "I've already heard about all of the recent commotion of the day's events. I've been expecting a visit from you. If I'm being honest, I've been waiting anxiously for you and looking forward to it."

"You were looking forward to a visit from me?" Dan was surprised at that. He wondered just what Aristotle knew of the events that had happened today.

"Well of course, my young friend. First of all, it's always a pleasure to share company with you. I enjoy it when you get a chance to visit. But when unusual happenings occur, like Earth cats deciding to come visit and mysterious artifacts being discovered, these are the times and events of which legends are born. It's always an honor to bear witness to such things." Dan could tell Aristotle was enjoying himself and seemed quite happy to see him. He thought he had made a good choice to come for a visit.

Dan hadn't considered that he was part of a legend in the making. He had already created Blankets Mountain and been responsible for Feathers Time. Now it appeared he was in the midst of doing something extraordinary again. Nothing had actually changed, but as Aristotle's words sank in, Dan could feel the heavy and serious weight of the mission as it settled more firmly on his shoulders. The main difference between now and those last times was a big one. This time he had his friends to help him.

Dan was pleased that Aristotle already knew an artifact was involved. But he wondered if he might know more about it that would be helpful. "Have you ever heard about the mystical powers of the headdress?"

Aristotle took a moment and considered his answer. "I have heard about artifacts with unique abilities. When they are identified they are taken to the university and kept under careful watch. Legends and history tell us that more often than not those types of artifacts lose their powers quickly, or disappear entirely, when the cat they were associated with goes to the Beyond. To answer your question however, no, I did not know the headdress was such an artifact."

Dan glanced at his friends, "Have you ever seen a sink bath cat?"

"Earth cat," Leroy, now sitting up respectfully, quickly corrected him. "I prefer to be referred to as an Earth cat. It's much more dignified sounding than a sink bath cat."

Amelia nodded in agreement with Leroy. Binx was just staring in awe at Aristotle and how magnificent he looked.

"This is the first time I've ever actually seen an Earth cat." Aristotle nodded at Leroy and smiled. "I've heard stories about Earth cats. Those stories have been passed down through the generations. It's actually been so many generations since anyone has actually seen an Earth cat that the other elders and many of the professors and I were beginning to wonder if they were even real. I see for myself now that they most certainly are."

Dan thought about Aristotle's words when they first got there. He was gaining more understanding of why Aristotle referred to this visit as the birth of a legendary time. He asked his next question. "Do the stories make any reference to any dangers for an Earth cat at the Rainbow Bridge?"

Aristotle's voice lowered, his tone turned ominous. "That my young friend is a very wise question. While the legends and stories do not make any reference to dangers, it is obvious what the gravest one is." He stopped and studied each of them closely. "The danger is time. The greatest danger is the same as for all of us but more so than ever for the Earth cats. For an Earth cat to be here at all is the same as being lost in the clouds after dark."

Dan saw that Binx, Amelia and Leroy were listening closely. Aristotle's words suddenly sounded more like a warning than an explanation to Dan's ears. "Should your person die while you are here, you have no way of helping them cross as you do not shine. At the same time if you do not return you will never be able to cross the Rainbow Bridge the way we are all intended. You would be lost here forever with no way of crossing to the Beyond."

Dan saw Leroy shiver. Dan always thought of Leroy as the responsible one. He was the one that always did the right things and made sure they were done the right way. It probably wasn't sitting well with him that he was doing something that could jeopardize his mum or dad or his siblings. Dan could see Leroy stiffen in resolve. Dan knew Leroy would take the job of making sure everyone made it back home safely very seriously. He was proud to call Leroy his friend.

"It is not only possible but likely that the twins have become lost in the clouds after dark." Aristotle mused.

When Aristotle's words penetrated his thoughts of Leroy and the danger his friends were in, his worry about the twins returned in full force. His words seemed to make it more certain in Dan's mind that his fears were correct and they were in very serious danger.

"If that is so then we must act quickly." Aristotle continued his earlier musing. "We'll need to organize all the cats in heaven to help us. We need to launch search parties at first light. To begin, I want you to organize a group to gather up all of the balls of yarn that can be found. Tie one end to Blankets Mountain and roll it out with the searchers as they go looking. They should travel in a straight line and when they run out of yarn they should anchor it there and leave it. With any luck the twins will eventually wander across one of the lines and be able to follow it back home."

Aristotle's idea got Dan thinking. He had an idea for a plan that he could put in place as well, but it would have to wait until the morning.

Aristotle looked at Dan with curiosity. Dan was sure he could tell he was thinking something, but Dan wasn't ready to share what just yet. Dan was grateful that Aristotle didn't press for more information.

After a brief pause, Aristotle continued, "I am going to spend the night reminiscing. I will try to recall anything else that might be of help. Get as many cats as you can to gather the yarn we'll need for the morning. In the meantime, I recommend that you all get some rest. Tomorrow is going to be a very busy and important day. Remember, you are now living in legendary times. Every action you take, every decision made must be thought out and the consequences considered."

Dan remained silent, looking over to his friends for support and courage to get done what was needed. They each returned his gaze with resolve in their eyes. Dan looked back at Aristotle when he spoke next.

"Dan, I have trust in you. Now go and do what must be done." Aristotle said. His tone was serious but Dan also found it to be encouraging, almost like he saw something in Dan and knew he could rise to the occasion.

"Thank you, Aristotle. We'll see to the yarn, and then get some sleep as you've advised." Turning to his friends, he walked towards and then past them. Binx and Amelia, followed by Leroy and Remy were soon on their feet and following Dan.

The group of friends was silent as they made the descent from Aristotle's ledge of the cat tree down to the streets below. The crowds were boisterous and the mood was celebratory which Dan couldn't help but realize was in stark contrast to how somber he and the rest of the group were currently feeling. They took their time walking back to Blankets Mountain. Dan stopped and spoke with several cats he knew personally and asked them to help find the Team Captains and to recruit them to organize the yarn gathering mission.

They left the commotion of the city streets and began to make their way up the main trail of Blankets Mountain. Things quieted considerably and Dan was grateful for the opportunity to clear his head. The crowds now behind them, for a brief time they were all quiet, lost in their own thoughts. It wasn't long before Binx started asking questions and got them all talking again. They recapped what had happened, what they had learned and most of all the seriousness of getting this mission finished as fast as possible. If time was their number one danger then there was no time to waste.

As they got to the top of Blankets Mountain, Dan saw Grace approach.

"Any sign of the twins." Dan forced himself to sound hopeful. He had a gut feeling that the twins would not have shown.

"No sign of them." Grace confirmed her collar jingling as she shook her head. "A few cats came by to visit with you. I asked them if they'd seen the twins, but none of them had."

Dan nodded his head. That's the answer he was expecting. "Thanks for watching for them Grace. You've been a great help today."

Dan looked around to find the others drooping. Not one of them had mentioned how tired they were, but now they couldn't hide it. Dan created a big soft fluffy cloud that would fit Binx, Amelia and Leroy as he explained what he was doing to Remy.

"Now you try." Dan said to Remy. "You should be able to create just the cloud you want to sleep in and anchor it to Blanket Mountain."

"Alright. Let me give it a go," Remy said. Dan watched as Remy appeared to concentrate on a spot just to the right of the cloud he made for Binx, Amelia and Leroy. Soon a small cloud formed and anchored itself. Dan looked over to see Remy beaming with happiness at his accomplishment.

"Well done, Remy." Dan praised him. "You catch on quick."

Dan looked up at Grace. "What about you my friend? You're always welcome on Blankets Mountain but do you need to get back to your own realm yet?"

"Nope." Grace said and she hopped up on the small cloud Dan had created for Leroy, Amelia and Binx. She turned in circles as she prepared to plop herself down and settle in for the night and as she did the cloud widened to accommodate her as well. Finally satisfied with the cloud she quit spinning in circles, took a deep breath and lay down. She curled into a tight ball with her chin resting on her paws.

Amelia beamed with happiness and jumped up with her. She rubbed up against her until she got comfortable herself then snuggled tight. Looking at Dan she smiled, "It's perfect."

Remy and the others quickly settled on their respective clouds. They were quiet, likely exhausted from all the excitement and activity. He was super proud of all of them.

"Look everybody; I have an errand I need to run." Dan said as they all turned their heads to look at him. Aristotle's idea with the yarn is a fantastic one and going to be critical in getting this mission done as efficiently as possible. I'm going to go speak with all of the teams from the Feathers Time games. They are the fastest cats at Rainbow Bridge. That is, after all, a large part of how they got on the teams. They should be the ones to run the yarn out and anchor it. They would get the job done the fastest.

"It would also free us up to go out on our own and continue the search where we left off. I'm very worried we'll find more Earth cats. It will take all of us to get them to their feathers and send them home."

The others agreed and Dan said, "Get some rest. I promise I'll be back soon."

With that Feather Dan turned and raced back down Blankets Mountain.

Chapter 11 – Sassy

Sassy ran as fast as she could to get away from the panther. She stuck close to the edges of the clouds, hoping to use those as some form of concealment. The night had her disoriented and she had no idea where she was going. She tried her best to travel in a straight line but she couldn't even tell if she was doing that. As she rounded the end of the cloud she was running along, she stopped. Confusion washed over her and made her momentarily dizzy. She closed her eyes, took a deep breath and counted to ten. She found herself overwhelmed with frustration. When she opened her eyes and tried to focus, a tear ran down her cheek making things even blurrier. She couldn't remember which way she had just come from. She couldn't remember how many clouds she'd already run past.

Frustration, anxiety, fears for her brother and a sense of dread for all of Rainbow Bridge filled her heart. More tears fell from her eyes to the soft cloud where she stood. Her instinct was to keep running, but she was worried she would accidentally circle back and find herself face to face with the beast. The panther had called himself Tremor. She'd never seen anything like it. It was a massive muscular creature with yellow stained fangs that were longer than her legs and its claws…those were the stuff of nightmares. Those claws were the most wicked looking, sharpest things she had ever seen. The panther had obviously never been given a nail trim.

Spotting a small entrance under an outcropping on the side of the cloud mountain just ahead of her, Sassy rushed over to it. She ducked into it and was pleased to see it went back inside the cloud a few yards. It was a perfect spot for her to catch her breath and try to think. She didn't know how long she'd been running. She couldn't remember how long it had been dark and wasn't sure how much longer it would be before the dawn.

"Bandit, what do I do?" Sassy blinked and shook her head as she realized she was speaking out loud. Her heart pulled hard with a sudden ache and she realized part of what she was feeling was loneliness. That was something she'd never experienced. She was never without her brother by her side. They were inseparable and had been even during their time on Earth. She never kept a thought to herself, she shared everything with Bandit and he did the same with her.

"Come on Sassy, get it together." She told herself. "This is your fault. You have to figure this out and make it better."

She wanted to sneak up to the top of the cloud to get a look around but didn't want to take the chance of being spotted by the panther. She didn't think she'd be able to see very far at night anyway. The colorful lights that were dancing across the night sky also managed to extremely impair the cats, normally impressive, night vision. She hoped it would do the same thing to Tremor.

"Oh, Bandit, I'm so sorry." More tears fell from her eyes, down the black mask of fur on her face and onto the ground. Poor Bandit; she couldn't believe that beast had her brother. She'd seen how hard the panther struck him. The last blow had sent him hurling through the air and slamming into the side of the cloud. He was slow to get up and was obviously feeling pain. That realization was absolutely terrifying. There was no pain at the Rainbow Bridge, it simply didn't exist. Or at least it wasn't supposed to, Sassy thought. Something was terribly wrong.

Her last glimpse of the normally confident and boastful Bandit had broken her heart. He looked so scared and defeated. Leaving him to fight alone was the most difficult thing she'd ever had to do. That moment when she turned and ran left her feeling completely distressed, her emotions torn. She wanted to stay and help him but in her heart she knew he was right to tell her to go. Regret plagued her.

In hindsight, she felt like she should have stayed so he wouldn't have to be alone.

Guilt ate at her. She was the one who decided to try to catch another feather and he was the one who had to pay the price. It should be her to stay behind and Bandit out running free trying to find help. She lost track of time as she dwelled on her circumstances. Finally pulling herself together, Sassy made the decision to stay hidden until the morning. Her hiding spot was an excellent one and it was small enough that Tremor wouldn't even be able to squeeze in if he did wander by.

Sassy thought it was the worst night ever. Time moved more slowly than she'd ever experienced before. The morning was taking a very long time to get here. She had too much time to worry about Bandit. Her guilt for abandoning him and worry for his safety gnawed at her. She reminded herself she had to stay alert to her surroundings. She strained her ears, flicking them forward and sideways hoping to catch some sound that would either let her know Bandit was okay or confirm Tremor had found her. She made herself very small and sat as far away from the entrance as possible. She remained very still and silent, with her belly pressed to the ground, all four legs under her in case she needed to escape quickly, and tail wrapped around her.

Tremor had threatened to eat them and she wondered if it were possible to be killed by the beast. They were already spirits at the Rainbow Bridge but she was so overcome with emotions that her thoughts ran wild. Without Bandit to talk to and bounce questions back and forth with her mind went to a dark place. In that dark place, her mind ran through scenario after scenario and each time her fear grew greater.

It was a surprise when the first rays of the sun started to light up the sky and touch the tops of the clouds. Sassy could feel her sense

135

of direction returning. It was like waking up from a very vivid dream and in this case the dream was a nightmare. Her mind returned to normal but it was a slow process. The confusion passed in the same way the sun chased away the fog.

As soon as she felt like herself again she knew it was time to be brave and inched up to the opening of her shelter. She stuck her head outside, prepared to duck back in if she spotted anything dangerous. Seeing nothing but clouds, Sassy thought it was likely safe to adventure out of her hiding spot. After spotting a nearby cloud that was high up and would give a good vantage point to see where she was, she decided to climb to the top of the cloud. She had to do something to get some sense of where she was so she could decide what direction to go. She'd have to move slowly and try her best to stay hidden. If Tremor was nearby she didn't want to be spotted. Without the confusion the dark night provided, she knew she could never outrun him. She'd simply have to outsmart him instead and somehow rescue Bandit.

When she made her way to the top of the high cloud her heart sank. All she saw were clouds; lots of clouds that went on forever and ever in every direction. She had hoped so hard that she'd at least catch a peak of Blankets Mountain or even the glow from the Rainbow Bridge. She saw neither and her tail dropped and her ears drooped. The earlier depression she'd battled during the night began to creep back in.

What she saw next made her hair stand on end and she shuddered. Below her, two clouds away and moving steadily in her direction, she saw the panther. Its massive body moved confidently and he held his head high as he scanned his surroundings. Sassy was gripped with fear and was about to duck back to find cover when she spotted Bandit. He was walking in front of Tremor, dragging the headdress by himself. Sassy watched, transfixed and unable to look away. At one point Tremor must have felt Bandit was moving too slow. He shoved Bandit causing him to stumble ahead. Bandit was obviously struggling to maintain the pace being set by Tremor while carrying the headdress by himself. It had been awkward to carry it together, but Bandit was doing a good job by himself, even if Tremor didn't appreciate it.

Her mind racing, Sassy slowly backed down behind the cloud. They hadn't seen her but they were very close. She had to do something. Since she didn't know the direction back to Rainbow Bridge, she decided to go in the same direction the panther and Bandit were traveling in. She couldn't bear the thought of losing track of Bandit. Even if they were lost, it was better to be lost together than without him. Traveling as fast as she could she began developing a plan as she went. She often had to refocus when thoughts of Bandit being tormented by the beast drifted in.

"Hang in there, Bandit." She whispered to herself. "We'll figure this out... somehow. We'll get out of this mess just like we did all the others. I won't leave you behind."

Chapter 12 – Bandit

In the seconds immediately following the devastating blow he'd taken from Tremor, Bandit took the opportunity to assess his injuries. He stretched his right leg to see how bad it was. His right shoulder felt bruised from where he had been struck but nothing felt broken. Bandit was deeply concerned about that hit he had taken from Tremor. It had actually hurt a lot, and left him with his ears ringing. There was no pain at the Rainbow Bridge. Everyone could rough house and play as hard as they wanted and it never caused any physical pain or injuries. Bandit had never heard of stories about pain or injuries occurring at Rainbow Bridge. He knew something had to be wrong for him to hurt at all.

Tremor growled at him again, "I said get up and I mean now."

Bandit started walking, slowly at first favoring his injured shoulder, up the cloud towards the headdress of feathers. He wished they would have fallen just a little farther away or that he could have gotten around the corner of the cloud so it would have been out of sight. If they hadn't been able to see the headdress they probably wouldn't have been able to remember how to get back to it.

Tremor followed Bandit and stayed right behind him. He stayed close enough that Bandit could feel his breath on his tail. Tremor wasn't taking any chances that Bandit was going to try to run again.

"Why were you two wandering around out here with such a ridiculous looking thing?" Tremor growled behind him. His voice was laced with both contempt and a promise of pain for not answering.

Bandit stopped and collapsed beside the headdress. Defeated and resigned to doing Tremor's bidding, Bandit sat let his injured shoulder rest. "It belongs to a friend. We wanted to play with it. We took the opportunity while everyone else was distracted to borrow it so we could check it out. We really just wanted to play with the feathers for a while."

Tremor snorted and scowled at Bandit, "So, you're a thief. There's no honor in that." Tremor paused for a moment then asked, "Who does this belong to?"

"It belongs to Feather Dan." Bandit answered without hesitation to avoid more pain from Tremor being his reward for delaying the inevitable.

"Is he a fierce hunter? I would assume that he must have hunted down a lot of birds to be able to create such a thing as this headdress."

"Oh," Bandit shook his head, "Dan didn't make it himself. According to him this was simply there after he made Blankets Mountain."

"What is a Blankets Mountain?" Tremor asked again.

Bandit knew Tremor was just looking for any information he could gather about his surroundings. He was also likely testing Bandit and looking for inconsistencies in his story. He and Sassy had already given him a description of Blankets Mountain. What else could he tell him that would sooth his anger without revealing anything that would cause too much damage in the wrong paws? Perhaps some of Dan's background? That should be safe enough, right? He wished Sassy was here. She'd know what to say.

"When Feather Dan first came to the Rainbow Bridge he missed his home so much he managed to manifest a cloud mountain that resembled something he loved from his home on Earth. It's really quite remarkable. He's quite a remarkable cat as well. He's a little guy but has such a big heart that everybody loves him. And he sure does love feathers. He has a magnificent collection of them and he's never had to hurt a single bird to get any of them. He has them displayed in a place he calls the Hall of Feathers."

Bandit abruptly stopped talking when he heard what he'd just revealed. Maybe it was part of the confusion of the dark but he hadn't meant to ramble on and give up so much information. He realized he said too much already and tried to get himself composed.

Tremor grunted in disgust. "Absolutely pathetic! What kind of weak coward of a cat collects feathers without even bothering to hunt the bird?"

Clearly agitated, Tremor started pacing back and forth. "The hunt is life! There is no life without the hunt! The hunt is where you find peace, joy and excitement all at once. My home is a vast jungle and no part of life is easy. Every day is a fight for survival. Incompetent hunters starve and die or are themselves eaten by other predators."

Tremor glared at Bandit, before getting right in his face. "In the jungle there are rumors of you house cats and the entire concept of it disgusts me. Your kind is weak. You make the entire feline species look like a joke to the rest of the animal kingdom." Bandit could smell his breath. It was like horribly dead things that died a long time ago. Completely repulsive.

Bandit didn't dare say anything or disagree. He sat there head bowed in compliance, tail tucked between his legs and body hunched low to the ground. Tremor was obviously rambling on in the same manner he had when he talked about Feather Dan. It must be another side effect of the dark. Just as Bandit realized what was happening, Tremor realized that he was rambling and became distracted.

Tremor stopped pacing and turned his attention back to Bandit. "How did I get summoned to this miserable place with no suitable prey, only clouds everywhere?"

Bandit thought fast. He knew he couldn't get caught in a lie but at the same time he didn't want the panther to know exactly what had happened. "I really don't know for sure what happened. Me and Sassy lost track of time and became lost after night fell. We were playing with the feathers all day and just running around and having fun. Once we realized it was doing more harm than good to keep traveling we decided to stay put and wait out the night. We curled up beside the headdress so we wouldn't lose it. I don't know what happened next but something felt funny and when we got up to look all of a sudden you were there."

Tremor lowered his head to be level with Bandits. He glared intently into Bandits eyes and Bandit felt like his soul was being interrogated under that gaze. "Are you sure that's the truth. If you are lying to me I will eat you right now and be done with your nonsense. So?"

Bandit nodded his head vigorously. "Yes, yes, I swear that's the truth. I have no reason to lie to you. If I knew how you got here I'd be quick to try to send you home!" Too much truth that time. He wasn't sure why he'd been so bold to utter he'd send him home like that.

The panther sat up and chuckled, "Very well. Now I want more details about this mountain you mentioned."

Bandit retold him the story about Dan. He explained how kind and generous Dan was. He told the panther how he would welcome anyone to Blanket Mountain and how he loved to share his feathers. Then explained how Blankets Mountain came to be and how it was a wonderful place that was home to many cats. It was also the tallest point in all of the Rainbow Bridge. He revealed that Dan had become a sort of celebrity and was even called King of the Mountain by some.

Tremor snorted in derision, "That is just the most abhorrent example of a cat that I have ever heard. Not only does he not hunt but he helps others so that they don't have to hunt either? This fool you call Feather Dan enables the weakness in our species. We are fierce hunters and we fight for what we need. It is how we make sure only the strongest survive."

Bandit quickly tried to defend Dan. "No, I don't think you quite understand. This is the land of the Rainbow Bridge. There isn't any hunger or suffering here. We don't hunt for food here. We play, groom so our coats shine, nap, visit with each other, and explore. We are all already the strongest we can be here."

Tremor was studying him and listening to his words. Bandit prayed he was getting through to him and continued. "Now our purpose is to be here for our humans when they pass away. We're here to help them find their way across their Rainbow Bridge. Once we're reunited we get to go to the Beyond where everyone we've ever known is reunited in eternity."

Bandit's hopes of getting through to Tremor were immediately shattered when Tremor began shouting in anger. "Absurd! Again I tell you this is the most pathetic existence I can even think of! The weakness is sickening!"

Tremor pawed at the ground and growled. "Lead me to Blankets Mountain immediately! I am going to teach all of you how to be true felines. I will remind you of the glory of the hunt and rekindle the predator that must still exist somewhere within your pathetic weakened souls. I am going to claim Blankets Mountain for my own and rule all of Rainbow Bridge from there."

Spit was flying from Tremors mouth as he worked himself into an even more heated frenzy. "I am going to make an example of Feather Dan! He will be my personal court jester. He will juggle feathers and dance for my pleasure. If he doesn't make me laugh, he'll get the claws!" Tremor raised his huge paw menacingly, fully extended his long wicked looking claws right at Bandit's hunched form. Seemingly satisfied he'd made his point, Bandit was relieved when Tremor withdrew his sharp claw. The ache in his shoulder was a reminder that they could do some damage Bandit thought. He wasn't anxious to experience that again.

"The rest of you will battle each other for the right to access the Rainbow Bridge when your human passes. I will laugh at the humans who never find their way. It will be justice for them to wander the clouds for eternity as punishment for domesticating the feline race. I will even make it a game and hunt the humans then drag them through the streets of the city for all to watch while I maul them and make them suffer. Perhaps that will toughen you pathetic creatures up. Maybe, just maybe, you'll learn to become true predators again and learn to love the hunt."

Tremor spun on Bandit and yelled, "Get moving! Drag that headdress and lead the way. Take me to the Rainbow Bridge!"

Bandit had never been more terrified in his life. He could never let Tremor find his way to Rainbow Bridge; not if that was what he had planned. It had been his most important duty to be the light for his human. His responsibility now was to stay lost forever and to lead Tremor as deep into the unknown as he could. He fought back tears as he remembered Hope. He wouldn't be there when her time came. He would never see Sassy again. He was going to miss her. He hoped Sassy had managed to get away and find her way back. If she could do that, she would be enough to help his human find the light so they would be able to peacefully go to the beyond without him.

He'd never felt so helpless, desperate and alone in his life. With no hope left that he could gain his freedom, he surrendered himself to his new existence and started walking. He prayed that he was going in any direction but that of the Rainbow Bridge. It was the only chance any of them had.

Chapter 13 – Rescue Plan

Feather Dan had the group up and assembled before the break of dawn. When the first rays of the sun touched the tops of the clouds there was a sizable crowd gathered at the foot of Blankets Mountain. Feather Dan, followed by Grace, Remy, Binx, Leroy and Amelia traveled the winding path down the back side of the mountain. The atmosphere among the crowd was a solemn one. There was none of the chaotic chattering and bombardment of questions like there had been the day before. Word of what had occurred and was now happening had spread quickly and those thousands of questions had transformed into helping paws. Dan was truly happy to see so many turn out to offer their assistance.

Dan had managed to find and speak with all of the Feather Time teams last night. Most expressed shock to have confirmation from Dan that sink bath cats, something out of myth and legends, were not only real but here among them. Dan knew it was difficult for most of them to accept. More concerning to Dan was the disappearance of Bandit and Sassy. It was entirely possible that neither of them would ever be seen again and that could spell doom for their human. Dan informed them all that Bandit and Sassy's human, Hope, was very old and that her time to cross would be coming soon. None of them would forsake their sacred duty to assist a human with a crossing. They had all agreed it was an urgent problem and to help Dan find Bandit and Sassy as quickly as possible.

While only four teams of the Feathers Time games made it to the playoffs there were twelve teams in total. All twelve teams were gathered and awaiting Dan's instructions. Cats across Cat Tree City had rallied to do their part as well. Many had gotten into their own toy stashes, others had even unraveled parts of their cat trees and tied the threads together and several giant balls of yarn were already delivered and waiting to be run out. There were dozens of additional cats, each of them representing hundreds of others, waiting to see how they could help as well.

Addressing the crowd, Dan asked for the cats that weren't part of a team to spread out and go to the top of the clouds to be look outs. He said they should go in teams of four so they could look in all directions at once. He said they also needed to have lookouts on Blankets Mountain and in Cat Tree City in case the twins managed to sneak back in. If any of the lookouts spotted them they needed to gather the twins immediately and let everyone else know.

Looking at the Feathers Time teams he told them that they were to go out in teams of two. Each team of two should run one ball of yarn out until there was no more yarn left. They were then to anchor it to someplace steady and return. The fifth member of their team should remain at Blankets Mountain and stay with the anchor point there. The teams could tug on the yarn to send signals back to Blankets Mountain.

The teams quickly established a simple yarn tug communication system. They determined that the team captains would stay behind and the rest of the group broke up into pairs. Once all of the teams had one end of the yarn anchored they began pushing the balls of yarn forward. They took turns kicking and swatting at it and in no time the yarn was moving as fast as they could run and they raced off into the clouds.

The rest of the crowd started heading off. Some of them returned to Cat Tree City where they said they would organize the cats still there and set up a lookout system. Another group was put on yarn collection duty and left to find more yarn. Another group of cats quickly organized and ran off to take up lookout positions among the cloud tops.

Remy looked at Dan, "That's a very thorough plan and some impressive leadership. I'm sure we'll find the twins now."

"Let's hope so," Dan nodded and sighed. "We need to get moving. We'll resume our search where we left off yesterday."

"Wait," Leroy said, a look of concern etched across his orange striped face. "I'm really worried about mum and dad back home. We've been gone for almost an entire day and I know they must be in a panic by now. I can't imagine poor mum even slept last night." He pawed at the ground, his ears drooping in concern. "Is there any way for us to let them know that we're safe?"

Surprised Leroy hadn't asked about them last night, Dan knew he must have really been exhausted from the adventure to be waiting until now. Dan smiled at Leroy. "Time moves differently here, brother. Although it's been an entire day here, not much time has passed on Earth."

Leroy didn't look very convinced by his words. Dan knew that Leroy wouldn't be able to focus while he was worried about mum and dad. He completely understood. He also realized that Amelia and Binx might be feeling the same way as Leroy. He knew how he could set their minds at ease and it wouldn't take much time at all.

"What if I go and peak in on them to make sure everything is okay?" Dan offered to put Leroy at ease.

Leroy lifted his head and his ears perked back up. "I forgot that you can do that. Could you do it now?"

Dan smiled and nodded his head, "Of course. Come on we'll just make a quick side stop at the Rainbow Bridge. Remy, I would have usually already shown you how this works but we've been so busy I just haven't had time. I'm sorry, we should have checked in on Patti yesterday."

"It's okay Dan, I understand." Remy responded, lifting his gaze from watching Binx. "I'd really like to know how to check on Patti." He stood up straighter and looked back at Dan with excitement. "If you're ready to go, I'll just grab Binx."

Dan watched as Remy caught Binx just before Binx was about to hop up and climb one of the cat trees. It took only a few seconds for Remy to nudge him back towards the group. Seeing he had Binx's attention again, Dan led the others toward Rainbow Bridge.

Dan kept his ears open listening for the soft patter of kitty paws behind him, to make sure they were all following him. If anyone fell behind, he knew Grace would help keep the group together. He knew they could only afford to make a brief stop. They really did have to focus on finding Bandit and Sassy. In just a few minutes, Rainbow Bridge appeared directly ahead. When they got to the beginning of the Rainbow Bridge, Dan stopped to sit and wait for everyone to join him.

Leroy, Amelia and Binx stared at it in awe. Dan agreed, it was a sight to behold.

"It's even more beautiful than what we see on Earth!" Amelia exclaimed.

"I didn't even know there were that many colors! Look at them all!" Binx was excited and ran up to it. Remy caught him by his tail just before he ran across it just as Grace gave a warning bark at Binx.

"Careful Binx," Dan cautioned. "I have no idea what will happen if you step on it. It's meant for spirits not for physical bodies."

Binx looked back at Remy, then changed directions and sat beside Amelia. Grace was sitting near her, her big goofy grin in place and tongue hanging out. Her tail wagged as Binx settled down.

Leroy stepped up next to Binx and gave him a stern look. "You stay put, let me test it first." Leroy cautiously reached a paw out and touched it.

Dan saw Leroy's paw pass through it as if it was only an illusion. It didn't hurt Leroy at all, so that was a good thing.

Leroy carefully pushed Binx back away from the Rainbow Bridge. "Sorry Binx, you stay away from that. It's like stepping on water but with no resistance. I think we'd fall right through it and who knows where we'd fall down to."

"Really?" Dan was fascinated by that discovery. But he put the idea of exploring it further aside. "Remy come with me and I'll show you how to check on Patti."

Together Remy and Dan walked out onto the Rainbow Bridge as if they were still walking on the clouds. "Okay, it's really easy to check in on your human. All you have to do is think really hard about your human and let that love you share pull you together. Then you stick your head inside the Rainbow Bridge and you'll see what they're doing."

Dan and Remy lowered their heads into the Rainbow Bridge. As Dan and Remy's heads passed into the Rainbow Bridge beautiful white angel wings materialized over their front shoulders.

Dan heard Amelia and Leroy gasp at the same time.

Binx yelled, "Holy cat! You both just grew wings!"

"I can see my mom!" Remy yelled excitedly. Then sorrow laced his voice when he reported, "She's crying. Oh she looks so sad! Dan what's wrong? She just looked up and I think she looked right at me."

"She can't see you, Remy, but she probably senses that you're there." Dan felt bad for him. It was hard to check on your humans so soon after crossing. Sometimes they grieved for a very long time. "She's sad because on Earth, hardly any time has passed since you crossed the Rainbow Bridge. It's hard to say exactly how much time passes here compared to there. I sometimes think that it's different every day." Dan remembered how much time he'd spent watching his humans after he first crossed. He knew it would be hard on Remy to see her in pain. "I spent lots of time checking in on Leroy, Amelia and Binx too."

Dan pulled his head back up and his wings vanished. "Only an hour or so has passed back home. Mum and dad haven't even gotten home from work yet."

Leroy walked up to the edge of the Rainbow Bridge. "Can I see mum and Dad, too?"

"You can try, but it may not work for you. You aren't a spirit yet." Dan told Leroy.

Leroy walked up and put his head in the rainbow bridge. Dan didn't see wings sprout from Leroy's front shoulders and wasn't surprised when a moment later Leroy lifted his head.

"I didn't see anything but rainbow colors." Leroy told the group, clearly disappointed. "I wish I could have seen them. Thank you for checking on them for me Dan. I feel much better now." Leroy walked back to rejoin Amelia and Binx.

"I could sit and watch Patti forever, or at least until she's not so sad." Remy was still on the Bridge, head tucked into the rainbow, wings drooped in concern.

150

"I understand," Dan told him. "But we need to go. I need your help finding the missing headdress and sending home any Earth cats we find. The mission can't wait. I promise you can come back later and check on Patti."

With a big sigh Remy pulled his head up. His wings faded away and he walked back to the group. Dan bumped noses with him and said, "Once you've been here for a while and had some practice you won't even need to be at the Bridge to check on her either. You can do it from anywhere it just takes more practice."

Dan led Remy back to the others patiently waiting at the edge of Rainbow Bridge. Dan could see that Binx was having a hard time sitting still. He was practically bouncing, waiting for Dan and Remy to reach him.

"Dan you and Remy had wings! Real angel wings! That was amazing! Can you fly when you have wings?' Binx practically exploded his thoughts at Dan.

Dan nodded, "Yes, we can fly down to Earth when we feel like we're needed. If they are going through hard times, having a bad day, or even when they're having a good day we can fly down to be near them and offer support. We just think of dropping through the Rainbow Bridge or through a cloud and fly to them. We can visit and talk to them, but they can't really see or hear us the way they used to when we were alive. Sometimes I think they know we're there with them. Mum and dad have both talked to me a few times when I've been there."

"Wow!" Binx said. "I've heard them do that, but I didn't think you were actually there. I didn't see you."

"You know those rays of sunshine that can sometimes be seen breaking through clouds and beaming down to Earth? Those are pets checking in. That's the only way to see us. We can only stay for so long and I think it depends on what they're going through. It's hard to describe but one day you'll understand." Dan explained to Binx. He really didn't have more time for talking, so he ran faster to discourage Binx from asking more questions that would slow him down. He liked the little guy, but the mission had to come first.

The group of friends rushed past Blankets Mountain and made excellent time getting to where they had left off the search the day before. Dan noted they had also crossed two lines of yarn along the way. The lines stretched off into the distance and out of sight. The other cats were on the job and that made Dan feel encouraged Aristotle's plan might just work.

They climbed to the top of the cloud to get a good look around, Grace leading the way this time. Dan noted a few yarn lines in between some other clouds but other than that there was nothing to give them any hints about what direction to try to search in next.

Dan looked out across the clouds still hoping to spot movement or anything that would help give them a clue. "Things are going to be more difficult now. If the twins traveled during the night it would have been in random and aimless directions. Using Binx's strategy of sticking to the clouds that provide the best concealment won't be much use anymore. Hopefully, now at least, they're trying to be found. The yarn lines might be our best bet. Even if we find them they won't be able to give us any directions to any other Earth cats that they pulled through."

Dan saw Grace was wandering around and sniffing, already on the job trying to find any scent trails for them to follow. It didn't look to him like she was having much luck though. She trotted back and sat next to him. She didn't look discouraged as she panted, looking at him with her signature one ear flopped over. Her tail wagged when Dan looked back at her.

Dan sighed in frustration, "I'm not sure what to do but we have to do something. I guess for now we'll stick to the same strategy that we used yesterday. They left here with at least another hour of daylight remaining. Maybe Binx will at least sniff out another feather collar."

"If we assume they were still trying to stay hidden, they'd likely go in that direction there." Binx pointed with his right paw to a nearby group of clouds. "I say we search between here and there, but that should be our next destination."

"It's a good plan," Grace agreed. "I'll search for the smell of Earth cats. Binx can search for the feathers and portals."

Grace and Binx lead the way. They traveled for an hour, and passed another line of yarn.

"I've got something here!" yelled Binx. "It smells like clouds."

Grace ran over and started sniffing around in a circular search pattern that extended from the spot Binx indicated. Dan figured she was hoping to catch the scent of an Earth cat that belonged to the feather or portal Binx detected. Everyone else spread out and looked around very carefully.

"I'm going to the top of the cloud to look around." Remy volunteered.

The rest of them found nothing on the first pass. Just when Dan decided they should double check themselves just to be sure but it just wasn't there to be found he heard Remy call out.

"Hey! I saw something pass behind a cloud. You might want to come take a look."

Dan, Leroy, Binx and Amelia took off toward Remy. When they got there Remy pointed out where he had seen the dark shape.

Dan could make out the shape of another cat. It wandered back out from behind the cloud Remy had pointed out. It was too far away to see if it was wearing a collar but not too far to tell it didn't shine.

Binx shouted, "I see him!"

Amelia said in a more reserved voice, "Good eye, Remy. You found another Earth cat."

Grace raced up to them, likely spurred on by Binx's shout. She let out an excited bark when she spotted the Earth cat.

The cat heard Grace bark and looked startled. Afraid the cat would run before they could help him, Dan yelled out to it, "We are here to help you! We're coming."

Everyone raced off toward the new Earth cat. When they did get to it the cat was obviously more confused than any of the others they had seen the day before.

Leroy was first to approach him. Grace hung back so as not to spook him. The Earth cat wasn't as shy as the others had been and Dan thought he must have been somewhat familiar with dogs. The cat didn't seem to mind Grace's presence.

"I've wandered all night," he said. "I've never been more confused in my life."

Leroy patiently explained about what happened to him and asked, "Have you seen any other cats?"

The Earth cat nodded, "Yes, there were two Siamese who told me what direction to go but I got confused. All of these clouds just look the same and sometimes I think they even change shape. Once it got dark things got even worse. I heard very strange sounds and thought I saw a goat on top of one of the clouds." He looked at Leroy with a paranoid expression. "Do you think I'm suffering from hallucinations? I don't know what's going on. I just want to go home."

"You'll be okay," Leroy told him. "At least you still have your feather collar. Just give that a good chomp and you'll go back home right away."

The cat looked pleased at the idea of finally getting back home. "Thank you for the help. I'll be glad to be home again." He gave the feather a chomp and was gone.

Grace sniffed the air and looked around. "Dan, do you think there's really a goat lost in the clouds or was that Earth cat seeing things?"

"I don't know," Dan thought about it for a second. "At this point anything's possible. I wish he could have remembered what direction he thought he saw the goat so we could go check it out."

Remy looked concerned, "Do you think that headdress can open a portal to anything other than cats?"

"I don't know. I guess it's possible but I sure hope not."

Binx was just finishing up grooming his orange tipped tail. "At least we have a new place that we know the twins were at. It gives us something to go on. I can keep on sniffing if you want."

"Binx is right," Dan put his worry aside. "Let's get back to the search."

They searched for several more hours and crossed four more lines of yarn. They didn't see any other cats and fortunately no goats either. It was disheartening to have searched for so long without any indication that they were even close to being on the right trail. The longer they searched without any clues the more pointless it felt like the search became.

Dan finally voiced his concerns to the group, "I'm very worried. I don't think actually being out here searching is doing any good anymore. We probably got lucky finding the one cat that we did. Once the night had come and gone the rules of the search changed."

Leroy nodded in agreement, "I'm afraid you're right but it's not like any of us to give up and do nothing."

"No, Leroy, we'll never give up but I think for now we need to head back to Blankets Mountain. Maybe the yarn lines worked or one of the other teams has stumbled across something. If we go back now we might still have enough daylight left to follow up on any new leads that may have developed."

The group was in agreement and they began the journey back to Blankets Mountain. Dan was worried about the twins. He couldn't imagine what last night must have been like for them. If they were lost for two nights would they ever be able to find their way home? What if they had wandered farther out and not in circles? Nobody knew what the clouds were like beyond a half a day's hike out. There were stories that the clouds actually faded away. There was speculation that large oceans of blue sky took their place with just occasional puffy clouds floating around like islands on the open sea.

One thing was certain. The twins were going to have one fantastic story to tell if they ever did get back. Dan stopped, and shook his head. He couldn't let himself get negative or think in terms of '*if*'. He made himself do a mental correction and told himself they would have a fantastic story to tell when they *did* get back.

Chapter 14 – Goats Eat Anything

Sassy spent the morning keeping an eye out for familiar landmarks that would help her figure out where she was. Whenever she found a nice high cloud to provide a vantage point, she would sneak up to its top and take a peek hoping to spot something familiar. Unfortunately, she didn't find anything to help her get a sense of her direction in relation to Rainbow Bridge. She was well and truly lost.

She was also maintaining a safe distance from the Panther tormenting her brother. Tremor was pushing Bandit hard to maintain a fast pace. Poor Bandit was doing his best to comply but kept stumbling with the burden of carrying the awkward headdress. Sassy was managing to keep between five and six clouds between them, fighting her instinct to flee as far from the panther as possible. Tremor was paying too much attention to Bandit. She admitted to herself that there wasn't going to be an opportunity to help Bandit escape. She was going to have to try to get help.

About midday she decided she couldn't wait any longer to find help. She caught a final glimpse of Bandit. She whispered a quick prayer and told him she loved him. Her mind made up, she picked a different direction than they were traveling and ran. She knew Bandit would do his best to lead the panther away from Rainbow Bridge. Running in the opposite direction from them made the most sense. Once she decided she had to go, she was all in. She ran as hard and as fast as she had in her entire life. She knew she was putting some serious distance between them. She was covering a lot more ground than they could due to the awkwardness of carrying the headdress.

She was not happy about being so far away from Bandit, but she couldn't take the chance of being this close to them if she was stuck out at night again. With no sense of direction and the confusion of the night, the odds of accidentally running into them were just too great. If she got caught, there was no one to help Bandit. She also needed to get home, to warn the others about the panther.

After an hour of running, she found a nice tall cloud bank that would give her some height to see farther in the direction she was traveling. When she climbed up to the top of a cloud to take a look around she saw the oddest thing. She spotted color breaking up the whiteness of the clouds. On one side of a cloud there was a line of blue yarn. Another cloud over there was a yellow line of yarn that did the same thing. They resembled spokes on a wheel but she couldn't tell what direction the center would be. She couldn't see where either end went because the clouds were in the way.

Sassy sat and thought about it for a minute. The yarn had to have been deliberately placed there. Why would someone place a line of yarn in a straight line like that? She took a moment to do some grooming while she thought it over. There was no way for her to know for certain but it did look like they were trying to help her and Bandit find their way back home. Somehow the other cats must have known that they hadn't made it back before dark. Maybe one of those sink bath cats had been seen or maybe Feather Dan realized that the headdress was missing. Either way she was grateful they had thought of a way to help.

For the first time since this began she felt like she wasn't completely lost. A sense of relief washed over her. She knew if she picked the wrong direction of the yarn to follow, when she reached the end of it she could just follow it back the other way. Now that she knew to look for the yarn to find her way back, she wasn't worried about being lost in the night again. All she had to do was stay near the yarn and she would be able to find her way. She was getting excited by the idea of being home and was about to pick a direction when she had another thought that made her shiver with fear.

If she'd been able to find the yarn, then so would Bandit and Tremor. That would lead them right back to Rainbow Bridge. She had no idea how many lines of yarn there were. Knowing the community and how worried they would be about them not being there to fulfil their sacred duty, she bet there were as many lines as balls of yarn they could find. That was a lot of yarn and all the panther had to spot was just one of them and they were doomed. She decided she needed to backtrack and see if she could locate the panther again. As much as she knew she needed to get back to the Rainbow Bridge, she knew she had to make sure Tremor didn't find it.

She ran back in the direction she had come. She took a gamble and stuck to the tops of the clouds as much as she could. Even though she increased her chances of being spotted by Tremor she couldn't risk missing them. She chose to stay closest to the blue yarn because she thought it would be the most likely one that Bandit and Tremor would end up stumbling upon.

She ran back for about an hour and finally caught a glimpse of Bandit. The panther must have realized he was pushing Bandit too hard and allowed him to rest because he was lying on his back sprawled out and breathing heavily. The panther was grooming himself right next to Bandit.

Sassy looked around and studied the situation. She quickly realized if they kept on going in the direction it looked like they were traveling that they would run into the blue yarn well before dark. If they went the other direction they would run into the yellow yarn in about the same time.

She still wasn't sure what direction to follow the yarn to get back to the Rainbow Bridge but she knew it was time to choose. It looked inevitable that the panther was going to find his way to Rainbow Bridge and she had to warn the others.

Sassy was scared. She was frustrated and absolutely terrified of making the wrong decision. If she went the wrong way and Tremor picked the right way he'd get there first and there was nothing she could do about it. Realizing that there was nothing she could do about the situation and that sitting and fretting about it was only giving Tremor more time, she finally decided she would follow the blue yarn. That was likely the same one that Tremor was going to find. If she got lucky and got back to the Rainbow Bridge first, she would at least be able to tell them exactly where the danger would be coming from.

Once her mind was made up she sprang into action. She ran to the blue yarn and had an idea just as she got to it. There was a chance that there would be another cat on the end that went to the Rainbow Bridge. She gave the yarn a tug in both directions and waited. She didn't have to wait long. Two tugs came back at her from the direction she had originally been coming from.

Just to be sure she gave it two short tugs and two long tugs. Two short tugs and two long tugs came back at her. She was excited, she knew she was going to go in the right direction and would be able to get to the Rainbow Bridge first. Despite being tired, she dug deep into her resolve and found energy she didn't realize she still had left. She ran as fast as she could and didn't stop once to look back.

It was getting close to dusk when she saw something that made her skid to a stop. On top of the cloud right in front of her was the goat. She groaned and said to herself, "Oh no, not him again." Her first instinct was to hide before it saw her. Then she remembered something that gave her an idea. She just hoped it would work.

She jumped and yelled at the goat until it saw her. When it did it jumped around and did a brief happy dance before it ran down the cloud towards her. When it ran up to her it was excited and tried to do head bops with her. She ducked just in time to miss the big curled up horns but gave it a quick mush on its legs so it wouldn't be offended. She led it up to the yarn in the direction she had come from.

She swatted at the yarn for a minute and chewed on it. The goat watched her and made that funny sounding bleating noise. She wished she could speak goat so she could just tell it what she wanted it to do but it only took a moment for the goat to figure it out. It watched her chewing on the yarn for a second and its own instincts to eat everything kicked in. It started chewing on the yarn and in no time he had bitten it in half and was starting to eat it. She walked beside it for a second to lead it back towards the direction she had come from.

Once the goat started eating the yarn it didn't seem like it wanted to stop. It must have been distracted by the yarn, because it completely forgot about Sassy. She thought it went into some kind of an odd trance and it just started chewing and walking. The yarn was disappearing into its mouth, rapidly erasing the yarn trail, just as Sassy had hoped. Sassy watched for a minute to make sure the goat would keep eating the yarn. When she was satisfied the goat would keep eating until he ran out of yarn, she knew her idea could work to buy her some time to get to Rainbow Bridge before the panther could.

She knew the panther would eventually stumble across another line of yarn but likely not before dark. If she could get back to the Rainbow Bridge and warn them, they could pull back all of the yarn. A tear ran down Sassy's cheek and her heart ached. She knew that by pulling in all of the lines of yarn it could save Rainbow Bridge but she would also be condemning her brother to wander for eternity with that horrible panther. She didn't know what else to do but she couldn't think of another option that would both save Rainbow Bridge and rescue Bandit. If she didn't hurry she might not get back in time to keep them from stumbling on another line of yarn. Even if her plan failed, she hoped that she could buy everyone at Rainbow Bridge at least one more day to figure out a plan to deal with Tremor.

She tied the severed end of the blue yarn that was still there to her tail. She intended to drag it back with her as she ran. She could at least eliminate one path back to Rainbow Bridge. Once the yarn was secured to her tail she ran off again. She hoped she could get there before nightfall. The yarn would keep her from getting lost but the confusion of another night wandering alone and lost was something she wanted to never experience again.

Chapter 15 – The Claws

With Tremor right on his heels, Bandit walked through the night and into the morning. The night walking was confusing and felt absolutely pointless. His mind and thoughts were in a constant state of chaos. It was like a tornado in his brain blowing him from one thought to another. He wandered from one cloud the next but didn't even try to pay attention to where he went. He just put one paw in front of the other and carried on with the headdress in tow. He had no idea where they were at any time and as far as he could tell they were just walking in circles.

He tried to tell Tremor that it would be better to rest and wait until dawn but he wasn't having any of it. The panther rambled on the entire night. He talked about what a powerful hunter he was and bragged of his many kills. Bandit was disgusted as Tremor spoke with such glee about violence. Bandit understood that predators in the wild had to hunt and kill to eat and survive but Tremor… He took absolute joy in the fear and suffering he was able to inflict. Bandit knew that not all of his species were so evil at heart.

When Tremor wasn't talking about his love of the hunt, he talked about what Rainbow Bridge would be like under his rule. He asked Bandit who their best fighters were. When Bandit told him they didn't fight Tremor became agitated. He asked if there was any competition in any way at all and Bandit told him about the Feathers Time games. The panther laughed in derision at that. He said he would allow the games to continue under his reign but the rules were going to change.

He said that one of the changes would be that the worst player on the losing team would be led out to the clouds and forced to stay the night. They wouldn't be welcome to return until they found their way back on their own. Tremor's cruel plans for the Rainbow Bridge and its inhabitants were both sickening and terrifying. It would mean turning their back on their sacred duty. That was something Bandit couldn't allow to happen.

When dawn finally came Bandit prayed hard that somehow he had managed to lead them in the opposite direction of home. He felt relieved that he hadn't seen Sassy or any sign of her. Hopefully that meant she had found her way back. Sassy was a very smart cat. If anyone could figure out a way to get back, she would do it.

He also knew that Sassy was stubborn and would want to be with him. They had never before spent time apart. They were born together, grew up together, lived and even died on Earth together. Even at the Rainbow Bridge they stuck to each other like glue. They were inseparable and he was missing her terribly. He knew she'd be even more worried about him because of the panther. Surely she wouldn't try to stay close to keep an eye on them. There was nothing she could do to help him. She had to get home and warn Rainbow Bridge.

Tremor stopped briefly as the morning came and the fog of confusion and disorientation began to burn away. He snarled at Bandit and asked him "Where are we now?" The confusion was gone from his voice. "What direction is Rainbow Bridge?"

Bandit took his time and looked around. He studied each cloud closely and said, "I have no idea. The clouds farther away from Rainbow Bridge change shape all the time. I have no idea where we are or even what direction we just came from."

Tremor studied Bandit closely trying to detect any deception but there was none and he nodded in agreement. "I feel the same. Make your best guess and begin walking."

Bandit didn't worry about making any guesses because it would have been pointless. He just kept walking in what he thought was the same direction that they had come from. Dragging the headdress along was slowing him down. While he thought that was a good thing because it gave him an excuse to move slower, he also knew it would be best to get rid of it. He didn't want Tremor playing with it and summoning any other animals. For all he knew Tremor might be more likely to bring in another panther or other predator and that was the last thing he wanted to see. In hindsight maybe it was a good thing Tremor insisted on walking through the night. There'd be little to do to pass the time except play with the headdress. That thought gave him chills and he decided then that, under the current conditions, leaving the headdress behind was the right thing to do.

Bandit stopped and turned around to face Tremor. "We'd be a lot faster if we left the headdress behind. At this pace I'm worried we'll be stuck out here after dark again and I can't handle another round of that maddening confusion."

Tremor snarled and swatted Bandit on the side of his head. "I don't care. I want the headdress so we're keeping it. If we get stuck out here again, so be it."

Bandit knew better than to argue. He turned back around and continued walking, dragging the headdress with him. He did the best he could to travel in a straight line and continually prayed that he was taking them farther out into the middle of nowhere.

Near midday Tremor allowed them to rest. Bandit was exhausted. He dropped the headdress and collapsed. He rolled over onto his back and stretched his legs. Tremor sat next to him, watching him closely and groomed for a bit.

A curious look passed across Tremor's face. "Why haven't I been hungry since I've been here?"

"There is no hunger at the Rainbow Bridge." Bandit answered as he allowed himself to rest.

Tremor snarled, clearly unhappy with the answer. "Hunger is a critical motivator for predators. This is just one more reason why you are all so weak. If there can be no hunger for food I will find something else to make everyone hunger for. Another powerful motivator for predators is fear. I can create enough of that for everyone."

Once again speaking about how powerful predators are, Tremor went off on another rambling tangent. Bandit was grateful for it. Tremor rambled on for so long that Bandit actually felt refreshed when Tremor realized they weren't traveling and made them walk again. Bandit acted like he was more tired than he actually was, so he had an excuse to keep up the slow pace.

It was well over an hour later when they came across something that Bandit had never seen before. He stopped in his tracks and stared at it trying to figure out what had happened. There was a line of blue yarn that stretched between the mountains.

Tremor spotted it as well. "What is that?"

Bandit shook his head. "It's a line of blue yarn. I have no idea how or why it got all the way out here though."

They sat and looked at it for a minute and Tremor said, "Well, it was obviously put here by someone and must lead to somewhere. I bet it goes to your precious Rainbow Bridge. We're going to follow it. Pick a direction and get going."

Bandit thought the yarn probably did lead to Rainbow Bridge. That had him worried. That was the last place he wanted to take the panther. He knew he sometimes needed a minute to process things, but he figured the others had realized he and Sassy hadn't come back and this was part of a rescue attempt. He felt a momentary spark of hope for Sassy and love for his community that would go to such trouble to help him find his way home. He hoped Sassy had found some yarn to lead her back to safety and wasn't lost out here on her own. If she had, she could warn the others about Tremor.

Tremor was still a big problem. He had terrible plans for Rainbow Bridge. The idea of the cruel changes he wanted to make left Bandit overwhelmed with despair. How was he going to keep Tremor from finding the Rainbow Bridge when there was an obvious blue trail leading right to it? He was thinking as fast as he could, but couldn't come up with any ideas on how to avoid the inevitable. He was frozen in fear and indecision.

Tremor swatted him across the back of his head. "I told you to pick a direction and get going. Move, NOW!"

Bandit was grateful that carrying the headdress at least allowed him to move more slowly. He had to stall as best he could, but Bandit did as he was told. He started to follow the yarn but he hadn't given up on the idea of coming up with a plan. He knew he didn't think quite as fast as Sassy did, but he usually could come up with a plan just as good as hers if he had a moment to think. He began to get an idea that just might work. It would be dangerous for him, but if he could keep them going slow enough, they would definitely be stuck in the night again. While they could easily follow the yarn in daylight, if they lost sight of the yarn after dark they might wander off and not be able to find it again. He was going to wait until the effects of the night set in then, make a run for it. He'd have to hope he found a good spot to hide the headdress. He couldn't afford to carry it but he couldn't let the panther have it either. He'd wait until they were near a cloud and try to get either around it or over it. He would have to keep up the chase long enough, without being caught, to get them out of the line of sight of the yarn. He didn't know what Tremor would do to him when he caught him and he knew he would catch him; but he couldn't think of any other options. He had to get them off of the trail the blue yarn provided and if possible lose the headdress at the same time.

They followed the yarn for the rest of the day. Tremor swatted him several times trying to get him to move faster but Bandit used the headdress as an excuse to keep moving slowly. They rounded a cloud and in front of them was the goat he and Sassy had outrun the previous day.

The goat had its head down and was happily walking towards them completely unaware of their presence. Bandit cheered inwardly with relief as he saw the yarn hanging out of the goat's mouth. He never thought he'd be happy to see a goat.

Tremor let out a guttural growl and then screamed so loud Bandit fell to his knees. That scream made him want to cower in terror. Tremor's anger was truly frightening. Bandit found the courage to look over at the goat. The goat's eyes were wide and his jaw hung open in shock. It panicked, dropped the yarn and ran in the opposite direction straight up the side of the cloud as fast as it could. Bandit feared it might not be fast enough to outrun Tremor.

Tremor let out a predatory roar, and then he started giving chase. The goat turned around briefly. It must have seen Tremor bounding after him. Bandit heard its terrified scream before it scrambled out of sight over the top of the cloud.

Bandit knew better than to waste his opportunity. He braced himself, preparing to make a run for it. He glanced quickly at the sky, the sun was dropping and the effects of the night would be settling in any minute. That worked in his favor. If Tremor chased the goat and ran over the top of the cloud he'd be out of sight. Once that happened, it would only be a matter of chance if Tremor could find him after that. Bandit had a moment of indecision and hesitated. He had only a second to choose. Should take the headdress with him or leave it behind? He was much faster without it but it would be a risk to leave it. He decided he better take it. He couldn't leave it and chance Tremor getting possession of it again.

As soon as Tremor crossed the top of the cloud and disappeared in pursuit of the goat, Bandit made his move. He ran as fast as he could, the headdress bouncing on the ground beside him. He knew this was a big risk. Tremor would be furious when he realized Bandit had disobeyed him and tried to get away. He hoped that Tremors' predatory instincts and love of the chase would keep him in pursuit of the goat for at least a few more seconds. He prayed the goat was fast.

Bandit made it to the top of the cloud and was about to drop out of sight when he caught sight of something he wasn't expecting. There was another line of yarn, this time yellow. It stretched like the blue yarn had as far as he could see between the clouds. Bandit blinked to make sure he wasn't hallucinating. Nope. It was still there where he last saw it. The effects of the night hadn't settled in yet but it wouldn't be long. He had to keep moving, there was no time to lose. He decided to run towards the yellow yarn. Just when he thought he was going to make it, he heard Tremor shout his name.

"Bandit!" Tremor roared loudly. "I am displeased. You did not have my permission to leave."

The hair across Bandit's back stood on end as dread swamped his thoughts yet again. He looked over his shoulder and Tremor was running at him. It was a mistake. He knew he shouldn't have looked.

Bandit didn't have time to think of what else to do. He just knew he couldn't let Tremor find the yellow yarn. Acting like he was panicked, Bandit ran in a different direction, back down the cloud at an angle away from Tremor. The headdress was slowing him down too much. He dropped it and it bounced to a stop behind him. There was no use in trying to take it now. He wouldn't have a chance at all if he kept it. He immediately picked up speed. Bandit risked a quick glance behind him. Tremor was gaining on him much too quickly.

He felt it the first time Tremor pounced at him. Bandit listened to his instincts and blindly dodged him. He was rewarded by seeing Tremor's giant black paw swipe right past him. With no time to ponder his good luck, Bandit spun around and raced off at a different angle. The only advantage he had over the panther was being smaller and more maneuverable. He zig-zagged at angles as sharp as he could. He managed to avoid Tremor catching him two more times.

The night darkened and the disorientation began to set in. Soon Bandit forgot where he'd dropped the headdress. He couldn't remember which way the yellow yarn was either. He thought he was running back the way they had come but wasn't sure any more. His mounting terror didn't allow him to forget that Tremor was still hard on his heels. He had to escape.

He kept running and felt the whoosh of air as Tremor tried several more times to pounce on him, narrowly missing him each time. The zig zag maneuvers were working but he just wasn't fast enough to get away. He knew he wasn't going to be able to keep it up forever but he wouldn't allow himself to completely panic just yet. His best chance was to get out of Tremor's line of sight. If he could get just a piece of a cloud between them he prayed that a second of being out of sight would disorient Tremor long enough.

He dug deep into his soul and forced himself to move faster. He changed up the zig zags. He moved two steps before dodging left, took three steps only to dodge right, then three steps before dodging right again. He was trying to keep it as unpredictable as he could. He was almost to the corner of the cloud he'd been trying to get to when he felt his back legs sweep out from under him. He knew he couldn't give up now.

Bandit scrambled and kicked with all four legs in an effort to get back up and run. He did for just a second but Tremor was right there. Tremor struck Bandit harder than he ever had before and the blow hurled him through the air. He slammed into a cloud. His entire body hurt from the impact. His ears were rung loudly and his vision blurred. His mind, already fuzzy with the effects of the night, was just too slow to snap out of it in time.

Before he could come to his senses, Tremor rolled him over on his back and towered over him. The rage in his eyes sent waves of fear through Bandit and he quivered. Tremor growled and showed his fangs. Drool from his fangs and tongue fell into Bandit's eyes.

Tremor snarled and said "I told you the next time you disobeyed you'd get the claws."

Tremor lifted a paw and Bandit could see the razor sharp claws unsheathe. He was frozen. The colorful dancing lights that had been out the night before were starting to flicker again. The lights reflected eerily off those claws.

Tremor reared his paw back as he prepared to strike. Bandit forgot about Sassy, Rainbow Bridge and the headdress. He only knew he was in tremendous pain. Bandit closed his eyes and waited for the end to come.

Chapter 16 – Team Mouser

Gypsy, The captain of Feathers Time team Mouser, was sitting on the anchor end of the blue and yellow yarn when the first tugs came. The tugs weren't in the pattern that she'd established with the rest of her team for communication so she decided to tug back. A moment later she got two light tugs and two hard tugs. She responded back with the same pattern.

"Team Mouser, assemble!" She yelled out to her team. She was pleased when her team gathered in front of her immediately. Gypsy knew she was a capable leader, but she still felt lucky to have such a great team to work with. They never complained about extra work, they just did what needed to be done. She was grateful and proud of them for pitching in to help find the lost cats. They had been working diligently all day to roll out yarn without a single complaint. She knew they had to be tired.

She had spent most of the day patiently passing the time making sure her short coat gleamed. It was mostly black with patches of orange randomly thrown in with some smaller white patches. She had a white bib, and a distinctive patch of white around her mouth and small pink nose. But now that something was happening, she was all business. She had a job to get done.

"I just got tugs on the blue line. Odds are it's Bandit and Sassy."

All four members of her team jumped to their feet and collectively said, "We're headed out to get them."

Gypsy knew they had only been back for about a half hour. It was getting late so going back out into the clouds wasn't a great idea but none of them wanted to give up just yet. Gypsy held up a paw. "Hold on. It's going to be night very soon. I'm not going to ask any of you to go back out there until morning. I think only two of you should go. I don't want to risk all four of you getting lost out there. Jack and Flynn, the blue yarn was yours so it is your call."

"We're going," Jack said without hesitation looking at Flynn who was nodding his agreement.

Gypsy nodded her consent but looked at them sternly. "I want each of you to promise me you'll stay with the yarn and do not go so far out that you can't see either Blankets Mountain or the light from the Rainbow Bridge."

Jack and Flynn each promised her they would follow her instructions. She knew they would. They had drilled together as a team often enough. Without another word they both turned tail and raced off. Gypsy knew they had the good sense to stay out of trouble, but if they should run into it anyway, she could trust them to get out of it. No one on her team was a slow learner, or they didn't last very long under her wrath.

Chapter 17 – Lost and Found

Jack and Flynn were fast and made good time. They both took turns looking back and making sure they could still see Blankets Mountain. Jack was starting to feel the confusion of the night set in. It was far more disorienting than he'd anticipated.

"You feeling it too?" Jack asked, looking at Flynn for his reaction.

"Yeah." Flynn confirmed Jack's suspicion.

Jack knew they didn't have long before they would be forced to head back. He took a moment to look around. He could still see Blankets Mountain, but once the night settled and the lights started dancing in the sky, he wasn't confident he would see the glow from Rainbow Bridge.

"Just a little farther?" Jack asked Flynn. There was still enough light he could see the way back and he was reluctant to give up on whoever Gypsy had felt tug on the line of yarn.

"Let's give it ten more minutes," agreed Flynn. He was studying the amount of darkness creeping in to darken the sky.

Together they raced off again. But Jack grew increasingly worried every time they went around a cloud that they would lose sight of Blankets Mountain. While he logically knew he'd catch a glimpse of it again as they traveled, his concern was they'd forget to look once the night lights set in to distract them. He made sure to stay right next to the blue yarn. If they got lost, they'd need it to get themselves home.

A few minutes later, with still no sign of Sassy or Bandit, it was looking like they needed to turn back. Jack knew he would regret it if he didn't keep his promise to Gypsy. He was reluctant to leave without seeing who had tugged on the string. He was just about to voice his thought that it was time to turn back to Flynn when Sassy came running around the cloud just ahead of them. Jack could tell she was running as fast as she could.

"Look, there's Sassy!" Flynn yelled, pointing in her direction. "I think she sees us."

Jack was relieved they had found Sassy. He ran towards her closing the gap between them, Flynn fast on his heels. He inwardly chuckled. He had always been just a little bit faster than Flynn. Enough so that it was usually a very close race between the two of them any time they were on the field. They played it up as a big rivalry, but everyone knew they were fast friends.

Flynn asked, "Where's Bandit?" as soon as they reached her.

Jack had never seen one without the other. They were practically inseparable. He also noticed the blue yarn tied to her tail. She must have a reason for bringing the yarn back in behind her. He looked at Flynn to see if he'd spotted the yarn tied to her tail too. Flynn gave him a side glance and a tiny nod. Good, he'd seen it too.

Huffing and puffing Sassy managed to say, "It's a long story, but he's in serious trouble. We need to get to Rainbow Bridge right now." She looked around desperately. "We're all in serious trouble."

Jack was shocked that Sassy wasn't turning back around to go get Bandit. "Sassy, what's going on?" He knew it had to be something serious to make Sassy this upset. But he didn't want to leave Bandit behind. He was willing to go farther out and look for him. "I'll go back out for Bandit. You follow Flynn home."

"No!" She shouted at Jack and shook him by the shoulders. "No! You can't go to him. Not now anyway." Sassy glanced toward

Blankets Mountain. "We have to go, NOW!" Without another word, she pointed her head in the direction of home and took off running. The blue yarn was following in her wake.

Jack and Flynn looked at each other then chased after her joining the long line of blue yarn that was following her. Jack took comfort in finding at least one of the missing twins. Sassy could at least be there to guide Hope, her human, when her time came. Sassy might also have an idea of where Bandit was and could tell everyone what had happened to separate them.

Jack and Flynn caught up to her easily. Her exhaustion was evident. Jack slowed their pace so she could keep up. Jack ran in front of her and Flynn ran behind her and to the side to avoid stepping on the yarn. Jack was amazed Sassy had managed to run and stay with the yarn the way she had. it was a tangled mess trailing behind her and the weight of it had to be pulling on her tail. It didn't look comfortable at all.

The disorientation of the approaching night was growing more intense. It was getting darker and harder to see the yarn. Jack was navigating by the glow of Blankets Mountain and Rainbow Bridge behind it. They both provided enough light that Jack didn't need to slow their pace to a walk and rely solely on the yarn to guide them home.

When they got closer, Jack could hear Grace barking. She was probably trying to help keep them focused and give them another means of navigating the night. Jack knew Grace was smart like that. Finally rounding the last cloud between them and Blankets Mountain, Jack could see Feather Dan and company waiting for them. Gypsy, stood next to Dan and began waving her paws when she saw them approaching. Jack was relieved. Dan would know what to do to help Sassy.

Chapter 18 – Cat University

Sassy came running up headed directly toward Dan. Her butt hadn't touched the ground before she started talking. "Feather Dan! The panther... You have to get everyone... ready for the panther!" She paused for a breath then launched back in, "I don't know how much.... time we have. Tonight, tomorrow... I don't know!"

She was babbling and not making much sense. Dan knew he had to get her to slow down and catch her breath. He rested a paw on her shoulder and said, "Hey, Sassy, slow down. It's all right, just breathe for a minute. Gather your thoughts and start from the beginning. I need to understand everything that happened so I can help you."

Sassy provided a brief recap of finding the headdress with Bandit and wanting to catch the feathers so they ran out past Blankets Mountain to play. She described how she tried really hard to catch the feathers after Bandit clinked the turquoise beads together. Then there was the appearance of a goat and then Tremor showed up. When she got to the part about the panther she started trembling and her speech sped up. Dan had to make her slow down again so they could get a good grasp of what exactly had happened. She told him about being lost and separated from Bandit and how she'd found him and then had to leave him again. When she finally got near the end of her story and finished telling them about finding the yarn. Knowing the yarn would also help Tremor find Rainbow Bridge, she was terrified until she ran into the goat. She managed to get the goat to eat the yarn in the middle separating it in two. She tied one end of the line of yarn to herself and ran to Rainbow Bridge to warn everyone.

"The rest of the yarn, how many lines are there?" Sassy demanded.

Desperation and panic laced Sassy's voice. Dan could hear her voice quiver with it. He didn't know the answer, so he looked at Gypsy to see if she knew. She'd been charged with anchoring the lines of yarn.

Gypsy glanced down the length of Blankets Mountain and nodded towards each of the Feather Time team leaders. Each sat diligently beside the anchor points of the yarn their teams had run out. "There are ten lines out there now. We were planning on running more out tomorrow."

Dan watched as Sassy's eyes went wide with fright, "No!" She screamed. "Pull them in! Pull them all in right now! The Panther! Tremor will find them!"

Dan put his paw on her shoulder again. She was gripped with panic and nearly hysterical. "Calm down, Sassy. You're not alone anymore. We're all here to help now." Feather Dan tried to console her. She'd had a terrible fright. He was very worried about her.

"No, you don't understand!" Sassy cried, her tail twitching wildly. "Tremor's plans for Rainbow Bridge are horrible. We can't let them happen," she said her voice breaking from her fear. "No, Dan. You have to tell them to pull those yarn lines back in right now or I will!"

Dan shook his head, he'd never seen Sassy act like this before. She was intelligent and he'd never known her to be prone to exaggeration. Dan was bewildered at how strongly Sassy was gripped by her fear. Although Dan was known as one of the quickest thinking cats around, the concept of fear at Rainbow Bridge was so foreign to him that he was struggling to understand her peril.

Sassy, a wild look in her eyes, shoved Dan back towards the other yarn lines. "Now Dan, give the order now!" Sassy shoved him again, this time much harder and he staggered backwards a couple of steps.

"Tremor means to take over the Rainbow Bridge. He will rule from Blankets Mountain. He will make us battle each other for the right to guide our humans to us. He will laugh when our humans become lost. He will send them out to be lost in the clouds forever and hunt them at his leisure! He wants us all to feel fear, to hurt; to hurt each other!" Sassy was becoming wild with her fear. Spit flew from her mouth as she became more frantic.

Flynn stepped up beside Dan and gently nudged Sassy. "We can't just pull the lines back in, Sassy. We anchored them really good so nothing could accidentally break them loose. We're going to have to wait until dawn before we can take care of them."

Sassy let out a cry of despair, lowered her head and wept. Dan knew she needed the release of a good cry. She'd been through a lot but he felt the need to console her. Watching anyone in pain wasn't something he could sit by and do without taking some action to help ease their burden.

"Sassy," Dan's voice was gentle and reassuring. "I'm certainly not going to let the panther take over Blankets Mountain."

Dozens of other cats chimed in with unanimous agreement. Dan knew they were all determined that they would fight and run the panther off. Dan hadn't noticed that the crowd had grown since Sassy had returned to tell her story of what happened to her. The crowd was becoming loud with outrage at the thought of being turned against one another and having their humans hunted. Rainbow Bridge had existed since the first human who had a pet passed away and that was thousands of years ago. He heard several in the crowd say they weren't going to sit back and let some sink bath panther destroy what the Rainbow Bridge was there for. Dan agreed with them. They couldn't let that come to pass.

"Sassy," Tears wet his paw as Dan touched her chin and raised her head. "There is just one panther. There are thousands of us. We'll find a way to handle the situation."

"I'm still worried," Sassy admitted to Dan. "Tremor did bad things to Bandit. When he'd been struck he felt pain, and not just a sting. I could tell by the look of horror on his face that it had been a terrible hurt." She sniffled.

She gave Dan a stern look then addressed the crowd. "You didn't see Bandit. You didn't see him get hit. He tumbled through the air and slammed into a cloud. There was a horrible sound of him hitting the cloud, the smack of Tremor's strike, those were very real and so was the look of agony that twisted Bandit's face. Don't you understand? There's never been pain here; not until now."

There was some nervous mumbling among the crowd. The atmosphere was very tense. None of them really had any idea of what to expect let alone how to handle the situation. The more Sassy talked, the more an undercurrent of fear began to spread among the gathered cats.

Dan felt it too and knew he had to keep things positive or the situation could easily break down into chaos. "Did the panther have a feathers collar around his neck?" He nodded towards Leroy, Binx and Amelia. "It would have looked similar to the ones they are wearing."

Sassy looked at the group and was shocked as she realized there were other sink bath cats right there at Blankets Mountain. She studied their collars for a moment. "Yes," She said, "So did the other sink bath cats that we saw appear." She thought for a second, "Tremor also said that he wasn't going to take it off. It was causing him some pain and he said the pain would keep him sharp and focused."

Although Tremor's reasoning for keeping the collar on was a surprise, Dan was relieved. "That means we just need to get him to chomp the feather and the problem should be solved."

Dan paced as his mind raced, his tail flicking back and forth. "We need to get the word out. Everyone needs to be alert."

He walked over to Feathers Time team Mouser and found their captain paying close attention to every word. "Gypsy, I need you to organize all of the teams again. You still need to make sure the yarn lines are monitored but I also need you to get the teams to go through Cat Tree City and make sure everyone knows what's going on. A lot has changed and the stakes are higher. We're not looking at just two lost cats anymore. We're looking at a threat to the Rainbow Bridge itself. This is a threat to all of us and all of our humans."

Gypsy nodded, and Dan noted she looked outright angry at the entire situation "We'll get it done, Dan. You can count on us." She turned towards her team and began whispering instructions. In just a moment they were racing off in different directions. Two ran towards Cat Tree City and two towards the other Feathers Time teams.

Dan turned back to his companions. He spoke loud enough that the crowd could hear him as well. He didn't want anyone wondering what was being done. He wanted all of them on the same page. Rumors would only blow things out of proportion and he needed everyone to be in unison.

"We need to go back and talk to Aristotle again. I don't think Rainbow Bridge has ever faced a threat before. Hopefully he'll have more good advice."

Dan glanced over to Grace but she stopped him before he could ask and said, "Yes, Dan I will stay here and keep watch. I'll bark as loud as I can if anything happens."

Dan nodded in thanks but didn't waste any time. He immediately turned and began running towards Cat Tree City. The group followed right behind him. They were silent; each of them lost in their own thoughts trying to think of anything they could do to help. Even Binx who normally became easily distracted and was always trying to wander off was abnormally quiet and followed obediently Dan noted.

The trip back to Aristotle's cat tree seemed to go by in the blink of an eye. Other cats they passed could tell by the grave look on Dan's face that something wasn't right and quickly moved aside so they could pass without breaking their stride. Unlike their first visit, Feather Dan didn't stop the group to do any grooming prior to climbing up to see him. When things were this dire, there was not time for formalities.

As Dan anticipated, Aristotle had been waiting for their arrival. He could no doubt sense the seriousness of the group. His brow was furrowed as he looked upon Sassy. She looked frantic and terrified. Her fur was all out of order, didn't shine at all, and looked like it hadn't been groomed in days.

"Feather Dan, my friend. It is good to see you. We shall forego the usual pleasantries this visit I think. I think that's most prudent. Let's get straight to business, shall we?"

Dan nodded in agreement. He nudged Sassy forward, silently urging her to tell her story. Once she started talking her words just kept on coming. Dan was relieved to see that her thoughts were more organized than earlier. It took a few minutes but Sassy filled Aristotle in on what had transpired and did a very thorough job of it. Aristotle stopped her a few times to ask questions but mostly he listened intently to her every word.

When she was finished Aristotle sat silently for a moment grooming his paw while he contemplated what he'd heard. After a moment he stopped, looked up and said, "What bothers me the most about everything transpiring is that physical pain has been introduced to the Rainbow Bridge. The Rainbow Bridge is a place where there is no pain and no fear. It's supposed to be a paradise free from the trappings of the living. But now that physical pain has been introduced, I can sense fear growing amongst the community."

Aristotle paused in thought a moment before continuing. "Dan, you should go to the professors at Cat University. If there is any way to figure this out, they should be able to do so. I will continue to ponder on things. I will also go out to visit with some friends who may have ideas as well."

Aristotle got to his feet and stretched. He meant to get moving immediately and told Dan he should go quickly as well. "Be sure to send back word of anything that may be of value as soon as you hear it."

Dan nodded, "I will. We'll go right away."

Dan turned to leave. His friends were ready to go. They quickly made the descent down the giant cat tree.

Binx, finally acting more like himself asked Dan "What's a university?"

Dan explained as they traveled. "The university is a series of cat trees that house a bunch of cats that had humans who were teachers. They spent hours and hours sitting on desks and snuggling in laps while their human professors studied books and papers. They learned a lot doing that. They wound up becoming experts of their own in the fields their humans taught and are the smartest cats here."

"Who do they teach?" Binx asked in a subdued voice.

Binx, ever curious, was sure to have more questions than Dan could answer. Dan didn't want to discourage him, despite the urgency of what they needed to do.

"They'll teach anyone who's curious and wants to learn. We also have lots of kittens who come to the Rainbow Bridge when they are very young. Many of them never had a chance to learn anything about being a cat while they were on Earth. There are a group of professors who specialize in helping the young ones understand what they were and who they are now."

Binx nodded his head in understanding but didn't ask any more questions right away. Soon the group of friends reached Cat Tree University. Dan was familiar with the sight but let his friends have a moment to take it in. There were dozens of cat trees of all shapes and sizes that formed what resembled a college campus. Trees would have one high perch for the professor, with nearby seating for the students to hear the professor on the lower ledges of the same cat tree. Dozens of lectures were normally going on at any given time. With most cats out helping to find Sassy and Bandit, gathering yarn, organizing to monitor for Tremor, or overseeing any of those projects, the number of students in attendance was much smaller than usual. Several popular lectures that were always taking place still had some students in attendance. Dan noted that most of the cat trees were empty of students and teachers.

Dan led his friends between several of them and around a well-worn path to what Dan called the professors lounge area. That was where the professors gathered when they had down time or wanted to put their heads together to work on a problem.

When they got there, two dozen professor cats were gathered about. They were talking to themselves excitedly but when the group walked in the room went quiet. The professors looked immediately to Leroy, Binx and Amelia. They resumed talking albeit quietly among themselves but none of them took their eyes off the Earth cats.

Dan didn't know all of the professors by name but he knew several. The first to step up was Professor George Washington, a regal grey and white long hair cat. He was known as an avid student and expert in history. His human had been a history professor at a very well-known college. Professor Washington had sought out and become fast friends with Feather Dan as soon as he learned about the creation of Blankets Mountain.

"Feather Dan, my friend!" George Washington bellowed in his usual boisterous voice, "Why didn't you bring your friends over for an introduction sooner? They've been the talk of Cat Tree City and we've barely been able to contain our curiosity."

Another cat, Professor Newton stepped forward as well. She had short sleek black fur and golden eyes. She was more widely known as Professor Newt. Her human had been a professor of sciences. "Yes, my dear Dan," she squeaked.

Dan heard Binx giggle at the sound of Professor Newt's voice. Dan knew she was used to getting strange reactions to the sound of her voice and it wouldn't bother her.

"How could you hide such curiosities from us for so long? We truly must take advantage of this exceptional occurrence and study them." She looked over the group and started walking up to Amelia, "Oh my!" she exclaimed. "This one's a polydactyl at that!"

Amelia took a step back and shook her head no, "Ugh, nope, paws off, sister. I'm not getting studied, whatever that means. We're here on business and that's it."

Dan, surprised that Amelia didn't hiss first, stepped up and interrupted them. "Aristotle sent us here for a purpose." Dan filled them in on the details of what had happened. When he explained that pain was occurring at the Rainbow Bridge the professors became both excited and agitated. Fascinated, they spoke amongst themselves for a moment. With so many quasi-conversations happening at the same time it was difficult for Dan to understand what was being said but the professors all seemed to be completely aware of each other's interactions and ultimately were all on the same page within a few minutes.

One of the professors named Dr. Paws, whose human had taught at a medical school, stepped forward. He was a hairless white Sphinx with intelligent blue eyes and missing whiskers. He was very proper and formal but his eyes shone with kindness and curiosity at the same time. "Might I touch one of the feather collars?" he asked, and then patted his yellow polka dot bow tie.

Excited, Binx volunteered, "You can look at mine, touch it or whatever you want. I'd really like to know more about it."

Several professors stepped up to get a closer look as Dr. Paws approached Binx. He looked it over closely for a minute. "Does it hurt or cause any discomfort?"

"Nope, it just feels like a collar." Binx answered right away.

"Very well," Dr. Paws leaned in closer. "I'm just going to lift the feather a bit off of your neck so I can get a look behind it."

"Okay," Binx nodded. He managed to sit very still while he was inspected, but his eyes remained alert and his ears swiveled to catch everything that might be said.

Dan could tell Binx was enjoying the attention. Dr. Paws carefully reached out for it. The other professors leaned in a bit more to get the best look possible. As soon as Dr. Paws touched it he gasped in pain and pulled his paw back quickly. Before he said a word he began bathing his paw. His eyes were focused and forehead wrinkled in concentration as he urgently licked at his toes.

He glanced up to the other professors who were staring, mouths agape wondering what had happened. Dr. Paws stopped grooming his foot for just a moment and said, "That burned quite badly; quite badly indeed. That was much unexpected. I'd rate that a nine or ten out of ten on the pain scale."

Dr. Paw's words and his reaction caused the other professors to huddle together. They talked for a moment again and like the last time, Dan could barely make out a word of what they were saying. There were too many different conversations being whispered at the same time. Like before, all of the professors seemed completely able to follow every conversation at once and they all stopped talking at the same time.

Another professor stepped forward. She was slender with glowing white fur that was short like Binx's but looked as soft as cotton. She looked at Binx with soft blue eyes that gleamed with a mix of intelligence and compassion. "Hi Binx." Dan thought her voice was melodic like wind chimes and enchanting. He knew Binx would like her.

"I'm Professor Dimension, but please just call me Demi. My human studies quantum physics and I tend to think differently and have odd ideas compared to my colleagues."

Binx stared at her and his eyes went wide. She was the most beautiful cat he'd seen yet at Rainbow Bridge. He opened his mouth to say something but the only thing that came out was a choked squeak.

Demi smiled and patiently sat down in front of him. Binx gazed into her eyes and for the first time in his life he found himself blushing. The sensation confused him and left him speechless.

Amelia saw Binx's reaction and snorted. She looked entertained with Binx's sudden discomfort. "Well would you look at that," she teased, "I do believe Binx is smitten with Professor Dimension."

Amelia looked over at Leroy to gage his reaction to Binx's enchantment of Demi. Leroy seemed to be suffering from the same condition as Binx. He was just sitting there with his jaw hanging open staring at Demi in fascination.

"Leroy!" She scolded. "Get a hold of yourself!" She looked over to Dan for support but he was looking at Demi and grinning ear to ear. "I can't believe this! Remy, look at these drooling fools." She looked over to Remy but he was a mirror image of Leroy. He was just sitting there with his jaw open staring in wonder.

Amelia snorted in utter annoyance. "Alright boys," she huffed, her tail flicking about erratically in irritation. "Get it together! Leroy," She stepped up to him and popped him under his chin, shutting his mouth for him. She followed it up with a light swat to his head. "Leroy!" she said again, more loudly. "Get it together right now, mister!"

Leroy blinked a few times and blushed at Amelia's scolding. He collected himself and said, "Professor Dimension, my name is Leroy and it's my pleasure to meet you."

"Oh my Cat," Amelia rolled her eyes. "Would you boys please pull yourselves together and at least try to act a bit more respectable?" She turned around and nudged Remy. He responded by blushing with embarrassment as well.

Dan giggled at everyone for a second then said, "Hi Demi, good to see you again. Have you made any new discoveries about why Blankets Mountain became permanent?"

"Hi Feather Dan, it's always nice to see you. You should stop by more often. I have some new theories I'm working on but we should discuss those another day."

"Of course," Dan said, his mind quickly coming back around to the mission at hand. "Your insight is always valuable. What are your initial thoughts on the collars?"

She nodded at Dan and turned her attention back to Binx. "I have an unusual request but I would like to ask that you trust me." Binx stared at her wide eyed as she spoke, but said nothing. "I would like you to try to prick my arm with your claw."

Binx blinked in confusion at her request.

"I want you to be gentle," She cautioned, "Don't go deep, just see if you can prick my skin a bit. Can you do that for me?"

Binx blinked several times and paused but after a moment simply said, "Sure."

Demi held out her arm and indicated where she wanted him to try. He reached out and extended his claw above where she had shown him and asked, "Right here?"

Demi nodded, "Yes, Binx, right there. Go ahead it'll be okay."

"Alright," he sounded unsure of himself but did as she asked.

When he started to prick her she winced and pulled her arm away.

"I'm sorry!" Binx sounded distressed.

"It's okay, Binx, you just did as I asked you to." She thought for a second, turned back towards the other professors and said, "That hurt but obviously not as bad as touching the collar hurt Doctor Paws."

The professors broke back into groups and talked among themselves again. They talked for several minutes this time. When they quieted down again and turned their attention back to Dan and the group. Dan thought they all looked like they had come up with something.

Demi stepped forward again, "We have a theory. Anything that comes from Earth without first crossing the Rainbow Bridge isn't supposed to be here. That seems obvious. Leroy, Amelia and Binx, are still Earth cats and not spirit cats. We believe that makes it possible for you, or anyone or anything else that comes here the way you did, to bring some measure of the physical world with you. Professor Newton has stated emphatically that science says that shouldn't be possible. Under the standard laws of science and physics, I am prone to agree with her but I can assure you that I have several theories using quantum physics and other sciences which cause me to believe otherwise."

Doctor Paws stepped forward and nodded his agreement. "The simplest way I can think to explain it to those not familiar with the various schools of science is that the spirit world's reaction to the physical world is like an allergic reaction. The reaction in this instance seems to be one of pain. That's something that doesn't exist at the Rainbow Bridge though, so it makes little sense all the way around."

Professor Dimension cleared her throat and spoke up, "Doctor Paws is correct that pain is not supposed to exist at Rainbow Bridge but then again neither are Earth cats. That creates a change in our known reality which forces us to change the way we look at our known science."

Doctor Paws nodded his head vigorously in agreement, "Yes, yes, Demi. As usual, you're quite right."

190

Feather Dan was accustomed to speaking with the professors and had learned to anticipate what they would be talking about next even before they were able to figure it out themselves. Dan interrupted and asked, "Do you think there is any possibility of danger beyond just the sensation of pain?"

Dan's question raised several eyebrows and the professors huddled up once more and talked for a minute. Professor Newton was the first to answer the question, "That is a very important question but we simply haven't conducted enough studies or gathered enough data yet. We really can't give a good answer to that question right now, but I'm afraid that it's quite possible."

Demi stepped forward and addressed the group again, "We have no way of knowing exactly what the consequences of having anything from Earth in the spirit realm could be. It's possible the consequences are simply limited to sensations of pain. Unfortunately, it's more probable that the repercussions will be much more far reaching than we can imagine now. It's quite likely that a chain of events has been unfolded. This type of thing would usually take years of study, calculations and complex formulas to even begin to understand it all."

Dan glanced at the other professors. They were quiet and stoic as they took in Demi's words. "Well," Dan broke the silence, "we don't have anywhere near that kind of time. Let's just stick with what we know for now. Do you have any ideas on how to fight off an Earth panther? Will spirit cats, those of us who came to the Rainbow Bridge the traditional way, be able to cause it pain? Do Earth cats experience the same type of allergic reaction as we do from them?"

Once again, the professors huddled together and talked it over. It took only a moment and they turned back to the group. Professor Dimension stepped forward. "The fastest way for us to find out is the simplest as well. I could do the same experiment I had Binx try on me on one of you."

Leroy volunteered before she was even done asking the question. "I'm at your service Lady Dimension." Leroy stepped up and bowed his head in respect.

"I volunteer too!" Binx chimed in, blushing again.

Amelia snorted, half in disgust and half in disbelief, "Oh good grief, here we go. She's a distinguished professor, behave yourselves."

Demi smiled at Binx then turned her attention to Leroy. Her voice was all business as she told him, "I'm going to prick your arm in the same place and in the same way Binx pricked mine. If it hurts at all I want you to pull your arm away immediately. We can determine different pain levels later, for now let's just try to establish if there is any reaction at all."

Leroy blushed and held out his arm. Amelia rolled her eyes and said, "Oh he's having a reaction all right."

Leroy didn't say anything but flipped his tail that conveniently caught her right on the nose. Demi pretended she never heard Amelia and reached out towards Leroy. She gently put her paw on his arm and pushed her nail into his skin. Leroy waited to feel the prick but he never felt anything.

Demi looked at him and raised her eyebrow, silently inquiring if it hurt. Leroy shook his head, "It doesn't hurt at all. It just feels like you're touching me. Try pushing harder."

Demi nodded and pressed her nail into his arm very firmly. He shook his head, "Still nothing. I'm used to Binx rough housing with me on Earth. Go ahead and see if you can scratch me. Give it a good hit just to see."

Demi looked concerned but nodded. She pulled her paw back and struck faster and harder than Leroy was expecting. He forced himself not to flinch and was shocked that he felt no pain at all. She had struck him fiercely and by all rights she should have drawn blood.

"Nothing?" Demi looked at Leroy with a mix of emotions on her face. She looked concerned that she actually may have hurt him.

Dan knew her scientific curiosity was likely bubbling over. Demi was known to push things a little too far when it came to some of her scientific studies and research. That was what caused her to go to the Rainbow Bridge sooner than she had expected she would. But Dan knew Demi would never intentionally hurt Leroy and could hold back her curiosity.

Leroy looked at his arm, still surprised he wasn't bleeding. "Nothing. I didn't feel a thing."

The professors gathered together and once again spoke briefly amongst themselves. Doctor Paws looked at Dan, "It doesn't seem the reaction goes both ways. We appear to have no effect at all on the Earth cats."

A look of concern flashed across Dan's face and he was quiet for a moment.

"Oh I'm telling you," Amelia snickered, "there's most certainly a reaction, at least to Professor Dimension, among a couple of these Earth cats."

Leroy glared at Amelia, "You hush up miss sassy pants."

Amelia chuckled in response. Then apparently decided to groom herself for a while and keep her thoughts to herself.

Dan sat down and shook his head. He looked at Demi, "How are we supposed to stop the panther if it can hurt us but we can't hurt it?"

This time instead of talking amongst themselves the professors went silent as they thought about Dan's question. He was worried they wouldn't be able to help after all. Demi looked at the group and shook her head, "I'm not sure Dan but we have the brightest minds in all of Rainbow Bridge trying to figure it out."

Doctor Paws spoke up, "Sometimes the best cure for an illness is the simplest one. If it's true that Tremor will simply vanish if he chomps on his feather collar then perhaps you can reason with him or appeal to his desire to return home. "

"Or…," interjected Professor Washington, "think of the panther as a parasite. A parasite needs to feed off of its host for it to survive. When there is nothing left for it to feed off of it leaves and finds a new host. It would seem that he is feeding off of his desire to inflict fear to achieve his goals. If it sees that there is nothing here he wants, then perhaps like most parasites, he will simply decide to leave."

Dan remembered what Sassy had told him about Tremors plans and he doubted that either Doctor Paw's or Professor Washington's idea's would be feasible. "Could you send a messenger to Aristotle? He needs to know everything we've learned as soon as possible."

"Of course we will," Professor George Washington said. He turned and briefly spoke to one of his younger students. The younger cat nodded and without a word rushed off towards Aristotle's cat tree.

Dan and company were preparing to head back towards Blankets Mountain when Demi spoke up, "Feather Dan, please come back with your friends when there is more time to talk. In the meantime, we will do all we can to try to figure out some way to help. I believe Doctor Paw's and myself will make haste to Blankets Mountain and work on our theories there so we don't have to wait for more information to come all the way out here."

Dan nodded to her then turned and led the group back towards Blankets Mountain. They walked at a brisk pace. They were all in a hurry to return and see if there were any new developments. Halfway back Amelia had a thought and turned towards Dan.

"Do you think that maybe an Earth cat could hurt the panther?"

Dan stopped in his tracks and said, "That's something I wished we'd thought to ask when we were with the professors. Great idea, Amelia!"

Binx giggled and said, "I don't need a professor to figure that out." Before anyone had time to figure out what he meant, he quickly reached out and poked Amelia on the butt with one of his claws.

Amelia jumped and hissed. She spun around and bopped Binx across the side of the head with her big polydactyl paw. Binx winced and shook it off then asked, "Did it hurt?"

She snapped at him and said "Yes it hurt! You do that again and I'll show you myself!"

Dan barely contained his laughter and smiled. "That answers that question. At least there are some options."

Dan thought back to his conversation with the spirit Doba back in the Hall of Feathers. Doba had been insistent that Dan be selective on who he chose to bring in to help. Dan smiled. He knew that he'd made the right decision. He couldn't figure out who else he could have called given his knowledge of the situation at the time but at the moment he was trying to figure out how three Earth cats were

195

going to have any chance against a panther. That was the moment when they all heard Grace barking.

They stopped for a second and glanced at each other in concern then sprang into action and ran as fast as they could towards Blankets Mountain.

Chapter 19 – Discoveries

As Feather Dan and company rounded the side of Blankets Mountain, towards where Grace was barking, they ran into another huge crowd of cats. Dan shook his head in disbelief. It seemed like every time he got back to Blankets Mountain, the crowd of cats was getting close to double in size. Most of the crowd was sitting in silence staring out towards the clouds. Dan spotted Demi and Dr. Paws whispering together quietly as they made their way to the activity as well. He also spotted Gypsy hanging back but watching what was going on around her.

Dan stopped dead in his tracks when he saw what it was everyone was gawking at.

Binx ran up ahead of the crowd a little bit to get a better look, "What in the world is that? It sure is one funny looking… Is it some type of dog? It's sure not a cat."

Dan walked up to stand beside Binx, the rest of the group right behind him. Dan shook his head and said, "That, Binx is a goat."

Sure enough, there was a medium sized goat walking towards them. It was covered in a short brown coat with a large white spot on its belly. Two legs had white mittens and it had interesting white stripes trailing, from a half circle white spot above its black nose, up over its eyes. Smallish black horns curled straight back behind its head. It had a stub for a tail with white fur sticking out the end. It was walking slowly and eating a line of orange yarn, seemingly unconcerned with its ears straight up and swiveled sideways.

Its head was held low as it chomped on the yarn and slowly walked forward at the same time. The goat was so intent on chewing the yarn, it didn't seem to notice the cats staring in its direction.

When it was only a few yards away it finally looked up and its eyes went wide when it saw them. The orange yarn string it had been chewing dropped from its mouth. The goat bleated at them in a cheerful greeting and hopped about excitedly, bouncing back and forth and kicking out its front and back legs. It was doing a goat version of a happy dance Dan realized.

Dan was pretty sure this goat was familiar with cats since it didn't seem concerned that a large crowd of cats was watching it intently. It appeared to like having an audience as well, Dan thought, inwardly chuckling to himself. He felt the crowd of cats around him relax when they realized the goat was mostly harmless.

It trotted up to them and started bleating away. Dan was aware of the cats around him looking around in confusion. He figured they didn't understand what the goat was saying, not many cats spoke goat. It looked like he was the only one who could help the goat and his suspicion was confirmed when most of the gathered cats backed up to get out of its path. Amidst the confusion of the other cats getting out of the way, Dan stepped up, made a noise that sounded like a goose honk, and started talking in what sounded like bahs, neighs, maas, and hahs. Dan actually asked the goat who he was, and if he remembered how he got here.

Obviously relieved that someone could finally understand him, the goat started talking in a rush of excited maas, bags and neighs. He told Dan his name was Bumper. Then about being suddenly in heaven and how he had then encountered two cats carrying something with a lot of feathers.

Bumper told Dan about wandering lost for a time before encountering one of the cats he'd met before. This time instead of running away from him, the cat approached and started chewing on the yarn that was nearby. He decided he should chew on the yarn too and soon after found himself walking along chewing yarn by himself until he heard a loud roar of rage.

The goat bleated in distress, the noise startling the rest of the group and they involuntarily took a step back. Its eyes went wide in fear, Bumper described how he had seen the panther up close, seen the blood lust in Tremors eyes. He told Dan that he had been more terrified than he ever had been in his entire life. He described how he'd run away as fast as he could knowing it wasn't fast enough and terrified the panther would catch him. When a while had passed and Bumper realized he was still running and wasn't dead yet, he turned around and the panther was gone. He had no idea why he wasn't dead or where the panther went.

Dan was aware that around him, most of the heaven cats had wandered off, no longer sticking around to check out the goat. Dan knew they couldn't understand what the goat was saying and had lost interest now that their curiosity about the goat had been satisfied. A few cats waited patiently nearby, listening and watching Dan talk to the goat. The remaining heaven cats were those that had organized to help track down Sassy and Bandit, like Gypsy and her team. He also noticed Dr. Paws and Demi were nearby and paying close attention.

He relayed as quickly as possible what the goat had said about meeting the twins, his experience with the panther, being chased, running into Sassy again and finding yarn to munch on.

Leroy gave Dan a funny look and asked, "When did you ever learn to speak goat? We sure didn't have any around our apartment."

Dan turned back to Leroy, "I'm no expert at it but I can get by. I picked it up while I was at the rescue shelter I lived at before mum and dad adopted me. There were all kinds of animals around there."

"I think we should move up to the top of Blankets Mountain." Dan told Leroy. "I'll see if the goat is willing to join us." Dan asked the goat to come and join him on the top of Blankets Mountain.

The goat looked up towards the top of Blankets Mountain, hopped around in another outburst of excitement and told Dan he would love to climb a mountain.

Dan turned back to the group, "He's agreed and seems to like the idea of climbing a mountain. Since he's here, I hope to convince him to help us get rid of Tremor. We need all the help we can get."

Dan thought about what they had to work with as they all climbed up to the top of Blanket Mountain. He counted three cats and a goat that could cause some form of physical pain to the panther. But they would all have to be willing to fight. He'd probably best start with the purpose of Rainbow Bridge and how important it was. He hoped that when the goat realized how serious a threat Tremor was that he'd agree to stay and help.

When they got to the top of Blankets Mountain everyone in the group except Grace gathered in a circle and got comfortable. Grace stepped aside and took up her lookout position on the edge of an outlook. He told Bumper where he was and made sure the goat understood he could go home anytime by chomping on the feather collar that was around its neck. If he decided to return home, there was no way for him to come back for a visit until he died on Earth.

Dan quickly told Bumper the story of Rainbow Bridge and the creation of Blankets Mountain. Dan explained the purpose of Rainbow Bridge as a meeting point to help humans and their beloved animals cross over together. Bumper was brought up to speed on how Tremor was a very real threat to the harmony and peace that existed here, that his presence introduced physical pain, something they had never experienced here before. Unfortunately, the heaven cats couldn't also hurt Tremor and were powerless to stop him by themselves.

Dan asked Bumper if there was a human he had bonded with on Earth. The goat excitedly told Dan all about how much he was best friends with a little girl named Cindy on a farm. They used to spend long afternoons playing together and she would bring him special treats and knew just where to scratch behind his ears. He told Dan how much he already missed her and the more he thought about it he was pretty sure he would just chomp his collar and go home.

At Bumper's mention of going home to be reunited with Cindy, Dan reminded the goat that if he crossed the Rainbow Bridge before his human he'd be here waiting for her until her time came. What he was going to do when his day came to guide Cindy from the Rainbow Bridge, but the panther was now in charge and decided he wasn't allowed to help Cindy. Cindy could become completely lost forever.

Dan asked Bumper what he would be willing to do to make sure Cindy had help when she needed it. Would he be willing to stay and help to battle the panther? If he went home without first making sure Tremor was dealt with, he might never have his chance to help Cindy find her way and join her in the beyond.

The goat was silent for a moment, then stomped his hoof a couple of times in frustration and anger. He bleated his frustration; froth was forming around his mouth. Bumper asked Dan what the plan was. Dan explained to him that they were working on that. He asked him to tag along and they'd all figure it out together.

Dan pulled Remy aside. "I know you are keeping up with Binx and you're doing a great job but could you and Grace also try to keep an eye on the goat too? I really just don't want him wandering into the Hall of Feathers and eating everything in there."

Remy's eyes went wide. Dan could tell that the idea of the goat finding its way into the Hall of Feathers and eating all Dan's carefully collected feathers didn't sit well with Remy. "You bet, Dan. I'll try to keep them both together," he responded.

"Thank you," Dan said to Remy. He knew he could count on Remy's help.

Dan noticed when Gypsy pulled Leroy aside and trotted over to join them. Amelia and Binx had already joined Leroy and Gypsy. As he approached he heard Gypsy ask, "Do you think we could practice some things with you guys? We really need to see what works on an Earth cat and what doesn't before we have to figure it out first hand on Tremor."

Dan made quick introductions, pointing out how Gypsy's team, Mouser, had been the one who's yarn Sassy had used to find her way back.

Leroy nodded his agreement. "That's a good idea, Gypsy. Of course I'd be happy to help out however I can."

"I want to help!" Binx raced forward and ran a few laps around Leroy and Gypsy. "Do you think we could play a game of Feathers Time while we try things?"

Leroy reached out a paw and grabbed Binx by the tail, stopping him from running more circles and making him dizzy. "I think it best we do something a bit more structured at the moment."

Gypsy nodded, "Leroy is right, Binx. We have some very specific things we need to figure out before we play."

"First," Gypsy looked at all three of them, "I'd like to see just how strong all of you are compared to us. I'd like to see how many of us it takes to pin you to the ground before you are stuck and can't get back up."

"Oh no, I don't think so!" Amelia piped in. "You can do all the rough housing you want with the boys but I'm not that kind of girl. You can count me out of that nonsense."

Binx jumped up, looked Amelia up and down and said, "Oh come on, Amelia. You got the biggest butt of everyone. I bet it will take a lot of them to hold you down."

Amelia's ears went flat on her head and she hissed at Binx, "Shut up you brat! You wiry little runt. They'll probably be able to hold you down with nothing more than the kitten brigade."

Dan chuckled, he sure had missed his friends and it felt really good to be among them again. "It's okay Amelia. You can help give team Mouser pointers on how to get Leroy down. He's strong as an ox. It'll probably take two full teams to get him down."

Dan knew Gypsy had a solid reputation as a team leader and was used to putting up with high spirited cats. But he could tell her patience with Binx's and Amelia's antics had reached its end. "Either way," she continued as if not interrupted. "We should get started. We don't know how much time we have before Tremor gets to us and we need to learn as much as we can now."

Gypsy pulled in the other team captains and told them what she was trying to accomplish. They agreed to watch and provide suggestions and help try to pin the Earth cats down. Gypsy coordinated the teams. Dan could see each cat become resolved in helping as best they could. They tried all types of moves on each other. They ran into each other, tumbled with each other, knocked each other down and appeared to have a lot of fun trying to pounce and pin each other down.

It became immediately obvious that the spirit cats were not going to be able to use claws or teeth to fight. The best they could manage was just to get a good grip and hold on. There were some tactics they discovered that would work though. Leroy, being a very large and muscular cat, was not easy to hold down. Just like Feather Dan had predicted, it took several cats, most of two full Feather Time teams, all at the same time to be able to pin him down but they were eventually able to do so with sheer numbers in a coordinated attack.

Dan hoped that with their great numbers, the heaven cats could swarm the panther and be able to pin it down. Team Mouser was also able to get Leroy and Binx both dizzy. They played a fast game of running in circles until all of them got dizzy and fell over. Leroy and Binx got dizzy twice as fast and it took them three times longer to recover than any of the spirit cats. Dan nodded, the beginning of crude strategy forming in his mind.

The Feather Time teams and Leroy and Binx continued to play and rough house to try to learn new things for another hour. Beyond their initial discoveries, they didn't find anything else that might be useful. During a brief break while the teams tried to come up with a new strategy that would work to pin down the Earth cats, he wasn't surprised that Demi approached and sat quietly next to him to watch and observe.

"I have some news for you, Dan." Demi said in a friendly but serious tone.

He was sure she had heard the rumors they were practicing on top of Blankets Mountain and had come to see for herself. She'd also brought Dr. Paws with her. He was sitting on Demi's other side, also watching intently. If he was here too, it was probably something serious they needed to discuss.

Dan turned his attention back to his friends when Leroy and Binx looked his way. They jumped up immediately and rushed over to greet Demi. Binx reached her first. Dan wasn't sure how after observing Binx twice tripping over his own feet as he attempted to do some grooming to straighten out his fur at the same time as running full speed. "Hi Demi!" he blushed as he picked himself up.

Leroy took just a moment to compose himself then, with a little more strut to his step than normal, casually approached. "Greetings, Professor Dimension." He bowed his head, his ears just a bit pink from blushing, "It's a pleasure to see you again."

Demi smiled, entertained at their obvious flirting. "Warm greetings to both of you as well my new friends."

Binx hopped up excitedly, "We're friends? Already? I still can't get Amelia to admit I'm her friend but she is mine."

Amelia arrived just in time to hear Binx. She grunted, "Oh boy, here we go again." She rolled her eyes and sat down next to Dan. She then proceeded to bathe her tail that Dan couldn't find any dirt on.

Demi laughed, "Of course you are my friend, Binx. How could I not find you to be fun? Your curiosity is adorable and reminds me of myself when I was younger. I was curious about different things…" Demi briefly remembered something but didn't seem to want to share it.

Binx's wide smile and shining blue eyes reminded Dan of the Cheshire Cat. "Binx," Dan interrupted, "I'm afraid that Demi is here with some serious news. We should all listen to her for a moment."

"Very true," Demi chimed in. "Leroy, remember where I had Binx poke me with his claw?"

Leroy nodded and turned his attention towards that spot on her arm.

"Well look here," Demi held out her arm so they could all see. "Look at the exact spot. I'm glad now that I didn't have Binx do more."

They all stepped closer and looked at the spot where Binx had poked her. Her pristine cotton white fur looked like it had a bit of dirt or a freckle on that exact spot. Once everyone had a look she pulled her arm back and said, "Watch this." She began to groom the area frantically. After a few seconds she stopped; the spot was unchanged and still there.

Dan studied her in concern, "May I look more closely?"

Demi nodded and held her arm back out. Dan gently took her paw and pulled it closer. He put his face as close as he could to it then gently moved the fur around. His eyes went wide in shock and disbelief when he realized what had happened.

He let her paw go and looked at her with great concern, "It looks like a bit of dirt because that spot no longer has the spirits glow!"

There was a gasp among the other nearby spirit cats who had been close enough to witness the exchange.

Concerned Dan asked. "Does it still hurt?"

Demi shook her head, "No, it doesn't hurt. It doesn't feel different at all but I can't get it to shine anymore." She didn't sound nearly as distressed as Dan. She had an air of intellectual curiosity about her and appeared to be completely unconcerned for her own wellbeing.

She looked over at Leroy and asked, "Could I take a look at where I scratched you?"

Leroy nodded and stepped forward immediately. "Of course, Demi, anything at all I can do to help just ask. I am at your service."

Demi studied him closely. She pushed his fur aside and studied his skin underneath. She rubbed his fur in different areas to see if it felt any different from the spot she'd scratched him but there was no difference at all. There was absolutely no indication that anything had happened to him. Leroy was startled when Doctor Paws stepped up beside Demi.

Doctor Paws consulted with Demi quickly in hushed tones then turned to Dan. "We need to get that information out to all of the others and quickly. It would appear that if the panther attacks us and does enough damage it is completely possible that we could lose a significant amount of our glow. If we can't recover our glow and we lose too much of it, we'd be unable to help our humans find their way to Rainbow Bridge."

"Doctor Paws?" Demi asked him, "Team Mouser was playing quite aggressively with Leroy and Binx. Would you mind checking them to be sure they are okay?"

Doctor Paws raised his eyebrows, "Most certainly my dear. Come here everyone. Let me do a quick exam."

The cats from team Mouser lined up in front of Doctor Paws and waited patiently as he examined them. Leroy and Binx both assured everyone that they had been careful not to use their claws or teeth but Doctor Paws continued his exam to be thorough. When he was finished he assured each of them that no one had taken any scratches or bites. The players from Team Mouser breathed a collective sigh of relief that none of them had inadvertently suffered any dulled fur.

They shared with Doctor Paws and Professor Dimension the discoveries they'd made while playing with Leroy and Binx. They explained how it took many of them to be able to hold down Leroy but how they were eventually able to do so. They also shared how Leroy and Binx got dizzy quicker than the others and that it took them longer to recover.

Doctor Paws nodded thoughtfully, "Great research everyone! We need to inform our best strategists with your results and have them see what plans they can come up with."

Leroy and Binx took extra care when playing and experimenting with Team Mouser.

"I feel bad about the dull mark Binx made on you." Leroy told Demi. "I hope you aren't upset about it," an earnest look on his face. "I take full responsibility for all of my siblings," he admitted, obviously feeling guilty that Binx left a permanent mark on her.

Dan watched Demi study Leroy. Even Dan could tell by the look on Leroy's face that he was worried about it.

"Thank you Leroy, but it's not something you should feel guilty about. I actually consider it a scar of honor. We needed to know it was possible and he helped us know for sure." She said in a soothing manner. "Rest easy, my friend. One tiny dull speck would not keep my human from being able to see me when her time comes." Demi patted Leroy on the shoulder in a comforting gesture.

After withdrawing her paw from Leroy, she smiled at him. "In fact, I'm rather excited about it and being a part of an important historical event this discovery will be sure to be included in the history books." She couldn't repress a tail twitch, the only departure from her reserved appearance.

Dan knew the Professors of History and the other historians were very particular about what was included in those books. But Demi was right, this was a major discovery and would be passed on

208

forever. He was just hopeful that it was a good historical event and not a tragedy that was recorded.

All of them continued to plan throughout the night. Dan and Gypsy saw to it that the community broke into groups, each specializing in something that would add value. It was decided that at first light, the Feathers Time teams would retrieve the yarn they'd put out the day before. The team captains and their teams were still hashing out the plan details getting everyone coordinated. Dan was unable to resist giving furtive glances to the mountain range of clouds. He feared seeing Tremor approaching before they were ready. He prayed their plan would be enough, and it would be in time to save Rainbow Bridge.

Chapter 20 – A Diversity of Plans

All of the Feathers Time team captains had assembled with their respective teams gathered behind each of them. The final pieces of their plan were taking shape and they were getting the teams coordinated for the coming morning.

It had been decided by the team captains that the yarn lines would be removed starting at the crack of dawn, at the earliest. The team members weren't happy with their plan to wait until morning. They argued that the gravity of the situation justified the risk of going out beyond the clouds at dark. The yarn would keep them from getting lost.

Because they were already familiar with the effects of the night, Jack and Flynn were nominated to speak for the team members who didn't want to wait. Flynn stepped forward, "We know it'll be extremely disorienting out there if we went now, but we can work around it. We can attach a loop to the yarn and tether ourselves to it. That will keep us from wandering off track and guarantee we can find our way home.

The Captains considered the idea amongst themselves. Captain Twitch of team Butt Wiggle stepped forward and shook his head. "Good thought but absolutely not. What happens if you cross paths with Tremor and have to run? Being tethered to the line would ensure he can easily catch you. The only sure way to make sure you aren't lost is to do this during daylight."

The other Captains nodded in agreement with Twitch.

Jack stepped up next, "We also think that it would be best to unhook the yarn from the Blankets Mountain side. It could be used to lead Tremor in another direction, away from Rainbow Bridge."

Again the team captains talked it over and overruled them. This time Gypsy spoke up, "If something happened and you were to lead Tremor away, the risk of it becoming dark before you were able to return would be too great. You need the line to guarantee a safe return home."

Twitch nodded in agreement, "The original plan is the safest option. We won't risk losing any of you. Our duty to our humans is far too great to gamble even one of you on such a risky plan. You'll just have to go as quickly as you can, get to the end, untie the yarn and bring it back here."

"No more debates on leaving before dawn. We will wait for daylight. Let's work out the communication strategy," Gypsy added to Twitch's response.

The teams established a more complex series of tugs that would notify the Captain on the other end of the line that the panther had found the yarn. Gypsy quizzed them repeatedly, making sure everyone had it memorized.

Twitch came up with the idea to activate the reserve team members. Each team kept two additional members in reserve in the event something came up and one of the regular players needed to be substituted. If the signal was sent that Tremor had found the yarn and was heading towards Rainbow Bridge, the reserves would deploy and try to misdirect the enemy. If they weren't able to throw Tremor off the trail they would at least be able to race back to warn the others and provide much needed intelligence on which direction Tremor would be coming from.

The captains had decided that for expediency's sake, the teams would initially rely on speed to run to where the yarn ended. Once the end of the yarn was untethered, the teams would need to be stealthier and more cautious to avoid detection. At that point, caution was more important than speed. It would mean taking opportunities to stick to the sides of the clouds, and when possible to minimize their visibility. The captains thought that if the panther hadn't found the yarn yet, it would be making frequent trips to the tops of the clouds to survey the landscape and look for landmarks. Tremor was obviously intelligent and would immediately understand what was going on if the teams were spotted retrieving the yarn. The yarn retrievers must take precautions to detect Tremor and hide the direction to Rainbow Bridge. With the team plan in place, the teams waited for the night to end.

~

Meanwhile, Dan had been working on a plan of his own. Dan knew that Leroy was a catnip junky and that had given him an idea. Once he shared his idea with Doctor Paws it didn't take long for a large feather stuffed, catnip toy to be delivered. When Leroy spotted it his eyes went wide. When he sniffed it he started drooling. It took only a few minutes of him rolling around with that toy before he went wild. He lost his senses and became loopy. He played hard for a few minutes then fell over and went to sleep. Despite Binx constantly pestering him and trying to get him to wake up, Leroy couldn't be roused. Satisfied it was a decent plan, several cats were tasked with rounding up as many as they could find.

When Leroy did get up he said he had his first ever catnip hangover. After his long nap, Leroy reported the after effects wore off quickly.

Sobered up and sitting stoically next to Dan, Leroy said, "That Rainbow Bridge catnip is much stronger than anything I've tried on Earth. I bet if we could get Tremor interested in it that he would probably fall asleep like I did. Then maybe we could trick it into chomping on its feather collar."

Dan nodded in agreement, "I bet it would too. I just wonder how much of it would be enough to make Tremor get to that point. I've

212

never seen one myself but I know that panthers are huge compared to us."

Dan smiled as he noticed Grace making her way up the side of Blankets Mountain. She was returning from her own small yet critical mission. Grace was one of the most affectionate animals he'd ever seen and she loved cats probably more than anything else. She was always a wonderful mother figure to all of the kittens that she came in contact with on Earth.

"Professor Dimension was able to convince Miss Honeybee to follow her plan. Miss Honeybee agreed it was the best plan for keeping the young ones out of harm's way." Grace informed everyone. "Pippin even volunteered to help keep an eye on the kittens."

Dan smiled at that. Pippin loved to play with the kittens and the kittens loved to play with him.

Dan knew Miss Honeybee was the primary cat in charge of all of the kittens that found their way to Rainbow Bridge so early in their lives. She could also be stubborn and difficult to convince. He was glad she listened to Demi's advice.

Leroy's ears perked up at hearing Demi's name. "Who would have thought that Binx would have helped come up with that plan?"

Grace nodded enthusiastically. "Yes, I'm pretty sure there will be no way Tremor can get to them now."

Dan smiled, "Don't discount your own role in this Leroy. If you hadn't been so worried about mum and dad missing everyone, I wouldn't have had the idea to go to Rainbow Bridge."

Dan recalled how Binx decided he had to run out and inspect it for himself. "If Binx hadn't tried to run out onto Rainbow Bridge, you would have never tested it. We still wouldn't know that Earth animals would fall through. The kittens will be safe on the Bridge. I'm sure they will enjoy the extra time checking in on their humans as well. Hopefully they'll never even know anything is amiss." Dan couldn't see any way Tremor could reach the kittens. It was a solid plan to keep them safe as long as they stayed put on Rainbow Bridge.

Grace started to make her way back to her usual lookout spot but paused and looked back at Dan. "Miss Honeybee also seems to think that if Tremor gets one look at all of those kittens in one spot that his heart will melt because of their irresistible cuteness and their innocence. I don't mean to be pessimistic, but I don't agree with her at all on that concept," Grace chuffed in disagreement before continuing her thought. "There are a few dogs in the dog realm of Rainbow Bridge that still have a very aggressive wolf instinct. Fortunately, they also have a pack and family mentality. We noticed the predator instinct is stronger for animals born in the wild. I hope the kittens stay safe and we don't need to find out."

"I think they will be safe. Thanks for helping make it possible, Grace." Dan responded as Grace was walking away.

Dan was also working with the biggest fans of the Feathers Time games. They were busy gathering all of the feathers they could find. The idea was that if he could give away hundreds or even thousands of feathers all at once, the free ones that appeared could be sent in like a swarm unleashing a blizzard of feathers. Dan hoped it would be effective in slowing Tremor down or at least buy them a moment.

~

Amelia, who had remained quietly observing, followed Grace over to her lookout ledge. Once Grace sat down, Amelia walked circles around her, rubbing up against her and singing.

"I really have missed you Grace. I wish you could have been around to help with Binx. Your infamous pit maneuver used on Binx is something I would have loved to see." Amelia found a comfortable spot and settled in next to Grace.

Grace was watching a large crowd of cats organizing into squads. The squads were practicing running together in formation and moving amongst each other as a team. They were putting into practice what had been learned from the experimenting done by the Feathers Time teams. That knowledge was being used to formulate new strategies by the squad leaders. They coordinated the squads into several large groups and had them practice charging in waves simultaneously. The goal was to at least knock the panther down so it could be pinned. The squads needed to practice working together to be able to pull it off without getting in each other's way.

~

Remy, having been tasked with keeping up with both Binx and Bumper, had found the perfect way to entertain and keep both of them out of trouble. Both he and Binx were trying to learn how to ride the goat. Remy and Binx were very dexterous and found they could ride on Bumper's back and shoulders without falling off no matter how hard and fast he kicked and hopped about. Before long, they were charging all over the place. They raced up and down Blankets Mountain and leaped over obstacles.

Bumper seemed amused and pleased that others were taking such an interest in him. His good nature made him easy to work with, and he had a lot of energy. Remy had managed to pick up some of the goat's language. He and Bumper were developing their own combination of hand signs, touches, and noises with a bit of cat and goat all mixed together to communicate with each other. It wasn't long before the squads of cats waved both of them over and started to include them in their training maneuvers.

~

Another group was busy twirling several strands of yarn together to make a type of rope. The Feathers Time team members would use it to tie up the panthers legs. If they could find something strong enough they hoped it could even be used to tie Tremor down.

Feather Dan and Leroy observed it all from the top of Blankets Mountain. Dan was overcome with a sense of humility to be among such an incredibly historic event. Dan and Leroy turned together to look behind them as they heard a slow shuffling of feet. Aristotle had come down from his cat tree to visit. Dan could only recall one other visit from Aristotle and that was immediately after Blankets Mountain had sprung into existence.

Dan smiled as Aristotle sat beside him. "I'm absolutely amazed at the ingenuity of everyone. It's almost like they've planned for such a thing for years." Dan spoke with reverence for all the hard work being put in around him. The spot they sat in made it easy to observe all that was going on.

Aristotle shook his head as he gazed across Blankets Mountain. "No, Feather Dan, this is something none of us have ever even dreamed could become a reality but look at them all." Aristotle waved his grey, aged paw in front of him to include everything happening. "Rainbow Bridge is all inclusive. We come from so many diverse backgrounds that we have every kind of skill and expertise available." His face cracked into a large smile, evidence of his happiness and pride for endeavors of his fellow cats. "It warms my heart to be able to bear witness to this. The entire community has come together for a common cause. All life would be better if this were always so."

Dan nodded in agreement. He and Aristotle spoke at length while they observed everything unfold below them. Every cat was busy. Every cat was pitching in however they could. Dan had never been more proud to be a part of something.

Chapter 21 – Trouble

When the first rays of sunlight brushed the tops of the clouds a sudden silence swept across the enormous assembly at Rainbow Bridge. The sky was clear with no evidence of mist shrouding the base of the clouds. It was going to be a bright sunny day. The silence lasted only for a moment before the raised voices of the Feathers Time teams captains began calling out orders. Each pair of runners was already in place and anxiously awaiting the command to go. The captains hesitated for just a moment for the rays of the sun to touch the peak of Blankets Mountain before they issued the order for the teams to run. The runners wasted no time, and in unison they burst forth from the crowd. Each pair followed along a line of yarn, one on either side. Their speed was incredible. The runners left wispy contrails of clouds behind them as they vanished into the distance.

Two of the runners, Flash and Sonic, from team Sky Raisins were among the first to vanish into the Cloud Mountains and disappear from sight. They ran for hours, barely speaking a word to each other as they went. Sonic knew the plan and what needed to be done. He and Flash were going to run the length of yarn until they got to the end. There would be no slowing down to peek from the tops of clouds, no side trips, no scouting of any kind, just a mad race to where the yarn was anchored.

They didn't speak a word to each other when they finally got to the end of the yarn line. They worked efficiently as a team to untether it from the cloud and began the process of heading back. Sonic hadn't seen or heard anything on their run out, but since they hadn't stopped to do any scouting either he knew it was possible that Tremor could be just a cloud away. Now that they were headed back, they had to be much more cautious. Flash carried the yarn. He hopped along rolling it into a ball with his paws. Once it became large enough he tossed it in front of him and began kicking it forward in a straight line. Flash was able to keep it rolling much like a soccer ball that constantly grew in size as it picked up more and more yarn. Flash stayed near the sides of the clouds as much as possible to reduce the chances of being spotted by Tremor should he happen to be looking from a mountain top.

Keeping up with the yarn slowed Flash down more than Sonic had anticipated. That did, however, provide Sonic an opportunity to scout ahead and take on the role of lookout. Sonic made sure to stay within sight of Flash while scouting forward and staying alert for danger. He scrambled up the side of the next cloud ahead of them. As he got up higher and near the top, he slowed down. He began to cautiously belly crawl to the peak. Once there he looked around peering over the top surveying the way ahead, making sure the coast was clear. As Flash began to approach the cloud he was on, Sonic hurried back down, ran ahead to the next cloud and repeated the process of scouting and searching the path ahead.

Working together, they managed to keep up a pace which Sonic knew was fast enough to safely make it back to Rainbow Bridge before dark. Sonic made sure to use as much caution as possible while scouting ahead. He was hoping to be able to bring back some information with them. Even if they didn't see the panther, that itself would be useful.

They traveled for what they estimated was at least half the distance back when Sonic spotted something. He was at the top of a smaller cloud, scanning around for any sign of Tremor when he spotted a dark object lying on the side of a nearby cloud. It was too far away yet to identify. But Sonic knew it wasn't just a shadow. Sonic strained his eyes trying to make some details that would give him an idea of what it was but it was just too far away. Anything out this far was unusual and needed investigation. There should be nothing at all except clouds this far away from Rainbow Bridge.

Sonic hurried down the mountain and ran up to Flash. "There's something laying on the side of one of the clouds off to the right. It's too far away to make out. I think we should at least get close enough to figure out what it is but it's a little bit off our path. What do you think?"

Flash didn't have to think about it at all. "Anything this far away from Rainbow Bridge needs to be investigated. We're making good time. We can spare a few minutes."

"Alright," Sonic said. "I don't think it's a good idea to get separated or out of sight from each other."

"I agree," Flash nodded and began unspooling some of the yarn so that he could push the ball out to the object without causing it to tug and accidentally signal Gypsy that there was trouble.

He gave Sonic a nod when he was ready and they ran around the base of the mountain they were skirting and then on towards the dark shape Sonic had spotted. When they got closer they immediately recognized what it was. Not wanting to be distracted for long, they ran as fast as they could. Within the few minutes they were running up right on top of it. They gasped at the same time when they realized what they'd found. It was the very headdress that was the source of all of this trouble. Flash whistled in amazement.

Sonic thought the headdress was absolutely beautiful. It had a very mysterious and mystical energy that radiated off of it. It was fascinating and tempting to play with but it also had his innate cat instinct ringing alarm bells in his head. If he'd still been on Earth and spotted this he'd have left it alone, he valued his nine lives too much to tempt fate and play with such a thing.

"Wow," Flash whispered. "I can appreciate why Feather Dan kept this safely tucked away in his Hall of Feathers. What in the world were the twins thinking? This is not a cat toy."

Sonic shook his head, "I have no idea. I know the stories of the twin's time on Earth are filled with recklessness and poor decisions. If they lacked enough instinct and common sense to leave *this* alone it's a wonder they lasted as long as they did before they came to the Rainbow Bridge."

"I agree," Flash gave Sonic a serious look. "We can't leave this here. It needs to come back with us."

Sonic knew they couldn't summon help to come and fetch the headdress. They hadn't worked out a signal complex enough to ask for that kind of help, just one to alert those waiting if Tremor was spotted. He didn't want to give a false alarm of Tremors approach if it could be helped. They had run miles from Blankets Mountain and it was too far to run back and get help. Sonic didn't like the idea of leaving Flash here, alone and vulnerable with both the yarn and the headdress. He realized he was going to have to carry it. They still had to get back before night came.

Sonic stepped up to the headdress and pulled at it trying to get a sense of its weight and how hard it would be to drag it back to Blankets Mountain. He hefted it up and took a couple of experimental steps.

Sonic sighed, "It's going to slow us down. We should still be able to make it back to Blankets Mountain before dark but I won't be able to run ahead and do anymore scouting if I carry it. I don't like the idea of us traveling without knowing if we are walking into danger. Tremor could be just around any corner."

Sonic looked at Flash. Flash looked directly back at him. Sonic knew that there wasn't a choice to be made. They couldn't leave the headdress here. Flash knew it as well, so there was no need to even consider not taking it with them.

"Well," Sonic grunted as he hefted the headdress and started to jog back towards where they came from. "There's nothing left to do except get it done. Let's hope Feather Dan can figure out a way to use it to battle Tremor."

Their pace was cut nearly in half but they moved as quickly as they could. Flash gathered the yarn, rolling it into a larger and larger ball while Sonic dragged the headdress behind him. Sonic was very careful not to let the beads click together. As he got used to carrying it, he was able to get a grip that better compensated for its drag and was able to pick up his pace. He held it in the middle with the trails of feathers falling on either side of him. He was forced to just look straight ahead, but kept a close look to the sky and his ears perked up listening for any sounds of trouble.

They were making the best speed they could, hoping darkness didn't come before they got home and that they didn't accidentally stumble head first into Tremor.

They developed a method of cautiously moving forward. Before they had to make their way around a cloud and head into the open, they slowed their pace and approached with caution. If the way looked clear of danger, they would race across the open space towards the base of the next cloud. Sonic didn't like being that exposed when they made their dash out in the open. But he didn't have the spare time needed to scout ahead and come back for the headdress. It would cost them too much time. They had to keep moving forward if they were going to make it back before nightfall. The closer they got to Blankets Mountain the more a sense of dread came over Sonic. He shared harried glances with Flash and knew he felt it too. Their cat instincts were trying to warn them of danger, but they couldn't see it even if they could sense it was nearby. He knew there was nothing they could do but move forward.

Again they slowed as they rounded the corner of the next cloud. They barely made the turn when they both froze in their tracks. There was the panther. It was standing half way between the cloud they were on and the one they were headed to. It had its back to them and was examining the yarn. Tremor raised his head and looked back and forth across its length. Sonic noted his massive muscles. Thick corded bands rippled under a sleek black coat as he moved. Sonic was overcome with a fear which he had ever experienced before. It was primal. He knew his life was in danger. Panic welled up in his heart. Tremor began to follow the string that was in their direction. Without glancing at Flash, they both walked backwards back to the cloud they had just left putting a cloud between them and Tremor.

Sonic remembered when Sassy had told everyone how big the panther was. She'd been very descriptive, her voice shaking with fear. Even just retelling her story it was obvious that she had been scared by what she had seen. The terror that gripped her seemed crazy at the time. But now… to be in the presence of the beast… to see it for themselves… Sonic immediately understood that Sassy's panic had been justified. He looked into Flash's wide eyes.

Flash risked another furtive peek around the side of the cloud. Sonic did too. Sure enough, Tremor was following the yarn and picking up speed as he walked towards them. Flash ducked back behind the cloud and pressed his back up against the cloud. Sonic wished they had a place to hide. Tremor was enormous, his size alone was intimidating but the way he moved was something out of a nightmare. Every step, every turn of his head and flick of his tail was intentional. He'd seen the monster's fangs. Tremor was epitome of a predator.

Sonic looked at Flash and gently shook him. Flash's eyes were wide with fright. "Flash, we need to send the signal back to Gypsy at Blankets Mountain. They need to know."

Sonic's voice snapped Flash out of the shock he'd been in. "No!" He whispered loudly. "Tremor will notice it. Even if we're gentle with our tugs, he'll certainly see or feel Gypsy respond. If she orders the yarn to be reeled in, Tremor will follow it right back to her. At least now he's heading the wrong way."

Sonic nodded his frustration obvious in his expression. "Well we better do something and I mean like right now!"

"I know," Flash told him, "I can only think of one solution. I'm going to have to run the yarn back out into the clouds as fast as I can."

Sonic gave Flash an unsettled look and started to shake his head in disagreement. He knew Flash would never find his way back if he ran out now. He opened his mouth to disagree, but Flash held up a paw, stopping Sonic before he could voice his protest.

"Look, we don't have a choice and you have a job to do. You need to circle around him and get back to warn the others at Rainbow Bridge. Hopefully there will be enough time to run the yarn back from that end. Drag it back out and try to make it lead to nowhere."

Sonic poked his head around the corner to get a quick peek. He looked for just a second and then looked back to Flash. A new concern was etched on his face. "Did you see Bandit anywhere?"

"No," Flash's heart sank in worry, "I didn't see him anywhere but then again I couldn't take my eyes off of Tremor."

Flash took another quick look. He turned his head back to Sonic, "I don't see him either." Sonic could read the fear for Bandit's safety on Flash's face. Flash looked back and took another look. He reached out and grabbed Sonic's arm. "Oh no Sonic! Tremor stopped. He's turning around!" his voice cracked as panic began to take hold.

Sonic gasped and quickly looked for himself. They both watched as Tremor sniffed the air for a moment then began following the yarn towards Blankets Mountain and Rainbow Bridge. "Things just went from bad to worse."

Tremor was walking at a pace much faster than they could travel with the headdress and winding up the yarn. Sonic got an idea. He knew what he needed to do, but he also knew he couldn't do it while he was carrying the headdress.

"Flash," Sonic called in a calm voice, causing Flash to stop watching Tremor and look at him. "We can't leave the headdress, but I can't do what I need to with it. Can you manage to take both by yourself for a while?"

Flash nodded slowly, "I won't be moving very fast at all but I can manage. I can carry the headdress and butt the ball of yarn with my head. I'm not sure I will be able to keep it in a straight line though. What's your plan?"

Sonic was thinking while he spoke, "I'm going to race ahead and get in front of Tremor. I'll cut the yarn and run it back to Blankets Mountain. Do you think you can create a false trail? Try to just make a big loop, we don't want a straight line. The tall cloud up head looks like a giant mushroom. You can use it to orient yourself then work your way back to Blankets Mountain as soon as you can."

Flash thought it over for just a second and agreed to the plan. "I can do it. Be careful though, Sonic. You remember what Sassy said. She and Bandit couldn't outrun the panther."

Without another word, Sonic sprinted up the cloud. Without the baggage of the headdress he was moving at full speed and within a minute he reached the top and ran down to the next cloud. He knew Flash wouldn't be able to see him now. He said a silent prayer that this wouldn't be the last time he saw his friend.

Sonic caught another glimpse of Tremor when he got to the top of the next cloud. The panther was trotting along but not running which was good. He was going to have to run as fast as he could to get far enough ahead to have enough time to chew through the yarn. He looked once more hoping to see Bandit but he just wasn't there. Knowing he had no more time to waste he took one last look back at Flash, silently prayed that they'd see each other again and sprinted ahead to do what needed to be done.

Chapter 22 – Battle Wounds

The unexpected appearance of the goat and Tremor's instinctive response to pursue it had provided Bandit an opportunity to escape but that attempt had failed. After a desperate chase Bandit now found himself truly caught and cowering under the panther.

Tremor loomed above him, his massive muscular frame quivering from exertion, his sides rising and falling with each heavy breath. Bandit felt paralyzed under his gaze. Pure hatred glared from Tremors eyes and Bandit understood that he was being confronted by pure evil. Tremor's face twisted with rage as he raised his massive midnight black paw and extended dagger-like razor sharp claws. Bandit's heart skipped a beat when he saw the Tremor meant to kill him. Bandit braced for the end.

Tremor's claw struck so quickly that Bandit couldn't even follow the paw as it came down. The weight of his massive paw bore down on Bandit and he felt the razor claws immediately. Bandit couldn't help emitting a scream of agony as he felt the claws tear across his side and down through his stomach. He was sure he'd been cut in half and his body convulsed. His scream choked off as he ran out of breath to scream. Bandit told himself to fight through the pain to take one last breath. He could tell from the pain, he had suffered a fatal would. He was afraid to look at the damage but couldn't stop himself from checking. His horror at seeing what he looked like gave way to astonishment. He couldn't believe what he was seeing. Instead of gruesome slashes in his side and belly, he was whole. The pain was still coming in excruciating waves, forcing him to howl in pain but he was whole.

Tremor roared his anger. Rearing back he struck Bandit again and again. Each strike caused Bandit to scream, then cry and whimper in pain. But when Bandit checked, he saw no obvious signs of damage on him. He remained motionless, laying on his side, belly exposed to Tremor. The pain made it unbearable to move. He knew he was helpless and couldn't avoid it if Tremor decided to keep hitting him.

Tremor snarled and opened his mouth roaring his hatred and frustration. Bandit watched as the saliva that hung in long gleaming tendrils dripped from his deadly, yellow stained fangs. He gave Bandit a rough swat that ended up rolling him over onto his stomach still facing Tremor.

He must realize by now that he couldn't kill him. Bandit hoped that Tremor would soon grow bored of hitting him and biting him. He hoped that when that happened, Tremor would lose interest and go away. Bandit watched in helpless horror as Tremor lunged at him. He felt pressure applied to his entire neck, throat and most of his head. When Tremor lifted him off the ground, he realized Tremor had him in his powerful jaws a split second before he felt pressure bearing down on his head and neck followed by searing pain everywhere his body was in contact with Tremor's jaws. The pain just added to what was already there. It became so unbearable Bandit couldn't stop the spine chilling scream that rushed out of him. He screamed with renewed desperation and terror until Tremor's jaws bore down and his throat was forced closed. His scream turned into a gurgle then went silent as Bandit's mind drifted toward blacking out from the pain.

"No blood!" Tremor yelled as fury completely overtook him. He shook Bandit like a rag doll then spit him out, dropping him to the ground. Tremor bared his fangs and screamed so loud that Bandit's ears rang with a high pitched whine that was deafening.

Bandit could see Tremor open his mouth as if screaming in rage, but couldn't hear anything. Bandit had never experienced such agony. The pain was too intense for him to do anything except writhe on the ground and whimper in pain. Tremor again lifted a giant paw and took a swipe at Bandit. In too much pain to move, the strike caught Bandit on his side and sent his limp body rolling several feet. His mind barely registered it when he crashed into the side of a cloud.

Overcome with excruciating pain, his mind surrendered to the pain and for a while everything went dark. He just lay motionless, drifting in and out of awareness, waiting for the next attack. During one of the black spells, Tremor must have decided Bandit was no longer prey worth playing with and left. Bandit awoke to find he was alone before drifting back into unconsciousness.

Bandit lost track of how long he lay there. Each breath was like inhaling fire. Pain flowed like lava all along the places where Tremor had touched him, then radiating outward to encompass every part of him. Trying to raise his head made him pass out. His entire body felt broken in hundreds of places. After a while the pain started to fade. He tested his body. Finally able to handle the pain enough, he moved for the first time, pulling himself up off of his side and into a more proper resting position. He was no longer blacking out from the pain. He thought that was a good thing, but being awake meant feeling the pain and he longed to not feel the pain. As more time passed, he was relieved that the pain continued to gradually diminish. It became easier for him to breathe. Once his head quit spinning, he sat up and began bathing himself to confirm he had no lasting injuries.

He was a mess. He was covered in the panther's slobber. His fur was matted, tangled and sticky and his glow was greatly diminished as a result. He worked determinedly at the fur on his stomach where Tremor had initially struck him. When he cleared away the slobber and began to get his fur all flowing in the right direction again, he noticed something that made him panic. Where Tremors claws had

229

struck him were long ragged scars of dull fur. His eyes went wide and his heart raced. There was no glow to his fur where he'd been clawed. This had to be a trick of his eyes!

He quickly worked on his shoulder and side, licking furiously to get the fur cleaned up and aligned properly. Again he saw dull ragged scars that had no shine. He cleaned furiously and with a greater purpose than he'd ever had before. When his entire body was finally cleaned of Tremors slobber, he'd examined every inch of himself. His stomach, back legs… each place where he'd been mauled was covered in ragged dull scars that failed to shine with a heavenly glow. A quiet panic settled over him but not knowing what else to do, he resumed his bathing. He worked frantically, desperately licking at the scars and praying they would fade. He stayed focused on the scar on his belly, picked just one spot and cleaned it for a long time but it never regained any shine.

He stopped and thought about his predicament. For the first time since Tremor attacked him he became aware of his surroundings. He was still stuck in the clouds at night. It was a terrible feeling but this time he had several things to be grateful for. Tremor had given up on him, he was finally free. He could decide what he wanted to do without any continued assaults. He also knew his gamble to run had resulted in a tremendous victory. His maneuverings had successfully placed the headdress out of sight. With the confusion of the night it was highly unlikely Tremor would stumble on it.

While he groomed he realized he was covered in scars. He would spend the time trying to clean them and see if they would ever start to regain their glow. If they wouldn't then it would be more important than ever for him to make sure the rest of his fur glowed as brightly as possible. Knowing that Tremor could scar them and destroy their glow, Bandit felt an even greater sense of urgency to get back and warn the others as soon as possible.

Despite his pain, when he tried to move he was moving much slower than normal. The more time that passed the better he felt. He would need to be much stronger if he was going to be able to carry the headdress. He still had to find it again and he couldn't do that if he was lost in the dark. Knowing that if he left before dawn he would likely be leaving the headdress behind, helped him feel better about waiting until the morning. When the morning came, he could climb to the top of the nearest cloud and see if he could spot the headdress or another line of yarn and try to make it back to Rainbow Bridge.

Once the first rays of the sun touched the tops of the clouds, Bandit picked the tallest one and started to run towards it. He only made it a few steps before he stumbled and collapsed. Every spot under his scars were weakened and still painful. He hadn't recovered from his injuries enough to run. He was stiff, sore and his body wasn't responding like it normally did. But he couldn't wait any longer to warn his friends.

Determined, he climbed to his feet and decided if he couldn't run he'd walk. It took more time but he managed to make it to the top of the cloud. Once there he looked around. He was disappointed when there were no yarn lines in sight. But hope returned when he spotted the headdress on the other side of the cloud below him. All he had to do was get down the cloud and retrieve it. Once he had the headdress, he could go up to the top of every cloud around him until he spotted a yarn line to guide him back to Feather Dan. He prayed he also wouldn't spot Tremor.

Bandit's gait was slow and steady but he made it down the cloud mountain to the headdress and sat next to it. He gave himself a minute to rest, and then got up to grab the headdress. He clutched on to it, careful not to let the beads bump together, and tried to walk away. He was able to drag the headdress just a few feet before the pain was too great and he was forced to stop. His previous hope was darkened with the realization that he wasn't going to be able to take it with him. He was still too weak and it hurt too much to drag it along. He'd be lucky to get it to the top of the next cloud.

He tried to think about what Sassy would do in this situation. Not having her there to talk to reminded him of how badly he missed her. His worry for her wasn't solving his dilemma though, so he forced his thoughts to stay on the issue at hand. He would have to leave the headdress behind and continue on without it. If he could find his way back before the night he could probably remember how to get back to it. Under the circumstances, that was simply the best he would be able to do.

He made mental notes to himself about where he was, got to his feet and continued to trek up the cloud. When he got to the top he breathed in relief. At the bottom of the other side of that cloud was the familiar yellow yarn he'd seen the day before. He took one last look at the headdress and walked down to the yellow yarn line. He stared at it and tried to decide what direction to go. He realized it didn't matter what direction he chose because he had no idea where he was so he picked a direction and started walking.

As he traveled, he decided that every three clouds he passed he would climb up to the top and look around. He traveled for a long time and climbed up and down many clouds never losing sight of the yellow yarn. While he was walking, he found himself with plenty of time to think. His thoughts turned to what a mess he and Sassy had made. All they wanted to do was have some fun and play with something new. They really never meant for any of this to happen but happen it did. He didn't imagine he'd have many friends left back at Rainbow Bridge by now. Feather Dan was sure to ban both of them from Blankets Mountain and the Feather Time games forever. He couldn't blame Dan if that's what he decided. What he and Sassy did was unforgivable.

It was well into the afternoon before Bandit realized how much time had passed with him following the yarn. He couldn't help but worry that he'd gone the wrong direction and should turn around and retrace his steps. He was mentally and emotionally preparing himself for another night lost in the dark as he climbed to the top of the next cloud. His head snapped up, his heart jumped and for the first time in what felt like an eternity he allowed himself to believe he might just be okay.

Ahead of him, on the horizon and barely visible between two smaller cloud tops was the unmistakable silhouette of Blankets Mountain. He looked behind him and studied the path the yellow yarn line made. He let out a breath he hadn't even realized he'd been holding. The yarn line twisted and turned in between clouds but was, without a doubt, heading directly in the direction of Blankets Mountain.

He was so relieved he teared up and had to take a minute to compose himself before he could continue. He hoped beyond hope that Sassy made it back and they would soon be reunited. He was still too stiff and in too much pain to be able to run but he had a renewed determination in his step and his pace increased as he continued to follow the yarn line home. He found himself smiling and crying at the same time; joy and sadness overcoming him simultaneously. He was going home.

The moment he stepped out from behind the side of the last cloud between him and Blankets Mountain he could hear Grace begin to bark excitedly. He'd never been so happy to hear a dog bark in his life. Although he moved with a severe limp that was almost a hobble he kept his head up as he walked forward. He refused to take his eyes off of Blankets Mountain. He was looking around everywhere, desperately praying he'd spot Sassy and that she had made it home.

Several cats ran out to greet him. He recognized them as Feathers Time team players, but didn't know them personally. They approached him cautiously once they spotted his obvious limp and scars that stood out in a stark dull contrast compared to his normal shine.

The next hour went by like he was in a whirlwind. Sassy appeared out of the crowd and ran up to greet him. Neither one of them spoke a word, none were necessary. They mushed each other hard and hugged each other tight. Bandit ignored the questions that were being asked, too intent on assuring himself that Sassy was okay.

They were escorted the rest of the way to Blankets Mountain. Bandit recognized Feather Dan, Grace, several professors from Cat University and the team leaders from the Feathers Time teams that had gathered around him. He didn't recognize the three sink bath cats. Bandit was bombarded with questions from the clowder of cats. Sassy by his side, he ignored them, intent on reaching Dan.

Eventually one of the professors, George Washington, stopped the commotion and got the gathering organized. Bandit shared as much information as he could remember, including the location of the headdress he'd had to leave behind. He told them how Tremor had demanded information about Rainbow Bridge and what he had told him about it, and how he had tried and failed to kill him. He pointed out the scars where he'd been attacked and about how worried he was that he couldn't make them shine. He told them how he got away from Tremor and how he'd lost the headdress somewhere along the way.

The professors inspected his fur, grave concern obvious in their expressions. But they showed relief at the news that Tremor was unable to kill Bandit. Sassy cried as she listened to Bandit describe how he'd gotten each scar. Bandit knew she felt sorry for him. She tried to help him groom his scars. He knew it was pointless, the shine wouldn't come back.

The other cats took turns filling him in on what had been going on at Blankets Mountain. It warmed his soul to hear how much effort the entire community had put into trying to rescue him. While he was uplifted at what everyone had done to find him and Sassy, he was also plagued with guilt about what harm they had managed to cause. It was their fault that Tremor was here in pet heaven.

Feather Dan decided it was too close to dark to send a team out to retrieve the headdress but that he would lead an expedition to go get it himself in the morning. Bandit hoped he would be feeling better by then so they could go with them. He would just slow them down if he was limited to walking. He'd left at first light that morning. He'd traveled steadily in one direction and now there were just a few hours of light left until dark. He knew he could do it in time if he could run but, at least at the moment, running was out of question and he really had no desire to be away from Rainbow Bridge at night ever again.

Bandit shared his concerns with those gathered. It had taken almost the whole day for him to walk home. Whoever retrieved the headdress had to get and get back before dark.

Feather Dan was quiet and looked thoughtful before he spoke up. "Don't worry Bandit. We'll get it figured out by morning. You need to rest and heal. Leave the rest to us."

"Thank you," Bandit said. His exhaustion was evident and he looked like he was about to collapse.

"Bandit," Dan called, his voice was filled with compassion and understanding. "And Sassy, you too, I want you to stay on Blankets Mountain tonight. It's a very long walk back to Cat Tree City. There's no reason you need to make that journey."

Bandit blinked in disbelief and said, "We don't deserve a spot on Blankets Mountain anymore. I've made it this far. I'll manage to get back to our ledge in Cat Tree City." Humiliated and completely ashamed of himself, Bandit struggled to his feet. With legs wobbling he began to walk in that direction, Sassy helping to support him.

Feather Dan stepped in front of him, blocking his path. "Nonsense," He said, his voice was firm but filled with understanding. "Yes, the two of you made a terrible mistake. There's no denying that."

Bandit dropped his head. Sassy's whiskers drooped and her tail fell between her back legs as she moved up next to her brother allowing him to lean on her. The crowd was silent but all eyes were on them.

"Every one of us," Dan motioned across the crowd, "know that you meant no ill will in the actions you took. Yes, they were reckless but you had no way of knowing what would happen. You made a mistake. That does not mean you are undeserving of our understanding and compassion."

Bandit watched Sassy as she sniffed back a tear. Bandit raised his head and humbly looked Dan in the eyes. Bandit saw Dan's words were sincere. However, guilt weighed on him as all-consuming as the fear he'd felt from Tremor earlier that day.

"Dan," Bandit barely managed to get the word out. He paused and spoke again. "I can barely walk, let alone stand with any of you against Tremor. I'd be in the way. I've done enough harm already. You've already done too much to help us get home. We don't deserve anything…"

"Stop," Dan said firmly. He stepped forward and put his tiny pink nose right up to Bandits. "That's enough and I don't ever want to hear you say you don't deserve anything again. You are our friend, both of you are." He gave Sassy a quick look too. His golden eyes were so filled with love and understanding that Sassy began to cry silent tears.

"We did what was needed to rescue you because you are our friends and we love you. We'd do it again without question. We're going to stand against Tremor and set things right too. But you, your fight is done for now. Please go to the top of Blankets Mountain and take refuge within the Hall of Feathers until this is done. Leroy and Amelia will help you make the climb."

At his words, two sink bath cats stepped forward. One was a blue short-haired domestic cat that Dan introduced as Amelia. The second cat was muscular and long. He had orange and white stripes with white mittens on his feet. Dan said he was named Leroy.

Leroy gazed at Dan with a look that Bandit didn't know exactly how to interpret. It appeared to Bandit that Leroy was pleased with Dan for some reason he didn't understand. He was equally confused when he noticed Amelia quickly wiped a tear from her face before she shared a glance full of hidden meaning with Leroy. Not knowing what to make of it, his thoughts returned to what Dan had said.

Bandit was awed at Dan's words. After all of this, after everything they'd done, had Dan really just invited them into the Hall of Feathers? He looked at Sassy and saw his disbelief mirrored on her face. Surely Dan knew that was where all of this trouble had begun. The Hall of Feathers was where they'd stolen the headdress; where they'd made the biggest mistake of their lives. Dan must have lost his mind if he was even considering allowing them to go back inside the Hall of Feathers. He couldn't be serious could he?

Bandit's gaze traveled to the silent crowd gathered around him and Sassy. None of the other cats were blaming him for what had happened. No one looked mad at them. No one was calling them names or making any accusations. They should be. He deserved their anger. Unbelievably, the entire gathering looked upon them with compassion and love. There wasn't a look of irritation, disappointment or anger on a single face. Was this really happening? He must be awake; he was in too much pain to be asleep and dreaming.

Feeling tears welling up in his eyes and unable to speak, Bandit gently pressed his forehead against Dan's in gratitude. Pain made him move slow but he turned, looked at the hundreds of friends that were there supporting him and Sassy then nodded his thanks. He silently began his slow walk up Blankets Mountain towards the Hall of Feathers.

Leroy and Amelia walked up beside Bandit as he made the climb up Blankets Mountain. They let him lean on them when it was needed, rested when he grew too weary to take another step and gave both him and Sassy words of encouragement along the way.

Chapter 23 – Decision's

Sonic ran as fast as he could. If he were to have enough time to chew through the yarn he was going to have to get some distance between himself and the panther but he faced a dilemma. The yarn was extremely well put together. It was meant to be played and rough housed with so it was thick and sturdy. Chewing through it was going to be tough and take time. As a result he wasn't sure how far ahead he needed to get before he started working on it. If he didn't get far enough ahead, Tremor would come up on him before he was finished. If he got too far ahead, it would be very possible that Blankets Mountain would be visible. If that happened Tremor wouldn't need the yarn to get to Rainbow Bridge anyway.

He counted the towering clouds as he ran. One, two, three, four… It still didn't feel like enough, … Five, six, seven… It still felt like he could feel Tremor breathing down his neck. He studied the yarn as he ran as well, hoping to find a thin spot. Finally when he passed the twelfth cloud he decided to stop. The yarn was just a tiny bit thinner there. He was also becoming increasingly worried about how close he must be getting to Blankets Mountain.

He skidded to a stop, his claws digging into the wispy cloud stuff below him for traction. He hadn't even stopped sliding before he latched his mouth onto the yarn and began working on it. He chewed it, chomped it and tried to grind it between his sharp cat teeth. He gnawed and twisted on it but was very careful not to pull it hard enough for either home or Tremor to notice. He attacked it with everything he had. He was over half way through and felt like he was starting to make some progress as his intuition kept nagging at him that he was running out of time.

Reluctantly, he decided to take a brief break from chewing the yarn and scout for just a minute. He looked around, picked the closest cloud and sprinted to the top. He crouched low, flattened his ears to reduce the profile his head would make against the sunny sky and eased up to take a peak around. When he did he gasped.

He didn't realize just how close he and Flash had gotten to returning home. In the distance, looming on the horizon behind two other clouds was the distinctive and familiar top of Blankets Mountain. It was still far enough away that it just looked like any other cloud and he'd be willing to bet that from here Tremor wouldn't be able to identify it, but there it was nonetheless. Another two or three clouds closer to home and Blankets Mountain would be impossible to miss.

His heart now racing, Sonic looked around intently to see if he could spot the panther. After just a minute scanning the distance and searching along the yellow yarn line he saw movement. It was a couple of clouds away. Instead of focusing intently, Sonic adjusted his vision so that he wasn't focusing on everything. He allowed his vision to blur a bit and waited. He only had to wait for a moment and he caught sight of the movement once again. The direction better identified, he now focused hard on what he'd seen.

Walking out from around a small puff of cloud was unmistakably Tremor. The panther was still following the yarn and heading his way. Fortunately he was still just walking and didn't seem to be in a hurry. Sonic understood the danger though. As large as Tremor was and with his long powerful legs, if he decided to run, he would be able to catch him in just a few minutes. Although frustrated and disappointed, it was obvious that there wasn't going to be enough time to chew through the yarn.

Sonic had to make a decision. The first option he thought of was racing directly to Blankets Mountain so he could warn them that the panther would be there before dark. Second, he could use himself as bait and lure Tremor off in another direction and hope he could get both lost at night in a direction that would take them away from Rainbow Bridge. Lastly, he could circle around and go back to Flash.

Flash had undertaken an enormous task and would be struggling to make progress. Although Sonic hoped that despite dragging the headdress and the yarn, Flash would make it back before dark, he knew the odds were not in his favor. The thought of his friend lost forever was distressing and his heart screamed for him to run and help Flash. Sonic knew that if they were together he could tell him to drop the yarn and together they could drag the headdress back to Blankets Mountain. They would never be able to beat Tremor home, but they would get back not too long after the panther got to Blankets Mountain. At least they'd both be there to help if there was a fight. There was also the possibility that Feather Dan could use the headdress as a weapon to give them the upper hand.

As Sonic debated his options, Tremor was steadily getting closer. Sonic studied him as he moved. He saw those powerful muscles rippling under the glimmering black fur and he shook his head at the sheer size of the panther. Tremor was more dangerous than anyone had believed. He was simply enormous.

Sonic took a deep breath and his jaw set firmly in resolution. He made his decision. He had to warn Blankets Mountain. The upcoming confrontation was inevitable. He would at least give them a little time to get prepared before the battle. Sonic had seen more than he wanted to of the panther. Without a second glance, his mind was made up, he turned and ran toward home.

Despite Blankets Mountain being visible on the horizon, it still took him over an hour to get there. As soon as he rounded the final cloud and Blankets Mountain came fully into view he heard Grace begin to bark. He had expected it, he knew that was her job but the sound echoed far and wide and made him cringe. He immediately spotted Gypsy and the rest of his team on her heels, racing out to greet him.

Sonic ran headlong into his team. He grabbed Ronny, the first teammate he could and said, "Stop Grace! Tremor is not far behind me. Tell her no more barking! She'll just guide him here faster."

Gypsy's eyes went wide. She turned to Ronny and commanded, "Go now!"

Without question or hesitation Ronny spirited away. Fortunately Grace had stopped barking when she was sure the others had seen Sonic. Now they just needed to make sure she stayed quiet. Ronny could see to that.

Gypsy looked to the clouds behind Sonic, "Where's Flash?"

Sonic's face grew taught with stress, "Still on the mission." He looked back to Blankets Mountain and saw Feather Dan as well as all of the other members of what were now considered the leaders of Rainbow Bridge hurrying down to meet with him. "Come on," Sonic said and started running to meet them, "Everyone needs to hear this and we don't have time for me to repeat myself."

As he and his team raced the remaining distance to Blankets Mountain, Sonic looked around him. He'd never seen the place so busy, not ever. There were cats positioned all about as lookouts. There were large squads practicing maneuvers, and other combat tactics. Runners were racing all over the place relaying information where it was needed. It looked like a full scale military training camp. He was astonished at how much had happened since he left that morning. He was impressed.

As all of the leaders assembled, Sonic shared his story. "Tremor is close, very close. There's little chance now that he won't find us. He's following the yellow yarn line."

"Well," Feather Dan said, "At least we know. We even know from where he'll first approach so he won't be able to surprise us."

Sonic nodded in acknowledgement. "Look everyone, Sassy was right. Tremor is an enormous and frightening animal. Until you see him for yourself it's impossible to understand but you need to be prepared for it or that first look will leave you momentarily in shock and unable to react like you normally would."

Dan shook his head. "How long would you estimate until he arrives?"

Sonic let his gaze wander over the group before he spoke, "Tremor will be here before the sun fully sets."

Professor George Washington looked at the sky, let out a long quiet whistle and said. "That gives us two, maybe three hours at best to put our final preparations in place."

Sonic knew from his earlier observations of the activities taking place that things were well underway and he wouldn't be needed. Pulling Gypsy aside, he told her "I'm going back out for Flash. I can't leave him behind. He needs my help if he's going to make it home before dark."

"Very well," Gypsy nodded. "I know better than to argue with you about going back out for Flash, but I can at least send you with some help." Turning to her team, she singled out his remaining team member to help him. "Raven, go with him. Take this end of the yarn with you. Just maybe Tremor won't know what he's looking for and you can get him to circle back the other direction."

With that Sonic and Raven raced away towards the horizon. It took only a minute before they were behind another cloud and out of sight.

~

Dan observed as the rest of the Feathers Time captains jumped into action immediately following Sonic and Raven's departure. They started shouting orders to their teams and to the other cats who had volunteered to fight on the front line. If negotiations failed and it came to a battle, Dan knew every one of them would have an important role to play. Each team member was in charge of thirty five other cats, which the military cats organizing everything were loosely referring to as platoons.

General Bradley, recently voted to be in charge of all combat operations, stepped forward. "We've had very little time to prepare for this." His voice was deep but loud and carried clearly across Blankets Mountain and the open field below it. "Every one of you has pitched in, stepped up, and made me proud for all that we've managed to accomplish so far."

Bradley stopped to survey all of them before continuing. "The time for training, practice and drills is behind us. Now is the time for all of you to remember what you've learned and take your positions. Trust in yourselves and your teams. We will do what needs to be done. Rainbow Bridge will not fall under our watch." With that General Bradley nodded at Feather Dan and Professor George Washington then marched off to take his own position. He exuded confidence and determination to lead them into whatever situation arose. Dan felt he was a good choice to lead them.

Feather Dan nodded back to General Bradley thanked him and then turned his attention to his friends. "Grace," he motioned her to come over. Her bark could be heard a long ways off and they didn't want to make finding Blankets Mountain any easier for Tremor. "No more barking unless it's absolutely necessary."

Grace, wagging her tail, nodded in understanding. "I understand," she said. "I've been in the cat realm a very long time now without getting back to my own. I really have to go check on something. I shouldn't be long though. I promise I'll be as quick as I can."

Dan frowned with worry as he looked at Grace. It was true she had never stayed even close to this long in the cat realm without returning to her home. It was completely unknown what side effects, if any, there could be for her to stay away so long. "Are you feeling okay?" He asked her, his concern for her evident. "Do you want me to send for Doctor Paws or Demi?"

Grace was staring off into the distance, as if she was seeing something that none of them could see. Dan could tell she was only partially listening to him, with her head turned away and one ear cocked. She didn't seem stressed to him, just a little distracted maybe.

She glanced back down at him, gave him a quick lick on top of the head and said, "No, Dan, I'm okay. I really just need to go for a bit and I really can't put it off any longer."

"Sure, Grace." Dan provided his acceptance of her needing to go. "Go do what you need to do and come back to us as quickly as you can. We need you here."

Grace took two fast steps forward eager to be off when Amelia whimpered. Grace stopped in her tracks and turned around to look at Amelia. With a happy gleam in her eye, tail high and wagging she gave a quiet muffled 'woof', ran up to Amelia, rolled her over upside down and gave her several wet kisses on her belly.

"Grace!" Amelia shouted in surprise. "Now is NOT the time to be playing and giving me the pit maneuver!"

Grace chuckled then as Amelia got back to her feet. Grace took the opportunity to nuzzle Amelia's neck. "I'll be back before you have a chance to leave. Promise me you'll be careful while I'm gone."

Amelia nodded, "Well of course I will." She pointed over at Binx, "That's the one you should be telling to be careful."

Grace chuckled, turned and ran off as fast as she could. Dan and Amelia watched her go. Just as she got to the edge of the nearest cloud and was about to run behind it she simply vanished.

Amelia's eyes misted over and she took a deep breath. Dan knew she was already missing Grace. Grace was a wonderful friend. He didn't blame Amelia for missing her the second she was out of sight. He already missed her steady, confident, and happy personality being by his side.

Feather Dan, accustomed to Grace vanishing like that turned his attention to other matters. He decided it was time to check on Remy and Bumper, the goat. He ran up Blankets Mountain, where he knew he'd find them. They had remained on lookout during the conversation below and needed to be apprised of the situation. At the top, he spotted them up at the highest spot, which provided a good view of the surrounding area and was his favorite spot for that very reason.

Dan was surprised to see that Remy was still riding on Bumper's back. Not only was the goat not complaining but the two of them were obviously having a great time together. Their system of communication had continued to develop throughout their time together. Dan had been making visits to keep tabs on their progress. Bumper had learned quite a bit of the cat language and Remy was picking up goat fast. He wondered if Remy was a natural linguist and how many other languages he might know.

The two of them had selected a few spots at the top of Blankets Mountain that they kept running back and forth between. Dan knew each spot had a different vantage point of not only Blankets Mountain but the landscape below. Each spot also had blanket formations and outcroppings that made for ideal spots to charge down. Bumper had made several practice charges and Dan was impressed at how much speed they could pick up in a very short time. If they had to charge the panther it would certainly knock him off his feet. How Remy stayed balanced on Bumpers back the entire time and made it look effortless at that, was simply beyond Dan's comprehension.

When Remy and the goat had started working as a team, Leroy and Amelia had agreed to assume responsibility for Binx. They were used to keeping an eye out for him. Binx seemed fascinated by how much was going on that he mostly ran in circles checking things out and he didn't stray far away.

Now that things were getting more serious, Leroy, Binx and Amelia stayed close to Feather Dan. They had agreed that as long as they were together they'd be able to work as a team. If things went bad and an opportunity presented itself they were prepared to strike as one.

Amelia paced back and forth, over and over again. She kept mumbling to herself about how she was a lover, not a fighter. She mumbled that she was too delicate to be jumping on giant panthers. She mumbled more than once about things being terrifying and she wanted to go into the Hall of Feathers and hide with Bandit and Sassy. Dan knew that despite her fear, she could be a fierce fighter when cornered. She would always prefer not to engage in any kind of aggression. He knew this was taking its toll on her and without Grace here to keep her steady, he'd have to keep a close eye on her.

"Look Amelia," Leroy reminded her, "how many times have you flattened Binx with one hit when he gets to rough housing too much?"

She looked irritated and flicked her tail, "More times than I want to remember." She said as she gave Binx a dirty look.

"Please calm down, Amelia," Leroy continued. "You're the one who has those huge paws and extra toes. That's like having a superpower."

Amelia snorted, she didn't agree. "I don't plan on getting close enough to Tremor to have to use them."

While Leroy tried to keep an eye on Binx and stave off Amelia's panic, Dan was surveying everything. The team captains were nearly finished getting their squads in order. The field generals had taken up positions along the sides of Blankets Mountain where the orders they shouted would be heard. Despite the impending danger the entire assembly, minus Amelia, was acting with confidence. Dan felt a calmness settle over Rainbow Bridge as they waited to see what would unfold.

Dan, sensing he was being watched, glanced back towards Cat Tree City. He spotted Aristotle, along with all of the remaining professors who were not already present, on the other side of Blankets Mountain quickly approaching him. Aristotle waved to him in a friendly greeting. Dan was surprised to see him. Aristotle seldom left his cat tree, so his visits were an incredibly rare occurrence.

As they came up Dan asked, "Welcome Aristotle! It's my honor to have you here."

"Thank you Feather Dan. I should visit you here more often. The view is breathtaking and the tranquility here is unmatched." Aristotle responded with genuine warmth.

"You're welcome any time, my friend," Dan looked at all of them inquisitively. "Wouldn't it be safer if you observed from your ledge in Cat Tree City? I'm sure you'd have a decent view from up there."

"Oh yes," Aristotle agreed. "I have a marvelous view of everything from up there. But up there simply isn't right here now is it?"

Dan was confused. Aristotle and a few of the other professors chuckled in a friendly way. "Feather Dan, you're truly remarkable. You only see what needs to be done and aren't weighed down by the rest."

Dan looked even more confused. Had he missed something? It would be terrible if he'd missed a solution that could have avoided this entire pending conflict.

"History Dan," Aristotle stated. "We're in the midst of history being made. This is something we must witness up close for ourselves. This is a rare moment in time. It is quite possibly the rarest moment ever to happen at Rainbow Bridge. Stories from today will be told for generations… perhaps for as long as Rainbow Bridge exits."

The excitement and anticipation he saw in Aristotle as well as all of the gathered professors confused him. Dan didn't care much about history or stories. He cared about making sure everything got back to being right again. He cared about making sure that when his mum and dad came to find him at the Rainbow Bridge that it would be safe for them to do so. He cared about that the most. But his concern wasn't just for his family. He felt a sense of responsibility to all of the humans of every cat here.

This was his Blankets Mountain. If he hadn't somehow summoned it, the headdress might never have been discovered. As far as he was concerned he hoped history would leave him out of it and just let things go back to the way they were supposed to be.

Aristotle, carefully studying Dan and looking into his golden eyes, took a moment to read Dan. Resting his paw on Dan's shoulder he looked at him and their eyes locked. His voice turned serious and respectful as he said, "And that, my young friend, is why this is happening now. The headdress was surely there all along."

Dan was surprised Aristotle knew exactly where his thoughts had been. Was he that easy to read? Or was Aristotle just that wise? Before he could ponder it further, Aristotle interrupted his thoughts.

"At some point it would have come to the surface. There are many of us here who believe that this day was preordained. We have faith that it happened with you because it is you who have the heart to make the right decisions. We believe it will be because of you, that we will carry the day."

Dan felt lightheaded as Aristotle's words swam in his head. What he was saying instinctively felt right but a sense of unease began to creep back into his thoughts. He was overlooking something important. Unfortunately, Aristotle and the other professors were missing it as well. Dan felt sure it was something terribly important but Dan had no idea what it was. The sudden sound of Professor George Washington's loud booming voice broke Dan free from his thoughts.

"Hello, my distinguished colleagues!" Professor Washington shuffled up front and center to stand behind Dan. Professor Dimension was close on his heels. She took one look at Dan and Dan could tell she didn't like what she saw. She moved beside him and gave him a gentle nudge to let him know things were okay. He appreciated her concern, but didn't like making her worry unnecessarily.

"Yes, Professor Simon," Washington was answering a question from another professor that Dan, who was still lost in his thoughts, hadn't even heard asked. "We still believe that Tremor doesn't know that we can't hurt him. We're hoping that as long as he believes he could be in danger as well, that he'll be more willing to negotiate with us. Surely we can convince him that Rainbow Bridge is simply too boring a place for one as mighty as he." With that, the professors broke off to speak amongst themselves and Dan took the opportunity to get away from being dragged into their academic discussions. He wasn't surprised when Demi followed after him and stayed close.

"I heard what Aristotle said, Dan." Her voice was soothing and just listening to her helped Dan to relax a bit. "Don't listen too much to their mumbo jumbo. They've been around for a long time, and they got way too "people book smart" while they were on Earth. Some of them are a bit too bored and looking for a good story to witness."

Dan nodded, he appreciated her words but the conversation with Aristotle still left him feeling unsettled. "I know Demi, and thank you. But…" Dan hesitated to verbalize his emotions and what he'd sensed.

"But what, Dan?" Demi asked concern in her voice, "I know there's something you aren't saying. What is it?" Demi slowed to a halt and Dan stopped with her.

Dan shook his head. It was a confusing sensation and he didn't quite know how to put it into words that anyone could understand. "I've got a terrible feeling that there's just something that's not quite right. There's something we've missed and it's important."

She put her paw on his cheek and turned his head to face her. Her bright blue eyes looked into his bright golden eyes and they stared at each other for a moment. "I can sense it too. Well actually, I sense it through you…" Demi flicked her cotton white tail. "It's confusing to explain. I deal with quantum physics and most of that doesn't make much sense either. Ugh." Demi shook her head, "I'll just get both of us confused if I start talking about that." She took a couple of steps away, turned around and walked back up to Dan.

Dan waited for her to gather her thoughts. He knew she cared about him and wanted to help. She often helped him organize his own thoughts and sometimes gave him clues or helpful advice to solve his own problems. It was worth waiting to see what she had to say.

"Look," she said firmly, "You just do what you do. Do what feels right. Don't question your instincts. I've seen very few cats with such a well-developed sixth sense and I've never seen even one with such a good heart. I know you'll know what to do. I trust in you. Now you trust in yourself. And trust in everyone else too." Demi waved her arms around, "Look at this Dan! Look at everyone. You're not alone. All of Rainbow Bridge stands together and they're following you. They're not following Aristotle or the generals or professors. They're following you. And you know why?"

Dan was staring at her, his eyes wide, his jaw open and his heart singing. He felt his worry fading away as her words sank in. The light, hope and trust in the world were returning to him. Demi asked him again, "Do you know why everyone is following you and nobody else?"

Demi answered for him. "It's because they see what I see. That you don't see it is why we follow you. Feather Dan it's because none of us have ever met someone with a heart and soul as pure as yours."

Dan didn't know what to say so he just stared at Demi. Demi stared back at him, waiting for some kind of response. When Dan didn't respond quickly enough, she stepped forward, bumped her head with his forehead and kissed him on the cheek. She held the kiss for just a moment then leaned forward and whispered in his ear, "Feather Dan… Just be yourself and all of this will turn out okay."

"Oooooh!" Binx, pointing at Dan and hopping up and down excitedly started yelling loudly, "Dan's got a girlfriend! Dan's got a girlfriend!"

Startled, Dan and Demi jumped in surprise. Dan had forgotten Binx was around. Dan glanced at Binx as he broke out in a fit of giggles, drawing attention with his antics. Binx had successfully ruined the moment, but Demi's kind words lingered instilling Dan with confidence. Dan returned his attention to Demi. He watched in wonder as her white cheeks flushed pink in embarrassment. He thought she looked lovely, she always did. Dan found himself even more pleased to have her attention when she leaned in and touched noses with Dan affectionately.

She gave Binx an ugly look and fussed at him, "Hush you!" She started to walk off, back towards the other professors. Blushing bright red himself, Dan turned back around and realized all of his friends had been following right behind him during his conversation with Demi. Not just Binx had heard what Demi said. Binx was still giggling when Demi passed him. When no one could see, she flashed Dan a quick wink and a smile, playfully ruffled the fur on the top of Binx's head and kept on going.

Amelia was the first to speak, "Well Dan! Look at you mister, aren't you quite the smoothie!"

Leroy was grinning too but was enough of a gentleman to keep quiet. Dan knew better than to encourage Amelia. He didn't say a word to her. He just started walking back up towards the top of Blankets Mountain. The others fell in behind him.

He heard a soft swat then Amelia whisper "You keep your mouth shut, Binx. That was a very sweet moment and you better not try to ruin it."

As they passed by gathered professors, Doctor Paws could be heard updating them that while Bandit's pain was gradually decreasing, his scars were unchanged. It looked like those were going to be permanent and his glow would be forever diminished.

Dan hoped that wasn't the case. He felt bad for Bandit. No one deserved to be that permanently branded for one mistake.

"Binx!" Leroy yelled, "What is it?"

Leroy's yell caught Dan's immediate attention. He turned his head to see Leroy watching Binx. He saw Binx jump up and down and then stop to stare intently out into the clouds, his orange tipped oversize ears perked and pivoting around searching for something. His pupils went wide, his cheeks got puffy and his tail poofed.

"What's wrong?" Dan heard Leroy demand, clearly alarmed by Binx's actions.

Binx responded in a very serious tone, "I heard it."

Dan saw the fur on Leroy's neck stand on edge. He didn't have to ask what it was that Binx heard. Without a doubt it was the panther.

"It did it again! It's a strange snarling screaming noise." Binx informed them. Binx pointed in the direction the sound had come from.

Amelia spotted it and she gasped. Tremor was still a few clouds away but there he was. He was standing on the top of a cloud in the distance. Dan focused on it. Although Tremor was too far away to see them clearly, Dan knew he was looking right at them.

Dan heard General Bradley telling all the platoons to get ready. He'd already seen to it that everyone was in place and ready to carry out their instructions.

What they'd been dreading was finally here. Dan saw Tremors tail thrash before he took one giant leap down the cloud and disappeared again. A few moments later he showed up on top of the next cloud. He was running at full speed and Dan knew he would get to them in just a few minutes.

Chapter 24 – Negotiations

Tremor charged across the landscape. His massive muscular frame appearing at the top of clouds then disappearing again as he descended. Each time he reappeared he knew he looked bigger and more imposing to the house cats watching his approach. As he topped the final cloud between him and Blankets Mountain he quit running and proceeded with a slow deliberate pace. He surveyed everything before him.

Standing between him and a tall and wide cloud formation, thousands of house cats were lined up and organized into pathetic formations as if they intended to stand against him. The tall cloud was covered with so many cats it gave the illusion that the Mountain was breathing. This had to be the Blankets Mountain that Bandit had described. The yellow yarn had led him right to it. Tremor studied his weak opponents with an experienced eye before he took in the rest of his new domain. Beyond Blankets Mountain was a large sprawling city made of thousands of cat trees, just as Bandit had described. Some of the cat trees reached farther into the sky than the real trees in the jungle from which he'd come. The city was more impressive than he'd anticipated. In a strange way he was reminded of home. Perhaps these house cats would prove useful after all. Beyond the city he could see a steady multi-hued light that must be the Rainbow Bridge. He was going to enjoy owning all of it.

Tremor stalked forward with deliberately slow steps giving them time to bask in the glory of his presence. To drink him in and realize they were his to do with as he pleased. He was their new master. There would be no option for them but to serve him. He assessed the assembly before him. He admired their level of organization and that they had not run when he'd first appeared. But they were hardly worthy subjects. They did not hunt. That was unacceptable.

Once he stepped to within pouncing distance of the first line of defenders he stopped. Knowing he was going to have to make an example of them he took a moment to gaze into the eyes of those cats in the front line. Very soon they will know true pain. They would be the first to feel his wrath. He could see tremendous fear in their eyes but he also saw a fierce determination. He had a great deal of respect for their courage and acknowledged to himself that it was possible they would make worthy servants once they were broken and bowed to his will, of course.

Tremor stood before them, his size dwarfing those nearest to him. As his gaze looked into their eyes, not one cat flinched or made a sound. Tremor stood still, knowing the silence was menacing, letting the tension continue building. Their preparations were for nothing. They could not defeat him. They had no chance against his mighty claws. They were pathetic and weak, just like Bandit.

A loud voice carried clearly to where Tremor stood. He pinpointed it as coming from the top of Blankets Mountain. One of the house cats was daring to speak to him. It looked old, hardly a threat to him. "Tremor, my name is Aristotle. We welcome you to Rainbow Bridge as our guest. We understand how confusing this landscape must be to you. We would be honored if you would grace us with the opportunity to speak with one another."

Tremor snorted, a burst of mocking laughter erupting from him. He looked up to the top of Blankets Mountain in amusement. He could see several cats standing on the edge looking down. So be it. It begins now. He will teach them the true meaning of fear. Slowly he turned to the side and began to pace back and forth in front of several squads, intentionally unsheathing his claws so the closest troops could see them. Most were hardly bigger than his paw. Let them see how magnificent and powerful he was.

He looked up and spotted Aristotle standing slightly in front of the others. "Yes, old one. We do need to talk. Surely you realize that I am now your new master. I am making several changes immediately and all of you need to learn the new rules. If you fail to follow my rules there will be consequences. It's best you learn them quickly and obey."

Aristotle spoke up again, "Tremor, there are no rulers at Rainbow Bridge. Everyone is honored and respected equally here. Rainbow Bridge serves a greater purpose than any one of us and we are all here to fulfill that purpose. There is nothing here to rule over. There is no treasure, nothing to covet. Here there is only love."

Tremor stopped his pacing and looked up to Aristotle. He squinted but couldn't make out Aristotle's eyes from that distance. "You, old one, are very wrong." Tremors voice was deep, a bit of growl creeping through yet loud enough to be heard by all. "You were all weak in life and you are weak in death as well. Your kind has brought shame to the feline name. Among the wild animals you are laughed at and mocked as weak and pathetic house cats. Domesticated to serve man, you are a disgrace. Great predators, like me, have to endure the shame you have brought to our kind."

Tremor looked back down to the army assembled before him and his voice full of contempt he addressed them as well. "You were weak in life. That cannot be changed." He cocked his head and a wicked gleam sparkled from his eyes. "But you don't have to be weak in death. You can learn the ways of your ancestors. You can remember the true thrill of the hunt. Feel the true power of your claws and teeth when used the way they were meant to be used." Tremors voice rose with excitement. "You can experience the bloodlust you were denied in life. You can awaken that part of you that is a true feline and become a true predator." Tremor was breathing hard in his excitement, but his voice remained steady as he continued. "Your days of being weak are over. I'll make sure of that. You will hate me for a time," He hesitated and nodded to let his words sink in before he finished, "but once you become an awakened predator you will learn to respect me for the gift I will have given to you."

Tremors words were met with silence. He could feel the uneasiness settling into the army in front of him like a fog descending in the night to send shivers of uncertainty and fear to all of those assembled before him. Like scared prey, they no doubt felt the predator in their midst. He waited for the fear to cause the first of them to run in terror. The first glimpse of motion he noticed came instead from the top of Blankets Mountain. He looked up eagerly looking forward to whatever came next.

A small orange striped cat with large eyes stepped forward. Tremor suspected from what Bandit had told him that this would be the famous and respected Feather Dan. He was finally able to get a look at their so-called leader. He looked as weak as he expected him to look. The new cat was shaking his head in bewilderment as he stepped up next to Aristotle. He looked down and Tremor could feel the weight of those soft eyes looking at him. It was the first uneasy feeling he'd gotten since he arrived. It felt more like the small orange cat was looking into his soul. Well, Tremor chuckled as he thought, let the little one have a look into the soul of his new master. He'd know he was already defeated before this even began.

Feather Dan looked down at him and said, without a hint of fear or discomfort, "Yeah, that's not really going to work for us Tremor. Our purpose for being here is something you don't understand. You've never felt the love of a human. It's something you'll never be able to change. It wouldn't matter what you did to us."

Dan paused before continuing, "You see, Tremor, something that wild animals don't know is this. We, as well as a very select few other animals, are blessed to have a soul connection with our humans. We chose them." Feather Dan stopped as if to consider his next words. "They did not domesticate us as is commonly believed. The truth is we helped to domesticate them. We teach them to feel love for something tiny, helpless and completely different than themselves. They learn compassion for those weaker than themselves. In doing so, humans also learn to respect and understand animals that are stronger than themselves. They gain empathy and less fear of all animals, to see the world differently as something that belongs not to just them."

Feather Dan stopped and gazed calmly at him. Tremor recognized that the mood had changed as if the words had shined a light to chase away the fog and any lingering fear that Tremor had been able to instill. Tremor looked at the assembled cats against him. They appeared calm and at peace. Irritated and surprised at the sudden turn of events, Tremor was debating his next move and snarled in frustration just as Dan continued speaking.

"Do you not understand what would have happened without us?" Tremor could feel Dan's gaze on him as he asked the question. When he didn't answer Dan continued, "We showed them that animals love their young just as people do. We showed them that love could be felt mutually among all species great and small. Without those lessons the humans would have had no reason to allow the larger of our kind to exist on Earth. Without compassion they would have hunted down every feline and every other animal that was a threat to them and wiped them from existence."

Tremor laughed a giant belly laugh that echoed across the clouds as well as Cat Tree City. He laughed for a long time at their audacity to think of themselves as heroes of weak pathetic humans. Humans had no claws, no teeth. He wasn't sure which was more absurd, the story he'd just heard or the fact that everyone here seemed to believe such nonsense. It took him a moment to gain his composure and when he did he looked across the army of cats. He was surprised at what he saw. Reverence, conviction, and pride radiated from every cat within sight. They still had not said one word or given any indication of doing anything about resisting him. They sat in their formations and just looked at him.

Tremors patience gave out all at once. He wasn't finding any of this amusing anymore. It was becoming obvious that he was going to have to do this the hard way and that, he believed, was for the best. They would need to experience his strength and witness the true ability of a predator before they would be able to discard this fairy tale nonsense and embrace their new reality.

The old cat, Aristotle, spoke once again, "Tremor, this isn't your world. You will not find happiness here. All you have to do to go home is to bite on the feather collar that is around your neck. Do that and you'll be right back where you were before you showed up here. Go! Go home, return to your jungle. Go there and be what you are."

Tremor looked up, his lips twisting into a smirk. He raised a paw, flicked at his feather collar with a claw and said, "Good to know about the collar."

Tremor lowered his paw and firmly planted his feet. Lowering his gaze from Aristotle he glared at the army before him. He could feel his bloodlust rising, creeping into his eyes. Tremor snarled and his voice low and threatening, "So be it. You will be made to learn. Let the lessons begin!"

Tremor let out a terrifying battle scream and leapt into the middle of the squad closest to him. The battle had begun. This pleased Tremor. Words were wasted on the weak minded. They learned best from action.

Chapter 25 – War

Tremor moved faster than anyone would have expected. His claws were everywhere; slashing, stabbing and swatting. He roared and growled as he picked up cats with his mouth and flung them away. He decimated the first squad in seconds. All thirty five cats were down. Most writhed in pain while others lay unconscious.

Once the initial shock of Tremor's sudden and fierce attack wore off the cat army sprang into action. They began running, forming up behind each other. He thought their movements resembled a massive snake uncoiling. That was unexpected. In only a moment they were running a circular pattern around Tremor. Keeping their distance, they circled waiting for him to make his next move.

Tremor turned to advance on a squad at his left. He was tracking them with his eyes and knew that as fast as they were running he'd have to aim in front of them to strike where he wanted. As he crouched and began to make his move the squad he'd targeted unexpectedly broke ranks. That squad and three others all charged at him at once. They began zigging and zagging in between each other the closer they got, making it difficult for him to select a single target. Tremor roared in frustration. Tremor was not used to fighting this kind of coordinated attack from a large group of much weaker animals. They were aggravatingly persistent in evading him. Before he could prevent it, they were racing under his legs. Tremor tripped over them, staggered and fell on his left side. The cats that had just tripped him quickly retreated and rejoined the formation before he could swat them. The groups of cats resumed circling him, staying out of his reach. He knew they were waiting for another opportunity to strike at him. He had enough of being on the defensive. He needed to teach them a lesson.

Angered, Tremor got to his feet, roared and leapt blindly into the circling army. He caught the tail end of another squad. He landed directly on them and his claws went to work. More cats were quickly tossed through the air. Five more lay motionless on the ground, joining the earlier squad he had decimated and put out of commission. He roared in triumph. He was determined to make them all pay.

The squad behind the one he'd attacked struck back. They launched themselves into Tremor's side. The thirty five cats weren't enough to knock him down but they were enough to distract him. He didn't see the next squad approaching from behind and as he went to attack he was once again tripped up. He growled in frustration as he staggered falling onto his left side again.

Tremor went with the fall and let gravity work for him. He wanted to crush some of them beneath him, but they were too fast and zipped away out of his reach. He rolled over, sprung up and without hesitation charged directly at the closest squad in front of him. The house cats were much quicker than he'd imagined they could be. Before he reached his first target, two squads rushed him, got under him and tripped up his back legs. His legs kicked frantically as he tried to regain his balance and he felt a couple of cats get caught under his claws. He smiled knowing it would be a long time before they got up again.

When he got to his feet he assessed the situation again. He was getting irritated, but he wasn't mad, not yet anyway. He was grudgingly impressed that these house cats had managed to find any way to mount any kind of a defense against him. Tremor wasn't a fool. He had survived for years in the wild as the top predator in his jungle not only because of his incredible physical abilities but mostly for his intellect and ability to adapt. He was done playing the game they had started. It was time to change things up. It was time for them to play under his rules.

He took a giant leap and landed outside of the encircling army. When he glanced behind him the army had slowed its pace but not stopped. They were obviously waiting for orders from someone on how to respond. If he could eliminate the leader the army would fall into confusion and he could end this much quicker. Taking advantage of their hesitation, he made three more great leaps in rapid succession before landing at the base of Blankets Mountain. He looked up and saw a small group at the top staring down at him. He snarled, showing his fangs then roared in challenge. Aristotle, Feather Dan and whoever else stood beside them was now his primary target.

Blankets Mountain was already swarming with so many cats it didn't seem possible one more could squeeze on yet somehow cats began forming up in front of him, more effectively blocking his path. There were thousands of them. It was more animals than he'd ever seen before. Each one of them looked at him without fear and boldly stood between him and his destination. He shrugged, leapt forward and went to work. Within just a few moments he had cut down nearly one hundred cats and was creating his own path forward. Tremor was steadily moving up Blankets Mountain.

Tremor was dumbfounded at this new strategy the cats were deploying. They did nothing but continue to file in front of him to obstruct his path. He kept swiping at them and tossing them aside with his huge paws. He'd swipe aside ten, get a half step forward and have to stop to attack again. They refused to run, determined to slow him from reaching the top. Tremor had been attacking non-stop for so long that he felt himself beginning to tire. That's when he realized what their true strategy was. He had to admit that their persistence was starting to pay off.

The cats were not trying to attack him. They just swarmed him and moved to block his way up the mountain. Tremor stopped his assault for a moment to reassess the situation. He'd made it about a quarter of the way up Blankets Mountain. It was obvious that the group at the top consisted of their leaders. They had been observing the entire time but had done nothing to join the battle. He still hadn't found the signal caller who he believed was the key to ending the fight. Whoever that was had successfully avoided his detection. But it was only a matter of time and that time was fast approaching. The night was coming and he wanted to sit as the new king of Blankets Mountain before dark.

As he studied the cats around him he could tell they were tightening their ranks. They were attempting to make it even harder to get through them. He knew he could shred them all but it would take time he didn't want to spend letting them dictate how the battle would play out. He didn't have to battle each cat between him and the top when there was a quicker way. Leaping over them would be much easier and vastly quicker.

He crouched, looked up at the top and began to calculate how many jumps it would take to reach that small group. When he made the first leap there was a collective gasp of surprise from the cats around him. Their mistake had been thinking he would just keep charging forward. His jump took him easily a dozen yards up the mountain. As he sailed above them he nearly laughed at the look of shock on the cats below.

When he landed he landed hard, crushing and clawing at any cats under or near him. He made a savage display of the ones he got his claws on. However, the army of cats didn't hesitate. They surged in from all sides trying to fill the void and get under his feet. He leaped again and made short work of the cats that were unfortunate enough to be where he landed. Several savage swipes of his claws and he'd cleared enough room to jump again. Yes, he was pleased with himself.

At this rate he'd be at the top well before dark. He was looking forward to dealing with their leaders. He knew once they were gone the others would more than likely fall into line. The cat army would have an uphill battle and at that point the logistics of the battle would change when he had the higher ground. He was finally close enough to lock eyes with Aristotle as he prepared to make another jump. He'd give him a more proper jungle style welcome shortly.

Chapter 26 – The Battle of Blankets Mountain

Feather Dan and Aristotle stood side by side looking down an overlook at the top of Blankets Mountain. Leroy, Amelia and Binx were on a neighboring ledge doing the same. Remy, still riding on Bumper's back, had run up to a higher spot. The Battle for Blankets Mountain was playing out below them. It was a nightmarish and savage thing to witness. The fighting part of the battle was entirely one sided and Tremor was leaving piles of wounded everywhere he went. Feather Dan felt terrible for all of the cats who were getting mauled. Tremor wasn't holding back and even from his high vantage point Dan could see the glow diminish from those who'd been caught in the path of destruction.

From a strictly strategic perspective the battle seemed to be going well. The squad tactics they'd formulated and practiced so hard on were working exactly as they had hoped. The strategy had been to wear Tremor out. The harder and longer he had to fight the more tired he would become. Eventually they hoped that he would need a rest and stop fighting. That would provide them with another opportunity to talk with him. They hoped that once he was exhausted and unsuccessful that they could speak rationally with him and convince him to just go home.

If he still wouldn't leave then they would press their attack in full. Without a chance to physically recover he should become so exhausted that he would collapse. If they could wear him out to that extent the next stage of the plan was to pile on and try to get his feather collar off. Once they had it all they had to do was sneak it into his mouth. The next bite he took and poof he'd unknowingly send himself home.

After Tremor had grown frustrated by the circling army and jumped free of them, they all waited to see how long it would be before exhaustion would claim him. By the time he was starting to fight his way up Blankets Mountain it looked like the plan was working. He was stopping to pause and his swings were getting slower each time. Heaven cats filed in, keeping up their strategy of making him fight for every step. Each swipe to swat cats out of his way to take a step forward was sapping his energy and he wasn't making much forward progress.

But Dan knew Tremor was an intelligent opponent and could change his tactics in ways they hadn't anticipated. His fears were realized when Tremor began leaping up the mountain. His jumps were expending much less energy than was the constant battling. He was also making much faster progress without wasting his time in battle. At the pace he was going all of the companions would be greeting Tremor face to face at the top of Blankets Mountain shortly. Dan looked around to check the placement of his companions and make sure they were all ready.

Remy and Bumper had found a place between two large blanket outcroppings at the very top of Blankets Mountain. Dan knew the spot served as the perfect lookout position, depending on which way Bumper turned he had a three hundred and sixty degree field of view of the entire Mountain and area below it. He'd scouted it out earlier with Remy, so he knew Remy could also see several of the other army officer cats who would flash him signals. He would then flash those signals back to the designated cats embedded into the center of the squads of cats, who in turn verbally relay the command signal to their squad. This helped prevent Tremor from detecting how they were coordinating their attacks. If all the cats were looking at Remy to know what to do, Tremor would easily catch on. Dan knew their best advantage was Tremor's underestimation of what they were capable of. Having lived his life in a jungle and not learned side-by-side with humans, he would have a distinct disadvantage of their large scale war tactics and strategy.

Once Tremor had leapt over the encircling army that was being led by the Feathers Time teams, Remy began sending them signals to engage a secondary strategy. That portion of the army reorganized and made its way around the other side of Blankets Mountain. They were now climbing up it as fast as they could. They were preparing to get above Tremor then circle down to him and intercept him. The timing would be crucial. They had to get into position so they could build enough momentum and hit him just at the right moment. Remy, mounted on Bumper, would attack right behind them with a follow up strike to knock Tremor off balance. Their objective then was to try to either push or have momentum carry Tremor back down to the bottom of the mountain. If he had to repeat the entire fight to reach the top of Blankets Mountain again, that should be enough to force him to stop and rest.

Much to Dan's dismay, Tremor was making incredible progress. Remy flashed frantic signals to the Feather Time teams encouraging them to hurry. Dan knew they needed to get into their attack positions before launching the assault or they wouldn't have enough momentum to carry Tremor back down the Mountain. Feather Dan shared a look with Remy. It was obvious Tremor would be at the top before they would be able to strike. There wasn't enough time for them to get in place.

General Bradley turned to Dan. "We need more time for them to get into place. We have to stall. Five minutes should be enough."

Feather Dan nodded in understanding at Remy then turned to his friends. "It's going to be up to us to hold him off. The Feathers Time teams need more time to get into position. It's our job to make sure they get it."

Amelia was all but in a complete panic. She was running back and forth frantically and begging for Grace to hurry up and get back. Binx had been jumping up and down with excitement during the entire engagement. His whiskers were pushed forward, his white cheeks were puffed out and his orange striped tail had poofed out like a Christmas tree again. Leroy was sitting nearby, but not paying attention to Binx. Aristotle had backed up and was trying to blend in with his surroundings.

"Brace yourselves," Dan said, his orange tail held high and confident, his voice steady. "We just need to dodge his attacks long enough to buy the others a little time."

Tremor was only three jumps away from making it to them and was in clear view of all of them. Dan could see the rage in his eyes and the closer he got the more imposing he looked. Sassy and Bandit had been right about how terrifying he was up close. He thought he was prepared for it, but seeing Tremor this close he knew he could never have been prepared for just how terrifying and massive he was.

Leroy looked Tremor over and nodded in acceptance of what was likely going to be a bad day. He kept a stoic smile on his face as he said, "Alright then big fella let's get this done."

Together, Dan, Amelia, Leroy and Binx walked ahead, protectively placing the other cats behind them by several yards. Dan knew they would need to keep Tremor close enough to the center of the top of Blankets Mountain so the others could keep out of danger, escaping if they needed to.

Tremor made his final launch. The Mountain around them shuddered when he landed right in front of them. He carefully looked over the group. Snarling, his gaze settled on Dan, "You must be Feather Dan. I have plans for you. Yield the fight. Your entire community, let alone this pathetic group, can't stop me. Show me

271

some of that wisdom I've heard so much about. Accept what is to come."

Dan had never in his life felt smaller standing in front of anything before. He was small for a cat to start with and compared to Tremor he was barely larger than one of his massive paws. But Tremor's words had given Dan an idea and his ears perked up with interest. If Tremor was the type to gloat and brag then Dan would encourage him. If he could keep him talking long enough they might be able to avoid a physical conflict all together.

Dan lowered his head for a moment and scratched his chin while his mind raced for ways to drag out this coming conversation. "Nice to meet you Tremor, my name is Feather Dan. Although you already figured that out I do still believe in polite introductions. First impressions are important after all."

Tremor looked irritated but before he could speak Dan continued, "I have to ask since I haven't heard yet. What exactly are your plans for me?"

Tremor snorted in amusement and his eyes gleamed as they looked hungrily at Dan. "You will be my court jester. You will dance and do every foolish thing you can think of to entertain me and make me laugh. If you don't, you'll get the claws."

"Wow!" Binx interjected. "That sounds like a fun job! Well except for the claws that is… I do that all the time and I'm really good at it too. If Dan doesn't want to do that I could…" Binx's words were interrupted by a strong swat on the back of the head from Leroy.

Dan did his best to ignore Binx's antics, remaining focused on Tremor. Tremor gave Binx a disgusted look. Tremor unsheathed his deadly claws which he used to rip at the ground with ease. Dan knew the twins hadn't exaggerated about those claws either. They looked very sharp and painful. He remembered all the scars on Bandit's body and shivered. Dan forced himself to take his eyes off of Tremors claws and look back up and into his eyes. "What are your plans for Rainbow Bridge?"

Tremors attention snapped back to Dan immediately. "This pathetic defense you've brought against me is pointless. You lost before the battle even began. You can't defeat me. It's no use trying, it only prolongs the inevitable. Submit to me now if you want to avoid more pain. I will not make this offer again. You'd be wise to take it."

Dan nodded at him in agreement, "That's surely true but what of my question? What are your plans for Rainbow Bridge?"

"As your new ruler I will see to it that you all learn what it is to be a true predator." Dan saw Tremors eyes gleam with anticipation of setting his plans into motion. "There will be no more escorting your humans to some magical place. You will all have to fight one another and win my blessings to do that. The greatest of predators will earn such honors. Those who fall short will be expelled into the clouds to wander the nights alone forever. When the banished ones humans cross, should they manage to find their way here, they will be hunted to provide sport and standing among the remaining fighters."

No sooner had Tremor finished telling Dan about his plans than the Feathers Time teams charged around the top of Blankets Mountain. They were going at full speed but moving silently. Tremor was so caught up in his bragging that he never saw them coming until they hit him. Dan dove backwards out of the way. He saw Amelia, Leroy and Binx dive with him out of the path of the inbound squads.

The squads managed to tangle Tremors feet before slamming into his side. Several cats clung to his face obstructing his eyes. He

273

clawed away the cats on his face and when he put his foot down to get his balance, he was tripped by too many cats and stumbled. He tried to rebalance himself but there was nowhere he could step that was free of cats. Dan thought it looked like Blankets Mountain had come alive and was writhing beneath him throwing him off balance. Tremor was forced to ignore the cats clinging to his eyes in an attempt to get all of his feet on the ground but he was too late and began stumbling towards the edge of Blankets Mountain.

That's when Dan heard Remy shout, "Charge!"

In response, Bumper did a hop to gain height, lowered his head and horns, and charged at Tremor. Racing full speed after just a few steps, Bumper struck hard. Tremor took the heavy blow from those curled horns directly to his ribs. Dan watched Tremor's face twist with pain. Dan's eyes went wide with hope at that confirmation that they could hurt him.

The blow from the goat and the onslaught of the cats was more than Tremor could recover from. He slipped, stumbled then tumbled head over heels as he fell over the edge of the mountain. Dan ran forward to watch. Tremor tumbled a long way down. He fell hard, landing heavily several times as his momentum continued to carry him down the mountain. A number of the cats involved in the attack went over as well followed by more cats that leaped over on purpose, charging after him to continue their attack. Just as soon as Tremor started to come to a sliding stop and regain his balance, the cats were on him again. A cheer went up as once again Tremor was overwhelmed and was forced to continue falling down the mountain.

Binx ran over to Dan and pointed excitedly. "Dan, look! Is that your missing headdress?"

So engrossed with watching the battle Dan had completely missed seeing Flash and Sonic return with the headdress. Dan immediately located Sonic and Flash who were running as fast as

274

they could. He knew carrying the headdress made it difficult for them to look up. Concern crossed his face as he realized they were running right at the spot where Tremor was about to land. There was no time to warn them to get to safety.

Tremor landed hard at the bottom of Blankets Mountain and right in front of Flash and Sonic. All three of them stopped, shocked to be facing each other. Tremor had caught both of them off guard. Dan couldn't hear Tremor's words but he saw how fast the fight was over for poor Flash and Sonic. The attack was unbelievably fast, leaving Sonic and Flash lying prone on either side of the headdress. Dan reminded himself that Tremor couldn't kill them. Only cause them tremendous pain and leave them with dull scars. But it was still painful to watch such brave cats be laid low.

He turned around and looked back up Blankets Mountain and saw Dan and company looking down on him. He let out a rage filled, ear splitting scream. His fury was obvious and it appeared to have renewed his energy. He hooked the discarded headdress with a paw and flung it up onto his head. It conformed to fit perfectly and the long flowing tail of feathers draped down his neck and off to his side.

Tremor wasted no time in leaping back up Blankets Mountain. Any cats that were unfortunate enough to be caught under him when he landed were mercilessly beaten and left on the ground crying in pain. He moved much quicker than he had before, clearly determined to reach the top in record time. Tremor launched himself up, the tail of the headdress waving in the air like the tail of a kite. When he landed he attacked anything near him and launched again. He repeated that over and over again. He moved too quickly for the army to respond or try to predict where to maneuver next. In just a few short minutes and with his final leap he landed back at the top. He stood nearly at the exact spot from which he'd initially been taken down.

This time, Dan knew he wasn't in the mood to talk.

Remy, still riding Bumper, had managed to get repositioned at their communications ledge. The Feather Time teams were a mess. Nearly a third of them had fallen to Tremor during their assault and the rest were scattered about the sides and bottom of Blankets Mountain where they had followed him down. Dan knew Remy was signaling again, attempting to get the Feather Time teams organized and back in formation. Dan knew the game was almost up when Tremor glared at Remy, but turned his attention back to Feather Dan and the group of cats near him. Dan hoped Remy could get the Feathers Time teams re-organized for another attempt to knock Tremor off the mountain again.

Tremor didn't speak another word this time. He just attacked the cat closest to him. He leapt forward and landed directly in front of Amelia. He growled and swiped at her with a massive paw. Luckily, Amelia was able to dodge. She shrieked in panic and ran underneath him as he landed. Dan felt a moment of relief that she had managed to evade him.

"Leave my sister alone!" Binx shouted at the top of his lungs and made a vicious leaping attack of his own. He landed directly on Tremors face, hooked in his claws and bit him as hard as he could on the nose. Shocked, Tremors eyes went wide. The pain from the bite likely surprised him. He gave his head a vicious shake and Binx flew off.

Dan was proud of Binx's bravery and desperately worried about Amelia. Despite Binx's attack, Tremor was still focused on Amelia. He quickly slid to the side and turned back to face Amelia. She screamed again, her face showing nothing but blind panic. She managed to dodge the attack. But this time when she tried to run away, she was too slow. The outside edge of his paw grazed her just

276

enough to make her lose her balance, but didn't cause any damage. She responded by screaming in fear.

Tremor laughed watching her run around in a blind panic. His ears flat along his head caused the headdress to slide back a bit, his long dagger like fangs dripping with saliva and a gleam in his eye he leaned forward towards her and said "Now I'm going to eat you!"

That was it for Amelia. Dan knew she was in a full blown panic and her only thought was to escape. She stumbled, landing on her back looking up at Tremor. She scrambled to right herself, and frantically tried to pull herself in four directions at once, effectively going nowhere. He could hear her whimper and mumble, "I'm not a warrior cat, please leave me alone. I shouldn't be here. Please go away!"

Tremors next laugh came from deep within his belly. He was enjoying her torment. It made Dan feel sick watching him inflict harm on others.

"No!" he snapped at her and his mouth wide open he lunged in to devour her. Without even thinking she jumped straight up in the air. Tremor bit onto the ground and she landed on top of his head right in the middle of the headdress.

Tears of fear streamed down her cheeks. Panicked and screaming she tried to run down his back in an attempt to escape but got tangled in the feathers of the headdress. She hit the ground hard and was badly entangled in the tail of the headdress. She tried to roll out of the way but got herself more wrapped up in the bead strings. She couldn't move her back legs. Dan knew she was stuck and feared Tremor would harm her.

Tremor turned and saw her predicament. He laughed, shrugged off the headdress to face her squarely and opened his mouth, preparing to take a bite out of her. As his head neared her, Amelia shrieked. In sheer desperation, she grabbed her feather collar and chomped it. She was gone. She disappeared immediately. Dan's relief that she was safe from Tremor was instantaneous.

Tremor stopped, momentarily confused by Amelia's sudden disappearance. Dan knew he had seen her chomp on her feather. He would surely remember Aristotle told him doing so would send him home. He had to know that Amelia was now out of his reach.

Sure enough, Tremor flipped the headdress back on his head and turned back to the others. Chuckling he mocked, "Well that gets rid of the chubby one. Who's next?"

The remaining group spread out in front of Tremor making it harder for him to take more than one of them at a time. Binx, no doubt furious for Amelia's treatment, went back on the attack and jumped at Tremors face again before Dan or Leroy could stop him. Tremor saw him coming and easily swatted him out of the air. Binx was thrown several feet away and slammed into a cloud. He jumped right back up, shaking his head, not out of the fight by a long shot.

Dan spared a moment to make sure Binx looked unharmed. Then Leroy and Dan attacked at the same time. Leroy went high and Dan went low. Dan slid under Tremor and latched onto the back of an ankle on his back leg. Leroy landed on the side of his back near his neck. He dug in his claws and raked as hard and fast as he could with his back legs.

Tremor swung his head around and tried to bite Dan but Dan was expecting it and ran clockwise around to Tremors other side. Tremor turned with Dan, chasing him, trying to catch him while he shook his powerful shoulders attempting to dislodge Leroy.

Dan was dodging Tremor, trying to get back underneath him and latch onto him and slow him down. He saw it when Binx took advantage of his distraction and jumped back on Tremors face. He

278

latched on to the top of his snout, clawing and biting. Tremor roared and shook his head trying to dislodge Binx. Binx managed to hold on tight by digging his front claws in as deep as possible to keep him in place. Using his back legs to rake Tremor's nose Binx also used his sharp teeth to bite him on the face over and over again. Binx was growling ferociously, and leaving gouges in Tremor's nose. His bites were drawing blood as well. He was definitely hurting Tremor.

Furious, Tremor slammed his own face into the ground. Dan knew that would have knocked the breath out of Binx and momentarily stunned him. Dan let go of Tremor's back leg and ran toward Binx, hoping to distract Tremor enough for Binx to recover and get away.

Seizing his advantage, Tremor kept Binx pinned with his face before he hooked him with a claw to keep him still. Rearing back Tremor attacked, this time with his teeth. His mouth covered Binx's entire body as he shook him viciously before throwing him over the edge of Blankets Mountain.

Leroy had been tossed off during the exchange between Binx and Tremor. He yelled in horror when he saw Binx thrown over the edge. Now, even more furious, Leroy leaped back at Tremor and managed to land on top of Tremor's head. Leroy's head was facing Tremor's back and his body was dangling over one of his ears and an eye. He bit into Tremors neck behind his ears, clutched on as tight as he could with his front claws and began to savagely rake his rear claws across one of Tremors eyes. Dan was hopeful that Leroy might be able to blind the panther.

Tremor shrieked then roared in shock and agony. He attacked, slashing at the cause of the intense pain. He managed to hook one claw into Leroy's back. Leroy jumped away at the last second but not unscathed. Dan retreated with a now limping Leroy and they watched Tremor carefully hoping to anticipate his next move and avoid it.

Tremor licked at his nose and rubbed at his eye. There were red claw marks and nasty looking bites where Binx and Leroy had gotten him. Dan looked at Leroy and saw two very long ragged looking red lines running down the length of his back. There was blood oozing out and matting Leroy's fur. He was grateful it was a shallow wound and not more serious. Leroy didn't pay it any attention. He was focused on Tremor. Dan couldn't help his worry about his friend.

Dan didn't like the way the odds were looking at the moment. Leroy was injured, Binx was out of the fight, and Amelia was safely at home. Only Leroy and Bumper were left of those who could actually hurt the panther. Dan couldn't lose his friends. He had to come up with a way to stop the panther.

Dan heard it when Remy yelled "Charge!" His head popped up as he looked for the direction Remy would come from. A flurry of cats streamed back around the top of Blankets Mountain shouting their own battle cries as they attacked Tremor. Dan and Leroy got out of their way to watch them work.

They charged right at Tremor but this time they had lost the element of surprise. Tremor was in full battle mode and better prepared for their assault. He jumped to the side before they could get under his legs and savagely assaulted any of them that came close. As they began to close on his right he jumped to a different spot. He repeated it each time they pressed and as a result cats were falling as fast as they could attack. Some of the injured were crawling away, some barely moved and a few lay motionless on the field of battle.

Remy charged in on the goat but once again but Tremor was ready. He waited for the goat and Remy to get right to him then slid to the side and struck the goat on its backside, digging his claws in deep as it passed. Bumper panicked, leaped forward and jumped right off Blankets Mountain taking Remy with him.

The Feathers Time cats were still attacking but making no progress. Leroy kept a close eye on the battle's progress. Dan knew by the look in his eyes that Leroy was preparing to attack again. He also noticed Leroy was in more pain that he wanted to reveal, moving more slowly as he shifted position looking for an opportunity to strike.

If he was going to come up with a plan to save the day, he was running out of time to do it in. The sun was setting and it was going to be a night of dancing lights, which meant it would be too hard to see to continue the fight. Having never been put in such a position before, Dan didn't know what to do. He wished someone would step up and help him out. Then someone did.

Aristotle appeared out of thin air right next to him. He laid a gentle paw on his shoulder and nodded in understanding at Dan's predicament. Aristotle's next words were painful for Dan to hear, even if they were true.

"Blankets Mountain is lost." Aristotle choked out the words as if giving voice to them pained him. "It's time to retreat. There is nothing more we can do now. We were able to learn much. Now we need another plan. We need to collect our wounded and regroup. Sound the retreat. It's time."

Dan, tears streaming down both cheeks only to form a puddle at his feet, nodded and signaled the team captains to sound the retreat. Dan looked at General Bradley, who caught his eye and nodded before signaling Remy to signal the retreat.

Chapter 27 – Regroup

Tremor didn't try to interfere with the retreat in any way. He was content to pace across the top of Blankets Mountain and gloat. His voice was loud and projected clearly across Cat Tree City. He preached about how things were going to change. He told them over and over again how he expected them to battle each other. He insisted that all honor was in the hunt and that until they could embrace their true nature they would never know themselves for what they were meant to be. He promised they would hate him in the beginning but would embrace being a predator and love him for revealing their true nature to them.

Dan and Leroy immediately went looking for and found Binx. He wasn't in bad shape at all, just angry he was forced out of the fight. He'd landed on a ledge not far down from the top but couldn't get back up by climbing. He'd had to work his way all the way down the mountain hopping between cloud ledges.

Remy and Bumper were also fine. They had landed not too far down the mountain and were on their way back up to the top. Bumper was an excellent climber. They heard the retreat sound but were glad to be of some use. They made several runs out to the battlefield, draping cats unable to walk across Bumper's back in order to assist with getting the immobile cats back to Cat Tree City.

It took hours to move all of the wounded into Cat Tree City. They pulled the more critically injured as far back towards Rainbow Bridge as they could. It was remarkable how quickly many of them were recovering but it would be days before others would be up and moving again.

Dan was most worried for Bandit and Sassy. They were left hiding alone in the Hall of Feathers. Tremor paced back and forth in front of the concealed entrance. Dan normally wouldn't have given it a thought, after all, it had taken him a long time to figure out it was there at all. The problem was that Bandit and Sassy had already revealed its existence. Dan hoped that Tremor was so caught up in his own narcism that he'd remain too busy gloating and preaching to stop long enough to remember it was there at all. If Tremor did find it, Bandit and Sassy would have an endless series of passageways and tunnels to hide in that the panther was too big to reach. That was, if Bandit could move fast enough to hide before he was spotted.

Feather Dan and company met with Aristotle, the professors and the remaining uninjured captains of the Feathers Time teams at Cat University. They were analyzing the battle, sharing perspectives from different areas of the battlefield. Despite losing Blankets Mountain, their strategies were successful in tripping and impeding Tremor. They were able to tire him out. They reviewed the tactics they still hadn't used that would be useful.

Dan had the most valuable information to relay. "When Leroy managed to damage Tremor's left eye, it glazed over with a milky white substance. He is effectively blind in that eye. I don't know how long it will stay that way."

General Bradley nodded in approval, "Yes that is a critical piece of knowledge and must be used to our advantage in our counterattack strategy."

"I would expect," George Washington chimed in, "that we'd only need the blindness to last a few minutes to achieve our objective."

Demi, standing beside Dan spoke next, "Getting his collar needs to be our primary focus. His greatest weakness is that when he is angry he attacks with blind rage. He can be easily baited."

Dan remembered the catnip that had been gathered. "What of our plan to deploy catnip to subdue Tremor?"

General Bradley groaned. "We've decided that it won't work. When we sent a platoon to deploy what we'd gathered they became overcome with the aroma and intoxicated. Trying to keep an entire platoon of intoxicated cats organized and functional is maddening beyond words."

Dan chuckled inwardly and forced himself to remain stoic. He could only imagine General Bradley running around shouting orders at a platoon of nip crazed cats. There were other strategies they'd planned on that wound up being dismissed once Tremors tactics were evaluated.

Feather Dan looked at the assembled cats. Despite his terrible grief that his beloved Blankets Mountain, a symbol of safety, hope and light had forever been marred by the tragedy that occurred on it today, he was grateful for those standing with him. He was grateful for their optimism in the face of adversity, their courage and hope for the future, their intelligence and bravery. While he admired them all and valued their opinions, he thought tricking Tremor into returning home would be the most expedient way to make sure no more of his friends suffered.

"I believe," Dan spoke up, "that if we attempt going for Tremor's eyes first then follow it up with a swarm at his feet to trip him, he would not notice a smaller group attempting to capture his collar."

Remy, standing next to Bumper, said, "If you need an additional distraction just give the word and I'll yell 'Charge' again. That sure got his attention last time. He hasn't forgotten how much it hurt when Bumper struck his side on our initial engagement." Bumper bleated in agreement.

Together they discussed ideas until they formed a plan of attack that they felt would be successful. Everyone was given a task that was best suited to their strengths. Dan admired the ingenuity of his friends. He felt more confident than when he'd first arrived that things would return to normal.

"It's settled then. Our plans are made. We attack at first light." George Washington looked at each cat in attendance silently asking if anyone had questions. When no one voiced any, he dismissed the gathering.

Dan was lingering behind with Demi, Leroy and Binx when Professor Newton approached. Dan thought her short black fur had a remarkable sheen and sparkle to it. It reminded him he was overdue for a bath of his own. He shouldn't neglect it and would need to attend to it very soon.

"Leroy and Binx?" Professor Newton inquired her squeaky voice sure to get their attention. "If you'll remember I am the professor of sciences here. I've developed a special scratching post that I believe you would find very beneficial given your tasks for tomorrow."

At the sound of her unique voice, Leroy turned to look at her, but only nodded in response.

Binx, ever curious, asked, "What's special about it? You said it was special but what makes it better than something like a couch?"

Leroy groaned, "Binx, you're not supposed to use the couch. That gets mum and dad in a bad mood, remember?"

Newt smiled in amusement, "Well first of all Binx, you don't have time to go back to Earth and do any sharpening on a couch. The way time moves you might not make it back here before the battle is over. I've modified a post here that I've been experimenting on. The sharper your claws are the more catnip comes out of it."

Binx's blue eyes went wide. "You mean it gives out that special Rainbow Bridge catnip?"

That was all Leroy needed to hear. "You heard the Professor, Binx, shut up and let's get going. We have to be prepared to do our part after all."

Feather Dan smiled, "You two don't overdo it so much you can't get up in the morning. Meet me back at the main road to Blankets Mountain when you are done."

Leroy and Binx followed Professor Newt into a series of cat tunnels to go find the special scratching post and sharpen their claws. Dan knew the most important factor was the catnip. Sharpening their claws was just a bonus. He inwardly chuckled. Demi leaned up against Dan and gave him an affectionate hug, jarring him out of his thoughts of Leroy and Binx.

"How about you Dan, are you ready for tomorrow?"

"Yes," Dan answered without hesitation. "This madness needs to end. We've been incredibly lucky that no humans have crossed the Rainbow Bridge since Tremor's been here. That luck won't last much longer."

"I know and you're right. I was thinking the same thing, but was hesitant to speak of it earlier. It wouldn't have helped us figure out a plan any sooner, only distract us." Demi grew quiet, just looking at Dan in that quiet way she had.

Dan looked up to Demi, grateful to have someone he could speak openly with, "Tremor won't be content to sit on Blankets Mountain for very long. If our first attempt doesn't take him down he'll be prowling through Cat Tree City before midday. Then it's only a matter of time before he finds the Rainbow Bridge."

"I believe you are right about that as well." Demi agreed. "Our plan is a good one. We have more information and a better idea of what will actually work against him. We knew the first battle was going to be trial and error."

Dan took a deep breath but didn't speak. He only wished that they could have reasoned with Tremor and avoided the necessity of having to fight. He couldn't help but feel a terrible weight of guilt for all of the cats who were now scarred with diminished glows.

"Plus," Demi continued, "You have amazing friends. You picked really well. The spirit, Doba, was right to trust in you."

Dan took another deep breath and stared up at the dancing lights in the night sky. "I hope so Demi. I sure do hope so."

Chapter 28 – We Attack at First Light

Feather Dan spent most of the night reviewing the strategies they'd made. He kept looking for ways things could go wrong or if anything could be improved. He still felt like he was missing something. He shook his head, he knew he was missing something. He kept staring at the sky as if that would provide him the answers he sought but he just couldn't put his paw on it. The distraction and doubt were both something that he didn't have time to dwell on.

Demi repeatedly reassured him that the plans they made were enough. She reminded him that General Bradley would adapt as the situation called for but the plan was sound even if it was similar to what they already tried. They were going to gather every able bodied cat and surround Blankets Mountain. Then they would begin slowly marching up maintaining a steady pace until either he pounced or they reached him. At that point several groups would rush and swarm him to distract him while other groups would try to bring him to the ground and force his collar in his mouth. As for whatever it was that he was convinced he was missing, she assured him that he'd figure it out when he was supposed to.

The rest of the night went by quickly. Those that were injured used it to rest and heal. By morning, several hundred cats had recovered enough to re-join the fight. Others would be days yet before they would fully recover. Grace had not returned yet and Dan was worried about her. It wasn't like her to say she'd return soon and be gone for so long. Grace had never stayed in the cat realm for nearly that long before and he wondered if she simply had to go back to the dog realm for a while or if time ran differently between the two realms. He just didn't know and worrying about something he had no control over was only compounding with the worry that he'd missed something. It was adding up and his nerves were feeling frayed. He put his worry for Grace out of his mind and refocused on the task at hand.

Dan marveled at the sight of thousands of cats gathered and organized into five large army units consisting of smaller squads of cats. Gypsy, Twitch and the remaining captains of the Feather Time teams each led a squad of cats, overseeing and coordinating those underneath them to accomplish their assignments. Feathers Time was proving to be more than just a game. It had trained their new army leaders and given them valuable experience managing teams and coordinating strategies to accomplish team goals. Dan realized he would forever be grateful for the Feathers Time game having created leaders they could count on to get the job done and teams that were used to working together. Every cat assembled here today was united in purpose and determined not to lose the ability to fulfill their sacred duty at Rainbow Bridge.

The armies were in place, ready to head forward and surround Blankets Mountain at first light. Feather Dan and his friends gathered with the army that was going to be moving directly up the main path to the top. Remy was still riding on Bumper's back. The two had formed a strong bond and friendship. They were instinctively communicating with each other now, and were practically inseparable. Dan was pleased that Remy fit right in and was so determined to fight even after only being at Rainbow Bridge for such a short time. It spoke volumes about his character. He worried how he would cope when Bumper returned to Earth.

Dan decided that this was the best opportunity to use those feathers that had been gathered. He'd never seen so many of them in his life and wondered just how many he could give away at a time. He looked across the army, picked out a platoon then thought of a pile of feathers and gave it to them. As soon as he did hundreds of feathers appeared before him. His view of the battlefield was completely obscured which made him smile. His idea would work.

He blew on those feathers and they raced up in the air above the platoon he'd given the feathers too. Once they settled above them the feathers drifted down, falling in pace with their advance. He repeated the move nearly a hundred times and when he was done the landscape before him looked like a winter wonderland.

It worked, by the time he ran out of feathers the army had moved in unseen and were beginning to advance. They were intentionally marching in step – one step and stop, another step and stop. They wouldn't be fatigued when they reached the top and they would get there at the same time. They were also waiting to see how Tremor would respond to their advance.

As soon as the sun had come up Tremor became easily visible due to his massive size and dark coat. Dan could see him pacing back and forth circling around the top of Blankets Mountain to get a good look at the advancing cats. He began yelling at them and taunting them. They could hear his words but they didn't change their pace or respond in any way.

Aristotle turned to his left and reached upwards to tap Remy on the leg. Remy looked down at Aristotle from his perch on Bumper. "Make a run past all of the armies. Inform every leader you see that no one is to respond to anything Tremor says. Our silence will agitate him and increase his anxiety."

Remy smiled before he spoke, "Consider it done." Then he leaned down to Bumper's ear and whispered. A second later they were off making the rounds Aristotle had requested. With how slowly the armies were marching, Dan figured Remy and Bumper would be back quickly.

Aristotle looked to his right side where Feather Dan and Demi were walking next to each other. "Tremor obviously likes to brag and engage in threatening banter. Ignoring it is another way we can take away his power."

Just then Binx passed Dan again. Binx was running in circles extremely energetic for so early in the morning. He was also pestering Leroy mostly just rambling and asking random questions. "Leroy, do you still have a little of Professor Newton's nip from last night?"

"Binx!" Leroy growled in frustration. "No, I don't have any nip. None, none at all. Now stop asking."

"That's too bad." Binx sounded dejected for just a second before his perkiness was back. "That was some really good nip though wasn't it Leroy?"

Leroy chuckled despite his earlier frustration at Binx's pestering. "Yes, Binx, it was."

"Was it the best though? Was it the best nip you've ever had? Amelia says you're like a catnip expert."

"Yes, now for the last time please be quiet and focus." Leroy took a couple of quick steps to get between Dan and Aristotle. Dan knew it wouldn't help him avoid more questions from Binx. Binx was just too wired to settle down yet.

Other than Binx's constant ramblings to whoever would listen, there was very little communication among the cat army. Everyone knew the simple and straightforward plan. Unless Tremor made a move they had nothing more to do or say.

After a couple of hours of marching the distance was closing between them and Tremor. The armies reached three quarters of the way up Blankets Mountain without any interference. Tremor had stopped trying to taunt them or verbally engage them once he realized he was met with nothing but stoic silence for his efforts. Dan was close enough to see Tremor was obviously agitated. His pacing was erratic. He was snarling and growling as he paced, biding his time for something. He couldn't have missed that he was being surrounded by cats.

Dan and Demi, including the professors and General Bradley hung back allowing the rest of the armies to move ahead of them. They needed to be able to observe what was going on and if they got any closer it would be too easy for Tremor to advance on them directly. General Bradley had insisted during their planning that if Tremor were to make a move on the leadership that it must cost him the high ground.

As much it bothered Dan to allow others, including Leroy, Binx and Remy to advance while he held back he understood that Bradley's strategy was a sound one. Remy was easy to spot as he raced between the different armies relaying information as needed. Leroy and Binx were harder to track but he knew instinctively where they were. They were nearer the front but holding back just far enough to remain out of Tremors range. If Tremor were to land on the troops near them they would be close enough to slip in with the reinforcements and make their move. He hoped they were staying well enough disguised so that they would be able to retain the element of surprise if they opportunity presented itself.

Dan felt some satisfaction as he watched the armies continue to climb and tighten their circle around Tremor. He knew that Tremor must have begun to feel it closing around him like a noose. They had wanted to unnerve the panther. By the looks of his restless pacing, they had reminded him they could be a threat.

The closer they got the tighter the cats were pressed together by the formation of the clouds leading up to the top of Blankets Mountain. Their ranks were narrower, stretched all the way to the bottom of Blankets Mountain. The cats in the front ranks soon reached the top of Blankets Mountain where the clouds formed a wide flat area. When they got to within a dozen yards Tremor let out a mighty roar and leapt into the middle of one of the armies.

Tremors attack was savage. Each cat that he struck was sent flying through the air. They either disappeared over Blankets Mountain or crashed into the ranks of other cats. In just a few seconds he cleared away nearly a hundred of them.

Without hesitation a surge of cats closed in around him aiming to get under his feet. Before they could he leapt again. He was striking with his claws and fangs before he even hit the ground. He dived into the squad near him sending cats flying. Then he jumped away before the surging cats could close in and get underneath him to trip him. He moved incredibly fast.

The next time he pounced the cats were trying to adjust to his strategy. They tried to give him a place to land so they could swarm in but the battlefield was too congested for the small area they had to work in. There was simply nowhere to go to get out of each other's way. Tremor avoided the small open gaps, instead jumping only into large groups he could scatter with his paw and knock out of the fight. On his next attack, just as he leapt away, he snatched up a cat by its head and held it in his jaws. The cat's body hung limp when he jumped away. Midway through his jump he let it go and watched as it dropped into a group of horrified onlookers.

The move was devastating to morale. The Feathers Time team captains were adjusting their strategies quickly. They started to change formations which allowed for more space between the ranks. They also started sending word to recover those who had been struck down.

Tremor saw what they were doing and adjusted his own tactics. He landed in areas that hadn't had time to get formations adjusted. He didn't stay in any one place long enough for the squads to mobilize and get underneath him to knock him off balance. He was simply outsmarting them and keeping them from properly organizing against him. In under an hour nearly a quarter of the cats were down and another quarter of them were trying to get the wounded to safety.

Aristotle and General Bradley were in deep conversation. Dan was listening as closely as he could without taking his eyes off the battle. Aristotle pointed, "Look, Tremor is keeping his attacks near the top of Blankets Mountain."

"Very true," Bradley never took his eyes off of his opponent. "He'll jump down lower when there's an opportunity to cause mass damage but jumps back near the top as soon as he's done."

Demi, still side by side with Dan said, "He has also been very careful to avoid landing anywhere near where Leroy, Binx, or Bumper are. Clearly he seeks to keep the high ground."

Dan watched as Tremor attacked then retreated to the top again. Demi was right. The area around Leroy and Binx had been left unbothered. Tremor was trying to cause as much damage as he could before he had to face anything that could actually hurt him back.

"We need to get Remy and Bumper up there." Dan pointed to the very top of Blankets Mountain where Remy had taken his position the day before. "If they could get just one good charge and knock him off his feet one time we could swarm him before he recovered. With a little distraction they should be able to force his fall towards Leroy and Binx."

General Bradley nodded eagerly in agreement but Aristotle warned, "Remy and Bumper may only get one chance. Tremor won't fall for it twice."

"True," General Bradley grumbled, "but Feather Dan is right. We have to do something soon. Dan, give the word."

Dan looked off to his right to see Remy and Bumper were headed their way. Remy was returning from running messages back and forth. Dan gave Remy three fast waves and yelled "Top of the world to you friend!"

Remy nodded in acknowledgment of the command to obtain high ground. Bumper stopped and they looked around, turned and raced off trying to stay out of Tremors immediate line of sight.

Leroy saw Dan give the signal. When Remy and Bumper began working their way up, he nudged Binx and gave him a serious look. "We need to be there to attack him," Binx didn't say a word but he nodded in agreement and they began to charge forward. The rest of the army caught on immediately and all of them surged ahead together.

Dan didn't miss the anger that flashed across Tremor's face and he knew immediately that Tremor hadn't been deceived. Indeed, it became obvious to Dan that they'd underestimated him. Tremor had been keeping close tabs on each of the animals he'd already identified as a threat. There was no doubt he spotted their move as soon as it happened, betrayed by the flick of his eyes directly at Remy and Bumper.

Dan tried to shout a warning to Remy as he watched Tremor feign ignorance but his warning went unheard. Dan yelled again; panic welling up in his chest, as he watched Remy and Bumper crest the top of the mountain. As soon as they did Tremor snarled, turned directly towards them and charged them. Dan cringed, with one mighty leap Tremor landed directly on top of them. Remy was knocked off Bumper's back and rolled several yards away managing to get clear of the panther's attacks. Bumper wasn't so lucky.

Tremors attack drove Bumper off of his feet and onto his side. Bumper screamed the sound a horrifying mix of agony and terror. Tremor tore into the goat with his fangs, tearing at him while he gouged and raked his powerful back claws across Bumper's stomach. In only a moment the goat fell silent. Seemingly not content to just maim Bumper, Tremor snatched his body up by his hind leg with his sharp fangs. He dragged Bumper a few feet closer towards an outcropping before swinging Bumper in a giant circle using him to knock back the swarm of cats that were rushing forward in an attempt to help. Bumper was then dragged by his leg to the edge of the mountain. Without hesitation Tremor slung him over the edge. Bumper's limp body twirled through the air then disappeared from sight. Remy screamed in helpless despair as he watched his friend fall.

Tremor turned and surveyed the attackers before him. Dan saw what Tremor did, the horrified looks on the faces of those who'd seen the savagery. Tremor laughed. "Look at you!" Tremor shook his head in disgust. "You're weak, powerless to control your fates, pathetic!"

Tremor chuckled menacingly. Squads of cats were still advancing, but more slowly after witnessing the horror of what happened to Bumper. "Half of you are already finished for the day and what have you to show for it? Nothing but pain and more scars to steal away your glow. Do you truly think your precious humans are worth all of this?" Tremor paused his speech to look around at those arrayed against him.

Dan knew what Tremor would see on the faces of the cats assembled near him. They would never forsake their sacred duty. They would fight, even knowing they could ultimately lose. His words would never sway them to accept defeat.

"You can't escape fate forever. I'll rule you all before the day is done. I'll give you one more chance to accept fate and surrender. Why continue this foolishness, why risk…" Tremor stopped in mid-sentence. His ears perked up as he listened carefully.

The gathered armies did the same, pausing to listen as they swiveled their ears to catch the sound. The sound came again and every cat stopped marching as they turned their attention away from Tremor and looked out to the clouds. A sound they'd never before heard at the Rainbow Bridge was echoing loudly up Blankets Mountain.

Chapter 29 – Grace's Pack

The howling of dozens of dogs interspersed with loud barks drifted out from the clouds and echoed across Blankets Mountain. The howling grew louder very quickly as the dogs approached. One by one, dogs started to appear out of the side of the Feather Time Arena and rushed towards Blankets Mountain. A moment later and an entire army of dogs were rushing the battlefield and Grace was leading their charge. The dogs she'd brought with her were all large breeds. Great Danes, Newfoundland's, St. Bernard's , Cane Corsos, Great Pyrenees, Black Russian Terriers, Dobermans, Mastiffs, and Irish Wolfhounds were all barking and howling as they followed Grace racing toward them.

Feather Dan rushed ahead and caught up with Leroy and Binx just as Grace appeared. He looked at his friends in disbelief then looked back to the dogs that were charging up Blankets Mountain. He was relieved when they ignored the cat armies and raced to the top of Blankets Mountain. Dan knew Grace must have warned them not to chase the much smaller cats. The determination of the cat army was so steadfast, that they simply smiled in welcome then shifted out of the way to give them room to pass as the dogs charged through their midst. Every cat knew Grace on sight and trusted she knew what she was doing. Dan felt his heart almost burst with hope and pride seeing Grace leading the dogs that had come to help them fight.

Aristotle caught up to them and said in wonder, "I've never seen so many dogs in the cat Kingdom of Rainbow Bridge. This is truly remarkable, and a story for the legends."

Leroy was watching in amazement. "There must be over a hundred of them. Did you see how big they all were? They looked like they could eat panthers for breakfast."

Cats scrambled out of the way, clearing a straight line path leading towards Tremor. As the dogs caught sight of Tremor the howls, barks and growls grew more menacing and threatening. The dogs weren't in any particular formation but the eclectic pack looked like they were working together. Dan remembered Grace always talking about the 'pack mentality' and how it was intuitive. Feather Dan guessed he was about to witness it in action. He couldn't remember a time when he'd ever been this happy to have his friend back. Several dogs began running round Tremor, while others slowly closed in leaving Tremor nowhere to run for safety. Grace hung back, barking and keeping the panther aware that she was a threat.

Tremor let out a battle cry, snarled and hissed. He flattened his ears, his hair puffed out and he balanced on all his feet, tail held out to the side ready to shift at a moment's notice. Dan recognized the feline battle stance. Even a large predator like Tremor, would be wary of a pack of large dogs working in unison.

As the dogs were within range, Tremor sprung at them. He caught the first one with his front claws, tore at it briefly then tossed it into the others charging behind him. The maneuver slowed a few of them but that was all. Dogs began circling him on all sides. They'd rush in, find an opening and nip at him before retreating before he could swipe at them. The nips and bites were catching him everywhere and leaving him no clear dog to focus on. After just a minute they were doing more than nipping. They were latching onto his legs and tail attempting to drag him to the ground. A couple Great Pyrenees were making lunges for his throat but were forced to back away to avoid Tremor's fangs and claws. Grace must have warned them that the panther could seriously hurt them even if they were spirit dogs.

Despite the dog's advantage of sheer numbers, Tremor had the advantage of desperation that comes from being in a life or death battle combined with the experience of a lifetime of killing for food nearly daily. Dan knew he would fight with everything he had and would not be an easy opponent for Grace's friends. Tremor maintained a savage volley of attacks and the dogs fell aside one after another but there were so many of them they kept coming. Several of the dogs had managed to lock their jaws on his legs and tail. He was prevented from escaping, weighed down by them and unable to jump away or shake them loose. Tremor was kept distracted trying to hold off the dogs that were nipping at him and trying to get at his throat. He swiped with his large paws, snapped with his teeth, shifted his weight, never staying completely still in his attempts to evade the attacking dogs. They kept harassing him, preventing him from focusing or counter attacking the dogs on his legs and tail. Where the cats had failed, the dogs succeeded in wearing out the panther. He was growing tired and slowing his strikes as more dogs were able to lock onto him. Before long they had immobilized his back legs and were starting to pull him to the ground.

Grace, seeing an opportunity, raced in and nipped at his feather collar in an attempt to take off with it but Tremor swatted her away at the last second. He finally managed to claw and bite until he got his left back leg free, then spun around and attacked the dogs on his right leg. He dropped three of them quickly but just as he freed his right leg others immediately latched on to his left leg again.

The cats watched as the dogs made progress in pinning down the panther. Their leaders knew they would be in the way and had ordered them to stand ready to assist. The dogs showed determination and organization, but the fight was also taking its toll on them. Tremor had already taken half of the dogs out of the fight.

Aristotle stepped up to Dan, "The dogs need our help."

Dan agreed, "You're right." He looked around and gathered all of the cats in the area. "Attack now. Get under Tremor's feet and trip him up. If you can get his feather collar do so." Dan looked over to his friends, "Leroy, Binx, we go with them. It's now or never."

Dan's squad quickly formed around him and began to charge, closing the distance quickly but not fast enough. As they got close enough, Tremor suddenly broke free of the dogs and took one giant leap in the opposite direction. He landed and quickly leaped again coming to a stop right at the top of Blankets Mountain. Dan could see Tremor was furious. The rage on his face, the hatred burning in his eyes, the long and wicked exposed fangs as he screamed his frustration reminded Dan that he was more than just a panther, he was pure evil. He also appeared to need a moment to regain his strength.

Dan and company changed directions and ran to Grace and her pack. Grace looked to Dan and said, "We couldn't hurt him. I was hoping that dogs... being from a different Kingdom of Rainbow Bridge... that we'd be able to do more damage." Grace was out of breath and panting. "Unfortunately it looks like we have the same limitations as you." Grace looked around at all of the fallen animals then up at Tremor. "I'm sorry it took so long. I had to look hard to find enough dogs that were bonded enough with cats to be able to make the transition between kingdoms."

"You've done well," Aristotle told Grace. "Your pack almost had Tremor."

"Indeed," General Bradley stepped up, his eyes surveying the top of Blankets Mountain. "We're going to have to mount one last coordinated attack. There is still enough of your pack to hold down Tremors legs. Working together hopefully we can hold Tremor down long enough to get the feather collar off and in his mouth."

Leroy spoke up, "Binx and I are the only ones who can cause Tremor any real pain. If we can get to his eyes, we can blind him. It won't last long but it should buy you a shot at getting his collar." Leroy looked at Binx to get his agreement.

Binx didn't hesitate, "Count me in."

"Excellent," General Bradley stated. "I think we have a plan then. Let's get everyone on the same page."

Grace trotted off to speak with her pack while General Bradley signaled the team captains. Within moments the cats and dogs were ready to go on the offensive. The dogs charged in first while the cats hung back waiting for an opportunity to strike.

Tremor remained snarling, unwilling to give up the fight or the high ground. At the first sign of the dogs running toward him, Tremor leapt at the front of the pack and attacked with a flurry of swipes. It was obvious that he knew he had to keep the dogs away from him before they could pin him and prevent his ability to leap away. He was also trying to injure as many as possible to keep them out of the fight. It was quickly becoming a battle of attrition for the panther. Dan hoped the gamble to reach his collar was successful. Both the dogs and cats were quickly losing able bodies to keep throwing at the panther.

The dogs struck quickly while the cats swarmed in right behind them. Grace was barking and acting as a distraction as much as possible for her larger canine friends. The biggest dogs focused on his rear legs and tail knowing that was the best way to prevent Tremor from leaping and regaining his mobility to dodge their attacks. The smaller dogs darted in and out like Grace, doing their best to get the panther's attention focused on them while staying out of injury range. When Tremor managed to get one dog off of him three more rushed in to take its place. Tremor wasn't able to keep them all away and they were gaining the advantage yet again.

With Tremor focused on getting the dogs off his back legs, the cats attacked next. Feather Dan leading the charge, they swarmed in and got under his front feet and belly making it harder for him to twist around to reach the dogs attached to him. They dug in with their teeth and claws wherever possible, further hampering Tremor's agility and flexibility.

Binx wasted no time, attacking with the swarming cats, landing on Tremor's head behind his ears and face. He dug his claws in as deep as he could and held on tight as Tremor shook his head attempting to dislodge him. Tremor roared at the unexpected pain from Binx's claws. Binx hissed his fury, clawing and scratching with hind feet, and biting his head and ears viciously.

When Binx didn't come off Tremor started clawing at him. Binx seemed to anticipate Tremor's retaliation and attempt to dislodge him, quickly released his grip, scurried forward and ducked Tremor's first swipe. Without any hesitation, Binx took the opportunity to pounce forward toward Tremor's left eye. He managed to dig in his back claws and find purchase with his teeth but not before Tremor managed to close his eye lid. Tremor roared in anger. Hissing in frustration, Binx took the moment he had to dig his claws at Tremors left eye and cause as much damage as possible. Tremor's second swipe didn't miss. The heavy weight of Tremor's paw smashed into him, making him lose his purchase and forcing him to the ground with the force of the blow. Dan was grateful that Tremor had retracted his own claws to spare himself injury. Binx landed on top of several cats Tremor had already knocked aside. He quickly set to work righting right himself and getting back on his feet.

Tremor's right rear leg began to buckle from the pull of too many dogs. He was forced to abandon his follow up attack on Binx. He spun back to attack the dogs that were the more immediate threat. The cats were everywhere, hampering his efforts. He stumbled and staggered several times as the cats deliberately placed themselves under his feet trying to keep him off balance. More cats clung to him, weighing him down. Each step Tremor made became a heavy stomp that was taking more cats out of the fight. The dogs were right there beside the cats doing their best to slow the panther's mobility and keep him off balance and unable to focus his attacks. The dogs were taking heavy casualties but were relentless. Some of them that had been hurt had gotten up and dragged themselves back into the fight. They couldn't do any real damage to Tremor, but they could still make him waste time and energy to bat them away which meant more cats got under him.

Leroy pounced at Tremor's face just as Tremor managed to rid himself of the dogs clinging to his back legs. Leroy landed and slashed at his right eye. Leroy's bold move took Tremor by surprise and he staggered as he roared in agony. Before he could regain his balance, Feather Dan pounced on his face and head, joining Leroy. Several other cats did likewise until Tremor's head and face was covered in cats. Dan knew they couldn't cause pain, that wasn't their goal. He did his best to be a distraction to give Leroy as much time as possible to blind Tremor while others worked on getting his collar.

Leroy pressed his attack with renewed determination, not wasting the distraction Dan and the other cats were giving him. Leroy lunged for Tremor's left eye hoping to add to the damage Binx had already managed to cause. Tremor, no dummy, had squeezed both his eyes shut tightly. Leroy growled his frustration when he couldn't get his claws through Tremor's eyelids. He lunged in to bite when Tremor suddenly reared up on his hind legs and caught both Leroy and Dan with his front claws. Dan and Leroy were knocked to the ground but managed to scramble up before Tremor could stomp on them. Tremor had kept his eyes closed tightly to avoid a counter attack and the temporary blindness allowed both Dan and Leroy to roll out of harm's way of Tremor's deadly claws.

Dan waited to see how much damage Leroy managed to do before he was knocked loose. When Tremor opened his eyes, Dan was heartened to see that his right eye had turned a cloudy white. Enraged, Tremor went into a frenzy first directed at the nearest dogs. When he had bitten and clawed his way through them, he pressed forward renewing his attacks on the cats closest to him in a murderous rage. Within moments, he had cleared his immediate area of cats and dogs. The remaining cats and dogs still capable of putting up a fight scrambled to get out of range of Tremor's claws and teeth, prepared to race back in if the opportunity presented itself.

Chapter 30 – Amelia, Mr. Owl and Mr. Squirrel

Dan looked around in sorrow at the number of cats and dogs that were much too still or writhing in obvious pain. The wounded covered nearly the entirety of Blankets Mountain. The rescue crews were doing their best to pull the wounded back to safety, but the sheer number of cats and dogs that were injured was nearly overwhelming. Dan looked back at the battle that was still being waged and knew that those who were still in the fight wouldn't last much longer without help.

Dan glanced at Leroy and Binx. They caught his look and raced towards him. "We need one more good attack to get that left eye. It's the only chance we've got. Binx, get Tremor's attention and try to get him to start circling. Make sure you stay in view of Tremor's left eye. Leroy, you're getting a second shot at his left eye. Sneak up on the Tremor's right side. Ambush him and do your best to make that left eye as blind as his right eye."

"You got it Dan!" Binx ran off with confidence in his step, headed directly for the panther's line of sight before he started taunting him. "Ha Ha! Tremor, you look like a one eyed pirate now! Where's your patch?"

Leroy shook his head at Binx and looked back at Dan, "The kitten is going to enjoy this too much. He'll be lucky if he lasts two minutes."

"I agree," Dan replied, "Go, Leroy. You need to get in position quicker than I thought you would."

Binx had just begun to tease Tremor. "Hey Tremor! I bet a one eyed panther is a pretty pathetic predator."

That last comment was enough to make Tremor furious. He turned his back on the retreating cats and dogs and looked directly at Binx. "I'll have both your eyes and then some before this day is done little runt."

Binx made sure to keep out of range of Tremor's claws but close enough the panther didn't have room to leap at him. Without making it too obvious, he kept dodging in the same direction forcing Tremor to circle counterclockwise to keep Binx within sight. The other cats and dogs seemed to realize Binx likely had a plan and managed to give him enough room to evade Tremor. They hung back taking the opportunity while Binx had him distracted to race in and drag back some of the wounded.

Grace and her friends continued to growl holding their protective positions to give the others time to get in attack position and provide cover to remove the wounded from the battlefield. They would dart in and distract the panther if he became too focused on Binx.

With Tremor now facing him, Binx started trotting off to the left forcing Tremor to follow to keep him in sight. Binx was doing his best to move fast enough so that Tremor couldn't effectively pounce on him while keeping up the banter. "Ouch! That sure looks like it must hurt." Binx started to tighten the circle he was walking to give Leroy a better chance at getting in position. "I can't believe you let a... what was it that you called us? Was it a pathetic house cat?" Binx dodged Tremor's swipe, shifting right and keeping Tremor's focus.

Tremor let out a snarl and growled at Binx. Tremor was getting more agitated every time Binx spoke. But the dogs proved to be effective at keeping Tremor distracted from taking out Binx by running in close to provide an immediate threat. Binx managed to buy them enough time to remove the most gravely injured and immobile from the battlefield.

"Whatever it was, a house cat sure did do a number on you." Binx continued to taunt Tremor. Ever circling to keep out of range, Binx continued his insults. "That's going to be a tough one to live down with the guys back in the jungle isn't it?"

Leroy shook his head at Binx's antics as he moved in as quickly as he could to get into position, cautiously approaching while staying in Tremor's blind spot. Grace quietly rallied the dozen remaining dogs and moved them into positions near Binx.

"Some king of the jungle you are. A housecat is a better hunter than you!" Binx called out.

Tremor gave in to his rage and charged after Binx. Seeing it, Grace and the remaining dogs began barking, growling and snarling, darting around to provide a distraction and tempt the panther to charge after them instead of Binx.

Out of time, Leroy was as close as he could be without being noticed. Deciding he wasn't going to get a better opportunity, he made his move timing it to land just as Tremor got close enough. He pounced, landing on the right side of Tremor's face. He struck out for the left eye as quickly as he could but Tremor got his eyes shut just in time. Desperate, Leroy hooked the nails of his left paw onto Tremor's eyelid and pulled hard trying to pry the eyelid open. He struck rapidly with his right paw in an attempt to get the job done.

Tremor reacted by raising his right paw to swat Leroy off his face. As soon as his paw made contact, his claws dug deep into Leroy's side, skewering him and drawing a painful yowl from Leroy. In one smooth movement, Tremor retracted his claws and slammed Leroy on the ground in front of him. Leroy bounced a couple feet forward and didn't move. Tremor looked down on him and roared his wicked yellowing fangs on full display.

"Leroy!" Binx screamed in warning.

"Move Leroy! " Dan shouted, fearing for his friend as Tremor lunged aiming for Leroy's head.

Before Tremor could bite Leroy, he was knocked aside as Grace rushed in and slammed her head into the side of Tremor's face as hard as she could. Grace spun and bit at his face. She latched onto his lip and snarled. She dropped her weight and tugged on his lip, shaking her head savagely at the same time. With two impressive tugs she managed to force Tremor's head down onto the ground facing in Binx's direction.

Binx didn't waste the opening Grace had given him. He pounced but his timing was awful. Tremor struck out at Grace with his massive paw resulting in lifting Grace off the ground and throwing her into the air. Binx crashed into the sailing Grace while in mid-leap and crashed to the ground with her.

Leroy took advantage of Grace's attack to roll out from under Tremor. Dan watched in fear as Leroy attempted to crawl out of the way. Dan could see that Leroy wasn't using his legs on his left side very well and his breathing was labored. Dan knew he would be in terrible pain from Tremor's last blow.

With Grace and Binx momentarily out of the fight, Tremor turned back to Leroy struggling just to crawl away. Tremor immediately started forward towards his prey. Dan knew he had to act now or Leroy would be finished. Tremor knew by now how much of a threat Binx and Leroy were and would target them first. Dan couldn't allow that to happen.

Feather Dan jumped between Leroy and Tremor. He planted his feet, raised his tail, flattened his ears, arched his back and hissed as menacingly as he could manage at Tremor. Dan was determined he wasn't going to let his brother suffer if he could do anything about it. A flash of white caught his attention from the peripheral of his right eye. He couldn't risk a quick glance behind him and remained focused on Tremor. He was caught off guard when Demi stepped up to stand beside him on his right instead of Binx. He heard more cats rushing in right behind her.

"We are here to help," Demi whispered to Dan.

Tremor disregarded everyone but Dan. He glared at him and with spit flying with each word he said, "Move aside now or I'll destroy you both."

Dan growled and hissed but refused to budge. A moment later, Leroy stepped forward with a severe limp, squared his shoulders, and stood shoulder to shoulder on Dan's left side. Although concerned for his injured friend, Dan couldn't help but be proud of Leroy's determination to stand by his side and continue the fight.

Dan glanced quickly behind him and saw the other professors were fanned out behind them, a look of determination on their faces. He also noted Grace and what remained of her pack, as well as a mightily perturbed Binx, approaching cautiously behind the professors. Dan felt it, the others likely did too. This was going to be their last stand. There were no more tricks, no more cats in reserve. Grace didn't have any other dogs to help. Win or lose this was it.

The utter silence on Blankets Mountain was disturbed only by Tremors heavy breathing at first. Then Dan heard a familiar sound he wasn't expecting. He knew that sound, he'd heard it thousands of times. It was the very subtle sound of blankets being pulled aside.

310

"Do you hear that, Demi?" Dan whispered, hoping the sound wasn't his imagination.

"No, Dan," Demi replied, never taking her eyes off of Tremor.

Dan's eyes went wide and he quickly looked to his right. He'd lost track of where on Blankets Mountain the combat had taken them. The battle had been fought all over Blankets Mountain but now they were near the top and Dan smiled as he realized they were right next to the entrance to the Hall of Feathers. It was appropriate he thought briefly, that this would end essentially where it had all begun.

Tremor gaped in confusion as the clouds parted revealing an entrance that suddenly popped open. Sassy and Bandit rushed out of the cave entrance side by side to stand next to Grace and her pack. Tremor watched them with squinted eyes before he started to chuckle, "I wondered where you two had been hiding. You will be very sorry that you..."

He was interrupted by an odd swooshing noise coming from the entrance where Sassy and Bandit had just emerged. The swooshing sound was followed by a "Hoot, Hoo, Whoo!" that echoed out of the Hall of Feathers. The moment Dan heard the sound he knew immediately what it was but he had no time to explain it.

Leroy asked in bewilderment, "Is that really Mr. Owl? From back home!?"

Mr. Owl's signature hoot was unmistakable. Dan couldn't understand how or even why Mr. Owl would be here now let alone inside the Hall of Feathers. He didn't have the answers for Leroy. When Dan heard a much louder and closer, "Hoot, Hoo, Whoo!" Dan knew he was right. The sound echoed again across the walls of the Hall of Feathers and from the entrance to the Hall of Feathers, a large brown owl with no glow swooped out and soared up into the sky.

Binx jumped up and down and shouted excitedly, "Look Leroy, its Mr. Owl!"

Dan watched as the owl, wings flapping hard as he circled upward, carried Amelia under him with his claws. Dan was further astonished when he noticed there was a bright eyed, grey bushy tailed squirrel on his back. Amelia had found Mr. Owl and Mr. Squirrel from back home on Earth! Mr. Owl circled around above their heads twice while Amelia was pointing to him which way to go.

Mr. Owl swooped around, climbed up into the sky and dove down towards Tremor. Tremor screamed at the owl and tensed his muscles. Before Tremor could take a swipe or leap to catch one of them, Mr. Owl pulled up sharply and Mr. Squirrel dove off his back.

After several acrobatic flips in midair, Mr. Squirrel landed on the back of Tremor's neck. Tremor shook his head at the unexpected nuisance. Dan knew how agile Mr. Squirrel was and that he was used to running along slender tree branches. It would be easy for him to keep his balance and stay on if Tremor attempted to dislodge him. Dan wasn't sure what Mr. Squirrel planned to do. He wasn't surprised when Tremor stayed focused on the owl carrying Amelia. Both had razor sharp talons that could do some damage. Tremor had to want to make sure his remaining good eye was protected.

Mr. Owl flew up, circled around and was once again making another dive at Tremor. Tremor tensed in preparation to make a move but he froze as Mr. Owl disappeared precisely before reaching Tremors pouncing range. The owl now gone, Dan watched as Amelia tumbled through the air right at Tremor, determination written all over her face. Without missing a beat, Tremor opened his mouth in anticipation of catching Amelia with it. That's when Mr.

Squirrel sprinted up Tremors back, onto his head, up to his nose and jumped as high as he could. He passed Amelia as she fell and handed her something Dan couldn't see before twisting and changing his momentum to land right back on Tremor's back. Dan watched in horror as Amelia tumbled right into Tremor's gaping mouth and Tremor immediately chomped on her. In a blink, Tremor and Amelia disappeared. They were both gone. There was a collective gasp then the battlefield was utterly silent and still for several seconds.

The first to recover from the surprise, Binx broke down into a fit of giggles. He started cheering as he ran up to Leroy. "Did you see that?!?" Binx started talking so fast his words were all jumbled together in his excitement. "I never knew Amelia was that sneaky?" He was so excited he was bouncing from foot to foot. "While everyone was watching Mr. Owl and Amelia, no one was paying attention to Mr. Squirrel. Mr. Squirrel got Tremors feather unfastened from his collar and was waiting for Amelia to get into position. When Mr. Owl dropped Amelia, he ran up Tremor's back and jumped right off his head towards Amelia. He passed her the feather in midair. Did you see that? That was so cool! When she fell into Tremor's mouth, Amelia chomped her collar right before he chomped her! He wound up biting his feather instead." Binx broke down into a fit of giggles. "Don't you see? Our plan worked, just not the way we planned it."

Feather Dan laughed in disbelief. While he'd been on Earth he'd constantly pestered Amelia to go ask Mr. Owl for one of his feathers. She had always hissed at him and given him a sassy retort. Now, not only had she actually gone and braved facing an owl but she put together a plan and had come to the rescue at the last moment. Dan was very impressed with her courage and determination to help her friends despite her fears.

Thinking of her bravery in the face of her fears reminded Dan of Bandit and Sassy. Those two had been through a lot. He knew they'd

313

done what they could to camouflage the entrance and stayed put. Tremor had paced back and forth right next to the entrance most of the night but never did find it. Dan looked at Bandit and Sassy. Dan had to know, "What happened in there you two?"

Sassy answered before Bandit could. "We were hiding out. I'm not really sure what point of the battle it was but we could hear fighting. We also started to hear someone yelling inside the Hall of Feathers. It sounded like they were a really long ways off."

"Yup," Bandit confirmed, "We decided that since we couldn't help with the battle we'd investigate the voice. We eventually found Amelia at what she said you told her was the bind point where Blankets Mountain on Earth was? Not sure about that, but anyway, there she was."

Sassy picked up the story from there. "She'd stuck her head in that entrance and was just screaming as loud as she could to get anyone's attention. When we found her she shared her plan with us."

Bandit continued, "She told us about the battle and how she almost got eaten. She said when she'd gotten tangled up in the headdress trying to get away that she'd pulled out two feathers. They came back with her when she chomped her feather that provided her with an emergency exit. She said getting those two feathers gave her the idea for her plan."

Sassy nodded enthusiastically, "Amelia sure is a brave one. I wish she was here so she could tell the story herself. But at least she's back at her home safe and sound."

"Yup," Bandit chimed in. "She said we were her back up plan to let Leroy and Binx know what happened to her if she was missing and they couldn't find her when they got home. She told us her plan was to speak to Mr. Owl and that he was dangerous and he might eat her before she got a chance to explain how she needed his help."

"She asked us to go and wait by the entrance to the Hall of Feathers," Sassy said as soon as Bandit paused for a breath. "She said if we heard an owl hooting that it meant she didn't get eaten and was on her way with help," Sassy smiled.

"Hearing that hoot was scary and exciting at the same time. We swung open the door and got out of the way just like she asked," Bandit concluded.

Mr. Squirrel ran over to fill them in on the rest of the story. As it turned out, Mr. Owl was full when she found him and he was in a good mood so let her tell her story. Mr. Squirrel had been a couple trees over and heard what she was saying. He volunteered to help and together they sat and came up with the plan of how best to use Amelia's two feathers to trick the panther into chomping on his own feather.

They decided they had to come right away. Amelia handed each of them the two feathers, Mr. Squirrel hopped up on Mr. Owl's back and Mr. Owl held onto Amelia. They took off, counted to three and chomped their feathers at the same time. They showed up at Amelia's bind point in the Hall of Feathers. Amelia told Mr. Owl to start hooting and the next thing he knew they were zooming out of the entrance and into a huge battle.

Aristotle applauded the group, "Amelia is a hero. All of you are! Everyone who stood against the destruction of the bonds of love that Rainbow Bridge stands for is a hero. Everyone fought bravely and should be proud of having helped to banish Tremor from our realm."

Dan looked around with pride at everyone he called his friends. The crowd was beginning to cheer.

Before his words would be drowned out with the celebrations, Aristotle yelled loudly. "Go forth and spread the word. Those of you who witnessed the final battle go share that story with the others. Tremor is gone. Rainbow Bridge has been saved!"

Chapter 31 – Celebrations and Goodbyes

The story of the final battle spread like wildfire across Rainbow Bridge. There were celebrations from Blankets Mountain and throughout all of Cat Tree City. The sense of relief that life had once again been returned to normal fell like a tidal wave of relief over all the cats. Plans were made to resume the Feathers Time championship games after everyone had a chance to heal.

There was laughter and tears of joy among the survivors as they shared battle stories recalling Binx's antics to taunt Tremor and the look on Tremor's face when Amelia disappeared twice. Those that had seen the owl described it to those that hadn't. Mr. Squirrel's bravery was also praised and his story told far and wide. They paid homage to the brave dogs that had come to help them.

The wounded were all healing, some quite fast and others a bit slower. There were cats with dull scars everywhere. They soon became known as battle cats. Their scars were seen as badges of honor, visible proof of those brave souls who engaged in combat with Tremor. Those special cats would be forever referred to as the veterans of what the professors were calling the Battle for Rainbow Bridge.

Grace and her pack stayed to celebrate with everyone on Blankets Mountain for a while before they decided they were all healed enough to go home together. They had spent some time trying to help each other with their wounds and scars but despite their best efforts the dull scars would remain with them as well. They would have their own stories to tell once they reached their own realm. Dan was visiting with Grace because she would be leaving soon. As the pack was finally organized and ready to go, Aristotle arrived to speak with her.

"Grace," Aristotle said warmly as he approached, "Surely you're pack can stay and enjoy this evening's celebration with us."

Grace wagged her tail at Aristotle's request. "I'm sorry Aristotle. Each dog here has a pack. Things work a bit differently between the animal realms. No doubt our packs in the dog realm are already very worried. I need to make sure we all get back before dark."

"I understand," Aristotle said. "You know you are welcome back anytime you like. We are forever in your debt. The pack you brought came in our greatest time of need to fight at our side. That will not be forgotten. I have made sure all of their names will be recorded in our histories."

"Thank you, Aristotle. We consider it an honor to fight at your side."

Grace took the lead spot in her pack, ready to lead them back to their own realm. She turned to Dan before she left. "I'll be back just as soon as I get everyone to their packs and settled."

Mr. Squirrel ran up and did a quick hop onto Grace's head then dropped down to her feet. In a chirpy voice he said, "It was good to see you again. The old neighborhood just isn't the same without hearing you barking at me while I'm out foraging."

Grace smiled and gave Mr. Squirrel a sloppy kiss on the head. She gave her pack one final look over to make sure everyone was accounted for, let out one loud bark and charged out towards the clouds. Dan watched quietly as Grace and her pack vanished as they approached the Arena Cloud.

"You know you can stay for a while as well," Aristotle sat down next to Mr. Squirrel and looked at him fondly. "You played a key role in the victory. Your bravery in riding on the back of an owl into a realm filled with cats is something quite remarkable. You'll be remembered as a legend among us."

Mr. Squirrel flipped his tail about and excitedly chirped. "I have a family waiting for me back home, a Mrs. and two babies. I really need to get back to them."

Aristotle nodded, "I understand."

"But you know something?" Mr. Squirrel asked as he pulled off his feather collar.

"What's that?" Aristotle asked.

"There are stories passed down among the squirrels that some of us have even been friends to the humans – pets, just like cats and dogs."

Smiling, Aristotle nodded, "Those stories are true."

Mr. Squirrel flicked his tail excitedly again, "Great! So there should be a realm here at the Rainbow Bridge for us as well."

Aristotle nodded again, "Yes, my new friend. All animals have a place at the Rainbow Bridge."

Mr. Squirrel studied his feather collar while he thought, "That's good. So maybe we'll see each other again one day."

"Yes," Aristotle responded warmly. "I would like to think we will as well."

Mr. Squirrel took the feather collar, put the feather in his mouth and chomped. In a blink he was gone.

Remy, head held low, walked up slowly to join Dan and Aristotle.

Aristotle nudged him gently with his head. "What is it Remy? Why are you so down when we are celebrating such a great victory? You and Bumper were crucial to our success."

Remy took a big breath and looked up to Aristotle. "I just said goodbye to Bumper. Tremor's last attack crippled him and he couldn't walk back here to celebrate with everyone. He was too big for us to drag over here so he decided he would go home." Remy sighed sadly. "Bumper's collar only had one chomp left to get him home. He won't be able to come back and visit like Amelia, Binx and Leroy can. Dan gave them a special feather so their collars were different from Bumper's."

Aristotle smiled and gently placed a paw on Remy's shoulder. "I'm quite sure you'll see him again."

"I sure hope so," Remy said and looked up to the sky.

Aristotle nodded in confirmation. "I'm quite sure he'll come here looking for you again when it is his time to cross the Rainbow Bridge. Do you think you would be up to helping him cross when that time comes?"

Remy's eyes lit up with excitement. "Oh yes!" He thought for a minute and said, "Do you really think I'll be able to greet him? You know, like Dan greeted me?"

Aristotle nodded, "I can think of no other cat he would rather see when he returns than you."

Remy smiled, wiped away a tear that had formed. "I think I'd like to check on Patti now." He trotted off in the direction of Rainbow Bridge.

~

That night's celebration was spectacular. Clowders of cats were everywhere grooming, exchanging news, singing, dancing, relaxing, resting, breaking out toys and catnip to share. Some were re-enacting key moments of the battle against Tremor in vivid detail as onlookers watched. There were hundreds of different stories being shared. Each battle cat with an audience listening to their own personal story of how they got their scars. The history professor, George Washington, was extremely busy trying to get everything documented.

Best of all, Leroy, Amelia and Binx were no longer being called sink bath cats. Gone was the fear and disgust for their dull coats. Instead they were praised for their bravery and much loved by everyone. Everyone was eager to make introductions with Leroy and Binx. There were many pats on the back, offers to share catnip and toys, and requests to tell their stories. Aristotle thought Leroy and Binx were gracious to everyone even if they were a bit too quick to accept the catnip.

Aristotle watched the cats lining up to tell Professor Washington their stories. He stopped to listen to a few and noticed a common theme of selfless sacrifice and love.

Professor Washington interrupted Aristotle's thoughts. "We're going to need a new wing in the Cat University Library. There'll be far too many new volumes to be added. We don't have the space."

Aristotle chuckled. It was good to see Professor Washington so excited about something new. He was always contemplating and studying the past. He would be busy for a long time making the new additions and living in the present. "We'll get it done, old friend. We'll get it done."

~

Grace was met with thunderous applause and cheering when she returned just before dawn. Feathers Time team captain Gypsy met her at the base of Blankets Mountain as she was about to run up and see Feather Dan. "Hi, Grace. All of us Feathers Time players have been talking it over and we've decided something. You can watch the next Feathers Time game."

Grace's eyes went wide with surprise and she hopped with enthusiasm.

"But," Gypsy held up a paw. "You have to promise not to chase anybody. Not even once." She gave Grace a stern look and smiled. "I bet if you can get through one game without chasing anyone we'll let you watch them all after that."

"I'll try!" Grace raced up Blankets Mountain barking excitedly. She couldn't wait to tell Dan about that!

~

When the sun came up that morning a remarkable thing happened. The sound of wind chimes and birds filled the air. A breeze kicked up and the smell of spring flowers settled over Cat Tree City. Cats ran to the streets and looked all over in anticipation. Dan knew what that meant and his excitement grew.

"There's no time to waste. Quickly, follow me!" Dan bade his friends to follow. Leroy and Binx followed Dan as he raced down Blankets Mountain and towards Rainbow Bridge.

"What's going on, Dan?" Leroy asked.

Feather Dan had a huge smile on his face. "I'm glad you two stayed the night. This is what happens when someone's human passes and begins to transition to the Rainbow Bridge. The sounds and smells are different every time and meaningful only to their pet. The sounds and smells are a representation of some of the happiest memories of the person who is crossing. It's a way to call to their pets and let them know it's time."

The streets were crowded by the time they reached Cat Tree City. Dan led them past cats that were blocking their path forward. They jumped on top of Cat Trees, hurried down alleys, scooted past groups weaving their way toward Rainbow Bridge. Cats were milling everywhere and looking around at each other as if waiting for something to happen.

Leroy noticed and asked Dan, "Why are they all looking at each other as if waiting for a surprise to be revealed?"

Dan told Leroy and Binx, "When a person crosses their cat's fur glows even brighter to make sure they know they need to get to the Rainbow Bridge. Everyone's trying to figure out who gets to go meet their human."

They could hear some excited cheering up ahead as Dan led them around a few more obstacles until they were at the front of the crowd. Dan knew they had found out which cat had a human crossing. When they finally arrived, Dan saw that Bandit and Sassy were sitting at the foot of Rainbow Bridge. They had an extra gleam to their fur but not the full brightness they would normally have. Dan watched as they were frantically working on cleaning their fur. Dan could hear Bandit was fretting about how badly he was scarred and his worry that Hope wouldn't see them. Sassy told him to not worry about it that together they would be bright enough.

Sassy looked over her shoulder and saw Feather Dan, Leroy and Binx watching. She raised her paw, whispered "Thank you." before waving goodbye. They waved back at her.

To greet your human was the happiest moment ever at the Rainbow Bridge and while he was sad Bandit and Sassy would be leaving there would be no tears. This was their purpose and it was an honor to witness. The clouds at the Earth end of Rainbow Bridge began to shift and glow. The silhouette of a person began to appear. Bandit and Sassy were rubbing against each other excitedly. It took only a moment before a young lady stepped out of the cloud. Dan knew that Hope had arrived. She saw Bandit and Sassy and gave a little gasp before her hands covered her mouth. She ran towards them, falling to her knees when she reached them. Dan watched as the three of them were reunited and loved on each other for several minutes. Nobody could hear their conversation. But everyone felt the joy of their reunion. Dan knew everything was, once again, as it should be.

Hope stood up and looked where Sassy was trying to lead her to. She followed Sassy and Bandit off the bridge towards a giant sparkling cloud. As the three of them passed through, the cloud sparkled intensely and glowed brightly. As they disappeared into the Beyond, waves of pure love pulsed out over the Rainbow Bridge leaving everyone left behind feeling peaceful and refreshed.

Feather Dan turned to Leroy and Binx. He looked Binx over and gave a nod of approval, "It was very nice to get to actually meet you in person. You are a very lucky cat. You live in one the best homes any animal could ever ask for."

Binx shook his head and stared at Dan hard. "Was that you? In the shelter when mum was walking around all sad. She was sad because you hadn't been gone long wasn't she?"

Dan nodded, "Yes, she was still feeling tremendous grief over my passing."

"But was it you?" Binx insisted with the question.

Leroy had no idea what Binx was talking about. "Was Dan what? Do I need to knock some cobwebs clear in that head of yours again?"

Binx quickly glanced at Leroy, "When I was in the shelter the day mum brought me home something weird was happening. I never told you or Amelia about it because you already think I'm goofy but I swear it was Dan."

"What was it that you think he did?" Leroy questioned him.

"I noticed mum and gramma as soon as they walked in. Gramma had knitted a bunch of cat mats and they came to drop them off and pet the kitties. I knew mum was my human, I just knew it. She kept getting distracted and wandering off. First people would chat with her, and then another kitten would cry. Every time she went to look at my kennel something distracted her. Then I felt something, like a presence was there but I couldn't see it. Then I could see it! It was a small orange glowing ball of light. Mum couldn't see it but it floated over to her, did a couple of circles around her head then settled on her shoulder. It guided her right to me and I was able to choose her."

Binx looked back at Dan, "You were that tiny orange ball of light weren't you? You were checking in and making sure mum didn't pass by me without giving me a chance. I just know it was you!"

Feather Dan was smiling from ear to ear. "Well Binx, mum and dad were still hurting and needed a little help just then. I knew that love was what they needed. I could sense you were the right one. You sure do have lots of love to share and your silly antics would make them laugh again."

"I knew it!" Binx shouted excitedly.

Dan laughed, "I believe you've helped both mum and dad heal. Thank you for that. Please help Leroy and Amelia take care of my humans until I can do it again myself."

Dan turned to Leroy, gave him a giant head bonk and said, "It sure has been wonderful being able to be together again brother. I knew you three would be the perfect ones to help save Rainbow Bridge but now our adventure here is done. You two need to get back home. Mum and dad aren't back yet but they will be soon."

Leroy nodded but didn't say a word. He just looked at Dan as if committing him to memory.

"Oh, just one more thing." Dan pointed to their feather collars. "I don't know how many times chomping on those feathers will get you back and forth between Earth and here but remember if they start to sting bad it means you've only got one chomp left. Don't chomp and come here if you can't get back home."

"I'll keep them safe." Leroy vowed.

Dan knew how responsible Leroy was and had no worries that he would. "I'll keep checking in from time to time. If Rainbow Bridge ever needs help again you'll know what signs to look for. Keep Blankets Mountain on Earth safe and give mum and dad extra kisses and luvins for me tonight."

They finished saying their goodbyes. Leroy and Binx took out their feather collars. They counted to three and chomped. Just like that they were gone.

~

Dan and Demi sat together on top of Blankets Mountain. They spent hours sharing stories of what their lives were like back home. Demi listened and asked questions when it seemed like he was leaving out pieces of his stories. Those were usually the embarrassing parts. She liked those stories the most.

Eventually they grew quiet and just sat together enjoying each other's company. The celebrations in Cat Tree City continued on well into the evening. The sounds of cheers of victory and laughter were welcome sounds after the trials of the past few days.

Leaned up against Dan and purring, Demi was startled when without warning Dan leapt to his feet. Standing up, she asked, "What is it, Dan? What's wrong?"

Dan was staring at the sky, his face covered in concern. There was a flock of seagulls flying above Blankets Mountain. It was unusual to see more than one bird at a time but not entirely unheard of. All he managed to get out was, "The birds."

Demi looked up to the sky. She looked back at Dan, "The seagulls? What of them?"

Dan turned his attention away from the gulls and looked hard at Demi. "Now I know what's been bothering me. I know what it was I missed. I can't believe I'm just now figuring this out."

Demi looked at the birds for a second then back at Dan her face twisted in confusion. "What is it?"

"The birds." Dan reiterated. "They're flying the wrong way."

Demi's eyes went wide as she realized what had gotten Dan's attention. She looked back to the sky, this time studying it more closely.

"Oh no," She said. "Dan, this isn't good!"

"Nope," he replied. "I was hoping, but I guess this isn't over after all."

Feather Dan and Demi each took a deep breath as they watched the birds fly back towards the Rainbow Bridge and out of sight.

Demi turned back towards Cat Tree City and said, "We need to…"

"Tell the other professors." Dan finished for her. Together they ran down Blankets Mountain in hopes of finding answers.

Epilogue

Leroy, Binx and Amelia were all sitting on the couch together back home. They were sharing stories and reminiscing about their Rainbow Bridge adventure with Dan. They had decided to hide their feather collars inside Blankets Mountain. They each chose their own hiding spot so they wouldn't accidentally take the wrong one. This was something of his that Leroy was pretty sure Binx wouldn't try to steal to play with.

Amelia rolled over on her back and stretched, "You know, both Mr. Squirrel and Mr. Owl still had their feather collars too." She reached under one of the couch cushions and pulled out a big brown feather. "Mr. Owl even gave me one of his feathers. He wants me to give it to Feather Dan if we ever have a reason to return to Rainbow Bridge."

Leroy smiled, "After all of those years of Dan asking, you finally got him an owl feather. You really are a good sister."

"Yup," Binx piped in. "She's just a big old softy behind all of those mean hisses."

Amelia swatted him on the head with her tail, "You hush."

Amelia groomed her tail and studied Leroy's orange striped chest, obviously pondering something. Leroy knew she'd ask whatever it was that was on her mind and he was right. She looked up at him and her eyes went soft with concern. "Do you think the spirit cat's scars will heal so they get their glow back? You and Binx got pretty beat up too and you were able to get your red battle wounds to wipe away just as easy as if you had fur settled in the wrong direction as soon as we got home"

Leroy had already thought about that. There was no way for any of them to know and while he hoped their scars would fade as well, his intuition told him they wouldn't. He also had a suspicion that the scars he and Binx were so easily able to wash away would return when they themselves returned to the Rainbow Bridge as spirits. It wasn't something he felt he needed to worry Amelia or Binx with though. He was thoughtful when as he worded his answer. "I hope so, Amelia. They truly need their glow at the Rainbow Bridge. As hard as it would have been for us to explain ours scars to mum and dad, they wouldn't have impaired us in any way. "

They chatted for a while longer before they heard the sound of a key turning in the front door. The door opened and they could hear their mum and dad talking as they walked into the living room. Mum looked at all three of them sprawled out together. Mum told dad they looked adorable all sitting quietly with each other and getting along. Dad told mum it looked like they were plotting something and he wondered what they were up to.

Binx looked at Leroy and asked him, "Can I please tell them about our adventure?"

"No," Leroy shook his head, "at least not yet."

Binx looked dejected, "But it's such a good adventure. I know they'd just love to hear how Dan is."

Amelia thought about it, sniffed and rolled over again so she was upright. "We could if we were careful."

Curious, Leroy asked, "What do you mean? I don't see how we can tell them about this until we're all at the Rainbow Bridge together and I mean being there the right way."

"What if we all take turns whispering the story into their ears while they're asleep? That way they can dream about the adventure and get to see Feather Dan again," Amelia suggested.

Leroy smiled, Amelia had the perfect idea. He looked over to Binx and saw him eagerly waiting for him to approve of Amelia's plan. "I think that's a marvelous idea." Another thought came to Leroy, "You never know. If we tell it well enough and repeat it over and over again, maybe, just maybe, it will get into their subconscious. Maybe they'll even think they came up with a great story and write a book about it. After all, everyone should know how wonderful it is and what they have to look forward to at the Rainbow Bridge."

About the Authors

Eric and Amanda Fish are Amazon bestselling authors who live in northwest Georgia. They each work full time jobs in their respective professions of security management and social services while they raise their two amazing grandchildren and of course their beloved pets.

You can follow Eric on his Amazon author page as well as on Facebook at ericfish-author

You can also follow Dan's siblings on Dan's original Facebook page at Neuro Dan – Feather Dan. They continue to post the ongoing shenanigans of Leroy, Amelia and Binx almost daily.

A brief statement from Eric:

"Born and raised in the expansive farm country of western New York, I spent a great deal of time enjoying the beauty of nature in all of its forms. I developed a love for reading which sparked my imagination which developed into a passion for writing.

In 2015 Amanda and I took on a new pet. We kept pets our entire life. Since we never had children our pets, both cats and dogs, were always special to us. This time we had no idea what we were getting into or what an adventure we were about to begin. Neuro-Dan was a small orange striped kitten with a rare and terminal neurological disease. An angel on Earth, Dan taught us that sometimes, the greatest love comes from the tiniest of God's creatures. The experience was one of the greatest blessings of our lives. Through his social media page, Neuro Dan - Feather Dan's stories of determination, hope and unconditional love touched tens of thousands of people from all over the world. We wrote stories of his daily adventures, both the soaring ups and devastating downs. Those stories inspired thousands of people with disabilities of their own as well as shined a light on the issue of adopting those pets labeled as 'special needs'.

When Dan passed away and made his journey across the Rainbow Bridge his fans began to ask for books about his life. Another unexpected part of our journey with Dan happened. His fans began to ask us to pray for Dan to help their pets cross the Rainbow Bridge when they passed. They also asked us how to explain the loss of a pet to children. As we wrote the stories of his life on Earth I decided to also write a story about his adventures beyond the Rainbow Bridge.

Thank you for taking the time to read this story. I hope you enjoyed it."

Eric Fish

If you enjoyed this book and would like to read more stories by Eric and Amanda Fish, or learn more about Neuro Dan – Feather Dan and his life on Earth with his siblings then check out these other books all of which are available on Amazon.com in both eBook and paperback formats.

Neuro Dan - Feather Dan Stories from Blankets Mountain Year one - My Forever Home

Eric Fish

Neuro Dan - Feather Dan

Stories From Blankets Mountain

Year Two -
Living Life to the Fullest

Eric Fish
Amanda Fish

Neuro Dan - Feather Dan
Stories from Blankets Mountain

Year Three
Feathers Time

Eric Fish and Amanda Fish

Made in the USA
Columbia, SC
02 September 2021